Light of the Dove

Light of the Dove

R.J.R. Black

In Loving Memory of R.J.R. Black

1946- 2023

Chapter One

"Chaek…chaek!"

At the height of midsummer in the year twelve B.C. the raucous cry of the mercenary bird known as the red-backed shrike rang eerily out in the suffocating darkness as high in the broad cross branches of an ancient oak tree, the slumbering child Vescala stirred restlessly from what had been an uneasy and intermittent sleep.

Suddenly, from out of a nearby tree, the dreamlike warbling of a songbird broke alongside the rapid scurrying of some unseen creature now foraging amongst the decaying vegetation that covered the floor of the vast forest. And with these sounds dramatically condensing into the diminishing starlight, the night's moonless sky slowly lightened as the trees surrounding the child became immersed in a veil of deep indigo hues. However, while the night's intimidating malevolence had for so long appeared impenetrable, towards the eastern horizon the hunter of the darkness − the sun god − began to ascend ever higher into an increasingly illuminated sky. Throughout the golden-painted foliage of the trees, the almighty rays of the eternal hunter now strove in a relentless onslaught, probing and dispersing each of the night's lingering shadows. Meanwhile, as if heralding the sun god's retribution over the darkness, the forest's multitudes of birds and plants united in a ceaseless riot of song and colour that soon bathed the glistening landscape in an atmosphere of true thanksgiving.

High on a leaf directly above the child, a cold crystalline dewdrop formed and, slipping down from it with the aid of a whispering breeze, it meandered slowly in a pathway predestined to kiss his small-uncovered shoulder. The sparkling cascade instantly released him from the sanctuary of his dreamless slumber, and, now finding himself in a bright living world, he shook his head vigorously and smiled happily on realising that he had survived the long night and all the terrors the darkness had always held for him. Banishing the last remnants of sleep from his mind, he slowly raised his reclining body into a seated position, only for the immediate awareness of his perilous predicament to suddenly invade his few fleeting moments of euphoria. Tears flowed uncontrollably from his wide misty eyes as the unhappy memories of the previous day surfaced in the storm of uncertainty now rampaging through his troubled mind. And as he thought of the other children in his village learning of his cowardly flight, his small round face contorted into a shamed expression. Instinctively longing for his mother's maternal protection, he pulled his long thin linen cloak up and around his shoulders and, using the hem to wipe away the tears trickling down his pale cheeks, he wondered how at this moment his mother and sister must be feeling. Suddenly his expression altered into one of anger as the memory of the two heavily robed and fearsome-looking druid priests became the predominant feature in his thoughts. For to what useful purpose could a child of a mere seven summers be to the priests whose sinister appearance the morning before had sent such a terrifying premonition of dread surging through him, he resentfully wondered. The previous morning his mother had awoken him directly before dawn. Slowly rising from the comfort of his straw bed, he immediately detected an atmosphere of foreboding pervading throughout the small circular hut that, ever since the day of his birth, had been his home. And by the flickering light from the solitary tallow-fuelled lamp, it had been apparent to him by the troubled expression on his elderly mother's face that something was far wrong.

"Vescala, my only son, shortly before this village awakens you are to be taken from this household by those of a far higher authority then even our village elders are endowed with!" she had stated in a delicate voice trembling with emotion, pausing momentarily to stare down at his small cowhide sandals, clasped tight in her frail wrinkled hands. Although deeply distressed she had continued to speak in broken phrases as to the reason why his destiny was to be governed by those other than herself. However, as Vescala had dressed into his ragged woollen shirt and ill-fitting deerskin trousers, he had ignored all further words coming from her quivering lips as his bewildered thoughts had wandered from the reality of the gloomy hut's sparsely furnished room into a world of inexpressible despair. For at that moment in time it had seemed as if all his childhood security had vanished forever.

Having finished speaking, his mother had then handed him his sandals before bidding him sit on the log beside the charcoal fire situated in the centre of the room. As Vescala had slipped into the sandals, she had then resumed with the preparation of the morning meal. Turning his head away from her, he had wept silently whilst staring across to the upright rickety loom which so reminded him of the dire poverty in which his small family were forced to live under. For since being widowed the year before, a little weaving was the only work his sickly mother had been capable of undertaking, in order to keep her family from starvation. By then his fifteen-year-old sister had risen and after dressing, she joined her mother in stirring the watery gruel simmering in the iron cauldron suspended above the fire. After ladling out and handing him a wooden bowlful of the steaming gruel along with a lump of stale bread, his sister had then tried to reassure him in her kindly tones that no harm would befall him; explaining to him that his future had been preordained by his long dead ancestors and that to struggle against his fate would anger not only anger the spirits of his forebears but almost certainly incur the wrath of the gods as well. However, her words had brought little comfort to him, and as he sat eating his brooding eyes stared vacantly into the fire's shimmering embers. He was to speak to neither woman again and having forced the tasteless gruel and bread beyond the lump in his throat, he bitterly wondered as to the reason why his mother had not previously informed him of his, by then imminent departure. But then, staring up at the long, prematurely silver hair hanging down the back of her ankle-length dress, compassion had filled his heart, only for his thoughts to end abruptly on hearing the powerful knocking on the household's wooden door.

The resonant sound had sent both women into a flurry of activity. After first unbarring the door, his mother had greeted the callers while his sister had pulled him to his feet to somewhat nervously wrap him in his cloak, all the time trying to reassure him in quiet whispers that he had nothing to fear. He had then turned sharply to see the two elderly bearded figures emerging through the dimly lit doorway. However, at the menacing appearance of his approaching priestly abductors some dark rebellious instinct within him had screamed at him to run. With his heart pounding, his instant decision to escape had overpowered any logic that might have remained in his troubled mind as without hesitating, he had brushed between his mother and the priests to run through the open doorway and out into the chilly morning air.

With the realms of his conscious mind having been engulfed in a confused terror, he had then sprinted headlong past the other village huts and, splashing ankle-deep through the dew pond, almost stumbled into an empty storage pit. Once past the open unguarded portcullis of the high trellis stockade surrounding the village he continued on running blindly past the cornfields lying to each side of the path that led out of the village before fleeing across the hay meadows and the treacherous marshlands lying beyond them; never daring to look back lest he see his predators stalking him. For at the time, he had felt as one with the terrified roe deer who is hunted into exhaustion and death by the merciless wolf pack.

It had been some time in the late morning when he entered into the sprawling forest, but it wasn't long before he had found himself hopelessly lost among its dense suffocating legions of trees and bushes. Later in the day, a few hastily gathered edible roots had helped alleviate his hunger, but the approach of nightfall had seen him preoccupied with seeking out a safe refuge from the forest's wild animals. A suitable ivy-enmeshed oak tree had provided him with a comfortable retreat, and after climbing it with ease he soon settled down among the thick branches to fall into a light, uneasy slumber.

That night had been a long and often terrifying ordeal for the child, but having been cradled safely in the tree's high branches, he began to feel optimistic regarding his future. Now in a benign mood, he openly prayed that the oncoming day would see him safely delivered from his wretched self-imposed exile. He was now, well aware that he had no alternative but to attempt to find his way back to his village, and moving nimbly between the tree's compact branches, he worked his way back down through the mesh of clinging ivy only to discover a strange excitement stealing into him as his feet sank into the dank mouldering humus at the base of the tree. It was as if some dormant self-confidence had surfaced from deep within him, bringing hope where before he had known only despair, and taking his first steps back into the primordial surroundings, the courage he had so foolishly forsaken the day before now seemed to burn from deep within his soul. Stooping down, he picked up a small sturdy branch lying among the rotting leaf mould, reckoning that if attacked by some wild animal, he could now at least attempt to defend himself. With the weapon enhancing his courage, he drew his cloak tight around his shoulders and remaining ever alert, glanced around the trees before choosing the direction through the wilderness from which he thought he had originally come.

Striving forward, the warmth of the blazing morning sun now surging down through the lofty treetops energised each of the tortured steps he was taking through the dense thicket. But with the entangled masses of bracken, nettles and scrub stinging and stripping the skin from his exposed ankles, his progress became painfully slow, and, wandering until all sense of direction had vanished, he concluded that any hope of a speedy return to his village was now gone. There were times when he was forced to stop and rest and his ever-watchful eyes would absorb the rich abundance of life forms that gave the forest a gentle and almost innocent appearance; with the purples, yellows, and pinks of the flora standing in sharp contrast against the towering backdrop of mottled green and brown shades. With the forest's sensuous atmosphere buzzing with countless numbers of droning insects that lazily weaved their paths through the still humid air, he observed almost laconically, that even the capture and demise of one of their numbers in the beak of a swooping whitethroat failed to prevent their rightful flights throughout the forest's heart. For a few brief moments, he allowed himself a smile on spotting a timid red squirrel skipping through the branches of a neighbouring tree. However, growing ever wearier he continued on his way, only to experience the discomfiture of hunger and thirst beginning to wrack his tired and bleeding body. Hopelessly lost, he was now aware that if he was to survive then he must quickly find food and water or the elusive pathway that would eventually lead him beyond the forest's perimeter. A little further on, he was fortunate to come upon a small clearing where a cluster of mushrooms grew near to a thicket of bramble bushes, and after eating his fill he stuffed as many as he could into the small pocket in his woollen shirt.

By this time the heat and humidity had become unbearable, with clouds of moisture rising steadily up from the forest floor, and pressing on he was forced into removing his cloak, which he promptly slung over his shoulder. After a while the ground ahead began to rise sharply and once again, he felt his courage falter, when recalling his mother's words as they powered their way out of his memory.

"Vescala, at no time are you to ever enter the forbidden forest – that lair of demons!" she had warned him from his earliest years and, this being the first time he had ever set foot in a forest, he struggled on upwards bitterly regretting having ignored her advice. The climb was difficult and, along with the streaming sweat from his forehead trickling down into his now stinging eyes, his weary legs began to cause him a considerable aggravation. But the further he ascended the incline the more he noticed the surrounding trees beginning to thin out, and, rapidly drawing in breath and with every muscle in his lean frame straining to the maximum of physical endurance, the changing landscape spurred him on in his desperation to reach the apex of the hill.

At the summit, he was delighted to see a wide steep ravine opening out before him, where a small stream, sparkling in the glistening sunlight, provided a small herd of red deer with a plentiful supply of cool water. At last, here was a place where he could drink, rest, and bathe his aching feet, he thought, feeling a certain relief. However, the journey down the ravine's slippery fern-infested slopes proved more difficult than he had anticipated, and stumbling on a loose rock, he fell, only to roll down the embankment and plummet headlong into the stream's fast-flowing waters with the commotion scattering the frightened deer. But the soothing water immediately invigorated his exhausted limbs and, had he not remembered the food in his pocket, he would have lain where he was for some considerable time. Clambering back onto the grassy bank, he quickly slaked his thirst and, after eating his remaining food, decided to follow the stream in the hope that this artery of the forest might provide the water supply for some nearby village or homestead out-with the forest's boundary.

Feeling heartened and refreshed, he returned to gather up his cloak and weapon that he had dropped further up the slope, and stepping briskly forward he remained fully alert as he walked along the banks of the stream's white waters, stopping occasionally to relieve his painful feet in its turbulence. As he progressed, he was to notice the steep sides of the ravine begin to recede, with the fern-covered slopes soon giving way to a rolling, rock-strewn landscape broken only by a few isolated clumps of thick bushes and tall erect conifers. And with the stream now bending sharply to his right he pressed on, but after only a short time his heart sank on seeing it to be no more than a tributary leading into a small lake. As his eyes scanned the waters spreading out before him, he remembered being told of the lake-dwelling tribes: a people who constructed their homes on offshore stilts, in order to give them protection against hostile tribes as well as predatory animals. But from where he stood it was apparent that no such people inhabited this region, for on all sides of the lake the forestry came to within an arm's length of the water's edge.

On the lake's far banks a family of beavers swam close to their lodges. Before them a large variety of wildfowl glided listlessly over the water's surface; their calm wanderings frequently shattered in a cacophony of beating wings, splashing water, and threatening calls as one species would suddenly encroach upon another's territory. The clamorous noise sent the profusion of multi-coloured insects hovering low above the lake's surface into a panic-stricken swarm back to the shore, only to return in the ensuing peaceful moments; all with the exception of one pale blue butterfly whose glorious fluttering was dramatically terminated in the frenzied grasp of a bright green-attired dragonfly.

Suddenly Vescala shuddered violently, feeling as one with the ill-fated butterfly and morbidly seeing in his mind's eye the dragonfly masquerading as the ever-threatening forestry. Hearing only the incessant chirping of the hedge crickets behind him, the child watched apprehensively as the butterfly's powdered wings gently floated down to come to their inevitable rest on the glassy waters.

With the high sun suddenly disappearing behind a lone cloud and the lake and all its inhabitants now enshrouded in a veil of menacing gloom, his sad heavy eyes stared upwards, uncertain if it was indeed a cloud or the dark retributive hand of the powerful thunder god Taranis, who in his anger had obliterated the light as if to inform him that his suffering must continue. His mother had often told him that the thunder god would exact a terrible vengeance against anyone, who had the temerity to defy the will of the Gods. But, as the cloud slipped slowly across the sky, he was more than relieved to see the landscape once again glow vibrantly in the sun's life-inducing rays.

By now it was mid-afternoon, and strolling almost complacently along the shore he suddenly spotted through a cluster of trees a gravel escarpment, rising up to stop at a line of gorse bushes at the summit. Seeing that it would not be too difficult to scale, he began to make his way up, only to find that by the time he reached the summit, he was drenched in a film of warm sweat. After struggling on through the prickly gorse, he saw ahead of him, a number of massive lichen-covered rocks dominating an undulating grass-covered terrain. And with the plateau stretching a fair distance before once again being surrounded by the forest, he reckoned on it being an excellent spot to take a short rest. By now his sandals were causing him some pain, and, removing them, he wrapped them in his cloak and tucked it under the arm holding the weapon. However, on passing between the two prominent rocks, he suddenly glimpsed from the corner of his eye a sight so horrific that it caused him to drop his belongings and stand frozen to the spot in utter terror. At first his gaping eyes could hardly take in the gruesome sight at his feet, for lying spread out in a mangled heap among a pile of smaller rocks lay the naked, blood-encrusted body of an adult male whose arms still clutched onto the maggot-infested entrails that had gushed from the gaping wound in his abdomen. Although Vescala's senses reeled at the macabre sight, it was the ghastly face of the corpse that struck his soul with the sharpness of a dagger. For beyond its grey mantle of death, he recognised the features as belonging to a close friend of Culain, the man shortly to marry his sister. Now panting with terror, the child recoiled sideways, retching, and spitting out in an attempt at cleansing his mouth and nostrils from the miasmal stench emanating from the decaying flesh. But on forcing his eyes to once again look down upon it, he was so terrified by the cursed look in the lifeless eyes staring back up at him that, leaving his belongings where they lay, he turned and fled the scene.

Running headlong back into the forest he soon found himself entombed within a nightmarish, sordid greenery flooding over his wide, glazed eyes as the forest's haunting permanence brought to him a chilling despair. And as he ran through the timeless Everglades, he now imagined every branch and every twig of the twisting, writhing trees to be mirroring the long skeletal hands of death, whose threatening fingers longed to grab and return his soul to the time beyond the womb!

With the day now flying by, and with the exhausted child almost on the verge of a mental and physical collapse, crude figures representing gods and roughly hewn out of the tree trunks suddenly appeared on either side of him, bringing from apparently nowhere a pebbled pathway now stretching out before him. With his strength almost gone, and now in a state of outright desperation, he ran in sporadic bursts following the narrow, man-made structure in one final effort to escape the forest's enticing but savage intimacy.

As the time elapsed, a cool evening breeze eerily rustled the treetops in a melodious sound that to the forsaken child appeared to be moving the swaying branches in some pre-ordained ritual that only the superior knowledge of the gods might understand. But now half-crazed in agony, he struggled on wondering if there was some message in the forest's music or if indeed the continuing lines of carved tree figures were beckoning him to safety or catastrophe.

With his mind and body having undergone a traumatic ordeal, he now saw and cared for nothing as he trundled on, passing by the crossroads where six long blood-stained wooden poles were erected around the circular grass mound where the four paths adjoined. Six newly severed human heads – freshly embalmed in cedar oil were mounted on top of the poles; their lifeless eyes staring eastwards towards the kingdom of the sun god.

Stumbling and falling and now guided by intuition alone, the child raised himself up only to struggle on and, following the path to his right, the encompassing world now revolved in his mind like some surrealistic netherworld as he became aware of a distinct pounding in his head. But a pounding that seemed to be urging and abetting his divine soul to some psychic provenance.

The child would never know just for how long he remained within the inhuman grasp of his mesmerising stupor. But now, sustained only by fate's decree and with dusk descending all around him, he suddenly became conscious of being surrounded by many shadowy human forms who immediately passed before him to reveal a vast clearing where towering on either side of him, stood two rows of artistically sculptured wooden totem poles. Swaying and staggering between them, he saw ahead of him a flame-encircled grassy knoll, where rising from its apex stood the most revered of all the forest's trees.

With the very stature of the ancient stag-headed oak appearing to dominate all other forms within the sacred glade, it stood as witness against the opaque purple of the falling twilight as the trembling, gaping-eyed child lurched towards it sensing the blissful contentment of a spiritual atonement. Suddenly the ethereal voices surrounding him became coherent words as many white-robed men and women swarmed around him, with each face bearing its own mask of incredulity.

Perspiring heavily in his ragged clothing, the child felt no fear, and even the recognition of his two would-be abductors among the excited throng meant nothing to him as, slumping to his knees in utter exhaustion, two words heard from unseen lips were to penetrate the ensuing mists of sleep now overwhelming him.

"Vescala…Deliverance!" the voices exclaimed, and having been raised to be carried in secure arms, the blackness of a gentle sleep soared over his mind just as his fading eyesight saw again the sacred oak tree. That mystical harbinger of life so worshipped by the druids as the Godhead of the forest. The mighty tree − that to the child Vescala had become a strange mentor that some inner sense informed him was destined to play a specific role in the unfolding drama of his life to come.

Chapter Two

By means of his long oaken staff, the old druid master raised himself up from the straw-covered earthen floor; his depressive eyes remaining fixed on the log fire in front of him. The voices in the warm cosy room suddenly abated, and clearing his throat, he then addressed his nine students who sat facing him in a semicircle around the fire's dying embers.

"Gentlemen, tomorrow each of you embark upon the journey into manhood," he said to his students, with his sincere, deep voice carrying as much authority as the resplendent white druidical robes he wore. "Over these past twelve years, you have studied hard and learned much from your other tutors as well as myself. For each of you the future horizon glows in the white of light, the blue of truth, and the purple of hope as depicted on the triple-coloured novitiate headbands that you don so proudly on this auspicious evening. However, for myself the horizon darkens! For tomorrow I retire to a life of solitude to await my approaching death. But in my seclusion, I will pray daily to the gods that each of you – whom I look upon as sons and not just mere students – will forever stand united against the ever-growing powers of darkness lying not only outside but also within the shores of our beloved islands."

As the old master paused his tear-filled eyes stared in turn at each of the young men's doleful expressions; perhaps it was the effect of the strong wine he had so joyfully consumed earlier in the evening, he wondered pensively. For at the sight of their carefree faces his own youthful memories suddenly surfaced in his mind, only to quickly recede. His day had gone, and it was an uncertain future that he now stared toward; a future that would only be safeguarded by these very students whom he had helped educate over these past twelve years.

A prolonged silence now filled the room as each of the young men's eyes glanced inquisitively toward their companions as if seeking an explanation for their master's sudden unhappiness. Surely this was an inappropriate time for such a serious diatribe, each of them thought. In the morning, they would be returning to their tribal lands for the first time since they were children, and might never set eyes upon one another again. However, the old master was well aware of their thoughts. Maybe it was unfair of him to spoil the evening's gaiety he now reckoned; nonetheless, he had things to say that he felt they must hear.

"I said within these shores, and believe me, what I said I meant!" he exclaimed, swaying slightly as his tall, wasted body leaned heavily onto the staff now held rigidly in his deeply wrinkled hands. "I'm sorry to say that there are those among our upper social strata, and many even in our own beloved priesthood, who, in their pernicious quest for gold and riches, abuse their high positions as they cling like parasites onto the cloaks of our tribal kings. My sons you must always remember that our priesthood is never tribal in its teachings – but universal. Many eons ago – long before our ancestors crossed over from Europe to colonise these British islands – our predecessors who built and worshipped in the great megalithic structures sited at Stonehenge and Avebury found to their tragic cost that their priesthood, when disunited, became directly responsible for the spiritual corruption that preceded the long centuries of inter-tribal warfare that erupted among them. This sent the original inhabitants of these islands plummeting headlong into an age of darkness and superstitious ignorance. For nigh on three hundred years, we druids have been attempting to unify all the tribal kingdoms of our islands – but as of yet, without success. It is now up to the likes of yourselves to ensure that what happened to the ancient Britons never happens to you. For today powerful Roman armies lie in wait across the channel separating us from Roman-occupied

Europe; their leaders longing for the time when they can return and complete the invasion they began exactly thirty-six years ago. Never forget that the Romans worship many gods, as indeed we do, but believe me when I tell you that they are demented gods fed on mass genocide and deified by the Romans merely to satisfy the depraved and avaricious lusts inherent within each of their incestuously bred generations."

Hesitating for a few moments, the old master then continued speaking, only this time in a voice trembling with anger. "If any among you ever take the oath of allegiance to their unholy state, you will pass beneath their yoke of worldwide slavery only to emerge as mindless creatures whose spirits will forever remain fossilised in time. My grandfather told me, when I was a mere child in Gaul, that when they came from their great stone-constructed citadel of Rome, he personally witnessed them spreading their misguided pestilence on the wings of a supremely well-organised duplicity. Firstly, they practised their deceptive philosophy under the guise of liberty and friendship, hoodwinking the gullible masses with empty promises of a future affluence that could never have known fulfilment. And after their emissaries and agents had sown the seeds of inter-tribal dissension among us, below the shadow of their pagan eagle came their marching armies, who raped, looted, and burned with a ruthless dexterity, murdering, and plundering on a scale unprecedented in all of history's bloodstained reality. In their wake we were promised freedom and equality but instead we received repression and bondage. As a youth, I escaped to these shores, and ever since Julius Caesar's aborted invasion, we have lived at peace with Rome. However, it's an uneasy peace and we must forever keep one eye on the channel separating us from Gaul. Our strength and commitment lie in the unity and bonding influence that our priesthood brings to the tribal fiefdoms. For never forget that in Caesar's time our gods favoured Rome, and only when we had exorcised the besmirching decadence that had so corrupted our priests and kings alike did, we once more find favour with them."

The old master paused and thoughtfully stroking the long grey beard adorning his noble features then continued, only this time in a grave voice fraught with anxiety. "Last night, in a terrible vision which came to me in the form of a dream, I witnessed the side profile of one among you standing alone against a background of many interchanging seasons. In his right hand, he held a bronze drinking vessel overflowing with the blood of human innocence, and in the left, clutched a small golden sickle dripping with the blood of human debauchery. His mouth was gagged, but the sinful expression in that one eye I will never forget. The seasons then flew before my eyes until summer engulfed the figure in its brightness. But then, raining down from a clear sky, countless numbers of blood-encrusted human heads slowly tumbled to the earth until they finally buried the figure against a darkening background, leaving sleep's mystery and I to share the vision's dark secret. As you all know, our yearly calendar cycle is broken up into fourteen months, with each month being associated with a different species of bird life: all that I have told you is set to occur in the month of the red-backed shrike, commonly known as the 'butcher bird.' Looking around, I see doubt cast on some faces, but you would do well to heed my words. For I warn you that one among you may, in time, be guilty of profane worship, and not only might his resulting crimes herald disaster for every tribe in the land, but he will bring shame and finally destruction upon our proud seat of learning! By the time such events have occurred, I will have been long dead; therefore, I beseech each of you to vigorously uphold and respect the laws and customs of the past generations of our glorious priesthood until the day you die!"

Once again, the old master paused, only to resume in a sympathetic manner. "Now it has been twelve long years since you last saw your families, and as you are aware, over the next year you must decide whether or not to remain in the priesthood. I too was once in your position and well remember that long year of soul searching before deciding to return to this hallowed island to accept the un-severable bonds that come with the priesthood's final vows. No one can force you into returning, but over the period of the next year, it is probable that most of you will choose an alternative lifestyle for yourselves. Perhaps some among you will marry and spend your lives in the world of trade and commerce, while others may choose to become nobles and warriors. However, if you should return you will be expected to work hard at your studies. For we druids are not only an elite body in the teaching of our religion, but also in the teaching of law and medicine. This is why all full members of our priesthood are granted dispensation by the tribal kings from paying taxes as well as taking up arms in times of war. Now at first light a slave will guide you to your point of departure where the ferryman will be waiting with his barge to ship you and your ponies over the straits to the mainland."

Content that he had taught them well, the old master stared down into the fire. "And so, gentlemen," he said solemnly as his fatigued eyes rose to meet each of theirs in turn, "I must leave you for the last time, but never forget that you live and will continue to live in dangerous times. You must always beware the month of the red-backed shrike and take great care that my terrible prophecy remains forever unfulfilled!"

At this point his nine students rose simultaneously and, one by one, each man silently embraced the master whose sorrow-filled eyes flooded with tears at the affection being shown to him. It was an emotional few moments, with some of his students openly weeping as he slowly turned to walk out of the room, and as he closed the door behind him each one of them felt as if he was losing a father rather than a tutor.

For a few reflective moments, everyone stood still with only the torch flames stirring as if swaying in unison to the sound of the bleak moaning wind outside. But their long flickering beams now danced around a room where joy had given vent to sorrow as each man returned to once more sit among the animal skins and straw covering the earthen floor. Some of them stared thoughtfully down at the long blue initiation robes covering their bodies, while others contented themselves in drinking the last of the wine that had flowed so freely earlier in the evening. But by now most of them were tired, with the songs and poetry that had inspired the joyous camaraderie experienced earlier, soon forgotten as each individual contemplated over the long journey lying ahead of him in the morning.

Lying flat out on his back, Vescala lazily spread himself across a massive brown bearskin as his thoughts returned to that far distant day when as a young child he had absconded from the two priests. A broad smile spread over his tired, drawn features as he recalled the fear he had felt then; over these past twelve years it had never failed to amaze him how he had come upon the sacred tree just when all hope had seemed lost. At the time, there were many in the upper echelons of the priesthood who had been astonished that one so young could have stumbled upon the sacred tree, particularly during the important midsummer ceremonial rites. Perhaps that fact alone had been the reason why he had always detected a certain goodwill having been directed towards him by his tutors, he thought morosely.

It was to be many years before he learned the truth as to the reason for his abduction with his mother having been forced into selling him to the druids to pay off a blood debt owed to a family in a neighbouring village, whose son had been murdered in a quarrel. Culain, his then future brother-in-law, along with one of his close friends, had stood accused of the crime, only to be tried under druidical law and subsequently found guilty. As the law stood, it was a common occurrence that when one family was wronged by another then, rather than risk a major feud developing between them, a financial settlement was made in restitution by the culprit's family to be paid either in silver or livestock. If it was acceptable to the wronged party then the matter, whether it be murder, rape, or theft, was promptly forgiven and forgotten. Such inter-family agreements were always initiated and supervised over by the protagonists of the law, namely the powerful body of druid priests. Had it not been for such intervention, Culain would almost certainly have shared the fate of his unfortunate accomplice who had no means by which to pay the blood debt. As a result, his mother had not only saved Culain's life but she had also prevented her family from suffering many further years of grinding poverty. For shortly after being released by the druids, Culain had indeed married his sister, and from the information novitiates were periodically given as to their families' welfare, he had learned that the marriage had been a great success; producing three fine sons whose very existence must surely delight his mother he reckoned. He was more than grateful to Culain for having provided so well for his loved ones over the years. And yet even if the druids had not bought him to free Culain, it was possible that he might still have been taken into the priesthood. For it was quite common that when a family faced extreme hardship the druids would 'buy,' via their village elders, a young child whose above-average intelligence was reported to them. Such children, as he himself had been, were subsequently taken along with the sons of nobles, warriors, and craftsmen to be educated at the main druidical seat of learning, sited on the holy island of Anglesey.

Thinking of home, he chuckled aloud wondering if his mother and sister would recognise him after such a lengthy time, having changed dramatically from the scrawny, ill-fed youngster whom they had last seen; indeed, he was almost afraid to think of their reactions when they saw the tall, lean bearded figure confronting them. Suddenly his heavy eyes stared up at the rectangular thatched ceiling that was the protective barrier between the inmates of the hut and the wind-driven rain now gusting violently outside. He recalled with sadness his father, and how as a six-year-old child he had watched him for the last time disappear into a heavy rain storm to join the village hunting party. It was a trip neither his father nor any of the others were to return from, and he vividly remembered the mourning in his village when their bodies had been discovered two days later; all having been the victims of a sudden flash flood. Had his father lived, his life might have been so very different, he now thought dejectedly, and although his twelve years of enforced study had been relatively happy, he had in recent times begun to have serious reservations regarding the druid teachings reservations that had started to trouble him!

A restless sleep now began to infiltrate his thoughts, but it was a light slumber constantly interrupted by the drumming of the heavy rain outside and the occasional murmurings of the others whose excitement at their homeward journey he somehow felt reluctant to share. Finding sound sleep almost impossible, his discomfort on seeing the formless shapes leaping up behind his closed eyelids became unbearable. Momentarily, he imagined the eyes of the old master's sinister vision staring directly into his own. It was as if he were looking back at his own reflection staring up from some dark, brackish pool containing the ever-interlocking phases of the past, present and future.

With the aura of the flickering torchlights slowly diminishing, a still and awful darkness fell around him smothering the room in an evil shroud of black, funereal menace. In the morbid darkness, his now open eyes strained desperately to see as his alert ears longed to hear some comforting sound, but nothing breached the total silence that spawned a terrifying primeval fear from within the depths of his pounding brain. With an embracing sweat bursting from his skin, he suddenly felt as if he was back in the womb of his sinless pre-existence, only now devoid of the life-giving cord that through some long-forgotten memory had imparted to him a knowledge of absolute assurance. With his sense of isolation fearfully accelerating, he became acutely aware of an indefinable horror bursting into life in the far corner of the room, and lying half stunned, his mind swam through the congealed flood of a dissipating presentiment as the terror of living fire swept over the entire length of his body.

His horror ended abruptly, leaving his tense body drenched in warm sweat with the sudden relief of awakening more than compensation for what had been such an uncanny and realistic nightmare. Frantically gulping in huge mouthfuls of the fresh morning air now infiltrating the room through the open doorway, he sat up to glimpse the tall figure of their slave guide standing silhouetted against the murky daybreak; the man being unwilling to enter the building without prior permission.

Struggling to his feet, Vescala smiled and beckoning with his hand to the slave to enter enquired of the slave if everything was prepared. For with the nightmare eclipsed, his homeward journey now loomed uppermost in his thoughts

"Yes, master," the tall, well-built slave replied in a quiet voice as he courteously bowed before entering the room. "I have the ponies and travelling packs ready outside. But I fear that unless the weather improves the crossing over the straits may well have to be delayed."

However, Vescala did not pay him much attention. He was too busy going around awakening the other eight, all of whom were lying sprawled across the floor, oblivious to the chill breeze now sweeping around their recumbent bodies.

"Master, I fear that time is short!" the slave exclaimed uneasily. "The weather may yet deteriorate, and with all due respect, I think it would be advisable if we could reach the straits by noon. That way I believe we should have an even chance of reaching the mainland today."

Vescala, who was now changing out of his initiation robes into heavier clothing, detected the man's concern. Staring sympathetically towards the tall, clean-shaven figure, it was not difficult for him to understand the slave's anxiety, recalling that it had been only a few years before when five novitiates had been drowned crossing over the straits in stormy weather. Foolishly, they had ignored the advice of their slave guide not to cross: nonetheless, the man had been put to death soon afterward for what the priesthood had classified as his negligence. No! It is a harsh injustice that these older men, slaves though they might be, are answerable for the folly of youths whom they have no direct authority over, he reckoned sympathetically.

"What's your name, slave?" he enquired through a smile.

"Brenas, sir," the dark-haired slave who was some ten years older than him replied. "All right, Brenas, I'll do all I can to ensure that you alone will decide when the time is right to make the crossing. But tell me, do we have enough time for breakfast?"

"No, sir! Rather than waste time, I took the liberty of telling the slave women to prepare some extra food and put it into the saddle packs."

"Excellent! Now if you return outside and wait, we will be with you shortly."

At this command, the slave's weather-beaten features broke into a pleasant smile, and taking his leave, he felt delighted that the youth had spoken to him as an equal and not like some underfoot dog, as would normally have been the case.

By now the others had risen and, with Vescala having explained to them the situation regarding the weather, pandemonium broke loose as they practically fell over one another in their attempts to dress and pack their robes and possessions. Having fully prepared himself, a grinning Vescala sat picking at the few leftover scraps of food lying scattered all around him when suddenly a deep voice boomed out. "Get a move on. I for one have no intention of spending another day on this god-forsaken island!" Ravala said menacingly as his dark eyes narrowed into a threatening frown. When this pampered son of a rich nobleman gave orders, few of his fellow novitiates dared to disagree with him, and as he sat chewing on a small piece of cold bacon, Vescala gripped the hilt of the dagger tucked beneath his beaver-skin cloak. Eyeing Ravala cautiously, he recalled the day some two years before when he and his close friend Straval had gone fishing in one of the many rivers that meander through the island's rambling forests. They hadn't gone far though when they had come upon the debauched Ravala standing over the raped, mutilated body of a young slave girl. It was a sight that neither he nor Straval would ever forget, with the tragic victim's nipples having been torn off by her murderer's teeth.

At the time both men had been sorely tempted to kill Ravala for the atrocity. And although having reported him to their druid masters, after only a short term of imprisonment Ravala's father's 'gold and influence' had bought his only son's 'innocence.' Both men were now afraid of Ravala and they had good reason to be. For he had sworn that they had falsely accused him and had vowed that the day would come when he would be fully avenged. Vescala knew that neither Straval nor himself would stand much chance alone in combat against such a powerfully built adversary. Over the years the braggart Ravala had never shown any aptitude in learning anything other than the handling of the sword and spear, and ever since the young girl's murder, both men had ensured never to be in a position where they were left alone with the man who had openly boasted to kill them. Unclasping his dagger, Vescala was more than grateful that the three of them would be travelling south together; reckoning that even a man as mean and vindictive as Ravala would never dare to tackle two of them at once.

Having finalised their preparations, each of them then made their way outside to where the guide stood waiting alongside the team of ponies. By now a small crowd had congregated around the animals, with some of the slaves and their children having come to bid the party farewell and wish them luck.

All around the compact village, consisting of no more than ten round heavily thatched mud huts, everything lay silent save for the sound of the wind and the occasional barking of a solitary dog. After shaking hands with each of the slaves in turn, Vescala mounted his chestnut pony and looked around for what he thought would probably be the last time at the misery-ingrained faces of the slaves, whose impoverished existences had, even as a child, filled him with compassion. For from the very moment when he and his fellow students had first arrived on the island, the slaves, as was their duty, had never failed to provide them with adequate food, lodgings, and clothing. Sullenly staring down at the animal skins only half-covering some of them, he was again reminded of Ravala's despicable crime.

With a sad smile on his face, he turned his pony and, with Straval accompanying him, guided the mount along the muddy track that led towards the rain-drenched forest. The sky was a thunderous grey as they cantered out through the portcullis of the high wooden stockade surrounding the village, only for the sounds of the mud-splashing hoof beats to be suddenly broken by a forbidden cry.

"May the gods go with you, Vescala!"

At no time was any slave permitted to address a master unless first spoken to, and turning astride his pony to acknowledge the comment, a laughing Vescala raised his fist at the man's open disregard of what to him had always been an absurd law.

Brenas and Ravala, both being accomplished horsemen, had taken leadership of the party, with both riders galloping along at a fair pace. However, much to Ravala's frustration they had to stop periodically and await the others who were finding the terrain difficult to negotiate, owing to the now torrential rain turning the track into a quagmire of slithering mud. But with the two leaders a good bit ahead of them, the others had not travelled very far when the gusting wind swirled violently and bent the trees with such force that an overhead branch snapped and came crashing down directly in front of Straval's pony. The resulting blow shattered one of the stricken animal's forelegs, causing it to throw its rider headlong against a massive uprooted tree lying among the high ferns skirting the track's edge.

Instantly pulling up and dismounting, Vescala ran back to his now unconscious friend, only to see on raising his head from the earth, a deep ragged wound opened up on the left of his skull and which rapidly flooded his pale features in a mass of running blood. Seeing the seriousness of the situation the others likewise dismounted and, in an effort, to end the hobbling pony's distress began pulling the animal to the ground. As this was going on Vescala hurriedly tore a strip from the coarse linen jacket beneath his cloak and with it desperately attempted to stem the blood pumping out from Straval's wound.

After a time, Brenas and Ravala, who had stopped to await the others, turned back to see what the delay was, whereupon reaching them Ravala promptly leapt down from his mount to loudly curse Straval for his ineptitude in handling his pony. By now the others had succeeded in grounding the afflicted animal, and as one of them severed an artery in its pulsating neck with his knife to end its misery, the beast's convulsive death throes drenched everyone in a cold shower of clinging mud. Now mud-spattered and badly shaken, Vescala rose slowly, leaving Brenas to tie a makeshift tourniquet around Straval's head, and walking up to Ravala, who stood totally unconcerned at the injured man's plight, he directed hate-filled eyes towards him.

"Listen to me you heartless murdering bastard!" he screamed through teeth clenched in anger. "It is a damned pity that it's Straval who possibly lies dying and not you. He is twice the man an arrogant bastard like you ever will be!"

Each of them had been equipped with swords for their journey, and swiftly drawing his from the scabbard beneath his cloak, a vexed Ravala made a quick reply.

"You would be ill-advised to push me any further, Vescala. I warn you now, my sword is as sharp as the rays of a new dawn. Believe me, in my hand, it is only too willing to sever your troublesome head!"

"Oh, I don't challenge you," Vescala replied through a scornful smile. "After all, there will be plenty of time to fight later, or have you forgotten that when we reach the mainland you and I will now be the only ones traveling south. I promise you this Ravala: when we are alone you may well discover to your dear cost that I'm no helpless slave girl."

At this remark, the others openly sneered in derision as Ravala's eyes blazed furiously. But sensing the futility of his position he replaced his sword and somewhat sheepishly grabbing at his pony's, reins quickly remounted to disappear at a blistering gallop back along the track. Although now being acclaimed by the others for his boldness, Vescala was nonetheless glad to see the back of Ravala, all be it only temporarily. He had to admit to himself that he had been afraid, but for one brief moment, he was sure he had detected a glimmer of uncertainty in the big man's eyes. Perhaps it had only been his imagination, he wondered to himself. However, if there was a flaw in Ravala's hitherto undeniable courage, he would fully exploit it if and when the time came.

Turning his attention to Straval, he pondered over what was to become of the friend who ever since the day of his arrival on Anglesey he had looked upon almost as a blood brother; indeed, such had been the powerful physical resemblance between them that many of their druid masters had found difficulty in distinguishing the one from the other. He could hardly believe Straval's misfortune for he had been a brilliant scholar as well as a brave and trustworthy ally. If ever a man was destined to advance in the world it was surely Straval, he thought sadly; all the time praying inwardly to the gods to spare his life as he watched the teeming rain thin and cleanse the blood from his head, now lying cradled in the slave's strong arm.

It was now apparent to him that the only course open was to dispatch him back to the village, whereby he would receive expert medical attention. Turning to where the others were standing in a huddled group, he asked if one of them would be willing to accompany Straval and Brenas back to the village, thereby ensuring that the slave wasn't held responsible for the accident. One of the youths readily volunteered, enquiring of him as to the reason why he wasn't going himself. But Vescala never answered although the thought had crossed his mind that to return with Straval was an easy way out of a fight with Ravala. However, he was now committed to face the inevitable confrontation that he sensed must lie in the very near future.

In a depressed atmosphere, everyone then began cutting enough suitable branches, in order to build a makeshift stretcher capable of transporting the injured man back to the village. After this was done, they carefully laid the still-unconscious Straval onto it. Removing his own cloak Brenas tore it into long strips, which he then roped together and tied from the stretcher to around his pony's neck, in order to drag it back along the ground.

The remainder of the group could only watch sadly as the small party trundled back along the track until they were out of sight: Vescala praying that the bumpy journey back was not going to further aggravate Straval's wound. By now everyone was drenched to the skin, with even the tightly knit canopy of branches and twigs above granting them little protection as the heavy rain continued to pour down from the dull heavens. Remounting their ponies, they set off in the direction taken by Ravala, and after a long, tedious ride none of them were sorry to see the island's sandy shoreline spreading directly ahead of them on either side of a rocky promontory.

Chapter Three

Without the slave to guide them, it had taken them some time to find their point of departure. However, once they had, it was to be mid-afternoon before the weather abated enough to allow the ferryman to ship them and their ponies on his barge over the strait's choppy waters over to the mainland.

From high on the mainland's steep slopes, a sullen Vescala stared down to the beach below where a few old women, having taken advantage of the improving weather, busily gathered large quantities of edible seaweed in round osier baskets. Above him, the sun's forceful rays had begun to break through the heavy banks of grey silver-lined clouds, and spreading slowly across the island's dark green forestry, the rays transfigured its solemnity in iridescent shards of light that were broken only by the languid flights of a few distant kittiwakes whose shrill echoing cries appeared to be bidding a relieved farewell to the dispersing storm clouds.

Gazing upon the sacred island for what could be the last time, Vescala's emotions were mixed. Maybe he would return one day, he momentarily considered, but something inside him told him that his destiny must follow another direction: a route that he secretly hoped would lead him away from the despotism of the inveterate druid. For ever since the day Ravala had been absolved of the slave girl's slaying, he had seriously begun to question some of the priesthood's practices; primarily the one concerning human sacrifice. He now found it inconceivable that the priesthood's all too frequent acts of deliberate murder could appease the gods, and although never having personally witnessed any major sacrificial ceremony, he knew that the rumours frequently circulating among the novitiates had a base of factuality. Even now he could never forget Culain's unfortunate accomplice, whose terrible injuries had borne the distinct mark of the sacrificial blade. He now felt the suffering such victims were forced to endure to be barbaric and uncivilised, although he was well aware, that such thinking could never be the subject of any open debate with his masters. No druidical law was ever open to question! And he well recalled the savage beating he had received as a young child when he had dared question the law forbidding the use of the written word. It was a law strictly enforced under penalty of death! For among the Celtic races all knowledge had to be transmitted orally and memorised, with the mystery of all language considered by the druids as being the secret of none but the gods. He now wondered if his disillusionment with the priesthood had surfaced in his childhood, with the bitterness experienced after his attempted abduction never having completely left him. And as his long years of tuition had passed by, he had gradually become aware that his mind was being manipulated by imperfect mortals who had delegated to themselves a mantle of omnipotence. He had long ago seen through their procedure of sterile brainwashing that their students were subjected to through an educational system cunningly contrived for what was predominantly the subjugation of the poor ignorant masses who comprised the tribal peasantry.

Sitting astride his pony, his dark brown eyes grew misty as he reflected over the good and bad times he had spent on the island. And yet, he was uncertain over his alternating thoughts. For there were times when he utterly detested the priesthood, while at others he was filled with admiration at the many creditable works they achieved. Scratching at his tanned cheek just above the line of his short straggly beard, his dark brown eyes grew misty as he felt the light breeze whip at his unruly charcoal-coloured hair held in check by the thick novitiate headband tied tight around his classically shaped forehead. Brushing his long hair to one side, he spotted the others below him following the eastern shoreline, and he emitted a burst of laughter as one of them slipped from his pony to plunge headlong into one of the many shimmering rock pools that lay spread out all along the coastline. Momentarily envying them, his smile quickly altered into a scowl, for their journey home would never be fraught with the danger he must now face, and drawing his hands from the pony's reins, the sweat on his palms was a reminder to him that fear was every bit as dangerous a companion as the sadist he was now having to travel alone with.

After the party had reached the ferryman's frugal dwelling place; being no more than a deep cave above the beach, he and the others had dried themselves and eaten whilst Ravala had remained aloof. But apart from a few exchanged cursory glances, neither man had made any attempt to cause trouble. Vescala prayed that the present situation would prevail for the next four days: this being the time he estimated that it would take Ravala to reach his homeland. His own journey would probably take a little longer. However, he knew with absolute conviction that from now on he must never let his defences falter, even if it meant having to go without sleep in the time, he would spend in Ravala's company.

Turning his pony, he viewed the barren landscape ahead, and seeing the sombre hues in the western sky that denoted nightfall, it was with a feeling of trepidation that he began trotting towards Ravala who by now was already a good way ahead of him. After reciting a short prayer for his safe deliverance to Epona, the goddess of the pony, he broke his mount into a fast gallop. For in wintertime men isolated from the sanctuary of the villages were endangered not only by the elements but also the roaming wolves, whose packs forever lurked among the countryside's unwelcoming shadows. But with the exception of a few moss-encrusted boulders, the land ahead lay desolate, and pulling up alongside the disinterested Ravala, they continued trotting along for only a short time before sighting the thin wisps of grey smoke rising up from the distant village fires. This village was the first overnight stop on their respective journeys, and arriving tired and hungry they were made welcome by the village elder and given food and shelter with the remainder of the night passing by without incident.

In the morning, they advanced south, with every village they stopped at providing them as was customary with their food and shelter. As the days passed by their novitiate headbands assured them of a safe passage beyond the many tribal frontiers they were having to pass through. Although the conversation between the two men had been minimal, their relationship continued to be one of mutual hatred: even so, neither had made any attempt to offend the other. Ravala had for some reason seemed loath to risk a confrontation, much to Vescala's delight, and by the time they had reached the frontiers of the Dobunni tribe on the shores of the great, southern river, the distrust between them appeared, at least to Vescala, to have decreased. By this time, they had reached their point of separation, and pulling their mounts up it was Vescala who spoke.

"There never has or is ever likely to be any bond of friendship between us Ravala. Nonetheless, I wish you well in the future," he said in a reasonably friendly manner as Ravala eyed him uneasily.

"Hear me well, Vescala! Regardless of whether you return to Anglesey to accept the final vows or not…the day will come when your troublesome head will hang from my war chariot!" Ravala replied stolidly, before turning his pony to canter eastwards along the river's wide gravel banks.

However, at the sight of his departing enemy Vescala felt only joy, with even the cold weather appearing more tolerable as the encircling wind swept away the paranoid depression he had felt ever since Straval's accident. Grinning at Ravala's threat with a mixture of relief and contempt, he turned his mount west and vociferously shouted his praises for his safekeeping to Teutates, the god of travellers.

With the wide choppy river being the last major obstacle lying between him and his tribal homeland on its far side, he began to follow its banks. It was not long before he reached the village whose priest, he had previously been informed, would provide the necessary craft by which he could make the crossing over the water.

The people of the small village were more akin to those of the northern coast in the fact that the sea provided them with their basic sustenance, for at this point the River Severn swept into the sea separating the southern mainland of Britain from Ireland. However, he did notice that outside the village's protective stockade, there was no shortage of livestock, with cattle, pigs, and goats roaming carefree among the patchwork of fields surrounding the circular stockade. The village within comprised of no more than twenty or so mud huts, and passing through the open portcullis he dismounted, only to be immediately spotted by the local druid priest who strolled over to greet him.

"I was told to expect two of you," the elderly man commented; a grim expression covering his heavily bearded countenance.

"Yes, sir. I'm afraid my friend met with an accident back on Anglesey," Vescala replied and then explained what had happened.

"So be it. But come, I expect you must be hungry."

Ushering him into a nearby hut the priest then ordered a slave to tend to his pony before summoning a slave woman to prepare him a meal. The priest then left him and although slightly apprehensive at the coolness of his reception, he was relieved to be sheltered from the biting wind. Quickly removing his cloak, he took a seat on the small wooden stool next to the glowing peat fire in the centre of the small room. After only a short time, the woman handed to him a clay bowl filled with a warm, tasty gruel concocted from a variety of seaweeds and molluscs. This was quickly followed by a plateful of salted herring which he washed down with a much-enjoyed flagon of heated wine. However, as he sat eating, he pondered over how he could ever repay the courtesy and generosity shown to him over these past few days. Finishing the meal the priest returned, but before he could thank his host the man somewhat abruptly raised his hand to signal for silence.

"I'm sorry to have to give you this news," the priest said as his furrowed brow lowered into a deep frown. "But I am afraid that over these past ten days, a severe plague has been raging among the unfortunate people of your tribe, the Durotriges. From what information I have received, it would appear, that many have died."

This news stunned Vescala who jumped up from the stool.

"However, you may have no cause to be alarmed," the priest then muttered consolingly. "It may be that the gods have spared your loved ones. But I must warn you that should you decide to cross the river, you will be prevented from returning here until the crisis is over. In order to prevent the disease from spreading all contact between your tribe and the neighbouring ones has for the time being ceased; this decision having been taken by the high priests the moment the outbreak became known. My advice to you is to stay here awhile but the decision is entirely yours."

Horrified by the implications in the man's words, Vescala never hesitated and, donning his cloak, begged that he and his pony be transported across the river immediately. With his request granted, he had to travel further downstream to his point of departure where he could see the other side of the river teeming with hundreds of stranded refugees who sat dejectedly among their few possessions; their route to safety effectively barred by the heavily armed warriors of the Dobunni tribe who were positioned just offshore in small rafts that stretched out all along the coastline.

It was early in the afternoon when along with his pony he clambered ashore from the barge, only to find himself surrounded by angry peasants and slaves who instantly bombarded him with questions. But he could render them no assurances as to when the situation might change, and it came as no surprise to him to hear many among them openly cursing not only their lords and masters but also the priesthood, for having abandoned them to a possibly slow and painful death.

For a time, he searched among them for any signs of his own relatives. But finding no trace of them, he subsequently questioned some of the despairing people in the hope that they might know of his family's fate – but none did! And praying nervously that they had remained in their village, he rode free from the crowds, deciding to travel around the sprawling forest stretching out to the south ahead of him. He knew that by choosing this route it would take a little longer to reach his village. But at least there was no chance of him losing his direction; this being the northern boundary of the very forest he had last entered as a child, with its southern perimeter lying close to his own home.

Riding flat out westwards the pony made good speed until reaching the forest's southern edge, where they unexpectedly came upon a wide tract of marshland. Dismounting, he led the animal through the quagmire only to be surprised to find the swamp more negotiable than he had anticipated, and reaching firmer ground he decided that it was an opportune time to take a short rest. Tethering the pony to a bush, he noticed a small gorse-covered hillock rising steeply up to his right. But sitting down on the moist grass, he at first took the low moaning sound to be coming from the breeze as it worked its way through the masses of tightly packed reeds growing around the side of the hillock. However, on hearing it a second time his instinct told him that it was no natural phenomenon but more akin to a cry of human anguish. Unsheathing his sword, he rose and made his way around the hillock towards the source of the sound. Creeping stealthily along, he was astounded to suddenly come upon the emaciated figure of a young woman kneeling helplessly among the bracken, and attired in no more than a soiled linen smock that only partially covered her small neat body, Vescala stepped back horrified on seeing that both her bloodied wrists had been securely bound to wooden stakes embedded into the ground on either side of her. Unhooking the ornate bronze clasps from down the front of his cloak, he bent down to stare beyond her mud-streaked face into her distressed, heavily swollen eyes.

"Who committed this outrage against you, woman?" he asked, furious that anyone could perpetrate such a barbarous act.

"Your headband betrays your pity, priest!" she snapped back through lips chapped numb by the cold weather. And although genuinely sympathetic to her plight, Vescala began to suspect that she was the victim of an expulsion order: a severe form of punishment whereby the offender was banished from all tribal contact for the duration of their life. Momentarily, he felt apprehensive with the law stipulating that anyone aiding such a person was himself likely to suffer a similar fate.

"What crime did you commit to be treated as an outcast?" he then asked, almost fearing her reply.

"My only crime, priest, was to have loved my dear husband!" she exclaimed, staring contemptuously up at him. "After he died last month, my two young sons and myself were ordered by our local priest to become the second family of my late husband's half-brother. When I refused to marry this man the priest denounced me, accusing me of heresy. You see my husband's half-brother is a cruel man, and in my heart, I know that even for the sake of my children, I could never have grown to love him. After my trial two days ago, my children were taken from me and I was brought here and left to die."

As she broke down sobbing through a veil of tears, Vescala stood erect, shaking his head, and hardly believing that such a trivial offence could warrant such a sentence. He knew there was nothing he could do to help the unfortunate woman. She had clearly defied the law and must therefore suffer the consequences. But looking down at her, he was suddenly filled with a capricious admiration for the courageous stance she had taken against a tyrannical law that, in respect of an individual's liberty, proved merciless. How unhappy she must have been to have first lost her children and then surrender herself to death's ever-welcoming door, he thought sombrely.

"Did you know about the plague?"

"Yes, I heard while awaiting my trial. I was brought here the morning the priests began to evacuate my village. Some of the women then stoned me, believing that my contempt for the law was responsible for their misfortune. Since then, I've awaited death, all the time praying that one day my sons would avenge their mother's inhuman treatment."

Beneath the dirt spattering her mottled face, he could see that she was little older than himself. Kneeling to gently scrape away the mud with his fingers, it became apparent to him that she was a woman of great beauty; her penetrating dove-grey eyes radiant with an assurance of inner purity. Suddenly he shuddered, on imagining her slow death from exposure and starvation. And yet if he did dare release her, then he too could expect no mercy if his action was somehow discovered, he thought warily.

"Look, if I release you, will you swear that if ever recaptured you will tell no one who helped you, even under pain of torture?" he asked through a kind smile.

"Y…yes…I promise," she stammered out, staring at him with a stunned expression covering her face. "But why should you help me? After all, I was condemned by your own kind!"

But making no reply, he quickly cut through the flaxen ropes binding her wrists with his sword before raising her up and then helping her over towards the tethered pony.

"Listen carefully, your only chance is to seek refuge in the forest," he said, removing his cloak as his eyes scanned the horizon in case anyone was about. "Here, take my cloak and this dagger…I'm afraid it's all I can do for you."

Taking hold of his belongings, the woman first thanked him before limping painfully off in the direction of the gloomy forest. Re-sheathing his sword and un-tethering the pony, Vescala slowly remounted, but watching her go, he sensed that within a short time, she would in all probability be dead anyway.

"May the gods be with you!" he shouted encouragingly to her, but the feeble reply that came back was tempered with bitterness.

"What gods, priest? There are none!"

By now it was late afternoon and continuing, on his way he remained uncertain if his decision to free her had been the correct one. Riding south away from the forest's edge, he soon came upon a small deserted village, not unlike his own, and where now only a few geese wandered aimlessly among the once lively abodes of the departed tenants. However, on passing by the place, he felt only despair on seeing the torn carcasses of the many sheep and cattle lying in the fields; their remaining flesh now in the process of being consumed by the black swarms of carrion crows that seemed to be perpetually descending from the dull skies. They, along with the grey wolves, had feasted well, he reckoned, praying with all his heart that his family had made good their escape.

Beyond the range of rolling hills ahead of him lay the village of his forefathers. And with the countryside now becoming familiar, long-forgotten memories began to resurface in his mind, reminding him of his happy childhood escapades.

As he advanced, he slowly cantered past the gurgling stream where his father had taught him to fish before passing beyond the cluster of craggy rocks where he had once played, pretending to be some fierce and gallant warrior. But on embracing those long peaceful summers, when his childhood innocence had stood alone as a safeguard against the world's many perils, he experienced an icy shiver shooting up his spine as somehow, he sensed that his family bonds were severed forever.

It was almost twilight when he reached the summit of the range where he could only stare down disbelievingly at the huge columns of thick black smoke slowly spiralling upwards from the blazing households of his village below, where masked slaves now busied themselves in carrying aloft fiery torches from hut to hut.

Steering his agitated pony downhill, he clearly heard above the crackling of the burning timbers the obsequious ritual chanting of the five white-robed priests who stood close by to the village centre. On trotting through the stockade's raised portcullis, he warily dismounted before introducing himself to the eldest of the priests, who immediately took him to one side, leaving the others to continue with their incantations. These they directed towards the darkening heavens as if seeking a divine explanation for the pestilence that had forced them into transforming the village into a wasteland.

The priest with Vescala was tall and elderly with an imperious bearing.

"My name is Durada, son," he proclaimed courteously, and as he spoke the fleshy folds on his stout bearded features twitched slightly. "Now you say that your family belongs here?"

"Yes, sir. I've just returned from the holy island," Vescala replied, and placing his arm across the young man's shoulders, Durada led him back towards the portcullis.

"I'm afraid I have tragic news for you. Neither man, woman nor child of your village survived the plague!" he exclaimed, with a genuine compassion prevalent in his deep voice, as Vescala recoiled backwards in despair. "In the hope that the disease can be contained, some sixteen of your tribal villages are being razed to the ground. All our fates now lie with the gods!"

But the man's sympathy brought little comfort to the despondency now being felt by Vescala, who could hardly believe that he would never again set eyes on the mother he had known only as a child, and as he thought of his sister and her sons, nephews he had never seen and never would, his stunned eyes filled with tears.

"If it's any consolation to you, I swear that those responsible for your agony will pay dearly," Durada declared with a trace of anger in his voice. But Vescala did not care for the priest's statement. Inwardly he was cursing the gods for having inflicted such a sorrow upon him: a sorrow that no vengeance directed against his fellow man could ever exorcize.

It was the sharp, distinctive smell of burning flesh that made him suddenly turn to see the flames leaping up from the narrow-consecrated ditch containing the remains of his loved ones. And despite burying his stricken features in his trembling hands, the vision behind his eyes kept showing their innocent bodies melting within the fire's cremating flames.

Chapter Four

Through the seasons' inevitable cycle, the long winter days slowly retreated against the spring's onslaught, thus allowing the life forms of the countryside to once again re-emerge from their sombre twilit world. Throughout the land, pale buds now bedecked forests longing to escape the inactivity of their long winter's slumber as birds sang, mating and building with meticulous care the nests destined to share the intimacy of regeneration. In the fresh lush meadows, young lambs skipped lightly, free, and unconcerned as to their role in the newborn creation, as everywhere all life lay bathed in the warm tender embrace of their cosmic redeemer, the indestructible sun god.

To a spiritually exhilarated Vescala this was indeed a time of hope, for in the two months elapsing since the tragic demise of his family, the proctorial Durada had, after a great deal of persuasive talking, finally convinced him that his future lay with the priesthood. He was treated by the old man almost like a son, having come to respect the many good works that the priest achieved in the large township that he had taken him to after the burning of his village. Although he had happily sworn the oath of allegiance to the priesthood, an oath which bound him to them for the rest of his life, he had done so mainly in the desire to heal the sick and comfort the distressed. However, Durada being a long-standing member of the druid hierarchy, had constantly emphasised to him how those fully qualified in the druidical faith became more than mere mortals, with they and they alone being the chosen intermediaries between the natural and spiritual worlds.

Over the past two months, Durada had employed him mainly in the supervision of the town's many slaves as they worked in the fields or in the building of one of the new hill forts now under construction in the possibility of a sudden Roman invasion. A recent massacre of many druids in Roman-occupied Gaul had at last convinced the tribal kings that the legions of the Roman emperor Augustus, might well cross over the channel in exactly the same manner as those of Julius Caesar had done some thirty-six years before. But the tribal kingdoms of Britain were disunited, with some to the south and east of the country openly trading with Roman provinces whilst others bickered and fought amongst themselves. This destroyed the possibility of the united front that the priesthood repeatedly called for. It was a classic case of history repeating itself. For among the priests even the finest optimist had to admit that, unless the tribal kings came to terms with one another, their armies brave as they undoubtedly were would stand little chance against Rome's well-disciplined and battle-accustomed legions.

Although temporarily barred from wearing his priestly garments, he had begun to take a certain pride in the novitiate headband he was still permitted to wear. For everywhere he went, people from all walks of life treated him with the utmost courtesy and respect. He did however, find the work Durada had allocated to him to be somewhat monotonous, but in his spare time, he would mingle in the township among the artists and craftsmen, ever willing to learn the intricate skills of the potters and metalworkers. He now felt a close camaraderie with the people he lived alongside, with life in the township totally unlike that in the village he had known as a child, or indeed even on Anglesey. In these places, the market day had been held on every tenth day, whereas here it appeared to be every day, and with the market lying in the town's centre the place always seemed alive with the sounds of commerce. Traders from many tribes thronged the narrow lanes between the circular huts, noisily selling for silver and bartering their goods above the incessant noise created by the goats, pigs, sheep, and cattle constantly being transported to and from the marketplace.

Working his way through the congested lanes, he was suddenly forced to leap into an open doorway to avoid the wheels of a frantically driven chariot. The powerfully constructed vehicle was carrying what he took to be a prince of the aristocracy, judging by the bronze breastplate he was wearing and the ornate rectangular bronze shield pulled tight against his side. The chariot's driver stood alongside his master, screaming at people and animals alike who were forced to scatter to allow the clattering vehicle to pass between the close-packed huts on either side of the lane. A badly shaken Vescala was infuriated at the arrogant selfishness so frequently shown by these upper classes. Too often the mangled body of some innocent bystander was the end product of their arrogance, and staring in disgust at the vanishing vehicle he wondered if even Roman autocracy allowed such flagrant violations of their citizen's rights. For the common peoples of Britain had no liberty whatsoever, with the kings, princes and noblemen wielding a totalitarian power over everyone. They constituted the top level of society, and not even the second level which comprised the powerful body of druids could overturn any decisions taken by them. The priests acted as mere advisors to the aristocracy, and although their power in religious matters was said to be absolute, it was only tolerated providing that none of their decisions countermanded or interfered with their master's own personal lives.

Standing in the clouds of swirling dust stirred up by the chariot's wheels, Vescala smiled wryly as he pondered over his society's structure. One part of him detested the rampant injustices that held so many in such insufferable bondage, whilst the other fully agreed with Durada's submissive philosophy that their social caste system lay in accordance with their religious protocol. He had often questioned his master as to the legitimacy of such inequality: no more than five per cent of the country's entire population made up their society's top two levels, with another ten per cent comprising the third level, the merchants, artists, and craftsmen such as carpenters and blacksmiths. All those below these levels were peasants and slaves; the unskilled manual workers whom he knew only too well to be responsible for the creation of the vast wealth that kept their masters living in luxury.

Durada had frowned upon such questioning, reminding him that those older and wiser than himself were blatantly aware of the injustices – to persistently voice his own personal views might well lead him into dangerous waters he had stated acrimoniously. It was a warning Vescala was careful to heed, knowing that such were the blatant injustices in the system, the only way in which he could ever help the unfortunate peasants was through the priesthood.

He proceeded on his way towards the court building that lay behind the marketplace. The building itself was no more than a long rectangular-shaped structure comprising of four high trellis walls. No roof covered the place, the reason being that the gods should witness for themselves the fair administration of druidical justice. Inside the near-empty arena, seating facilities had been provided for some two hundred spectators, and passing through the main entrance where two heavily armed sentries stood posted, it was on one of the rickety wooden benches up at the back that he took his seat. With the place quickly filling to capacity, he looked around the benches only to be surprised to see no sign of any priests. For throughout the five day-long hearings, it had been mainly priests and novitiates that had attended the trials. But now the audience included only a few novitiates, with the bulk being made up of peasants.

Behind the long oak table at the front of the arena, a door suddenly burst open, and he drew in a sharp breath when seeing, entering just ahead of the two druid priests; a figure he took to be the high priestess Trestania. Although it was the first time, he had actually set eyes on her, he was more than familiar with her physical description and the tales that told of her renowned brutality. He could only sit staring in awe at her deeply lined, ashen face and the long flame-red hair cascading down over the black robes covering her lean figure. In the druidical hierarchy, her powerful status was second only to the arch-druid himself, and it was with a feeling of dread that he watched her steady unwavering gaze of authority scan the now silent benches.

Almost simultaneously the spectators rose to acknowledge the three judges who then took their seats at the table. The atmosphere felt tense, almost ugly, as the middle-aged Trestania, who sat between the two male druids, motioned with her hands for the spectators to resume their seated positions. First uttering a few inaudible words towards the clear sky, she then recited a prayer before placing her vein-ridged right hand on top of a bronze cube resting in the centre of the table. Vescala reckoned that she was swearing some kind of oath, well-aware that the very shape of the cube – being the same no matter which way it was turned – was to his masters symbolic of the truth. Suddenly, to the side of the judges, another door burst open and the emaciated figures of seven men, each chained by their neck to the other, were ushered in at spear point by two heavily armed guards, only to be immediately made to stand in a straight line directly in front of the judges. Removing her hand from the cube and standing erect, Trestania curled her thin cruel lips to smirk at the appearance of the prisoners. However, none present at the proceedings could fail to notice how her malevolent expression stood in stark contrast to the blank emotionless faces of the two white-robed priests flanking her.

"Your heresy and crimes have resulted in unspeakable misery for hundreds of tragic families as well as their suffering tribe!" she exclaimed as her long bony finger pointed in turn to each of the prisoners, who winced at the vengeful tone in her croaking voice. "You adjudged guilty ones know only too well that you were responsible for the destructive plague that spread like wildfire throughout the tribal lands of the Durotriges; a plague that killed over five hundred people and forced us into laying waste to some sixteen villages. I now ask myself: is it just that the gods should punish the innocent for the crimes that you heathens committed?" as Trestania paused a low disapproving murmuring from the spectators spread throughout the arena. "I think not! Each of you standing before me was granted a fair hearing by judges of the highest order, and it is now my duty to inform you that they have no doubt whatsoever that by your imprudent behaviour you provoked the gods into sending among us a pestilence in the form of plague. Such were your callous abuses of the law that nowhere in my heart can I find any desire to show you mercy! Therefore, I have no hesitancy in pronouncing upon each of you the most horrific of all sentences. As the legal representative of the highest of all life forms upon our holy earth, I deem you unfit to ever again live among your fellow citizens. You have left me no choice but to command that you be taken to a place of execution on the moorlands. Your evil flesh and souls will then be placed within a wicker image in the shape of the god of darkness and dementia, whereupon you will perish for eternity within the fires of retribution that will fall upon you from the flames of the sun god himself."

In an attempt to plead for mercy some of the prisoners tried to cry aloud, but the heavy, choking bronze manacles around their throats meant that their words remained an unintelligible babble. But unperturbed at their plight, Trestania resumed speaking.

"I further decree that everyone from this township and the surrounding villages, including the youngest children, are to attend the sacrifices in the hope that the punishment will deter them from following the unholy pathway taken by the guilty ones! Now remove them and bring the others before me."

The openly weeping condemned were kicked and pushed back through the doorway by the warriors only in turn to be replaced by another seven chained together in an identical manner. By the time the second group had been sentenced, the high priestess was in a state tantamount to hysteria. It began to appear to Vescala as if she had been manifested from the darkest recesses of hell, for alongside her evil shrieking, the golden amulet dangling from her pale withered neck and down over her chest now gave her the appearance of some demented infernal goddess.

Throughout the rest of the morning, the sentencing continued, with each fresh batch of prisoners, some including women, receiving the same horrific fate as their predecessors.

So, this is the culmination of the purges initiated by the priesthood, Vescala thought uneasily. Suddenly he felt afraid, wondering how on earth he could have allowed himself be so easily coerced into returning to the priesthood; now finding it abhorrent that one day he himself might sit in judgment under similar circumstances. For over the five days since the commencement of the trials, some eighty men and women had been tried, denounced, and condemned. And whilst many of them were genuine criminals such as murderers and thieves, he found some of the so-called 'capital offences' that the people had stood accused of to be unfounded. How was it, he wondered dejectedly, that his masters could possibly justify burning alive a poor, uneducated twelve-year-old girl whose misfortune was to have concealed and buried her illegitimate stillborn child. This had been followed by the case of five men who had done no more than verbally protest against the extortionate taxes imposed on their trading by their tribal king. They likewise would die, and to Vescala such people in no way deserved to suffer the ultimate penalty. He also found it astonishing that none of the accused, who had been allowed only a minimum of defence, had been spared. It was anathema to him that such people should die for a plague that, as far as he was concerned, they could in no way be held responsible for.

A niggling uncertainty had been his constant companion ever since Durada had informed him that his attendance at the trials was compulsory, half-expecting the woman whom he had rescued in the marsh to be among the accused. However, his anxiety lifted with the pronouncement from Trestania that the trials were at an end and that the sentences were to be executed the following day: that being the official calendar timing of the commencement of springtime. To the polite ripple of applause from the spectators, Trestania and her two companions left the courtroom. But grimly watching her disappear, Vescala's eyes narrowed as he recalled the law that allows druid and priestess alike to sit in judgment of their fellow human beings. But as only women bring forth life, none but the highest of priestesses has the authority to invoke the death penalty!

He left the premises only to be stopped and questioned by the crowds waiting outside as to the trial's verdicts, with no one daring voice an opinion. But he could see by their faces that, like himself, they were shocked by the severity of the sentences.

With no sign of Durada, the afternoon saw him return to the site of the hill fort. This new fort was under construction only a short distance from the town and lay situated on top of a long flat hill, which gave a commanding view of the surrounding countryside. The site had been carefully chosen by the priesthood, having been laid out between the boundaries separating two tribal kingdoms: a geopolitical arrangement that satisfied both the tribal kings who, owing to the astronomical sum of money involved, had agreed to share the project's cost. Climbing towards the summit of the hill, he was surprised at the progress that had been made in the short period of time he had been attending the trials. Giant earthen mounds, which would form the fort's outer defences, now towered high above the deep ditches laboriously hewn out from the ground, and beyond them, great piles of large stones lay neatly stacked, with long columns of ox-drawn wagons constantly bringing in more supplies from distant quarries.

Directly below him, on the green plains stretching out to the northern forests, a hunting party of tribal nobles stood in their chariots alongside their entourages. For some time, they discussed the massive construction taking shape above them, and from where Vescala was standing, he found it a resplendent sight as he watched them manoeuvre their chariots around the base of the hill. He could clearly hear them shout their praises to Nodens, the god of hunting. Then with the sunlight flashing from the enamelled bronze shields and helmets adorning them, they first allowed their savage hunting dogs to roam ahead of them before gathering into one group and riding off towards the sprawling forest.

Strolling over to the project's druid overseer, he was then assigned some twenty slaves and told to deploy them in filling in the long ditches with the heavy stones which would form the foundations of the impregnable walls that would eventually rise to dominate the landscape. Being a novitiate priest, he was automatically excluded from participating in any manual labour, and as the day dragged slowly by his boredom increased to such an extent that he was finding it difficult to stay awake on his feet.

At last, the swiftly deepening twilight descended, bringing with it the horn signal indicating that the day's toil was at an end. And as the long columns of weary slaves began making their way down the wide earthen ramparts, he, as much as they were grateful that the long, tiring day had come to an end. With a chill evening breeze now slipping into the air, he ordered his slaves to join their comrades before stopping to view the contracting landscape, all the while tying up the cord fastenings on his sheepskin jacket. Suddenly his sharp eyes discerned two shadowy riders emerging from the distant forest. At first, he was uncertain, but with their slow approach, his face lit up on seeing what appeared to be Straval accompanied by the slave who had been their guide on Anglesey.

Running between the great earthen mounds, he stumbled past the slaves before rushing down the hill, all the time shouting and waving his arms to attempt to attract the riders' attention. Drawing closer to them, he was delighted to see his thoughts confirmed but pulling up only one of the riders dismounted, and running through the long moist grass toward them he was surprised to see Brenas coming in his direction leaving Straval seated on his by now grazing pony.

"My master is blind, sir!" Brenas whispered softly; his deep brown eyes betraying the lack of emotion in his voice. Staggered at this news, Vescala glanced sadly across at the vacant expression on Straval's face. Brushing past the slave, he moved slowly towards his friend.

"I…I…is that you, Vescala?" Straval stammered, as his wide staring eyes searched around for a comforting presence.

"Yes, it's me," Vescala replied consolingly, placing his hands over Straval's, whose grip on the pony's reins immediately slackened. "I knew you had survived the fall, but I was told nothing of your blindness!" he then exclaimed; his eyes looking up to scan the jagged scar running along the side of Straval's closely cropped scalp.

"I heard of your sad losses Vescala. It would appear, that the gods have struck us hard for having defied their authority!" Straval retorted, only this time in a harsh, uncompromising tone. Puzzled by the remark, Vescala glanced towards Brenas.

"Vescala, we grew up almost as brothers, and I knew some time ago that your views on the priesthood were in turmoil. You were not alone; I, myself cast serious doubts on certain teachings. But I now feel that had we accepted rather than questioned as we have so often done between us, neither of us would have found ourselves in our present predicament."

Hardly believing his ears, Vescala drew his hands away.

"I must disagree, Straval; all we have done was to question...I can't believe the gods would punish us for that by first taking your sight and then the lives of my…"

"Don't be so stupid!" Straval shouted, bitterly interrupting him. "I know we were wrong! And I pray that we will atone in the future. Now, for the good of your soul, you would do well to heed me…In my blindness, I see more than you ever will with your vision."

Sensing an ill-timed argument, Brenas promptly offered the stunned Vescala his mount with the three men then making their way over the deserted moors towards the town. The darkness was falling swiftly now, and only the pale moon overhead appeared content as Vescala's troubled thoughts struggled to find understanding in the unhappy silence. He was saddened by the abrupt manner in which he had been spoken to. But reflecting on Straval having to spend the rest of his life in a sightless world, his anger soon subsided into compassion.

Entering the township, they met Durada, who promptly offered Straval and his slave lodgings. Reaching the premises, Brenas busied himself by first rubbing down and then stabling the ponies in the courtyard at the rear of the building, leaving the other two to enter the hut where they sat by the table to await the meal being prepared for them by a slave woman. Neither man spoke though, and Vescala felt a certain relief when Brenas took his place at the table alongside Straval, with one of the slave's duties being to help his master in eating. But the welcome meal was soon finished, and excusing himself, Straval – aided by Brenas – left the table to retire to the sleeping quarters. With the long journey having sapped his strength, Straval was soon sound asleep, and with the slave woman now gone, Vescala and Brenas were left to sit opposite one another, directly below the hanging flickering tallow lamp.

"How was your journey?" Vescala enquired of the slave.

"It went well, sir. I hope you were not offended by my master's words earlier on; he was very tired."

"No. No," Vescala replied, shaking his head, and pretending not to have been hurt by Straval's pointed remarks.

"I'm afraid, sir, there are times when he gets severely depressed and feels it's pointless in going on; indeed, at one stage in the journey down here he pleaded with me to terminate his life!"

A look of sympathy now showed in Vescala's eyes, which were directed toward the sword strapped across the slave's back.

"I see you're carrying a sword."

"Yes, sir," Brenas answered bluntly, detecting an uncertainty in Vescala's voice. "As you know, sir, only under exceptional circumstances is a trustee slave like myself allowed to bear arms. I was granted the privilege in order to protect my master. My eyes are now his."

"You could have killed him and escaped."

"I could have, sir, but where would a man like me escape to?"

Vescala nodded solemnly. "I take it Straval hasn't met his family yet?"

"No, sir. We were on our way there when the priest at a nearby village informed us that our attendance at tomorrow's sacrifices was compulsory."

"Hmmm...I hardly think in Straval's case the required attendance is necessary." Vescala commented.

"That's true, sir – blindness has its advantages when it comes to witnessing such a sacrifice, as I once did," Brenas replied, staring thoughtfully at the remains of the boiled pork lying in the wooden bowl between them.

"Tell me about it?" Vescala asked as the slave drew in a deep breath.

"As a small child, sir, I was forced to watch the burnings. Afterward I was taken by the druids and given the mark you see on my face." as he spoke Brenas had caressed with his finger the ugly circular scar that had been branded deep into his right cheek; a mark carried by all slaves. "I was one of the fortunate ones. But until the day I die, I will never forget the terrifying screams of all those who were mercilessly burned alive!"

Staring into the slave's dull, distant eyes, Vescala began to sense a common bond growing between them. And although Brenas was far inferior to him in the social structure, he had been struck by the integrity and compassion with which the older man had spoken. However, sensing the man's distress he changed the subject.

"Does your master intend on returning to Anglesey?"

"Yes, sir. He feels that by giving his devout allegiance to the gods he will be forgiven for sins that, like yourself, I cannot comprehend. Sometimes he suffers greatly from the pains in his head and, as I've said, longs for death. Perhaps when he is reunited with his family the situation will change for the better."

"Let us hope so. The man you accompany appears to be a mere shadow of my former friend."

"What about yourself, sir, have you made any plans for the future?" the slave asked politely.

"Yes. I too am destined to return to the sacred island, probably after the next mid-winter ceremonies," Vescala declared solemnly, and raising his black, bushy eyebrows Brenas looked surprised at his reply.

"You see, Brenas, I have already sworn my allegiance to the priesthood. Oh, I had my reasons, but let us be honest, when any tyrannical system such as ours has to be changed, perhaps it's best achieved from the inside."

The slave's eyes lit up in disbelief at such a radical statement. "You would risk certain death, sir. No one individual could possibly hope to change this system. It is too deeply entrenched and has been for centuries," Brenas remarked, and for a few moments, both men eyed one another with distinct caution.

"Surely it's a man's moral duty to try?" Vescala retorted.

"Yes, sir, maybe. But have you forgotten the two harsh realities that rule us? Gold and fear. Our kings and nobles have the gold to buy the manpower and weapons which they all too frequently use against us, and your own priesthood the fear by which to intimidate and exploit the superstitious masses."

Vescala was about to disagree when suddenly there was a rap on the door. At his bidding, the slave woman came in carrying a jug of the strong ale for which the town was famous, and for the remainder of the evening, both men contented themselves in drinking heavily. However, by the end of the night, the tongue-loosening effect of the alcohol had them talking of the day when all men would taste the elixir from the cup of freedom.

Chapter Five

The bright sunlight streaming in through the shutters struck Vescala's half-open eyes with a sharpness that saw him jump up from his straw bed, only to experience a dull thumping ache in his head, an instant reminder of the previous night's drinking excesses. Careful not to awaken Straval, who lay asleep behind the drapes at the far side of the room, he dressed before half-staggering into the living area.

Soon afterwards, Brenas entered the lodgings; the slave having spent the night in the slaves' quarters beside the town's stables. The two men then began to discuss over breakfast the route they would take to the sacrificial site, with both men readily agreeing that, with Straval accompanying them, it would be wiser if they took the longer of the two routes, reckoning that it would be the least congested.

No one heard Straval rise, but seeing his outstretched, flailing arms entangled in the drapes, Brenas immediately jumped up from the table. After freeing and helping him to dress, the slave then sat him down beside Vescala, who placed a bowl of barley soup into his hands.

"I must apologise for my remarks last night, Vescala...I didn't mean to be offensive," Straval said in a quiet, conciliatory tone.

"No offence was taken," Vescala replied, smiling, and glancing over to Brenas who now sat opposite him.

Thank you, but tell me how you got on with Ravala. When I first heard of you two travelling together, I feared for your life!" Straval stated, before making a considerable noise as he strained the thick soup through the long moustache hanging over his upper lip.

"Oh, I had no problems. Ravala proved to me that he is no more than an obnoxious loudmouth. He did, however, emphasise the point that one day he would sever my head. But I have lost no sleep in worrying over such an idle threat," Vescala replied, chuckling derisively as Straval nodded in agreement.

Meanwhile outside, the townspeople had started congregating in the warm sunshine filtering down into the town's narrow lanes. However, on making their way out of the town in the direction of the southern moorlands, every face in the crowd began to express its apprehension.

Having fully prepared themselves, the three men warily joined the closely packed masses: Straval having insisted that they join the main group rather than make the longer journey. Passing slowly beyond the town's defensive stockade, the long procession wound its way along the dusty track, growing ever larger as it was joined on the route by the people from the small local villages. Vescala was relieved that the pushing and shoving Brenas and he had anticipated never materialised; all the time wondering if it was due to the priestly robes Durada had ordered Straval and himself to wear the previous night. For from the very moment they had joined the crowds, he was aware of the respectful stares they had received from the tense faces surrounding them.

It was to be a long, tedious trek though, and the sight of the three gigantic human-shaped images now looming up on the distant horizon saw the solemn Vescala shiver nervously. And with their feet marching steadily in unison to the resonant pounding of the far-off drumbeats, each step drew the teeming legions nearer to the plain of the holy executions. But any excitement that might previously have been experienced by them rapidly changed to fear as the evil images began to tower ever higher over the masses, who blindly surged forward as if drawn by some invisible power.

An anxious Vescala had never seen so many people gathered together in his life; it seemed to him as if the entire human race was attending this one ceremony. With an unimaginable terror beginning to rise in his soul, he cautiously scrutinised the facially hideous titanic constructions that stood within the lines of robed priests separating the crowds from the sacrificial site. Now he knew the reason why Durada and the other priests had been absent from the trials the preceding day. They had undoubtedly been supervising the construction of the vast images that he now felt could only have been conceived in the imagination of a madman.

Each of the monstrous fabrications stood at the height of ten grown men, with their huge torsos rising directly up from the ground to the long, horizontal outstretched arms high above. Beyond the arms, each of the human-like ghastly heads stared east towards the fiery kingdom of the sun god; their hollow constructions comprising of scaffolding of sturdy wooden poles covered in great mats of tightly knitted wickerwork. Over these lay broad white canvas sheets that all but covered the figures and which were painted with the symbols of various deities. A small ladder led up from the ground into the wide opening in the front of the torso, and all around the bases of the wickerwork images, massive bales of tinder-dry straw lay menacingly stacked.

Suddenly the three men found themselves being pushed towards the front of the crowds: this, unfortunately, gaining for them an excellent vantage point directly behind the line of floral-garlanded druids.

Over on the western side of the moor, the bejewelled kings, princes, and nobles of various tribes stood in their flower-adorned chariots in front of their entourages to watch with interest the lawful proceedings about to unfold. Glancing eastwards, Vescala recognised Durada among the thirty-strong inner council of priests. In front of them stood the most powerful of all the druids – the black-masked arch-druid himself. To his far right stood an unmasked black-clad Trestania, who busied herself in giving final instructions to her nine black-robed and masked priestesses by her side. They in turn were flanked by a druidical choir, whose flowing lyrics grew louder to the unceasing accompaniment of the, by now deafening, drumbeats. All the male druids wore white robes symbolic of purity, with the various motifs adorning their chests displaying a magical quality that overshadowed the array of gleaming golden amulets and torques dangling from their necks and wrists. Each of them also wore a crown of oak leaves freshly cut from the holiest of trees: all that is with the exception of Trestania and her priestesses, whose long hair was kept in check by a simple black headband.

The quiet, expectant murmurings of the crowd suddenly grew as all eyes focused on the appearance of a white-tailed eagle gliding listlessly across the heavens. The bird's flight path cast a long, dark shadow that moved slowly over the three towering constructions, whereon sighting this the chanting of the choir grew louder and faster as they kept time with the tireless and increasingly rapid rhythm of the drumbeats. With their archaic faces now showing the emotion by which they viewed the omen, the council of druids momentarily pointed in confusion towards the sky. However, as the arch-druid raised both his arms to the heavens, the audible shouts from the priests that the omen was favourable quickly spread throughout the crowds.

Beads of sweat now grew and fell from Vescala's forehead as he nervously clenched his fists to dig his trembling fingers deep into his sweating palms. Even the hitherto calm Straval looked uncertain, repeatedly questioning him as to the unrestrained excitement now engulfing the crowd surrounding them. Suddenly the tumult of drumbeats and chanting ceased, with the crowds immediately falling into a mute and respectful silence. In an ominous fashion the sulphur-yellow sun appeared to climb even higher in the sky, as if compelling the high priests to signal the end for the unhappy victims now being shoved towards the clearing through an avenue of heavily armed warriors. Behind them, slaves carried and dragged the condemned people's few pathetic possessions. For such was the law, that in order that no innocent person should be corrupted by anything contaminated by evil spirits, all property belonging to the victims, including their livestock, had to perish in the same fires as their owners. The only exceptions to this law were the victim's children, who were forced to witness their parent's fate. Counting some thirty such children, Vescala scowled, knowing that their own fate would be one of a lifelong slavery. Meanwhile, Brenas struggled hard within himself to control the gentle tears filling eyes that knew from bitter experience the misery and anguish that would soon be imprinted upon each of their innocent faces. Faces and minds, like his own had once been, and that must shortly absorb and carry for the rest of their lives the physical and mental scars of an evil inquisition.

After spitting and jeering at the intended victims, the crowds quickly fell silent as Trestania and her priestesses began to walk towards the centre of the clearing where the chained prisoners stood naked and huddled together, close by to where their children stood watching. Vescala sneered inwardly at the tyrannical appearance of the high priestess, and listening intently as their crimes were once again recounted by the vociferous Trestania, he became increasingly aware that the true evil lay not in the condemned but in their accusers – the druids.

Each exaggerated claim from Trestania's tongue drew false gasps of astonishment from the crowds, whose blood lust rose at the inflammatory tones in her bombastic voice. And with each of the sentences again confirmed, the chanting screams from the crowds to "Destroy them!" rose high towards the heavens as if imploring the sun god to relinquish such worthless lives.

As at their trials, the victims were chained to one another by their necks, with their hands having been securely bound behind their backs. The warriors then led each chained group of seven towards the images where they were collectively forced up the ladders and into the titans' hollow torsos. Their livestock, pigs, goats, and sheep that had been bound by their feet were then manhandled up the ladders by slaves to be placed alongside their owners. With the victims quickly interred a heavy trellis barrier was then dragged across the entrance to each of the images and tied to posts to effectively enclose the prisoners in almost total darkness.

Vescala was surprised by the ease with which the condemned had allowed themselves to be interred. He had half-expected a few of them to have shown some resistance – but none did. It now appeared to him as if their sense of destiny had somehow invoked in them an apathy so strong that their willpower seemed to hang suspended in the time-marked realms of their inescapable fate.

The sight of yet another six slaves, this time masked, puzzled him, with each of the three pairs of men carrying between them a large, circular convex-shaped, and highly polished silver disc which they then positioned at an angle, inclined between the straw-covered bases of the images and the blazing sun now in its zenith.

Everyone fell deathly silent as the priestesses, now in lines of three abreast, first ensured that the slaves were holding them at the correct angle, before placing themselves behind each of the dishes. Trestania then walked back into the centre of the clearing and stationing her eyes on the blazing sun above, she stretched her arms high above her head and began muttering an inaudible prayer.

As if on a parallel with human suffering, time became infinite to Vescala who by now had presumed the gruesome purpose of the mirroring dishes. Suddenly his anaesthetised mind harped back to the fearful time he had spent in the forest as a young child. Once more a terrifying sense of isolation invaded his thoughts: it was as if he had been drawn into a world where reality had died and where the external forces out with his mind were now appearing as automatic marionettes about to enact a seemingly never-ending story of human depravity.

"One alight!" The excited shout from someone in the crowd instantly broke the trance to return him into a reality that showed one of the 'effigies' aflame, with the straw around the base having been ignited by the powerful, magnified rays emanating from the perfectly positioned reflectors. However, no sooner had the first burst into flame when the other two followed, and on seeing this the blood-curdling scream emitted by Trestania immediately drowned out the whimpering pleas of the incarcerated victims. And as black, choking smoke slowly billowed upwards to hide the sun in a deathly haze, it was with an eager destructiveness that the leaping flames snaked up to lick at the outer framework of the structures. Suddenly the mephitic blanket of malevolent, curling smoke rapidly smothering the unholy creations erupted into a ravaging, white-hot holocaust, and as the petrified groans of the onlookers acknowledged the vengeance of the omnipotent sun god, the dying screams of the doomed pierced the air like hurtling spears.

By now, the priestesses and slaves had begun to move silently back towards the lines of priests, leaving the lone swaying figure of Trestania to harangue and denigrate the condemned, whose dying pleas had quickly succumbed to the roaring brilliance of the flames that now illuminated the dullness of the smoke-laden landscape.

One by one the giant figures collapsed to the scorched earth, with each throwing up huge clouds of sparkling embers high into the air, and within what seemed to Vescala to have been an incredibly short time, eighty-four human lives had been reduced to no more than three piles of grey, spluttering ash. It was a sight that would haunt forever all those who had witnessed the grotesque spectacle, and looking around him, Vescala now saw only pale, shocked faces, with the very same peasants who had earlier screamed for blood standing silent and visibly afraid. For no one could have failed to appreciate the explicit warning: "Obey the druid – or die!"

"Is it done with?" Straval asked in a low, unfeeling whisper, with he, unlike the others, being incapable of fully comprehending the terrifying impact the barbaric rite had on those around him.

"Yes, sir, it's over," Brenas replied, curtly biting his bottom lip in order to prevent himself from openly reviling the priesthood. Standing entrenched in a disconsolate mood, Vescala stared hard at the offspring of the deceased, knowing that similar tear-stained faces must cry down the centuries unless drastic changes were made in the priesthood's present-day thinking. However, his thoughts were ended abruptly though with the garbled pronouncement from Trestania that the cremations were at an end, and as she walked back through the priests bowing before her, he thought it beyond belief that any woman could show in her face such a cruel, inhuman composure.

Almost immediately the crowds began to disperse towards the eastern plains where many small bonfires were in the process of being lit from the "holy flames" kindled from the dying embers of the funeral pyres and now being transported aloft on torches by the priestesses.

After every major religious sacrifice, it was customary to celebrate the event with a thanksgiving feast, and impaled on rows of iron spits were hundreds of boars, oxen and sheep now being roasted by the many slave women drawn from all over the country for the occasion. Pony racing, wrestling bouts, dancing, and a variety of games as well as an unlimited supply of ale and cider had also been organised and provided for the people's entertainment by the priesthood.

As the three of them made their way alongside the masses towards the site of the feast, Vescala, his pale face drained of its natural colour, stopped momentarily to look back at the acrid smoke gradually dispersing across the heavens. However, as the day stole by the fading obituary was soon forgotten, with the food and drink quickly drowning any remorse that the spectators might still be feeling, as the day's proceedings soon degenerated into what was little more than a large-scale drunken orgy.

By the late afternoon Straval, being the worse for drink, lapsed into a deep sleep, leaving the other two to sit among the dry bracken watching the distant peasant mothers who, clasping their young babies in their arms, continuously leapt through the now low flames of the bonfires; a custom much venerated by the peasants who believed that by taking such an action the "holy fires" would purify their bodies and souls. Vescala sat back watching them in dismay, for to him they appeared to be totally unconcerned by the religious atrocities perpetually being engendered against them.

"Are they blind or just plain stupid?" he asked Brenas angrily. "Don't they understand that next year or the year after it might be them who are to be burned alive by the sun god?" he said, raising his dissonant voice above the laughter and shrieking of the peasants.

"No, sir. Their lives are governed by fear and superstition," Brenas replied, deliberately speaking in a low key as if intimating to Vescala the danger of his words carrying to the wrong ears. "To them, sir, rebellion is an indulgence in which they can ill afford to participate. After all, it's an indelible fact that the life expectancy of peasants and slaves alike is little more than forty years. Such a short life span is preferable to any insurrection which would be a long-protracted struggle and which would inevitably lead to a far greater destruction of innocent blood than anything we saw today."

Disgusted by his reckless statement, Vescala lay back lethargically where overhead the mottled red sky he stared up at in despondent uncertainty filled his eyes with a phosphorescent glow that savagely reminded him of the burnings. However, after only a few moments he returned to a seated position, allowing his weary head to rest on the blue robes covering his raised knees.

"I was sold into the priesthood, Brenas. Why is irrelevant," he declared quietly, now leaning back to recline on his elbows. "For twelve long years, I was forced to study law, linguistics, and mathematics, and was to learn by heart some five thousand verses of the history and mythological poetry of the successive generations of our people. Most of these years were happy and productive and in the latter stages of my education, my tutors constantly reminded me of my scholastic capabilities. They said that were I to return to the sacred island to undertake another eight years of study, I should easily pass the final examination necessary to become a fully ordained priest. I don't know if you're aware of it, Brenas, but these eight years are spent mainly in the tuition of medicine, astronomy, the interpretation of omens, and the uses of magical powers. I do feel that one would require a first-class knowledge of magic; it's well-known even among we novitiates that for every five men who enter into the final initiation rites of the priesthood, on average only three come out of it alive! Oh, I'm not afraid of what their initiation involves, but never before in my life have, I found myself to be so morally destitute as at this moment – from this day on I want no part in their revolting practices."

Looking embarrassed at having allowed himself to have been so easily coerced into remaining in the priesthood, Vescala bowed his head. But sensing the conflict raging within the young man's mind, Brenas smiled sympathetically.

"You have no choice, sir; you are one of them!" he exclaimed decisively. "But your depression will soon lift; tomorrow is a new day and with every fresh sunrise I like to think that hope is reborn. I may well be talking out of turn, sir, but the sun god no more killed those people than you or I did! Something inside tells me that the human soul, once created, remains forever free and indestructible, whether it be through natural death or murder within a wicker image. Anyway, as you said last night, you might eventually be in a position, to change the system from the inside."

Once again, Vescala began to sense a common purpose growing between himself and the slave, but, as yet it was a purpose he was unsure of.

"You never exactly explained last night how you came to be taken into slavery," he then commented. Brenas momentarily shivered, with his thoughts returning to the day so long ago that had changed the course of his life.

"One of my former masters, sir, once informed me that in the village where I lived as a child, there was an old hag who, for the right price, would procure miscarriages for the local women. After the sudden death of a young girl from another village, and whose family had somehow discovered what had taken place, the abortionist was reported to the priesthood. As a direct result of her vile practices, all those in my village over the age of fourteen years were taken and burned in the manner you witnessed today. Apparently, the priests believed that the entire village was involved. They assumed that everyone had been sharing in the payments she had received, for her hoard of gold was never discovered. According to my master, the majority of the women involved in the old hag's evil ways were the rich licentious wives of the local noblemen and merchants; they, naturally, were exempted from receiving any punishment. But not so my parents, two elder brothers, and my sister!"

For a time there existed a solemn silence between both men and, as they sat reflecting on the slave's story, a chill breeze crept briskly into the air with a refreshing coolness that swept over the moorlands as if cleansing the earth from the religious fanaticism that had so desecrated it.

With the crowds beginning to disperse, Vescala now sat wondering as to how some of them would possibly manage home seeing the drunken condition most of them were in when suddenly to his side a female voice rang out.

"Is he alright?" she asked, and both men rose to their feet on seeing the diminutive figure of a young, black-clad woman bending over the slumbering Straval.

"Yes, he's just sleeping," Vescala replied; his eyes absorbing the graceful deportment of the woman who by now was standing erect.

"But his eyes are wide open!" she exclaimed in amazement.

"I'm afraid my friend was blinded as a result of suffering an accident with his pony," he answered, unable to draw his eyes from hers, for they appeared to be as heavy and distressed as his own. Suddenly it struck him that she was a priestess and almost certainly one of the masked ones who had participated in the sacrifices. Although unable to pinpoint it, he found there to be something odd about her intriguing appearance, but peering down at her through the twilight gloom, he became instantly enamoured with the superb lineaments that granted her enchanting face such a pure and innocent disposition.

The young woman, who was around the same age as himself, wore a long black cloak trimmed with silver embroidery which almost covered the ankle-length black dress adorned from her slim neck with a meticulously forged golden amulet. He could see that her thin curved eyebrows were naturally formed as if simulating the plucked eyebrows of some Egyptian queen and through her long tawny hair, as lustrous as the rays of a midnight sun, a golden hairnet studded with pink freshwater pearls had been skilfully interwoven. Her exceptional beauty was further highlighted by a small mole lying situated to the right side of her mouth, just above the corner of her beautifully curved lips, which like her high cheekbones, had been cosmetically stained in the red juice of the elderberry. And as she smiled towards him, he saw that her teeth were as snow-white as they were perfectly formed.

"Delancia!" The harsh menace in the voice abruptly woke Straval as both Vescala and Brenas turned to see Trestania's imperious figure standing officiously behind them; the mistrust in her keen eyes firmly directed upon the stunned Vescala.

"I object to the way you were staring at my priestess, young man!" she exclaimed smugly as Vescala stared down at her.

"I wasn't aware that I was staring, Highness," he snapped back impertinently.

"Are you calling me a liar?" she then demanded, with the veins on the sides of her temple visibly protruding in her anger.

"With all due respect, Highness, you were in no position to see – after all, you were behind me," he replied cheekily, and fidgeting slightly he felt his mouth dry up as he cursed himself for having dared to contradict the high priestess.

"Never forget, young man, that I see all things!" she screamed out in her rage, but as she stormed up to him, Durada suddenly appeared on the scene.

"Does this imbecile belong to your school, Durada?" she then enquired as her long finger stabbed repeatedly into Vescala's cheek, with her sharp, pointed nail scouring his skin until it burst and bled.

"Yes, Highness," Durada answered meekly, glancing anxiously at his pupil who now stood rigid with shock. His presence however quickly pacified the irate Trestania, leaving him more than relieved to see her step back.

"Then I suggest you teach the insolent dog some manners! For if I have to, he will certainly lose his foul tongue! Now come, child," she commanded, walking over to Delancia who glanced compassionately toward the irked Vescala before departing the scene with her enraged mistress.

"What on earth happened here?" Durada then asked in a voice almost as fearful as the look in his eyes as Vescala and Brenas helped Straval onto his feet.

"It was no more than a slight misunderstanding, sir," Vescala replied apologetically, before explaining that he hadn't meant to be so blatantly offensive.

"You better understand, Vescala, that Her Highness will never forget your impertinence. Take great care in the future that you address her as befits her dignified position. Now I suggest that the three of you return to the town!" Durada said reprovingly, leaving Vescala relieved that no punishment other than a mild rebuke had been administered to him for what had, after all, been an act of insolence.

As Durada took his leave. Vescala felt a little better that the long, insufferable day was drawing to a close and as the three of them made their way past the now defunct remains of the hideous images, the terrible events earlier in the day seemed strangely remote to him. Throughout the journey back, Straval discussed with Brenas the possibility of them departing the following day to go to his parent's home, leaving Vescala to ponder over the young priestess whose exquisite beauty had so captivated him. Putting the horror of the sacrifices to the back of his mind, he recalled the complaisance in her enchanting eyes as she had directed her desire towards him and the tender smile that for a few brief moments had shown her shapely face flushed in an instant love. As the darkened township appeared in the distance, he was still scraping with his fingers the dried blood covering his swollen cheek when it suddenly dawned on him that it had been Delancia's unusual eyes that had so mystified him. For each of them had shone brighter than any evening star, with one coloured a sapphire blue and the other a pale aquamarine.

Chapter Six

With Straval and Brenas gone, the yearly festival held to celebrate the midsummer solstice came and went. However, much to Durada's annoyance, Vescala had been unable to participate, having sustained a broken leg while working manually alongside his slaves up at the hill fort. Vescala's defence for his indiscretion in having undertaken physical labour was simply that he had been bored to tears by the monotony of his supervisory role. Unfortunately, the head druid overseer at the site had thought otherwise, ordering that he be given ten lashes of the whip for his 'irrational behaviour.' But having intervened on his behalf, Durada was again content to reprimand his pupil, warning him in no uncertain terms that his future conduct must improve.

By now Durada had decided that the time was right for Vescala to embark upon a more meaningful form of education. He thought that by taking him under his direct jurisdiction and letting him work among the ordinary people it would lead him into adopting a more responsible attitude. Durada, was well aware that the young man's next eight years of study on Anglesey would be as difficult as they were dangerous, with only the strictest obedience to the law being tolerated by his superiors. It would be a tragic waste, he reckoned, that if simply through having an over-zealous nature such a bright young man should fail – and in failure prematurely die.

By this time, Vescala had been incapacitated for nearly three months, with his entire leg having been securely strapped between wooden splints. But after the splints were removed the strengthening of the leg took another month, with most of his time spent in taking long walks through the countryside and swimming in the nearby lake, dedicated to the water goddess

Coventina and renowned throughout the land for its healing properties.

Even beyond the town Durada's fame as a healer was almost legendary, and with his leg now completely healed, Vescala attained great satisfaction in assisting his master in his medical treatment of the local people; greatly admiring the priest's expertise in curing sick animals and diagnosing and even remedying crop blight in its earliest stages.

By now the summer was drawing to a close. But over the past four months, he had found it impossible to forget the beautiful priestess Delancia. Her memory haunted him, and although he had desperately tried to put her out of his mind, the few fleeting moments spent in her company had so mesmerised him that his feelings for her had grown into an unhealthy obsession. She was in his thoughts even at the daily prayer meetings held by Durada. But what he found intolerable to bear was the sad fact that even to contemplate, all be it in fantasy, any emotional union between priest and priestess was classified as utterly forbidden; nonetheless, he was fired with the hope that one day they would meet again.

Late summer brought with it the warmest weather of the year, with everyone looking forward to a bumper harvest. Unfortunately, a full-scale war had broken out between two of the powerful northern tribes; the cause – as nearly always in such cases – having stemmed from a territorial dispute between the two kings. In an attempt to terminate the hostilities, it was customary for the inner council of druids to arbitrate between the warring factions. It was for this reason that Durada had been called north, but before departing, he ordered Vescala to go to the coastal town of Iscal, which lay to the southwest of the country in the tribal lands of the Dobunni. Once there, he was to report to a former academic associate of Durada's; a priest named Ruadi whom Durada was convinced would ensure that his protégé's education remained under the strictest supervision. Vescala was sorry to see his master leave, for there was no telling how long it might take to settle the dispute. He had certainly learned a great deal from him in the short time he had been under his tuition. However, when informed of his temporary transfer he had not been too downhearted, with Iscal being the hometown of Straval.

Leaving at first light, he estimated his arrival at Iscal to be sometime before nightfall. He was careful to travel heavily armed though, for in recent times there had been reports of bands of robbers active in the southern regions, and he felt that he could hardly put his implicit faith in a mere headband under circumstances that had seen some twenty travellers found on the rural tracks with their throats cut.

Riding flat out south, a bright sun eventually erupted through the dull sky bringing with it the promise of a warm day, and by noon his progress had been so good that he stopped to rest, deliberately choosing a stretch of high ground that rose sharply up from the tree-lined track. Earlier on, he had noticed that not too far ahead the track branched off in two directions, with one route heading due west and the other running south to the coast. After tethering his pony to a bush at the summit of the hill, he reclined on a broad flat stone that granted him a panoramic view of the iridescent countryside surrounding him. There he ate and drank from the provisions taken from the saddle pack, with the bread and tender beef washing down well along with the ale drunk from the small bronze flask by his side. On raising his eyes, he glimpsed a sparrow hawk circling lazily against the clear blue sky with its keen eyes scanning the trees and meadows as warily as his own. Perhaps it was a sense of precognition for suddenly he felt a cold shiver run up his spine as it plummeted to the earth, only to slowly rise clutching in its ruthless talons the body of a motionless leveret.

Feeling refreshed, he rose to repack his leftover food back into the saddle pack, but due to the incessant buzzing from the many insects hovering around him, he at first failed to pick up the sounds of the distant slow-trotting hoof beats. On eventually hearing them, he rapidly grabbed his spear and unsheathed his sword before running down to crouch cautiously behind the camouflage of a nearby thicket. Just ahead of him, the track was partially hidden from his view by a dense hedgerow when suddenly he was amazed on sighting the unmistakable figure of a floral-garlanded Trestania rounding the bushes, leading in single file some dozen of her likewise-mounted priestesses.

As the silent procession made their way along the dusty track, he wondered why no armed guards were accompanying them. But then, as his eyes caught hold of Delancia's alluring presence, his pounding heart almost came to a stop. She was bringing up the group's rear, and as he stood erect to attain a better view of her, she glanced over to spot him with her wide eyes instantly glowing in surprised disbelief as she smiled towards him with the persisting affinity of an undeniable love. Momentarily mesmerised, he returned her ingratiating smile, knowing that ever since the very moment of their first meeting that hers was the tranquil presence that had moved so inspiringly through his very existence.

As the party trotted by, he could no more draw his eyes from hers than she could from his, and trembling uncontrollably he sensed a spiritual unification of their very souls. The encounter appeared to him to be an inexplicable act of destiny so pure that for a few sensuous moments, it felt as if he had transcended into paradise itself. Neither of their eyes left the others until the trees of the forest ahead obliterated their views, and with the spell broken, the smitten Vescala stood feeling a happiness that he had never imagined. In the past, he had experienced the sexual favours of a few women, with novitiates being well supplied with unmarried slave women. But never in any of these relationships had he discovered the entrancing desire of an overwhelming love that now appeared to embrace his entire being. Somehow, he would have to meet her again, of that he was convinced, and although he was fully aware that he would have to show great discretion, he was determined that when the time came, she must belong to him and not married into any priesthood. Creasing his face into an arrogant sneer, he laughed aloud at the moral code of the druidical laws before re-sheathing his sword and running back up the slope to quickly gather his belongings.

After guiding the pony back downhill and remounting the animal, he galloped off back along the track. However, no sooner had he reached the southern route when a dark, blurred object came rushing out from the trees ahead to strike him hard on the face. The unexpected blow almost unseated him from the startled pony, and with his nose bleeding profusely and tears streaming down his cheeks he found great difficulty in controlling the animal. After a struggle, he eventually succeeded in pulling it up, and cantering back he had to search for a while before finding the offending creature lying dead among the long grass by the track's edge. On turning it over with his spear, he was horrified on seeing it to be a tawny owl whose neck had been instantly broken by the impact of the collision. He knew only too well that to the druids the owl is classified as a harbinger of supernatural wisdom, and he was more than aware that to sight one in broad daylight, was considered to be an unlucky omen but to have one fly into him might well auger a future disaster.

Wiping the blood from his face with his sleeve, but feeling dazed and uneasy, he continued on his way with Trestania's words, spoken to him on the day of the burnings now swirling around in his mind.

"Never forget, young man, that I see all things!" she had remarked prophetically, and cantering along for only a short time, he broke his mount into a fast gallop, in order to escape the dark, gloomy forest that by now he had deeply penetrated.

It was not long before he came upon the high, stratified cliffs of the coastline rising steeply up from the calm ocean, and there for a few moments he stopped to stare in awe at the myriads of squawking gulls that flecked the rugged peaks of the cliffs as they wound their way to the east and west as far as his eyes could see. With the fresh sea breeze now clearing his head, he began to make his way westward along the narrow track running parallel with the edge of the cliffs. And as the day advanced, he passed by many of the coastal villages, mainly occupied by the mineworkers who were employed in the vast network of tin mines that had been worked in the southern regions of Britain for many centuries.

It was early in the evening when he reached the small, granite ridge that he knew to be the final obstacle on his journey. After ascending it with little difficulty he cast his eyes down onto the idyllic setting of Iscal, with the town's many close-packed abodes lying upon steep terrain that stretched up from a rock-strewn, sandy cove. He immediately noticed that a high timber stockade fully encompassed the entire township, stopping only when reaching the water's edge. But the stockade was poorly maintained, and spotting a wide gap in it directly below him, he dismounted to lead his pony down towards it. Perhaps it was unwise of him not to have taken the longer route and formally introduce himself to the town guard posted up at the northern portcullis he wondered momentarily, but he was tired and anyway his headband would ensure he received a friendly welcome, he confidently assured himself.

His journey down the eastern cliff's grass-covered slopes granted him an excellent view of the naturally formed stone harbour jutting out from the face of the western cliffs opposite, where a few moored fishing coracles bobbed gently on the ocean's azure waters. Once through the gap in the stockade, he remounted the pony to canter over to where a group of small children played happily on the blanched, seashell-encrusted sand. On enquiring where Ruadi's premises lay situated, they directed him up to the town's main square. However, he couldn't help noticing the uncertainty covering their sun-tanned faces when he had mentioned the priest by name.

Iscal wasn't as large a township as he had imagined it to be, and making his way along the narrow, twisting lanes separating the ornate rows of clay-built round huts, he was more than conscious of the suspicious eyes that seemed to be following his every movement. Most of the huts had their outer walls lime-coated, which stood in sharp contrast to the overhanging honey-coloured straw of their sloping thatched roofs. But unlike the abodes in the other parts of the country, each of these huts had motifs representing various deities stuck onto their walls: this affect having been achieved, by the use of thousands of multicoloured sea shells that gleamed and flashed even in the now-diminishing sunlight. In the past Straval had often spoken to him of his love for Iscal, describing it as a true paradise on earth. Vescala could easily see why, noticing that even the peasant women and children were adorned with beautiful bracelets and necklaces fashioned from the finest mother of pearl. It was by far the most opulent town he had ever seen.

He found the priest's hut with little difficulty and dismounting tethered the pony to the post outside the household. Entering through the open doorway, he was surprised to find the place deserted, but in the dark gloomy atmosphere of the main room, he suddenly found himself facing his own reflection staring back at him from an oval-shaped bronze mirror encircled by human skulls! All around the walls of the room, wooden plinths had been erected where carefully mounted on each of them were various specimens of butterflies, moths, insects, and bees. Inquisitively looking at each of them in turn, he was aware that all priests were acknowledged experts in all forms of wildlife; particularly bees owing to their intrinsic food value, but never before had he seen such a vast collection.

The hut was spacious enough, although sparsely furnished, and after searching behind the linen drapes where the sleeping quarters lay, only to find no one, he went back outside to feed and stable his pony. After tending to the animal, he returned into the main room with his belongings to sit down wearily at the table and finish the remainder of his provisions.

"Did no one inform you where I was to be found?" Ruadi asked, only to have to repeat himself before Vescala finally awoke. It took him a few moments to fully regain his senses as his watery eyes slowly focused on the swarthy facial features of the elderly priest who stood on the other side of the table.

"I can see you've had a hard journey, lad. Have you eaten?" the priest then asked through a smile. Rubbing the sleep from his eyes, Vescala suddenly realised at whom he was now staring, and rising from his seat to address his new master he pulled his linen jacket free from his perspiring body.

"Yes, sir, thank you...I had some provisions left over from the journey," he replied as Ruadi took a taper from the fire to light the torches lying in their iron cressets on the walls.

"Had I known you were arriving today I would have had a slave woman in attendance to have a hot meal awaiting you," the priest said, staring up at the flickering torchlights.

He was a smallish fat man of around fifty years old, with a thick, black beard almost covering his bloated jowls. However, unlike most of his fellow priests his mass of long black hair hung down untidily over his broad shoulders with his eyes, although hooded, standing out prominently; the pupils reminiscent to Vescala of black glass beads. Perhaps it was the effect of the glaring flames emblazoned against the priest's features, but suddenly he began to sense a certain eccentric trait lurking within the man's character.

"I'm sorry if I've put you to any inconvenience, sir, but my master assured me that I was to be expected on the sixth night of the full moon," he remarked, looking surprised.

"No! Durada's messenger distinctly said I was to expect you tomorrow. At least I could have sworn that's what he said. Anyway, it doesn't matter; the main thing is that you've arrived," Ruadi replied, pausing to glance at him in an almost sinister manner.

"How did you find the journey down here?" he enquired as Vescala then explained that the only incident that had worried him was when he had nearly mistaken Trestania and her party for robbers. He was, however, careful to make no reference regarding his unfortunate encounter with the owl.

"Oh, I wouldn't worry about those robbers again," Ruadi commented through a smirk. "A few days ago, I dispatched an undercover squad of warriors who, I am pleased to say, made short work of them. You would, of course, have seen their heads mounted on display by the northern trackside to serve as a warning to others!"

"Eh…no…sir," Vescala spluttered. "I came by way of the clifftops, entering the town through a damaged section of the stockade."

"Damn them! I ordered that gap to be repaired days ago," Ruadi shouted angrily. He then went through to the sleeping quarters only to return carrying a flagon of wine and two silver drinking goblets. Sitting down at the table, he slowly poured the wine, but as he did so his piercing eyes kept darting up into Vescala's.

"I understand that my student Straval is a very good friend of yours?" he asked gruffly, handing Vescala a filled goblet and intimating to him with his other hand to sit down opposite him.

"Yes, sir, we studied together for twelve years. It was a terrible tragedy when he lost his…"

"Ha!" Ruadi exclaimed, cutting short the amazed Vescala. "Forgive me, lad. I thought you might have heard the news," he then said, unfastening the cord on the white robes from around his throat.

"What news, sir?" Vescala enquired, as Ruadi sat grinning at him like an excited child.

"Some forty days ago, Straval, who I must say is an excellent scholar, had as usual left his parent's abode to come here for his tuition when a sudden burning pain behind his left eye forced him to his knees in agony. His accompanying slave immediately carried him here, but I could do no more for him than administer a potion that did little to relieve his excruciating pain. After undergoing an agonising night, he eventually managed to fall asleep, but on awakening found to his amazement that, not only was the pain gone, but the sight in his left eye had been partially restored."

At this news Vescala gasped, almost dropping the goblet.

"Well, the next few days saw a rapid improvement in his condition, and now the one eye is as good as it ever was. As a consequence of such a miracle, I ordered that a private ceremony of thanksgiving be held in his honour. This concluded in the sacrifice of two white bulls that I naturally dedicated to Sulis, our goddess of healing and that is why you found my home deserted; as you know the sixth night of a full moon is classified by us as a holy time."

For a few moments, Vescala sat speechless.

"I'm overwhelmed, sir, but tell me, had you been treating him previously? I have seen my master Durada accomplish many extraordinary cures, although I have to confess there's nothing to equal this."

"No, lad. His was a hopeless case! Only his unswerving faith in the power of the gods has brought the cure he so resolutely prayed for...I can assure you that the conversion in him has to be seen to be believed."

For a while longer Vescala chatted amiably enough with his new master, but after finishing his wine he politely asked for permission to retire. This he was granted, but only after Ruadi had insisted on delivering a longwinded exhortation that he dedicated to the benevolence of the goddess Sulis.

Having spent a restful night in the spare room of the house, the following day saw him reunited in the company of Straval and Brenas. However, their subsequent day-long drinking session, saw the three of them suffer from the worst hangovers of their lives the following morning. And although Vescala was more than delighted by Straval's good fortune, the strong bond of friendship that had united them in the past appeared to have been weakened, with Straval, who had taken to wearing a black eye patch over his blind eye, talking of nothing else but the priesthood.

Owing to the acceleration of Straval's religious mania, Vescala chose to lodge with Ruadi rather than accept his offer to share his parent's home. However, after only a month it was a decision that gave him cause to regret, with Ruadi insisting upon him observing every detail of religious protocol. There were times when he would wonder if half the gods to whom the priest prayed existed only in his head. He had certainly been much happier studying under Durada, whose tuition had never shown the blatant religious fanaticism that so often manifested itself in Ruadi's frequent violent outbursts.

At times the man's behaviour was highly erratic, and what he had previously taken to be mere eccentricity was dispelled in one sadistic action that totally convinced Vescala of the priest's dangerously unbalanced state of mind. Two young boys had been charged, tried, and found guilty of stealing eggs from a bird's nest: a common enough practice among village children, but frowned upon by the priesthood who regarded themselves as the trustees of the environment. The children's chastisement had personally been undertaken by Ruadi who, as far as Vescala was concerned, had grossly overstepped the mark by administering to each of the culprits some fifty strokes of the lash. The punishment terminating the youngest one's life, leaving the other permanently disabled.

By now Straval had become something of a local celebrity, choosing to spend nearly all of his time under Ruadi's direct tuition, leaving Vescala to content himself mostly by visiting the sick and infirm. For following the incident with the children, he began to avoid as much as possible the master whom he had now begun to despise. However, he was more than aware of the mutual dislike Ruadi held for him, by the manner in which he was often rebuked for the slightest misdemeanour. But Straval saw his master in an entirely different light, believing the priest to be his spiritual redeemer as he became increasingly obsessed by his miraculous cure; indeed, such was Straval's attitude that Brenas would often sarcastically remark to Vescala that he was none other than the saviour of the druidical faith, Ruadi's mad incantations were forever prophesying about.

Vescala could only laugh at the slave's insolence, but as the days rolled by, he began to find himself increasingly isolated by the powerful influence the priest was wielding over his one-time inseparable companion. These were unhappy times for Vescala, and only his endless daydreaming over the memory of the demure Delancia prevented him from falling into a black despondency.

Chapter Seven

The long hot summer quickly surrendered to the milder weather of the early autumn. However, with still no sign of Durada returning, and from the rumours circulating of a serious escalation in the northern conflict, Vescala unhappily resigned himself to the fact that he would have to remain in Iscal – at least for the time being.

One cold damp morning, he was glad to rise and dress and seat himself in the centre of the main room beside the blazing log fire where two slave women were busy preparing breakfast. Entering the room from the sleeping quarters, Ruadi spoke in a loud, surly voice to immediately command the women to leave the household, and taking a seat at the table he stared suspiciously down at Vescala, who sat with his back to him.

"Who is this woman Delancia whom you persistently refer to?" the priest asked almost mundanely, only for his question to momentarily confound Vescala, who on turning around managed to keep his face expressionless.

"Why, sir, do you ask such a question?" he asked; a hint of indignation singing in his voice.

"Oh, I overheard you speak of her in your sleep last night. Not for the first time I might add. I get the impression that you're somewhat preoccupied with her." Vescala detected a derisive smirk lurking behind the long black whiskers almost covering Ruadi's mouth, but pursing his lips, he shrugged his shoulders casually.

"Preoccupied – hardly, sir!" he answered, keeping his earnest eyes firmly fixed on Ruadi's. "She happened to be a very, pretty, young slave girl whom I was on intimate terms with when I stayed on Anglesey. Let's be honest, sir, no man ever forgets his first true love…even in the sanctity of his sleep."

Although feeling uncomfortable, Vescala remained outwardly calm, hoping that his hastily constructed answer would satisfy Ruadi's curiosity. For a few lingering moments the priest sat idly drumming his fingers on the table.

"I took the liberty of asking Straval if he knew of the existence of such a woman on Anglesey? He didn't!" Ruadi snapped. Although suddenly looking nervous, Vescala made an immediate reply.

"There are certain circumstances in which a man finds it advantageous in keeping the affairs of the heart to himself; jealousy can often lead to the destruction of friendship, and as you may or may not know, sir, Straval does have a certain way with the ladies. I just did not want him to know of her existence." Vescala realised that he was talking too fast and he paused to emit a false sigh. "I do, of course, understand that I was foolish to have fallen in love with her. However, I believe I learned a great deal from what was, at the time, a very enlightening emotional experience."

"I also put the same question to the slave Brenas," the serious-looking Ruadi retorted, leaving Vescala visibly shaken, and his eyelids flickered nervously as he desperately sought to find the words that might satisfy the priest's curiosity. For he couldn't be sure if Brenas had mentioned to him their meeting with the priestess on the day of the sacrificial burnings.

"A married woman is legally entitled to certain rights, sir," he replied, trying to remain calm. "I used the name Delancia merely as a pseudonym, not just to protect her from her husband's possible vengeance but also to protect myself from my master's fury in the event of him having discovered the affair. As you know, sir, any unmarried slave girl is sexually used at will by priests and novices alike, but once she marries, all be it to another slave, she comes under the protection of the law appertaining to adultery. Anyway, sir, I must emphasise that at the time I was a somewhat immature sixteen-year-old."

Raising his bushy eyebrows almost nonchalantly but saying no more, Ruadi merely nodded, and rising from the table he went out through the door at a brisk pace leaving Vescala to breakfast alone. But he was far from convinced that Ruadi had swallowed his hastily constructed story, and getting up to take his place at the table he kept inventing other tales to explain his talking in his sleep that seemed much more plausible than the one he had just related. Still, he had done rather well under the circumstances, he reckoned, tucking into the meal being served up to him by the returning slave women. But how on earth does any man safeguard a secret fantasy when asleep, he kept on wondering.

After finishing the meal, the question continued to trouble him. But with today being one of his all too infrequent rest days the idea suddenly struck him that it might be to his benefit if he were to collect samples of the various life forms infesting the many rock pools at the nearby shoreline, hoping that by undertaking such an educational task he might just impress Ruadi: allaying any future suspicions regarding him that might again arise in his master's insane head. However, a glance through the open doorway at the ashen autumnal sky convinced him that he would have to be sufficiently wrapped up against the likelihood of a probable rainstorm.

Leaving the abode, his long sealskin cloak protected him well against the strong easterly gale. On reaching the deserted shore, he spotted a tiny hermit crab lying in the first shallow rock pool he happened to come upon. Bending down to pick it up, and scrutinising it, he cursed inwardly at Ruadi's intrusion into his private life. Momentarily, he envied the creature for its wisdom in protecting itself within the secluded confines of an empty whelk shell. For in a world where there is no true morality in nature, it need answer to no one for its actions. Gently placing the creature back, his thoughts were abruptly ended by the sound of a shrill whistle carrying on the wind, and turning sharply he saw the approaching figure of Brenas working his way carefully along the sharp, slippery rocks towards him.

"Where's Straval?" he asked, somewhat surprised at seeing the slave alone.

"I don't know, sir. Ruadi came for him earlier on and ordered me to take one of the ponies to the farriers to be re-shod; that's where I was when I saw you come down here."

Knowing that he had some time on his hands before the farrier would be finished, Brenas then asked if he needed a hand. Vescala agreed and both men proceeded to collect samples of the seaweed and crustaceans that encrusted the surrounding rocks, with Vescala placing each specimen into the small shoulder sack he was carrying.

"Tell me, Brenas, has Ruadi ever asked if you knew of a slave girl on Anglesey by the name of Delancia?" he enquired apprehensively, turning to face the slave.

"Yes, sir… he asked me only yesterday."

"Then what did you tell him?" a perplexed Vescala then asked; his forehead set into a deep frown as Brenas looking puzzled by the alarm in his question.

"I told him it was possible, but that was all. The only time I think I ever heard such an uncommon name was on the day of the burnings when Trestania called out to her priestess. Oh, that reminds me, when I left Straval's place, I saw her and her priestesses entering the town; they were heading towards the large dwelling house just up from the harbour."

Relieved at this information and now grateful to have someone to confide in, Vescala first swore the slave to secrecy before explaining his predicament to him. For a few moments, Brenas pondered over Vescala's dilemma.

"From what you say, sir, there's no incriminating evidence to associate you with this priestess. But he has gone to the trouble of asking Straval, and it is possible Straval might have remembered the name; after all, it was Trestania's shout that woke him that day."

"Yes," Vescala commented solemnly. "If Ruadi was ever to discover my true feelings for this woman, I would in all probability be charged with heresy and banished from all tribal contact for the rest of my life. To be honest with you, I'm afraid even to ask Straval, but from what you've just told me it may not matter. Trestania will only have to address Delancia in Ruadi's company for him to put two and two together; it is as you said, Delancia is a very unusual name."

Pulling the collar of his thin linen jacket up to his ears as a protection against the cold, blustery wind, Brenas straightened up to stare across the water to the distant, murky horizon.

"The ways of love are strange, sir," he remarked, sympathising with Vescala's plight. "But you might as well face it…yours is a hopeless passion. I know only too well Ruadi's violent temperament. He would never have you excommunicated and banished; instead, he would have you put to death in the most brutal manner conceivable. And if he didn't, believe me, Trestania certainly would. I doubt if even Durada could save you under such circumstances!"

"You may be right. But to forget her is for my part impossible," Vescala declared, with a slight embarrassment overshadowing his downcast features. But Brenas, who by now had come to detest both Ruadi and Straval, saw his chance.

"Sir, don't you think that just as a precaution it might be wise to prepare an escape route for yourself? I would be more than willing to join you."

"No!" Vescala exclaimed, vigorously shaking his head. "I couldn't even contemplate leaving without her. It might sound crazy to you but she's in my thoughts every moment of the day and night. But tell me, how did she appear? Was she well?"

"No, sir, she looked as miserable as yourself."

"That doesn't surprise me. You see, unlike we priests, these so-called 'chosen women' are never permitted to form any relationships with men. They must remain virgins for the duration of their lives."

The rain that had been threatening began to fall with a penetrating force, with an embittered Vescala deciding that they should return to the town. Passing by the harbour, they saw that work had started on unloading the two single-mast merchant galleys lying moored within its shelter. Although all direct commerce with Rome itself had been discontinued ever since Julius Caesar's aborted invasion, the town, like most of its southern counterparts, still traded freely with the merchants from the Roman provinces; these being Gaul, Spain, and Northern Africa. Tin was the commodity usually exported from Iscal, but silver, lead, freshwater pearls, and frequently slaves were also in great demand. In exchange, the local merchants imported ivory, glassware, fine woven cloth, and wine, with such trade bringing considerable affluence to the coastal regions. To both men, the unloading of the ships was an incredible sight. In the recent past they had seen many similar vessels but none as large as these. Like everyone else they were familiar with the tales that told of the misery of the unfortunate galley slaves who spend most of their lives chained to the oars in the hold below the deck; counting the oars dangling from the sides of the vessels they estimated each ship to be carrying in the region of one-hundred slaves apiece. For a short while longer, they openly discussed the injustices of slavery before going their separate ways.

Back in his lodgings, Vescala occupied himself for some time in mounting his specimens onto a long wooden plinth hanging empty on the wall, and by the late afternoon, the task was complete.

Having eaten and seeing a slight improvement in the weather, he once more donned his cloak and decided to take a stroll along the western clifftops; this being something he had meant to do previously but had never found the time. His intention was to follow the steep path leading away from the town's northern portcullis. However, seeing that there were so few people about, and hoping to at least catch a glimpse of

Delancia, he began walking down into the town itself. Passing by the dwelling house Brenas had spoken of, he was disappointed at not sighting her, but strolling past the harbour he soon reached the town's defensive stockade, which ran down almost into the sea at the base of the cliffs. With the tide now racing in and a strong headwind at his back, he decided to cut around the stockade and scale the cliff face. It wasn't too difficult a climb and reaching the springy grass slopes stretching out along the summit, he walked westwards away from the town before stopping to admire the view. From the height he was now at, it was breath-taking, and carefully leaning over, he looked down to where the dull green waters of the heavy seas thundered over the rocks far below with the foaming surf temporarily submerging the daring cormorants who dived and swam beneath the white spluttering crests of the waves that moments later crashed mercilessly against the impregnable cliff face. Standing back, he smiled admiringly at the impressive manner by which they almost casually taunted the terrifying spasms of the waters that repeatedly threatened to swallow them forever.

Leaving the spot, he ventured on for a while longer before his attention was suddenly attracted to the appearance of a distant, solitary hooded figure heading towards him. Instinctively he knew who she was, and as they approached closer to one another his heart was pounding, as he felt as if he was being drawn into a dream. As the unique beauty advanced ever closer, he walked over to meet her; all the time her enraptured eyes gazing into his. However, now standing facing one another, each felt a little awkward at their chance meeting, although neither of them could deny the obvious passion that they somehow sensed existed from deep within their very spiritual existence. To the stunned Vescala it was an inexplicable compatibility that seemed to defy all human understanding. And as they smiled timidly at one another, he glimpsed her windblown, tawny hair now hanging down below the upturned hood of her long black cloak where it danced and coiled in fine wispy ringlets over her smooth, pale brow. For a brief moment he stood, uncertain of what to say to her only for his muteness to suddenly vanish.

"I…I did he…hear of your arrival in town this morning," he spluttered out in a loud trembling voice, and quickly drawing his eyes from hers, he inwardly cursed himself for stammering. But sensing his acute discomfort Delancia made a quick reply.

"We've come to participate in the thanksgiving festival soon to be held to mark the start of the harvest gathering. My mistress reckons on us being here for at least a month," she said through a happy smile; a faint pink glow becoming visible over her face now devoid of cosmetics, and which brought to it an even more natural and enchanting beauty. And with the blustery wind whipping at the front of her long cloak, Vescala glanced down to the resplendent golden amulet she wore around her neck.

"I'm surprised to see you without a chaperone," he commented falsely, being only too delighted to have met her unaccompanied.

"But my two friends were ahead of me, you must have passed them," she replied.

"No, I came up here by the cliff face."

"Then they must have re-joined the path over the ridge," she said, pointing to the range of low-lying hills running parallel with the cliffs. But both could see that the only other living creature near to them was a lone sea eagle circling overhead against the grey lustreless sky.

"Oh well!" Delancia exclaimed with a shrug as she smiled up at him. "They were a good way ahead of me. I came this way in order to attain an aerial view of the town. But tell me, what's your name?"

"I'm known as Vescala of the Durotriges tribe," the grinning Vescala replied, and at his invitation they strolled slowly back towards the town, with both of them careful to keep looking around in case anyone saw them together. For at no time was any young priestess ever permitted to be alone in the company of a male, with each of them being fully aware of the dangerous suspicions such an innocent meeting as theirs could arouse.

In turn, they explained to each other how they came to be taken into the priesthood, with Vescala surprised to learn that Delancia had been found abandoned as an infant child by a sister of Trestania who had died not long after. However, what struck him as strange about her story was the fact that she had been discovered at the base of an oak tree. How similar to his own case he thought wistfully. It was certainly odd that the oak, the godhead of all the forest's trees, should have manipulated their destinies in such a way. Ever since that fateful day, Delancia had known no other life but the priesthood, and from the way she spoke it was obvious that she loathed her mistress Trestania, whom she openly referred to as the 'red witch.' Many years after her discovery, Trestania had informed her that her very creation had been an act of conception between the tree and the mother earth. But even now, Delancia scoffed at such a preposterous idea, believing herself to have been no more than the abandoned child of some unfortunate, poverty-stricken peasant girl. Like Vescala, she admitted to despising the constant cruelties administered against the underclasses in the name of druidical justice before going on to tell him of how, in the past, she had twice absconded, only to suffer severe beatings after having been recaptured.

As they talked it became clearly evident to both of them that neither had experienced much happiness in their lives, and in Delancia's delicate emotional voice Vescala sensed an intense desire to escape the immoral vows that had been so callously enforced upon a sinless deserted infant. Suddenly he stopped in his tracks as did Delancia, who stared up at him; her compassionate crystalline eyes appearing to him to glow with an enticing ignorance of any evil. Over these past few months, he had made frequent attempts to forget her, often rebuking himself for what he had taken to be no more than an obsessive infatuation. However, at this moment in time he found himself totally entranced and captivated by his desperate love for her, and sensing that he might never again have an opportunity to express his feelings, he drew in a deep breath.

"Delancia, I am more than aware that we hardly know one another. But I have loved you from the very first moment we met, and in my heart, I feel that you are likewise afflicted," he said convincingly as Delancia's startled eyes darted to the ground, only to rise to again meet his. "We belong to each other, Delancia. Please say you'll come away with me. Any life for us is better than to remain here and live a lie."

For a moment her eyes clouded over with uncertainty.

"Vescala, believe me when I say that I likewise love you! But our world is a small place and we would be doomed to live forever in its shadows. You must surely know that they would never rest until they had hunted us into an eternal extinction," she replied despairingly as Vescala tenderly placed his hands onto her small shoulders.

"No, no my love!" he exclaimed forcefully, agitated by her compliant despondency. "Trestania and the others would have you believe that. But I do know that the druid priesthood in Gaul and Spain, at least what is left of it, is under increasing pressure owing to Rome's insistence that the practice of human sacrifice be ended. It's even said among our own priests that many of the tribes in these countries are openly reverting to and worshipping Roman gods. As you know, the island of Anglesey is, and still remains the sacred island of all the druids, including the Europeans. But I know for a fact that every year sees a sharp decline in the number of novitiates who travel over from Europe to study on the island. For when I was there, I saw for myself that they numbered no more than a hundred, whereas in the past it would have been thousands. Now the Roman emperor Augustus has publicly decreed that Rome's empire ends at the channel separating us from Europe, but can anyone honestly believe that their next emperor or indeed his successor will hold a similar opinion…I doubt it! The Romans, like all empire builders, will never be satisfied until they eventually achieve worldwide domination, and I personally feel that it's only a matter of time before our own islands are trampled beneath their vastly superior war machine. The last time they invaded us was merely an exercise to enhance the reputation of one man, namely Julius Caesar. But the next time they come I pray that they will wipe our misguided religion from the face of the earth!"

As he spoke, Vescala had felt a terrible hatred towards his druid masters, and now, caressing Delancia's smooth cheeks with his fingers, he continued, only this time in an altered tone filled with impassioned pleading.

"All I seek for us is our natural right to love one another. The two of us are all alone in this world and would be betraying no one. Now I think I know of a way to escape. Please say you'll come with me," he beseeched her, although as yet he had formulated no definite plan of escape. With her misty eyes lingering on his, and as assuredly as their destinies had so mysteriously intertwined, their impatient lips met in the serene kiss of an indestructible love.

Suddenly she drew her moist lips away.

"It must be soon…the harvest celebrations begin in four days from now."

"Then there are no doubts in your mind?" the trembling Vescala asked, smiling in relief as he began devising a plan to escape.

"The thought of being captured and what they might do to us terrifies me. But no, we'll go!" she exclaimed nervously, hugging him tight. But easing her away and gently cupping her angelic face in his hands, Vescala then spoke to her reassuringly.

"They will not catch us. Now do you remember the slave who was in my company on the day of the burnings?" he asked, as Delancia smiled and nodded. "He will be only too happy to come with us. He is my friend and more than deserves his freedom. Tomorrow, he, and I will begin organising the ponies and supplies we will require. Now rather than risk leaving by the stockade's portcullis, it will be safer for us to go the way that I first arrived in the town. It means going under cover of darkness and forcing a way through the newly repaired section of the stockade. After scaling the not-too-steep eastern cliff-face, and once free of Iscal, we then ride flat out towards the great chalk cliffs that look over to Gaul. When we reach the channel, we should be able to barter our ponies for a fishing raft capable of transporting us over the water. It will not be easy, but I don't think Trestania will expect us to try and reach Europe. She is more likely to suspect we went north or even attempted the crossing over to Ireland. Now, in order to try and deceive her, Brenas and I will steal one of the rafts in the harbour and hide it somewhere. Hopefully, she will reckon on us having set sail for Ireland."

"Why can't we use the raft to get us over to Gaul?" she then asked.

"It would take too long."

"And the hole left in the stockade?"

"Brenas and I will camouflage it as best as we can. Anyway, by the time it's discovered we should be well on our way. Now the day after tomorrow, as soon as it is dark, I'll come for you. Will you be able to leave your lodgings undetected?"

"Yes!" she exclaimed, clinging tightly onto his arms. "Fortunately, I have a small room to myself near to the entrance of the house. I will wait for you at the entrance, which is never guarded. However, if for any reason I'm not there, find somewhere safe to hide until I arrive. Sometimes Trestania's late-night prayer meetings drag on for ages."

"Excellent! We can only hope and pray that in some six days from now we will have escaped to a new world. Oh, I don't expect life under Roman authority to be all paradise – but at least we'll have each other forever." Placing his arm protectively around her shoulders, the two young lovers strolled for a little while longer all the time talking optimistically of their future together; both utterly convinced that they would experience a lasting happiness in their relationship. Nearing the township, they stopped to embrace again, with each longing to hold the other forever in their arms. However, with time stealing swiftly by, they reluctantly parted, and it was with a calm sense of remorse that Vescala watched her elegant figure walk along the narrow path that led down to the town's portcullis.

From where he stood, he saw her reunited with her two friends far below. Suddenly the brief melancholy he had felt on her departure surrendered to a sense of supreme ecstasy. He was more than aware of the great dangers lying ahead of them, but for the moment such dangers seemed irrelevant. The unbelievable had happened to him with a strange beautiful twist having occurred in his destiny. For he had encountered Delancia on only three occasions and yet it now seemed as if they had known and loved the other ever since the very moment of their earthly conception.

He waited until she disappeared from sight before beginning his own journey back down the cliff face. A few scattered drops of rain fell to strike his beaming face with an exhilarating impact, and on the way down he could think of nothing else but the fact that a few more days would see them on their way to a long-awaited freedom. But passing through the harbour area the sight of the many slaves manacled by their feet and busy unloading the galleys filled him with sadness. Suddenly, he felt ashamed of his own selfish desires, for from the moment of their captivity to the moment of their death, the only true freedom they would ever know would be in the isolation of the grave. And staring pityingly at them, he somehow sensed their inaudible screams crying out for the leadership that would smash their chains of bondage forever.

Arriving back at his lodgings, he was informed by the slave woman that Ruadi had returned earlier and, having eaten, had left hurriedly in order to pay a social visit to Trestania. This news left him praying that nothing unforeseen would happen in the short time remaining until their escape.

Sitting by the fire, he repeatedly went over in his mind the fragile plan he had conceived. However, with many doubts now scourging his thoughts, every moment of joy was equalled by a fit of nerve-wracking anxiety; indeed, would Brenas even come with them? And if he did, would they manage to escape safely from the town? Even if this was successful, would they then get far enough away to elude the search party, which would inevitably be dispatched by Trestania and Ruadi the moment their flight was detected? For the remainder of the day, these questions kept troubling him.

Returning after dark, much the worse for drink, Ruadi merely acknowledged his presence with a grunt before retiring for the night leaving Vescala to extinguish the torchlight; a task he undertook with a great deal of relish, having half-expected the priest to have discovered his dream lover's true- identity.

Lying back on his straw bed, sleep soon fell upon him. But somehow, he sensed that Delancia's mist-enshrouded face, now appearing in his dream, belonged to that of a doomed woman, and against a background of incandescent eternity, he could only watch in horror as she attempted to defend herself from the demented fluttering of the hideous alien bird circling her. However, with no more than his nightmare's eyes to struggle with, he was pathetically incapable of rescuing her from the torrential and savage blows that tore in bloody lumps the flesh and eyes from her face until only a cleanly picked skull remained, held forever in the ghastly visitant's cruel, retributive talons!

To the unwary Vescala the previous day had been a glorious one, but time never sleeps, and it had completely escaped him that at the turn of the night – in the druidical calendar – the oncoming day would herald in the month of the owl!

Chapter Eight

It was almost daybreak when the piercing cries of distant drama shattered Vescala's violent nightmare. Mentally disorientated, he awoke to find one of the slave women kneeling beside him, shaking his shoulder, and screaming hysterically at him to get up. Although stupefied, his perception of danger saw him leap to his feet and quickly dress in the dark gloom of his sleeping quarters. Half-naked, the cursing Ruadi suddenly darted past him and out through the open door. Grabbing hold of a sword, Vescala followed only to see that outside pandemonium ensued all around, with half-naked men, women, and children running in all directions. In desperation, he attempted to question some of them, with no one being quite sure as to the exact reason for the panic. Suddenly a huge sheet of flame leapt upwards from the harbour area, illuminating the darkened streets of the town, and showering them with embers whose fiery tresses spread rapidly over the thatched roofs of the houses

The screamed statement from someone that Trestania had been murdered caused him to fear for the safety of his beloved Delancia. However, by the time he made his way through the swarming masses and down to the harbour area, what fighting that had taken place was virtually over. Frantic with worry, he was shocked to see many dead bodies lying in the streets, some of whom were being ritually beheaded by roaming packs of armed local men and women. Turning towards Delancia's lodgings, he stopped in his tracks when seeing that all that remained of the building was the smoking skeleton of its walls and rafters. But searching through the smouldering ruins, his terror became more acute on discovering many badly charred bodies whose physical features were burned beyond all recognition.

With the first light of the dawn now infiltrating the stormy grey sky, he made a thorough search of the immediate area but again failed to find any trace of Delancia. By now the fires that had threatened to annihilate the town were in the process of being extinguished by hastily formed chains of fire-fighters frantically pouring bucket after bucket of water onto the flames, with the heavy, wind-swept rain that by now had begun to fall aiding them in their task.

Numbed by his grief, a bewildered Vescala stood watching one of the fleeing Roman galleys, all the time contemplating over what had caused such carnage. For although short, the conflict had been exceptionally bloody, and in the dim morning light his sad eyes roamed over the seething rain-swept waters now stained a deep crimson by the many bleeding corpses floating on the surface.

"This is indeed a black day for us all," he heard, turning to see Ruadi's grim hooded figure standing beside him. "The gods have placed a dreadful curse upon us. There is no other explanation for this defilement of our sacred women. Only our holy Trestania has survived, although I hold out little hope for her recovery," Ruadi muttered despairingly.

"What the hell happened?" Vescala demanded, with the pouring rain now streaming down his unhappy features.

"It seems that the crews from the two galleys were drinking and whoring it up in the town when one of our merchants took it upon himself to check out one of the ship's cargoes. He had apparently suspected that the ship's captain was short-measuring him with merchandise. Anyway, whilst below the deck he came upon a Roman centurion, but before being killed managed to raise the alarm. The news, of course, spread like wildfire. However, by the time our people were fully aware of what was happening, the ship's crews had attacked and set fire to most of the houses around the harbour area; doubtless hoping that their action would give them more time to prepare their ships for sailing. As you can see, they partially succeeded. I have heard though that the ship that escaped has taken hostages! But this has yet to be confirmed. We will not know until all the dead have been officially accounted for."

Vescala sighed, feeling a little more hopeful on learning that hostages may have been taken.

"How on earth was our security so bloody inefficient?" he demanded, almost spitting the question at the strangely placid Ruadi, who shrugged sullenly.

"I do not know! Personally, I feel that we have allowed ourselves to be lulled into a false sense of security, by the manner in which we allot our trust to these merchant vessels. I have warned our chieftains many times that, under the guise of legitimate trading, the Romans merely use these ships to reconnoitre our coasts. Tragically, it would appear, that I have been proved right."

Both men then watched the fleeing vessel, and although she was a good distance out from the shore, they could see she was making little headway against the heavy seas repeatedly buffeting her.

"You say there could be hostages aboard?" Vescala asked, trying desperately to remain optimistic regarding Delancia's fate. "Don't you think it might be a good idea to have the ship followed? After all, in weather like this she will probably have to sail close inshore and in doing so might well strike a reef and run aground."

"Yes, all right," Ruadi replied, readily agreeing to the suggestion. "I'll tell you what, you form an armed party to track her. I, of course, will be unable to go with you…I'll be needed here to tend to Trestania's wounds…I'm afraid she was struck down by a spear."

But totally unconcerned regarding Trestania's welfare, an anxious Vescala took his leave and immediately began to organise the men and ponies he required.

Returning to his lodgings to obtain dry clothing and more weapons, he met Straval and asked his permission to take

Brenas with him. Straval willingly agreed, although he himself rejected the offer to go, electing to stay and help Ruadi.

Soon everything was prepared, with the heavily armed band of some twenty riders having quickly gathered in a group in the town's main square. All around them, chaos reigned, with many people, including children, still attempting to extinguish the last of the smouldering fires. Twelve prisoners, including a Roman centurion, had been captured from the galley lying stranded in the harbour. For a few moments, the party watched as they were pushed at spearpoint into one of the undamaged communal huts where they were to undergo their interrogation with Vescala praying that the town's chieftains would, for the time being, keep them alive in the hope that they might be exchanged for any hostages.

Riding flat out, the party set off along the rain-lashed clifftops with Vescala beseeching the gods to deliver his loved one safely back to him. Meanwhile, Brenas had been able to inform him that one of the eyewitnesses to the attack had witnessed one druidess and two slaves being dragged aboard the ship that had escaped. According to the description Brenas had obtained from the man, it appeared that the priestess had indeed been Delancia; this news strengthening Vescala's determination to find her.

It wasn't long before they reached the point where the vessel was struggling to maintain a steady course. But from their towering position, they could clearly see the helmsman skilfully steering her through the treacherous reefs and sand-banks that stretched well out from the shore all along the coast. However, as several days quickly elapsed the weather steadily deteriorated, and with the little food they were able to eat along with their lack of sleep, the party's morale began to sink.

Throughout the tiresome journey, Vescala remained preoccupied with Delancia. Had she been wounded like Trestania? Or would the same fate befall her as had happened to the slave girl, whom Ravala had so cruelly debauched? The questions kept circling in his mind as he repeatedly asked himself why everything had turned against him just when the future had looked so promising. His only hope against this savage twist of fate lay in the defiance of his spirit. He was now obsessed with finding and rescuing her, even if it meant journeying to the very ends of the earth.

On the third day, the ship's progress remained painfully slow. But by the evening the tempestuous weather suddenly changed, bringing a thick fog that totally obscured their view.

The first light of the following dawn brought with it clear visibility but with no sign whatsoever of the galley. Vescala decided to press on even further along the coast in the forlorn hope that they might again sight her. Deep in his heart though, he thought it highly unlikely, reckoning that the ship's captain had probably taken advantage of the calmer weather and headed towards one of the not-too-distant Gaulish ports. With still no sighting of the ship, that evening brought winds of almost hurricane force that whipped the sea into a foaming frenzy, and with gigantic waves crashing all along the shore and heavy rain driving mercilessly against them, he had no alternative but to order the party inland in order to seek shelter in the nearest village. With the next day having to be spent indoors in order to avoid the storm's ferocity, a marked lassitude now afflicted his entire being.

Early the following day, a lone trapper came to the village bringing news that the severe flooding engulfing the whole of the southern regions had destroyed many of the crops. He was also able to inform Vescala that, owing to the weather conditions and the attack on Iscal, the priesthood had decreed that the harvest celebrations were to be postponed indefinitely. But for Vescala that night was to bring the most disheartening news of all with yet another traveller reporting to him that a merchant galley matching the description of the one that had fled from Iscal had been sighted in the channel just south of the great chalk cliffs. From the man's account it appeared that the ship, whose mast had been shattered in the storm, had been struggling to remain afloat in the turbulent sea. The man also stated that he personally had witnessed yet another merchant galley break up and sink close to the channel, with some driftwood having come ashore although he had seen no sign of any bodies. With these events having occurred two days previously, the news virtually confirmed Vescala's worst fears. He was now resigned to the reality that no human being could possibly have survived at sea in such a tempest. That night he spent alone, utterly convinced that his beloved Delancia was dead, and as he sat morosely drinking the strong ale, he experienced a degree of loneliness that in the past had seemed unimaginable. In his dismay, he recalled the strange incident with the owl and then the nightmare with all its prophetic qualities. Had he not chosen to ignore such macabre omens, his beloved Delancia might not now be lying entombed forever within the ocean's silent shroud. In his isolation, it now seemed as if some evil thorn had pierced his chilled heart as he shuddered violently on recalling his old master's prophetic words: "For I warn you that one among you may, in time, be guilty of profane worship, and not only might his resulting crimes herald disaster for every tribe in the land, but he will bring shame and finally destruction upon our proud seat of learning!"

If only he had recognised the authority of the druid instead of pursuing a life of irreverent desire, then perhaps none of the recent carnage might have occurred, he thought sadly. All his short life he had regarded love as being the finest of all human emotions. Yet, it was a tragic fact that, in his own case, love was as fatal as the ill-timed spark that lays waste an entire forest. In his ruptured soul he relived the all-too-short times he had spent in Delancia's mystical company, only for the effects of the alcohol see him lapse into a deep, dreamless slumber.

At first light the following morning, the party left the village to begin the long journey home, and with the weather now calm and settled they rode off at a fast gallop. Even so, it took them three full days to reach the outskirts of Iscal, with every coastal village they passed by having suffered severe storm damage, and with much of the countryside around them still lying under deep flood water.

Reaching Iscal, it was just as they feared, with the riders finding the damage to their hometown to be horrendous; the fire and subsequent storm having destroyed half the dwelling houses. However, once through the town's portcullis the party immediately split up, leaving Vescala and Brenas to head through the ruins towards Ruadi's house. By this time many of the homeless families had erected makeshift tents of animal skins to temporarily replace their ruined property; the sad sight reminding Vescala of the unfortunate refugees he had encountered at the time of the plague. And although some rebuilding work had already begun, both men knew that it would be a long time before the once-magnificent town would be restored to its former glory.

Exhausted by their hard journey, they longed to rest, only for a large, curious crowd to quickly assemble with the townspeople enquiring as to what news they brought. On hearing the commotion, Ruadi suddenly appeared from his own undamaged property only to see by the riders' downcast expressions that their journey had been in vain. With his eyes heavy with fatigue, Vescala wearily dismounted, leaving Brenas to tend to the ponies, and at Ruadi's invitation the two men entered the hut.

"Tell me what happened, but keep your voice low," Ruadi whispered. Vescala then explained all that had occurred, somehow managing to disguise his true feelings, by the complacent manner in which he spoke.

"Well, that's that then," Ruadi said softly. "However, I'm pleased to inform you that the high priestess is improving. For the time being she is recuperating in the back room. She mustn't be told of your news until she's regained her full strength. By then our druid brothers in Gaul should have confirmed whether the ship returned to port or sank. I'll get word to them as soon as possible…I must confess though; it looks certain she went down."

Surprised to learn that Trestania had survived the attack, Vescala stared thoughtfully down into the fire.

"What's to become of the prisoners who were captured?" he asked bluntly.

"For the time being I'm keeping them alive in the hope that we can exchange them for any hostages that might have been taken. If by the end of the month we have heard nothing from Gaul − then they die!"

Ruadi's words brought a certain comfort to Vescala leaving him feeling uneasy. How, he wondered, could Ruadi so easily condemn the men. After all, they had merely been acting under orders issued by some despotic emperor who neither knew nor cared about the suffering of an impoverished people in a far-distant land. But the compulsion to spill blood in vengeance continued to compete in his thoughts alongside a virtuous desire to show the prisoners mercy − even allowing for the indisputable fact that their crimes had ruined his life.

The constant flow of important dignitaries visiting Trestania convinced Ruadi that Vescala would have to obtain alternative lodgings, at least until Trestania was well enough to leave with Vescala only too happy to accept the offer once more proposed by Straval that he now lodge at his parent's house.

The misery-laden days came and went with no respite from the lingering heartache that was now a permanent feature of his existence. He spent every passing moment praying that good news would soon arrive from Gaul only for his intuition to tell him that the tiny flame of hope still burning in him, and that prompted him to believe that Delancia was still alive, must soon be extinguished forever. There were times when he desperately tried to erase her memory but it was futile; deep in his aching heart he knew that such an all-consuming love, once experienced and lost forever, must leave a life-long emptiness in his soul. Only in the phantom realms of his dreams would the fleeting perception of her presence be once again personified.

As the floodwaters receded the harvest gathering began in earnest. The druids had taken it as a good omen that the crops were not as badly affected as had at first been anticipated, with the flooding and high winds having destroyed less than a third of the plants. By now all work had ceased in the tin mines with the labour having been redeployed, either in the gathering and storing of the harvest or in the rebuilding programme Ruadi had devised for the town; tasks in which Vescala and Straval had been given part-time supervisory roles. But there now existed a deep mistrust between the two young men with Vescala's once inseparable companion now treating almost everything he said or did with an arrogant disdain. The sinister, black eye patch Straval had taken to wearing appeared to Vescala to emphasise the change that had occurred in him since his return from Anglesey. For with the miraculous restoration of his sight, his religious fervour had increased to such an extent that even Ruadi's fanaticism seemed mild in comparison.

After a month, news at last reached them that the merchant ship had officially been lost at sea, with the Roman garrison stationed at Boulogne having publicly named some ten members of their armed forces who had gone down with her. The order was now issued throughout the land that all Roman ships trading with the southern ports were to be thoroughly searched, and that none of their crew were to be permitted to disembark to enjoy the local hospitality. The priesthood had attempted to prevent trading altogether, only to be overruled by the kings and merchants who had insisted that such a reprisal might well stretch Roman patience to breaking point, leading to a full-scale invasion being mounted against Britain.

However, it was common knowledge that the real reason for continuing the trade lay in their personal avarice.

The autumn soon surrendered to the first frost of winter, bringing to Ruadi a sense of urgency regarding the rebuilding of the huts still to be completed. The priesthood had decreed that a harsh winter lay ahead, and as the late harvest celebrations culminated in the annual sacrifice of six black sheep, everyone was relieved to see the granaries amply filled thus ensuring that the food shortages they had feared would be effectively avoided.

With the harvesting over, Ruadi assigned his two pupils full-time onto the rebuilding programme. Slaves were quickly called in from every available source, and although some work had been completed, fifty families were still living in makeshift accommodation. With priority given to those families with the most children, Vescala and his team redoubled their efforts. But nothing he did seemed to satisfy Ruadi, who persistently complained that the work was progressing too slowly. Vescala bitterly wondered how anyone was expected to accomplish such a task in the ridiculously short time his slaves had been allotted with Ruadi having given his team just twenty days in which to erect and complete ten round houses. Although labour was in plentiful supply, his problem lay in the acute shortage of the materials he required. This factor, along with the harsh weather, meant production was constantly being interrupted. As a result, and after only a few frustrating days, he began to despair of even achieving a third of his set target. Seeing productivity falling behind schedule, Ruadi ordered him to split his men into two shifts with one working through the day and the other at night by torchlight. At this command Vescala openly cursed his master, disregarding the fact that his slaves overheard him. Why, he asked himself angrily, had Straval received the same job allocation and yet had been given twice the amount of men and tools. Even the building materials were being delivered direct to Straval while he was forced to send his men on a long journey for the timber and clay. The slaves had been shocked at their overseer's rebellious attitude towards his master: nonetheless, he was a young man they openly respected, with Vescala ensuring by fraudulent means that they ate far more than the subsistence level diet they would normally expect to receive.

The days and nights were insufferably long for the ever-weary Vescala, who was forced into resting at irregular intervals with only sleep temporarily releasing him from the despair that was now a permanent feature of his existence. There were times when he felt an overwhelming desire to run away from Iscal and far from the reality that he himself was now little better off than the slaves under his supervision. But every time he gathered up the courage to do so a strange, dream-like apathy would claw its way into his soul.

Owing to their extra food rations the slave's morale remained reasonably high; this being shown in the way they enthusiastically undertook even the most difficult of tasks, and after eighteen days and nights hard work, all that remained to be done was to complete the thatching of two roofs. But Ruadi showed no appreciation at the achievement, and throughout the rebuilding programme had frequently chastised Vescala over his men's poor workmanship, at times going as far as to threaten him with a public flogging. However, Vescala now cared nothing for his master's veiled threats; indeed, every time Ruadi had complained, he had spat contemptuously at his master's feet; an action that infuriated the priest, and by the time the buildings were complete the relationship between the two men had evolved into a deep mutual hatred. But by now, Vescala had finally decided to make a determined attempt to escape and free himself from the physical and spiritual bondage of the vows that he had so foolishly sworn to the priesthood.

Chapter Nine

T he bejewelled Trestania was now seen in public for the first time since having been wounded. Addressing the townspeople from Ruadi's doorway, her appearance brought wild cheering from the large crowds who greeted her. But although deathly pale and unsteady on her feet, she had no difficulty in informing the people that the twelve prisoners captured on the morning of the attack were to be executed the following day; the sacrifices, however, being conducted in a strictly private ceremony. The crowds cheered even louder when she further announced that the sacrificial date had been declared a public holiday, with even the slaves being rewarded for their industrious work by being permitted to participate in the feasting and celebrations that would follow the killings.

After her brief public address, Trestania's ever-sinister eyes suddenly darted over to where Vescala stood among the crowd, only to betray no obvious recognition, and aided by Ruadi and Straval, she returned back into the house.

"She didn't appear to recognise you, sir," Brenas remarked as Vescala turned to see the slave grinning broadly.

"No, she knew me all right – a witch like her never forgets," Vescala retorted, as both men stood staring in disgust at the few misguided peasants who were attempting to follow her into the house, only to be forced back by Straval. But after she disappeared from their view the crowds soon dispersed, leaving the two men alone.

"I'm being sent back to Anglesey, sir," Brenas said sadly. "I'm told it's to be after the midwinter ceremonies. My present master has no further use for me, frequently referring to me as lazy, inefficient, and insolent. Although I disagree with the first two allegations, the last one is undoubtedly true.

Vescala smirked at the slave's remark, knowing only too well the infectious religious mania Straval had contracted from the fanatical Ruadi.

"Don't worry about it, Brenas, the day of our freedom isn't far away," he said, turning serious as the slave's eyes narrowed.

"No, sir," Brenas mumbled, shaking his head. "There would be no point in my escaping. Oh, I know I offered to join you in the past. But let's be honest, no matter where we went, the tell-tale scar on my face would always give me away."

"No, you're wrong," Vescala replied with conviction: "I don't think the Romans would care too much for a man's past life − especially a rich man. The jewels worn by the red witch will more than compensate you for the years of ingratitude shown by those you address as masters. All we have to do is deprive her of them, and between us…I think we are more than capable of achieving that goal."

"Sir, you speak as if only I'm going?"

"You are − to Europe," Vescala replied, glancing up at the bleak evening sky: "I'll help you all I can to first steal Trestania's jewels and then get you over to Gaul. As for me, I'll travel in the opposite direction following a western route that will take me beyond Ireland. A route beyond the Atlantic Ocean that I hope will eventually lead me to true freedom."

For a moment the fraught Brenas looked stunned at the absurdity of his statement.

"But, sir, the Atlantic! Such a journey would be suici…" he said, hesitating in order not to offend Vescala.

"Suicidal?" Vescala asked, staring at him almost laconically. "Perhaps, but I do assure you I'm perfectly serious. Let me explain. A few years ago, when I was at my studies, my old master told me about a great archipelago that once existed in the middle of the Atlantic Ocean. Now these islands of peace and plenty were supposedly inhabited by the most advanced civilisation mankind has ever known. However, owing to a natural catastrophe the sea swallowed them up a thousand years ago. As you know, Brenas, there are many who say the legend of Atlantis is pure mythology but others are not so sure. Every religion on earth – and there are many other than our own – tells of a great calamity that once befell mankind. Do not forget, even some of our own beliefs stem from an obscure knowledge of a flood that once swept over the world many thousands of years ago. However, no man can seek out a civilisation that no longer exists, and that's what fascinated me about the story. You see, my master believed that even further to the west, well beyond the sunken archipelago, lay an even greater land mass where some of the surviving Atlanteans had resumed their idyllic way of life. The old master had based his assumptions on the accounts handed down from the priests of ancient Egypt, who believed themselves to have been directly descended from those Atlanteans who had escaped the destruction and sailed east."

"Supposing you were to discover such a land, what then?" Brenas asked, lowering his eyebrows cynically.

"I'm not sure. But this I do know, ever since Delancia's death my life here has become spiritually impotent. Maybe if a man searches hard enough, he might discover a reason to justify his existence. I'll tell you this Brenas: whatever's left of our own Celtic civilisation must inevitably be absorbed into Rome's ever-expanding empire. In time an even greater power will rise to engulf Rome. So, it will go on, just as it always has done. At some point in history Egypt, Babylon, Persia, Carthage, and Greece have all been thriving empires, albeit built on social and economic immorality. Yet each was doomed to be devoured by an even more powerful and decadent one. To my way of thinking, any empire created through forceful conquest, and whose foundations are based on the injustice of slavery, is doomed to an eventual demise. But perhaps, in a far distant and as yet undiscovered land, there still exist the descendants of the original Atlanteans. Hopefully, they continue to share the peace, prosperity, and happiness that must surely be found in mankind's true desire to live in harmony with one another and not as emperors, kings, and nobles ruling over servile slaves. Such was the story of Atlantis: a land of equality, tolerance, and affluence where power, greed, corruption, war, and famine had long been eradicated. Maybe it's an insane idea, but to go there and discover the secret of their paradisiacal coexistence and then to return and pass on such a wealth of knowledge would more than justify any man's life's work."

"Sir, you are only assuming all this. If you fail in your quest, what happens to those of us left on these islands? Are we doomed to eternal servitude and suffering while idealists seek a dreamer's solution to the age-old problems you spoke of?" Brenas commented through a sigh, and detecting a caustic tone in the slave's voice, Vescala shrugged.

"It's as you said before, Brenas. If the slaves and peasants resorted to arms to overthrow the system, it would be they who suffer most. No, the present-day establishment is too deeply entrenched to be beaten into submission by what would only be a disorganised rabble. Anyway, the revolt I would hope to spearhead would be a peaceful one; indeed, it would be a crusade…a crusade led by an enlightened priesthood."

"When do you intend leaving, sir?" Brenas asked, suddenly impressed by Vescala's sincerity.

"Hopefully within the next year. When I was on Anglesey, we often used to mess around on the lake in small rafts not much bigger than coracles. I was also taught a good knowledge of carpentry and that I hope to put to good use. First, though, I'll have to make good my escape, and then find a suitable refuge in which to design and construct the strong, seaworthy craft essential to undertake such a voyage. I then hope to sail the craft over to the west coast of Ireland where I'll make a number of practice runs before actually embarking on the voyage itself."

"Then take me with you, sir!" Brenas exclaimed enthusiastically. And although he found the whole idea somewhat fanciful, he knew that such a venture would mean his long-desired freedom. "I've no need of Trestania's jewels or any other material wealth. All I seek from life is a free man's natural right to think and express what he truly feels and to be allowed to travel where he wishes…I place such simple desires above all others."

Vescala looked surprised although delighted at the slave's request.

"If you wish…I must warn you though that such a lengthy sea trip will be fraught with unknown danger."

Jerking his broad shoulders back Brenas suddenly gave him an agitated glance.

"I only wish we could leave today, sir. I've been detailed for tomorrow's execution squad."

"Have you ever killed a man before?"

"No, sir, I always hoped the day would never come when I had to."

"Do you know how the prisoners are to be put to death?"

"No, sir. I have heard that from the first day of their captivity, they've been staked out naked to the ground. Apparently, the skin was then stripped from the soles of their feet with hunting dogs periodically allowed to lick at the uncovered salty flesh!"

Vescala winced, knowing that only Ruadi's perverted mind could have conceived such a torture.

"Is there no way of avoiding the task?" he enquired as the scowling Brenas shook his head.

"No, sir, I wish there was. But any slave who refuses to do their dirty work is himself put to death; usually in the most bloodthirsty way imaginable!"

"Yes…I'll probably be forced to attend myself. And although my own feelings towards the prisoners are hardly merciful, I would rather see them face a quick death than suffer the bestial undertaking Trestania has undoubtedly planned."

For a little while longer they discussed a time schedule for their escape, but then a young messenger, sent by Ruadi, came up to Vescala to inform him that his attendance at the following day's ceremony was compulsory. However, this he was expecting, and parting company with Brenas, who went to rejoin Straval, he returned to his lodgings. But with Straval's parents attending to some family business in a nearby village, he was left alone to enjoy the flagon of ale lying on the table alongside the evening meal, and retiring early, the oblivion of a much-needed sleep soon erased all his earthly problems.

Morning, though, came in an instant, with his first thoughts reminding him of the ordeal lying ahead. Straval and Brenas had spent the night at Ruadi's leaving him to breakfast alone; the old slave woman having prepared breakfast for him the moment he awoke. But as he sat at the table imagining the gruesome deaths of the intended sacrificial victims, he found the thick meaty gruel repulsive to eat, and with his passive eyes staring into the dancing flames of the blood-red fire, he rose to once more don the blue robes of the novitiate priest that he now associated with butchery.

As the morning advanced a feeling of nausea began to grow in his stomach. And although leaving early enough, by the time he reached the marketplace, now a hive of activity with people and animals scampering everywhere, most of the priests and the few novitiates that were to attend the ceremony had already arrived. By this time, Straval stood alongside Ruadi, both of whom totally ignored Vescala who stood alone wondering as to when the prisoners would arrive, having yet seen no sign of them nor any slaves. Suddenly, alongside two of her priestesses and an elderly druid, Trestania made her appearance and immediately ordered the priests and novitiates, now numbering around thirty, to begin organising themselves into columns three abreast. The black-robed high priestess and the priest were the only ones mounted on ponies, with the white-robed druid the only priest wearing a crown of oak leaves. However, as she led the party towards the portcullis they were followed and constantly applauded by the many townspeople who had turned out to see their departure. Vescala now found himself placed at the rear of the columns beside his fellow novitiates, with Straval having been granted the privilege of accompanying Ruadi at the head of the columns, directly behind Trestania and her priestesses. Making their way out through the portcullis towards the forest where the sacrifices were to be conducted, the priests, led by Ruadi, then began to chant a prayer dedicated to Lug, the god of the harvest.

It wasn't long before a pale, watery sun forced its way through the grey sky; its sudden appearance being hailed by Trestania as a good omen. By now the hoar frost of the early morning had yielded to a more temperate climate that rapidly melted the thin ice covering the many pools lying along the winding track. Vescala was grateful for his decision to wear his thick cowhide boots. However, after only a short a time, he cursed himself for having donned a heavy fur jacket beneath his robes, and which now caused him to sweat copiously.

By mid-afternoon, they had reached the perimeter of the forest, with, as yet no sign of either the slaves or prisoners. Trestania now commanded the monotonous chanting to cease. But on entering into the forest, it seemed to Vescala as if the powerful silence had in some strange way become almost audible as the warm perspiration covering those on foot began to grow cold as the semi-naked trees now enclosed them in an intensely suffocating atmosphere. It was as if the forest was mocking the presence of mere mortals, whose inferiority appeared to be enhanced by the anxious expressions now masking most faces. Vescala allowed himself a wry smile when wondering just how many of those present would have been courageous enough to enter such a forest alone as he himself had done as a child. Soon, they entered in to a broad grass-covered glade ringed by giant oak trees, and where lying situated in the centre of the clearing stood a massive, moss-speckled black rock, surrounded by a wide circular border of flaming charcoal. At the opposite end of the glade, some twenty or so armed warriors suddenly appeared, bringing with them the slaves and the naked and bound captives one of whom was a Roman centurion. However, on seeing how some of the prisoners had to be carried by the slaves, Vescala screwed his face up in disgust, as a result of the mutilations they had endured, most of them were visibly suffering from the horrific gangrene that in certain cases had travelled halfway up their legs. Suddenly he glimpsed a tense-looking Brenas walking alongside another slave; the two men carrying between them a large, heavy bronze cauldron which they were ordered to place not far in front of the straight line that the druids had by now formed into. Aided by Ruadi, a calm but serious-looking Trestania dismounted, and after allowing her sandals to be removed by one of her priestesses, her feet were then gently bathed in an ornate silver bowl filled with water that, moments before, had been consecrated by the senior druid. Raising her robes up to her knees, the high priestess then proceeded to walk impassively towards the rock and over the outer red-hot coals, with the flames clearly seen to be licking at her naked legs. Sensing that her inflamed blood lust was responsible for her fire-walking feat, Vescala couldn't help noticing how her condition had improved dramatically from the previous day with Trestania now walking like some predator stalking its prey. Reaching the rock, she was immediately followed by the senior druid, who like her, showed no visible sign of suffering any pain. Standing between the rock and the fire, Trestania then stepped back to allow the priest to ascend the steps cut deep into it. Once at the top, the man raised his arms towards the now clear blue sky and with the exception of the slaves and prisoners, Ruadi commanded all the others to do likewise.

The bearded priest then began to sing in a strange, haunting tongue that neither Vescala nor any of his fellow novitiates were familiar with. However, as his singing degenerated into a repetitious chant, now being repeated by the other priests, and after what seemed to Vescala to be an eternity, he drew his eyes from the druid on the rock – who by this time stood in a trance-like state – to stare at the sombre, dusk-darkened trees around him. For a moment he blinked rapidly, reckoning that his imagination was playing tricks, but on staring up towards the diminishing sunlight he became fearfully convinced that the sky was gradually darkening! And with the perverse chanting now quickly accelerating into a deafening noise, he glanced around to the faces of his fellow novitiates who like his own, showed an intense fright. For with every passing moment, the air grew colder, as the sky grew darker and darker.

In the weak light, he could just discern that, like himself, all the slaves and prisoners were in a state of bewildered terror – the lone exception being the Roman centurion who stood apparently unperturbed by the phenomenon. With the now almost hysterical chanting striking ever deeper into Vescala's reeling senses, only the spectral figure of the lone swaying druid aloft on the rock appeared to be maintaining any sense of composure in the malevolent blackness now swiftly encompassing the entire sacrificial site. But with time itself appearing to stand imprisoned, the rapidly breathing Vescala swept away with his shaking fingers the ice-cold rivulets of sweat trickling down his forehead when suddenly Trestania ejaculated a long, hellish-sounding wail, and at Ruadi's shouted command the chanting immediately ceased.

Freed from his trance, the priest on the rock once more began to sing – only now unaccompanied – and with the slow return of the tremulous daylight the panic of Vescala and the others slowly eased. Soon the clearing lay bathed in warm sunshine, and ceasing singing the priest descended from the rock to walk back through the ring of fire with his place immediately taken by Trestania who, standing erect, carefully eyed all those in front of her.

"Are you fools dominated by false magic? No god extinguished the sunlight. There is a perfectly logical explanation for such a phenomenon!" the tall, olive-skinned centurion screamed out angrily in Latin; a language Vescala had obtained a rudimentary knowledge of while studying on Anglesey. But the man was unable to complete his statement, having been swiftly rendered unconscious by a blow from the flat blade of a warrior's sword.

Visibly flustered Trestania quickly composed herself to address her audience. But Vescala was far more interested in what the Roman had said. Was it possible that there existed some rational explanation for the darkness? He wondered bewildered at the man's statement.

"You have all witnessed the almighty power of the sun god, who in his anger gave us the eclipse of the light!" Trestania then exclaimed loudly, her face now as pale as a corpse. "He will repeat his action unless blood is spilled in his holy name and that of Lug! Does anyone among you deny what he saw with his own eyes?"

No one dared say anything regarding the Roman's statement, for by its menacing tone Trestania's voice conveyed a very real threat. There remained a prolonged silence among the audience as the high priestess stood in her elevated position, glowering, and scanning each individual's face for any trace of doubt that might inadvertently appear.

"You, do you doubt?" she demanded, spitting her words out through clenched teeth as Vescala gulped nervously, for her long spindly finger was now pointing directly at him.

"No, Highness! No one could deny that only a god could have achieved such a miracle," he answered loud and clear. Slowly her arm dropped to her side, but still glaring fiercely, her malevolent eyes then darted over to Brenas who stood in front of the other slaves.

"You, slave, will make the first kill," she snarled at him, and sweating heavily, Vescala fearfully wondered why she had first picked on him and then Brenas. Perhaps only coincidence, he thought uneasily as her ever-mistrusting eyes once more fell on his before finally settling on the prisoners.

"Proceed!" she exclaimed, hissing out the order. Two warriors immediately took hold of the first prisoner in the line, and after untying his hands, they held the man's arms rigid by his side. The senior druid then handed Brenas a short bronze sword and showed him the exact point in the man's back where the fatal blow was to be struck. With the prisoner having been turned to face the east, Brenas took up his position directly behind him. Momentarily hesitant, he first glanced up to Trestania before drawing his strong arm back to plunge the weapon's blade straight through his victim's heart until its blood-stained tip protruded from the groaning man's chest. On the weapon's withdrawal, the senior priest along with Ruadi eagerly gathered around the jerking body that the warriors had allowed to fall face down to the springy turf; the priests being able to tell by the victim's spasmodic contractions whether good or evil was portended by the sacrifice. Now ashen-faced and panting heavily, Brenas glanced over to where the engrossed Vescala stood watching the priests. However, after some discussion and deliberation, they quickly raised their right arms to the sky; a sign that told him the auspices were favourable, whereupon after screeching her praises to the sun god, a delighted Trestania commanded that the main sacrifices were to begin.

The next prisoner was then taken over to the cauldron and made to kneel before it, with the two slaves flanking him holding tightly onto his shoulders. A third slave then forced the grimacing man's head back by his hair, and with the bronze sword used by Brenas, now given to yet another slave Trestania then ordered him to cut into the petrified man's throat. This he achieved with one slashing stroke that severed his victim's taut windpipe, causing bright red, foaming blood to gush into the cauldron's deep bottom. At Ruadi's instruction, the body was then held over the cauldron to allow the man's blood to drain into it; the sight severely sickening Vescala who had to struggle hard within himself to prevent the gruel he had taken earlier from coming back up his tense, dry gullet.

With the exception of the centurion all the other prisoners suffered a similar fate until the grass around the cauldron lay heavily discoloured in fresh blood. Having been drained of their blood, the bodies were ritualistically decapitated with the heads then being skewered onto long wooden poles which in turn were mounted around the rock just outside the ring of fire. And with each of the victim's lifeless eyes having been carefully arranged to face the eastern domain of the sun god, the remains of the bloodless corpses were then carried and cast upon a cremation pyre that had been lit at the far end of the clearing. Trestania now ordered that the lone centurion be revived and dragged over to the cauldron.

"Pagan butchers!" he screamed aloud on regaining consciousness, having spotted the mounted heads, with his defiant shout echoing eerily back from the mute, motionless trees. The bronze collar he wore around his neck showed him to be a man of exemplary courage: Vescala being aware that it was an award granted to only the bravest of Roman soldiers for their distinguished battle service. Although more than aware of Roman crimes, he could only stand impotently admiring the man, whose feet were grotesquely swollen by the torture he had endured during his confinement. And searching beyond the crop of dishevelled, matted hair hanging down and over the centurion's bruised face, he could almost sense the pride motivating his contemptuous defiance. But once again Trestania was visibly incensed at the soldier's intransigence, and in a seizure of uncontrollable temper, she suddenly ejaculated a torrent of vituperative curses. Descending from the rock, she rushed back through the fires toward the senior druid where she whispered fiercely in his ear before taking hold of the sacrificial sword from the slave. Walking back over to the ring of fire, she proceeded to place the tip of the blade over the shimmering, red-hot coals.

"I want four of you slaves to hold the prisoner down on his back," the senior druid commanded, signalling to yet another slave with his hand to prepare to strike. The small, stocky-built slave immediately ran across to kneel over the heaving chest of the now pinned-down Roman; his teeth clenched tightly in his grinning jaws, that showed a desire for sadism. The two sharp punches delivered to the prisoner's nose from his large knotted fist rendered the Roman semi-conscious, allowing his assailant's powerful, stubby fingers to grab and stretch taut his tongue. The druid then handed him a small dagger, and slowly he began to cut at the back of the Roman's throat, causing his victim to instantly convulse with shock; the spray of blood as the man attempted to scream now covering the two slaves holding his shoulders rigid. Once again losing consciousness, the prisoner was then quickly revived by a warrior who flooded his bloodied features with water poured out from a goatskin pitcher. The long lump of flesh that had been his tongue was then handed by the slave to Trestania, who laughed as she casually strolled over to throw it into the fire. Taking hold of the sacrificial sword; its tip now white hot, she returned and handed it to the still-kneeling slave who unhesitatingly plunged it deep into his victim's eyeball. But with brown molten globules of smoking, spluttering flesh spouting up from the Roman's distorted features, the victim was only capable of emitting a short, high-pitched croak to replace the impossible scream desperately desired to express the excruciating pain now searing through his brain. His other eye was then cremated in the same brutal manner, and standing over him Trestania's gloating eyes remained transfixed on his now-inhuman features.

"So much for the invincibility of the degenerate puppets of the so-called divine Emperor Augustus Caesar: puppets who, you can all see, will never again usurp and terrorise our innocent citizens," she loudly commented, with her words flicked out as if from the tongue of a viper. The senior druid then first consulted with her before shouting his command for the slaves to hang the centurion by his distended ankles from the branch of a nearby tree. After this was done the man's ghastly head hung suspended by an arm's length from the ground, with the blood-mixed saliva dripping audibly from his gaping jaws into the leaf mould lying beneath his slowly revolving body.

Vescala wondered how even druidical hatred of their sworn enemy could drag them into such depths of bloodthirsty debauchery. As his stunned eyes wandered over to the misanthropic high priestess, he was suddenly incensed by the blandness in which she smiled without any pity at the mutilated and now docile centurion. Of all those present, he had a far more legitimate reason to have hated the victims than any of the others, but in his heart, he could find no earthly reason to justify such deliberately executed barbarism.

After allowing her sandals to be replaced by one of her priestesses, Trestania calmly remounted her pony to begin leading the party away from the glade's gloom-laden atmosphere. Once more everyone formed themselves into columns behind her, and although no words were exchanged between them, Vescala detected in the eyes of his fellow novitiates – excluding Straval – the anguish he himself was suffering. The procession, now including the warriors and slaves, moved silently back through the darkening forest, leaving the unconscious Roman alone with the dying embers of the funeral pyre.

Throughout the dismal homeward journey, Vescala prayed for death to release the man's tortured soul from the pain-wracked limbo of his earthly existence, and on reaching the forest's edge, he was still breathing in huge amounts of the cold night air in an attempt to cleanse his nostrils of the rancid stench of burning flesh. However, by the time the weary party had reached the outskirts of Iscal total darkness had fallen, bringing with it the hoar frost of the early morning.

Meanwhile, back in the town the celebrations were already under way. But along with the two slaves carrying the blood-filled cauldron, one of whom was Brenas, the novitiates in the party were commanded by Ruadi to remain outside the stockade. The cauldron was then taken by the slaves to the nearest field where Ruadi recited a short prayer that he dedicated to the god of the harvest. By the light of the moon and the star-strewn sky, each novitiate was then ordered to cup their hands and scoop from the cauldron the freezing viscid sacrificial blood and sprinkle it through their fingers into the charred stubble covering the earth.

One by one, every field surrounding the town was consecrated in the same manner with Straval eagerly pursuing the task, all the time shouting to the others to show more diligence in their ritualistic devotions. Cold, miserable and with his temper almost at breaking point, Vescala stared down to his blood-tainted robes to quietly curse the bestiality of the man whom he had once looked upon as a brother. At long last the final field lay completed, with the earth's fertility having been replenished in human blood, and wiping their cold, sticky fingers across their robes, each novitiate, again with the exception of Straval, was more than grateful to hear Ruadi end the macabre ritual with a prayer that he delivered in his customary fanatical tones.

In the township, the celebrations continued until late into the night. But the brooding Vescala preferred to sit apart from the others, and although incapable of eating, he drank the wine and mead in such quantities that Ruadi had to eventually order Brenas to carry him home.

Meanwhile, in the silence encompassing the moonlit forest, the last remnants of life begin to stir in the dying centurion's body.

"Am I alive or dead?" he asked himself in trepidation, and with an indescribable pain now surging through his brutalised body, he gradually becomes aware of the inescapable reality of his situation. In the numbing cold, only the instinctive rubbing of his bound hands against his backbone attains for him any physical warmth. And in the insufferable darkness, into which his mind is now totally incarcerated, his dead eyes long to shed a relieving tear as his charred eye sockets scan the trees blindly searching for some comforting presence. Stricken in terror, he longs to scream but is unable as slowly the smells of the surrounding trees and foliage drift into his nostrils. Suddenly he convulses in a seizure of panic as, deep in the forest, his hearing catches a faint but distinct rustling of leaves. With his body and soul now scourged in a callous pain, all the sins committed from his formative years begin to surface in his memory as in his tormented mind a terrible vengeance is conceived.

"I, Lancer, will one day return to inflict upon my murderers their decisive extermination," he swears inwardly.

Deep in the forest, below the trees, and palpitating leaves, the scent of fresh blood attracts an inspired howl from the jaws of his final executioner – an approaching lone wolf!

Chapter Ten

"Master, master," Brenas whispered, anxious not to awaken Straval, who lay sleeping alongside a young, naked slave girl at the far end of the small, dark room.

Vescala rolled over onto his side, insensible to the dried vomit half-covering the straw bed on which he lay and half-opening his crusty eyelids, his loud, surly grunts forced the slave to place his hand gently over his mouth. Brenas then glanced cautiously over to Straval and his bed companion, only to see that neither had been disturbed by the noise. Although still half-asleep Vescala slowly rose, at the same time hoarsely cursing the splitting headache that suddenly struck him.

"Sir, I bring good news. Durada's back!" the slave exclaimed in an excited whisper. But unresponsive to his words Vescala, his head spinning from the previous night's hard-drinking, pushed the kneeling Brenas aside to begin removing the blood and vomit-stained robes he had slept in. Beneath his robes, he was still fully dressed, and after helping him outside to the courtyard, Brenas stood watch as he splashed his face in the freezing water lying in the bucket by the side of the well. With his shaking hands rubbing at his puffed eyes, temporarily blinded by the glare of the shimmering moonlight, he drew in a deep breath of the frosty early morning air, only now realising that it had been Brenas who had addressed him. The slave then handed him the hem of his rough woven cloak on which he dried himself.

"Sir, I don't think you heard me the first time but Durada's arrived back in town."

"Thank the gods for that," Vescala retorted angrily, now facing the slave, and recalling in his mind the previous day's butchery. "I pray I never again have to witness anything like yesterday's atrocities. At least now I'll be free of that detestable bastard Ruadi."

"There's more, sir, much more, but the news I bring is…well…incredible!" Brenas then exclaimed, unable to control his excitement as Vescala queried the slave's wry grin with raised eyebrows. "Sir, it's possible that your Delancia is alive!"

Utterly confounded by the impact the slave's statement had on him, Vescala's wet lips quivered nervously.

"I could, of course, be wrong, sir, but from what I heard it must be her. Unfortunately, I only overheard snatches of their conversation."

"What are you talking about, man?" Vescala demanded.

"Well, sir, with yesterday's event still fresh in my mind, I found myself unable to sleep and so I rose and dressed. From the open doorway of the slave's quarters, I saw two robed horsemen heading towards Ruadi's place, one of whom I recognised as Durada. Following a distance behind, I saw them dismount and overheard Durada say in a loud voice to the other druid that Trestania would be overjoyed at the news. Seeing that there was no one around, I then went up to the house and eavesdropped on the conversation they had with Trestania and Ruadi. I didn't hear everything though, but apparently about a month ago a Roman ship was wrecked far up on the northeastern coastline of these islands, and that only one person survived. That person was definitely a woman with Trestania exuberantly referring to her as her daughter. What convinced me that it had to be your Delancia was when the other priest clearly mentioned the fact that the lone survivor had different coloured eyes."

"You're quite certain that's what you heard?"

As Brenas paused Vescala could feel his very blood singing.

"Go on…go on," he pleaded.

"Yes, sir. They then went on to talk of a far northern race of people and some emissary who would accompany them.

However, owing to Trestania's exasperating interruptions, I was unable to make out much more. Oh, tattoos…something was mentioned about tattoos."

Brushing away with his trembling hand the tears of joy trickling from his eyes, a now almost clear-headed Vescala quickly evaluated the situation.

"There will have to be changes in your plans now, sir," Brenas stated through a broad grin.

"Yes, but you say to the far north; that and the reference to tattoos leads me to believe that if definitely alive then she's in the lands of the tattooed races. If indeed that's the case, then there might be some difficulty in extricating her; the Picts are a people notorious for their lawlessness and barbarism."

"Yes, sir, I've heard of them. Do you think they could be holding her to ransom?"

"It's possible," Vescala answered cautiously. "You must understand, Brenas, our druidical order has no influence over their affairs. Although in theological matters there are many similarities between their priesthood and ours, they keep themselves strictly to themselves. Somehow though, I can't see a fellow priesthood holding her to ransom. Did you find out anything else about this emissary?"

"No, sir, there was so much excitement in their conversation, that was the only information I was able to glean."

"I'm truly grateful for a friend such as you, Brenas," Vescala declared through a smile, and staring up at the bright moonlight he suddenly felt all the despondency of the past month evaporating within its heavenly light.

"Sir, I can soon organise ponies and provisions," Brenas said, interrupting his thoughts as Vescala turned to him shaking his head.

"No! Before we even consider formulating any plan, I'll first have to see Durada to discover exactly what's happened. Only then will we find out what Trestania's intentions are," he answered forcefully.

Hearing a nearby noise they decided to separate, with Vescala returning into Straval's parent's house where the slave women had begun to prepare breakfast. However, at the very thought of his Delancia being alive, even the bloodthirsty sacrifices of the preceding day appeared far distant to him as once again his heart was immersed in the supreme joy of his love for her.

Merrily eating his breakfast, it wasn't long before Straval and his parents joined him, with the young slave girl having been ejected from the house by a still half-drunken Straval. At the table, the conversation between the four of them dealt mainly with the previous night's celebrations, with Straval's elderly father still chuckling over the comic antics of a skillful group of artistes whose display of acrobatics had enthralled the large, boisterous crowds. In the short period of time that he had lived at the house, Vescala had grown fond of Straval's parents, often noticing their outward displeasure at their only son's insidious behaviour. He particularly liked Straval's father, who was employed by the tribal king as a woodcarver, and they had often sat discussing his work, with the old man appreciating Vescala's knowledge of the arts. After a time, the messenger, he was half-expecting, arrived to inform Straval and Vescala that Ruadi required their immediate attendance. By now the dawn had begun to break over a clear sky, and donning their cloaks, they set off for Ruadi's place.

Entering the house, they were immediately confronted by the standing Ruadi whilst Durada and another priest remained seated at the table; the two men eating heartily from bowls of steaming stew and vegetables. Durada acknowledged his pupil with a curt nod, but not so Ruadi, whose narrow eyes conveyed his obvious annoyance.

"Good morning, gentlemen," he said through a cruel scowl. "I trust the two of you have recovered from the disgraceful exhibition you made of yourselves last night. Never have I witnessed such deplorable conduct from two so young. Must I forever keep reminding you of your holy vows."

As the two young men stood staring sheepishly down at the straw-covered floor, Ruadi became more enraged.

"Novitiates are not expected to behave as the common people do at such events. You, Vescala, owing to the paralytic state you managed to drink yourself into, had to be carried home. And as far as you're concerned Straval, making a pass at the wife of one of our most venerable merchants fills me with absolute disgust."

The priest's stern features were now scarlet with rage, but unable to control himself Vescala nervously burst out laughing as he suddenly recalled seeing Straval make a grab for the promiscuous woman Ruadi had spoken of. And there was no doubting in his mind that Straval's blindness must have temporarily returned with the notoriously ugly Leona being as fine a whore as Celtic womanhood had ever produced.

"I fear, sir, that Straval's lust must have overcome his normally good taste in women: I think he might have obtained more satisfaction in directing his pass at you," he commented, boldly blurting out his words, at the same time still sniggering at the thought of Straval and the ugly Leona. As for the stricken Straval, he could only stand red-faced and hideously embarrassed at the public denunciation of his outrageous behaviour. But now incensed, Ruadi made to strike the still smirking Vescala.

"Alright, gentlemen, that's enough!" Durada exclaimed acridly as he stood up.

"Vescala, you will dispense with your impertinence and apologise."

But Ruadi's hate-filled eyes gave way more to Durada's high authority than to Vescala's grudged apology.

"And now, gentlemen, be seated," Durada commanded, resuming his seat only to then call on the slave woman to pour wine for all five of them. "What I am about to say is very important so pay attention," he sternly demanded; his eyes darting from Vescala's to Straval's. "As no doubt you will recall, an attack was made on this town which led to a tragic loss of life. At the time it was believed that some hostages had been taken; indeed, I'm informed that you, Vescala, gallantly led an armed party to track the fleeing vessel."

Vescala nodded, anxious for his master to continue.

"We now know that only one hostage was taken! And after the galley reached the channel, such was the fury of the storm that occurred that the ship was driven far to the north. This we know for certain owing to a priest from the Iceni tribe having seen her adrift some four days after Vescala lost sight of her. At the time no one realised that it was one of the two galleys that had attacked this town. Anyway, she wasn't seen again and when news of the attack eventually reached us, I, like you, thought that the ship had probably perished and gave up all hope of ever seeing the hostage alive again.

As you know, we in the inner council of druids were called upon to arbitrate in the conflict between the Iceni and Trinovante tribes. Well, after a great deal of negotiating, in which at one stage we had to threaten the Trinovantes with excommunication, we succeeded in bringing to that region what is hopefully a lasting peace. However, just as we were preparing to return home news reached us of a civil war in the lands of the Caledonian peoples, in the far northern regions of our islands. The emissary sent to us by the rebel faction then told us of a long-standing feud between two stepbrothers. This had resulted in hostilities breaking out between them; hostilities apparently caused by the discovery of a young woman who had been washed up onto their eastern shores along with many dead bodies and the wreckage from a very large ship. From the information we now have, it would appear, that this woman is the very one who was abducted from here. At this moment in time, she's being held prisoner behind the walls of the king's imperial fortress by the elder of these stepbrothers…a man named King Ferdra." As Durada paused to clear his throat, Vescala felt a calm exhilaration surging through him.

"And now we must rescue her! But it won't be easy as the king's stepbrother, Gerant and his rebel forces have him completely surrounded. Owing to Ferdra's impregnable position and the severity of the northern winter, the present state of affairs between them is one of deadlock. Now what Gerant requires from us are enough men and arms to aid him in his cause. In return we receive the hostage, providing that is, we can rescue her unharmed. I must add that if we do succeed in getting her back, it's imperative we return her to our own lands as soon as is humanly possible. My intention is to leave at noon, along with the high priestess, both of you novices and a few slaves."

"Why the urgency, sir? Especially when the northern weather probably prevents any assault," Straval asked, only for his question to go unheeded by Durada. However, Vescala, who had shown no outward emotion at the staggering news, privately feared that the hostage wasn't Delancia.

"Master, it would seem improbable for any person to have survived such a storm. How can you be certain she's the one who was abducted from here?" he asked in an almost disparaging manner.

"There are certain distinct characteristics predominant in this young woman's physical features that have assured us the emissary speaks the truth," Durada replied assuredly, leaving Vescala convinced as he recalled what Brenas had said about her eyes.

"Forgive me, Durada. Is it necessary to take both novitiates? After all, there's still a great deal of work to be done here," Ruadi then asked.

"Yes, I understand. Very well, I'll take Vescala and Straval's slave and leave your pupil with you – alright?"

Ruadi acknowledged him with a curt nod as Durada directed his attention to Straval.

"Tell me, young man, how's your health these days?" he enquired.

"Excellent, sir, thank you."

"Good. Your faith must be exceptionally strong. You do realise that you're now quite a celebrity among we druids."

"So, I believe, sir: I must confess, were it not for my master's guidance, I fear I would have remained totally blind."

"You must continue in your diligent ways. Let's pray that in the near future, it will culminate in the gods restoring your original sight back to you."

With his face radiant with pride at Durada's kind platitudes, Straval bowed his head. Meanwhile, the thought of an armed conflict endangering Delancia brought to Vescala a considerable apprehension regarding the journey.

"Master, what tribe will provide us with the warriors and arms we will require?"

"The Atrebates. Now I suggest you return to your lodgings to collect your arms and belongings. I'll meet you at the marketplace at noon. Oh, you had better bring along all the heavy clothing you can muster."

Vescala then took his leave feeling slightly bemused at the strange twist in his fate only for the rest of the morning to fly by as he organised and double-checked all the equipment he was expected to take. By the time noon arrived, word of the impending journey had spread throughout the township, and in the marketplace, a large crowd had congregated to praise the bravery of those who were courageously risking their lives in travelling to the little-known lands of the fierce tattooed peoples.

Although optimistic, Vescala was perspiring nervously as he made his way on his pony to the meeting place. Reaching the square, he paid little attention to the cheering crowds as his thoughts were now obsessed by a desperate desire to be reunited with Delancia. However, it wasn't long before the mounted trio of Trestania, Durada and another priest arrived on the scene with their very appearance now seeming to Vescala to be tainted with evil. Behind them came Brenas alongside another heavily armed slave who he instantly recognised as the sadist who had so savagely butchered the Roman centurion the previous day. With a wave of his arm, Durada indicated to the noisy encircling crowds to clear a way for the high priestess who immediately led the small party towards the stockade's portcullis. They were then followed all the way there by Ruadi, who ran along behind them reciting his truculent prayers, and as they passed through the portcullis, Vescala was more than relieved to see the back of him and the suffocating crowds.

The hard frost of the earlier part of the day soon surrendered to milder weather with a cold breeze blowing over the dark green moorlands of the open countryside. At Trestania's instigation, the party of six suddenly broke into a fast gallop, with the high priestess now looking almost human to Vescala: a calm serenity now predominant in her blue eyes replacing the deadly glaring menace that he felt forever haunted them, causing him to wonder if this was due to the therapeutic value of the good news she had received.

Throughout the long, miserable ride no one conversed, and with dusk approaching, the now exhausted party, at Trestania's order, commandeered a merchant's house in a small village in which to eat and rest for the night.

The following day at first light they resumed their journey, only this time at a more leisurely pace. By noon they had penetrated the tribal frontiers of the Atrebates, and entering through the portcullis of the imperial township, where Durada had arranged to meet the main expeditionary force, they found a welcoming committee headed by the tribal king and Gerant's emissary. After the introductory formalities were quickly concluded, a local priest then took them to their various accommodations.

That evening the king held a banquet in Trestania's honour. However, it was an event Vescala declined to attend, excusing himself on grounds of exhaustion but, actually, preferring to seek out the company of Brenas to begin to plan as best as they could for the future. Brenas had been placed in the slaves' quarters located at the other end of the town, and leaving his own lodgings he asked directions from the local inhabitants as to its location. But the town itself was as large as Iscal but nowhere near as affluent, and as he went on his way, he couldn't help noticing the long rows of foul-smelling dwellings housing the ill-clad and miserable-looking peasants. With darkness rapidly closing in, he soon lost his way, and spotting two men standing in a doorway he enquired of them if they could guide him to the slaves' quarters.

"By all the gods, if it isn't the devious dog Vescala!" the grating voice exclaimed through the murky gloom. Although stunned, Vescala immediately recognised the voice as belonging to the tall-silhouetted figure of Ravala now emerging from the shadow of the doorway. In the incredible events of the past few days, he had completely overlooked the fact that it was Ravala's tribe who were providing the men and arms for the northern assault.

"It takes one devious dog to know another, Ravala," he boldly retorted, stepping forward to stare defiantly into the big man's eyes: Ravala showed his embarrassment by glancing over to the look on his astonished companion's face. Suddenly his mood changed as he stared into Vescala's unwavering eyes.

"So, I believe we will be travelling companions once again," he stated with his voice now carrying a pleasant civility as he thrust out his right hand in what appeared to be a genuine conciliatory gesture. "Ha! Vescala, let's forget the past. Grown men can hardly be expected to fight over the disagreements of their youth," he said, and prudently unclasping the dagger that he had instinctively made for on sighting Ravala, a cautious

Vescala shook his hand. However, as he did so his eyes, fearful of treachery, darted from one man to the other.

"Now tell me, have you decided whether or not to remain in the priesthood?" Ravala then asked.

"Yes, I remain in."

"Good, I hope the gods guide you to an illustrious future."

"I thank you for your good wishes, Ravala. Let's pray that good fortune smiles on both of us. Now you say we are once more travelling companions?"

"Yes, it's me who will lead the army north," Ravala proclaimed as Vescala nodded warily, hearing the customary arrogance now predominant in Ravala's voice.

After being shown the direction, he took his leave. But as he walked along, he remained mystified by the sudden transformation in the man who not so long ago had sworn to kill him.

Reaching the slaves' quarters, he was disappointed to find the place deserted, but spotting a large communal building a little further down the dingy road, he decided to make for it. Passing through the open doorway of the building, he entered into a spacious, smoke-laden hall where long, artistically painted crossbeams stretched out low above the feasting crowds seated at extended rows of tables hewn out from massive tree trunks. The place was teeming with people and, jostling through them, he made his way over to where a group of his fellow novitiates sat staring inquisitively up at him.

"Excuse me, gentlemen. I wonder if any of you know the whereabouts of a slave called Brenas who arrived with Trestania's party?" he enquired, feeling a little awkward.

"He's probably with the other slaves preparing the requisites for tomorrow's journey," one of the young men cheerfully replied. He then invited Vescala to join them at the table, before summoning one of the many slave women who were serving the food and ale. Having accepted the kind offer, Vescala was quickly served up a flagon of ale along with a hedgehog baked in clay, which he greatly enjoyed. But soon the conversation at the table centred on the druidess who had been taken hostage.

"How is it that you're the only novitiate going on this mission?" the youth who had invited him to join the company enquired.

"I assume it's because I'm Durada's solitary student," Vescala answered with a shrug.

The others seemed impressed, with some of them commenting on how envious they were of him going on such an adventure. But as the night advanced, he began to sense an uneasy, niggling doubt growing at the back of his mind. However, as yet it was an uncertainty that he was, for the time being, unable to pinpoint.

It was late when he bid the company farewell, and half-drunk he went back over to the slaves' quarters, reckoning that by now Brenas must have returned. But with still no sign of him he staggered merrily on his way back to his own frugal lodgings.

The following morning all those embarking on the mission were aroused well before first light. After breakfasting they were ordered to make their way with their mounts and equipment to the northern moors. It was bitterly cold with an unceasing drizzle falling as Durada organised, by the dusky glare of the many torchlights, the forty slaves who would be responsible for the ten ox-driven cartloads of arms and provisions they were taking on the journey. The warriors were under Ravala's direct command who by personal authority from the king, took his orders from none but Trestania, now seated on her pony watching the proceedings alongside two other druids and Gerant's emissary who would be acting as their guide. At Ravala's command, the army of some two hundred mounted warriors began to form themselves into columns two abreast, with the slaves quickly moving the carts into position behind the main army. Vescala and five warriors were then ordered by Durada to bring up the columns' rear.

Soon everything lay prepared as Trestania, who along with Durada and the other priests were stationed at the head of the army, began praying to the sun god, imploring him to send a victorious end to the campaign they were undertaking. But after the prayer ended in her usual garrulous hysteria, the high priestess screeched out the order to begin the long, arduous march north.

By mid-morning, they had reached the forests, and as the long columns snaked their way through the dense thickets, the incantatory pounding of the lone drummer at the head of the army brought to the buoyant Vescala a transient sense of impending fulfilment. However, after only a short time a persecuting terror was born in his mind. For why should such a force be mobilised in the rescue of one mere druidess, he asked himself fearfully. The question put to him the previous night by his fellow novitiate as to why he was the only novice going on the mission also kept returning to him, and recalling his encounter with Ravala he cursed himself for being so naïve in believing that this former enemy, of all people, would befriend him. Placing these facts alongside Durada's refusal to answer Straval's question as to the urgency of the mission, he began to experience an almost overpowering sense of paranoia. "Imperative!" Durada had said regarding Delancia's return. Now he asked himself why there was such urgency in the priesthood's desire to have her back; being fully aware that in just over two months it would be midwinter and the time when the sun god demands the yearly sacrifice of a virgin bride. With the nullifying drumbeats thundering in his head, his thoughts seethed in anguish…Were they in reality going to the rescue of an already condemned woman he morbidly concluded? But was Trestania aware of their forbidden love? He pondered over the question only to quickly refute the idea, reckoning that if she was, she would have had him killed long ago. And yet he couldn't be certain. Even a high priestess must have irrefutable proof before pronouncing a death sentence on anyone. But if she did know, what would happen when she eventually confronted Delancia and himself with the truth?

The euphoria experienced over the past few days suddenly vanished as he shivered violently at the demonic retribution Trestania might even now be formulating in the cesspit of her mind.

Calmly recollecting his senses, he began to recount everything that had occurred to him ever since that fateful moment when he had first set eyes on Delancia. He remembered that, on the day of her fire-walking exploit, Trestania had first picked on him and then Brenas. At the time he had put it down to mere coincidence, but he was now convinced that there had been more to it. Even so, he thought, there would be no point in his escaping from the army. As yet, he was clueless as to Delancia's exact whereabouts. Anyway, his absconding would be all the proof Trestania would require to have a more than eager Ravala dispatched to pursue and kill him.

As they advanced north the ever-impatient Trestania cared little for the welfare of the army. Often their food had to be rationed as she permitted little hunting, and with their sleeping time intolerably short, the days seemed endless. However, by the time they reached the lowland hills of the Caledonian provinces, he had still been unable to communicate with Brenas, who at all times was kept beside the other slaves. But he was well aware of being watched, with the eyes of the warrior who had accompanied Ravala on the night they had met never leaving him. And although the man was always careful to keep his distance, he now felt almost imprisoned. However, he knew that he must take no chances…the situation was bad enough for him without involving Brenas he thought dejectedly.

As the days dragged by, the journey became murderous, with many swamps being encountered and, alongside this factor and the monotonous damp weather continuing to lower the army's morale, their progress became painfully slow. On reaching firmer ground though Trestania, at last, gave permission for larger hunting parties to ride ahead of the main army. By now the landscape had transformed into a rampant sea of coniferous woodland that provided them with an abundance of fresh meat. This, alongside the longer sleeping periods she granted, soon brought its benefits with an increasing distance now being covered daily.

Occasionally – and content to watch from afar – a local tribal scouting party would take an interest in them. Whenever this occurred, Gerant's emissary would ride out to inform and assure them of their peaceful intentions. And with permission granted to them to continue, Trestania ordered that all animal skins accrued from the hunting were to be left behind as a token of their friendship.

Having been forced into making long detours in order to ford many wide rivers they had to cross, thirty days passed before they, at last, reached the highland regions where stretching out in the distance ahead of them lay the formidable snow-clad mountains known to the northern peoples as 'The Mountains of the Wolf.' Suddenly the weather deteriorated, bringing a severe whiteout blizzard of powdery choking snow that forced them to hastily erect a camp within the shelter of a nearby pine forest. And as the storm intensified, everyone was forced into huddling close together inside their animal skin tents to escape from the most intense cold any of them had ever experienced.

Three miserable days passed before the storm subsided enough to permit them to resume the journey, but owing to the severe conditions, and with the hunters returning daily with less and less game, their food was now strictly rationed. With the few reindeer, they managed to kill being insufficient for their needs, they were eventually forced into killing some of the oxen; an action that left the slaves to push the carts through snow that in places was knee-deep. Many of the mountain passes held treacherous snow drifts, and owing to further losses of equipment they were often forced into taking lengthy detours, which sapped the strength of the hardiest men. However, Trestania's endurance appeared to Vescala to grow daily, and he would often wonder what unearthly power kept her going. Even in these harsh conditions her savagery remained unstifled as frequently her fur-clad figure would ride through the long columns cursing and threatening any exhausted stragglers with decapitation. Only when the high mountain peaks were obliterated by low lying lead-coloured cloud formations did she ever look afraid with it now appearing as if they had reached the very roof of the world itself.

On the thirty-seventh day after their departure, they at last sighted their destination. The journey had exacted a heavy toll on human life, with some fifteen slaves having perished from the frostbite inflicted on them by their lack of suitable clothing. But for the best part, the warriors and arms remained almost intact, with seven carts surviving out of the original ten.

From high upon a great precipice, they stared down at the barely visible snow-enshrouded fortress in the valley far below. Vescala, whose hands, face and clothing were covered in deer fat to protect him against the cold, now experienced a justifiable insurgency welling up within him. Slowly wiping away the snowflakes lazily drifting against his partially hooded face, he knew in his heart that for Delancia and himself there would be no second chance. Failure to rescue her would result in either lifelong unhappiness or death! But he was now determined and fully prepared to challenge all the powers in hell that the fortress below might hold. Somewhere in there his captive lover was waiting, every bit as lonely and afraid as he himself now felt.

Chapter Eleven

Sweeping down from high on the majestic mountain peaks to the valley below, the bitterly cold winds had piled the snow into massive drifts against the sturdy walls of the rectangular-shaped fort, whose steep vitrified stone walls well protected its inhabitants from the intertribal warfare that was an integral part of this Pictish kingdom's way of life. As King Ferdra strolled along the wide parapets of the walls, he felt safe in the knowledge that his stepbrother's forces could never contemplate launching any assault against him in these conditions. Such was his confidence, that he had placed only four guards along the parapets where normally he would have positioned four times their number. His piercing blue eyes looked up to the turbulent grey morning sky. As he thought about his stepbrother Gerant, he grinned broadly through his frost-matted red beard that stood in sharp contrast against the black wolf-headed tattoos almost covering the rest of his course facial features. This was the sign of the wolf tribe; with each of the tribes in these highland regions taking for their tribal emblem an animal associated with their environment.

With his tattooed hand tightly grasping the silver hilt of the serrated iron sword hanging from his waistband, Ferdra quietly swore to personally behead not only Gerant but also each of the priestly vermin sharing the same nest. Now approaching his fiftieth year, Ferdra remained a fierce adversary, with his fame in having killed and beheaded over a hundred men in one-to-one combat being renowned throughout the land. His late mother, who had ruled his tribe just as ruthlessly before him, had lived for more than sixty years, and although three attempted assassinations on his life had left him lonely and embittered, he was determined to improve on her longevity regardless of what the price might be in terms of human life.

Unlike Gerant and his followers who were suffering great hardship, he at least had the satisfaction of knowing that in the comparative safety of his fortress both food and fuel were plentiful, with an entire winter's supply having been brought into the fortress some two months before the rebellion.

However, not so Gerant, who dutifully practiced his faith under the guidance of the Pictish priests whom Ferdra was convinced had been responsible for turning his step-brother against him. And yet perhaps all this turmoil might have been averted had he acted more decisively in the past instead of allowing the priests to roam at will throughout his imperial fortress sowing their seeds of discontentment he thought angrily.

The vast amounts of gold that he had accumulated over the long murderous years of his tyrannical rule had certainly ensured the loyalty of his well-armed soldiers, he thought approvingly; indeed, the only problem troubling him was the fact that Gerants forces were numerically superior to his own, outnumbering his by some three to one, but with the weather deteriorating daily, even that fact failed to cause him too much concern.

In the past, Gerant had reprimanded him many times, openly accusing him of heresy and blasphemy — but even now it never failed to amaze him that his weakly stepbrother had been capable of organising a rebellion on such a scale. Ferdra detested Gerant! Even as children there had never been the fraternal bond between them that would normally exist among kinsmen, and drawing his brooding eyes from the sky, he stared contemptuously toward the enemy camp where the make-shift tents of Gerant's rebel forces lay partially submerged in the deep snow.

To the atheistic Ferdra all religion was meaningless. He was a man utterly devoid of conscience but it had been his excessive cruelty towards his subjects that had gradually driven the normally passive Gerant to breaking point. The people had endured years of deprivation and repression on a mass scale, having been unable to protest for fear of their king's well-trained mercenaries who were little more than a highly organised band of criminals and cut throats, drawn from all around the country and deployed by Ferdra predominantly in the gathering of his taxes and supervision of his many slaves. Over the years their crimes had escalated into a slow genocide that Gerant and his priests had found impossible to tolerate any longer. At the slightest provocation, women would be savagely raped, and any man failing to pay the tolls and taxes imposed on them by the king, or who dared to even murmur against his authority, were usually first emasculated before being beheaded.

Noticing that Gerant's lookouts were still posted in their poorly camouflaged positions, he decided to return to his lavish dwellings to take breakfast. As he carefully clambered down the ice-covered stone steps, large white flakes of snow began falling heavily through the wispy smoke escaping from the turfed roofs of the close-packed round huts housing his soldiers and the few misguided slaves who had remained loyal to their king. Suddenly he recalled the words of one of Gerant's priests who had stated that 'conforming to the will of the gods is the ultimate aim in any man's life.' Ferdra sniggered aloud, knowing that only a small-minded weakling like Gerant could ever believe such nonsense. As far as he was concerned his stepbrother was a man who, if he were ever to ascend to kingship, would quickly bend and wilt under the brainwashing yoke of his priestly advisors. And yet, Ferdra had good reason to be thankful, for had it not been for an informer in Gerant's own ranks then the uprising would almost certainly have succeeded. For at the time of the uprising, what fighting that had taken place had been furious and bloody until his better-trained forces had finally succeeded in driving the inadequately armed rebels and their families out of the fort and into the wilderness.

With his flaring nostrils pouring misty breath angrily out into the freezing air, Ferdra stamped along feeling ashamed that any blood relative of his should have shown himself to be such a miserable coward. If Gerant had been so dissatisfied by the way in which he ruled the tribe then why didn't he challenge his king to a duel to the death? That's what he would have done had their roles been reversed. After all, throughout Pictish history single combat to the death had always been the method by which men of honour settled their differences. But Ferdra's shame was quickly stifled as he suddenly recalled the threat screamed up at him only a few days after the revolt by one of Gerant's priests, who had foolishly dared to come within spear-striking distance of the fortress's walls. Ferdra had taken delight in having killed the man with his well-directed spear, but the very thought of being burned alive as retribution for his so-called sins had struck more than a note of terror into him. For ever since the earliest days of his childhood, the thought of dying by fire had always tormented him. More than anything else, it had been the virulence in the man's threat that had effectively prevented him from forcibly taking the woman whom Gerant's priests so eloquently referred to as "flesh of the earth, spirit of the tree, and bride of the sun." "She whose chastity must remain undisturbed lest all hell be unleashed upon the earth," another of the priests had gone on to say. However, as far as Ferdra was concerned the priests' words were no more than some nonsensical riddle doubtless based on their preposterous superstitious beliefs.

At the time when Delancia had first arrived at the fortress, her unique beauty had instantly mesmerised him as no woman had ever done before. But when he sought to add her to his large concubine of young women, an enraged Gerant, manipulated by his priests, had firmly opposed such a union, describing it as the ultimate sacrilege. Even now he dared not touch her. For if he was eventually defeated and the priests discovered that she had been molested then he would assuredly die by fire!

Stalking up to the small prison hut incarcerating his hostage, he commanded the heavily armed guard outside the door to stand aside. Drawing back the tiny shutter covering the barred window in the doorway, he peered with a certain curiosity at the outline of the solitary figure seated on a small stool directly opposite him. Smiling wryly, he was more than grateful in the knowledge that as long as she remained in his possession, he was safe. And yet, it was certainly strange how she alone had survived the ship's sinking when everyone else had perished he thought solemnly. Good fortune had certainly been with her, for had the hunting party, that he had dispatched that fateful day, not been diverted by the foul weather, she would almost certainly have died from exposure. From the first moment he saw her being brought into his fortress, he had known only an overpowering desire to take her as his wife. Unfortunately, one of Gerant's priests, who had accompanied the hunting party, had noticed the unusual tattoo etched into the right breast of her partially clad body; with such a sign deemed by the priest to be universally sacred. However, over only a short period, Gerant had cunningly used her presence among them to instigate his rebellion. By claiming that the gods had delivered her to them to help them expel the monster that had so ruthlessly exploited them over the past twenty years.

The lonely figure of Delancia stared aimlessly towards the window, indifferent to the lust-fuelled menace in the eyes gazing down at her. Ever since her abduction from Iscal, she had lost all track of time as she sat incarcerated in an almost perpetual darkness. There were times when the past events were clear enough in her mind, but at others they were no more than blurred recollections, leaving her uncertain if what had happened to her was factual or imaginary. Her miserable existence now mainly comprised of desperate attempts to relive the beautiful memory of her last meeting with Vescala, high on the windswept cliffs, and with it the promise of a long-desired freedom. But then morbidly, she would suddenly recall the night the Romans attacked Iscal, clearly remembering the red witch falling when struck by a spear. To this day she remained mystified as to how she had escaped death when her many friends had been so indiscriminately butchered before the building had been set alight. Nor would she ever be able to dismiss from her mind the terrible reality of almost choking to death in the enveloping smoke which had resulted in her lapsing into a long unconsciousness, only to regain her senses trapped in the black hold of the fleeing Roman galley. Now shrinking fearfully back on the seat, she again saw in her mind's eye the ship's sturdy timbers splitting apart in the violent storm that had blown the vessel so far north. The very weight of her waterlogged robes had repeatedly dragged her struggling body beneath the fury of the churning waves, and even now she could still clearly sense the suffocating embrace of the numbing icy waters when totally immersed into the sea's terrifying silence. Frightened and shivering uncontrollably she had suddenly found herself lying on some alien beach among her tattered robes; her semi-naked body lying spread-eagled over the cold silver sands. In desperation, she had longed for the protective embrace of her distant lover Vescala before falling into a deep sleep.

Freezing cold, she had awoken to the onrushing daybreak and with it the warm sympathetic look on an elderly priest's face. His presence had brought to her a fleeting renascence, but the words uttered by him had been spoken in a tongue she was unfamiliar with. All around her, the shoreline lay littered with bodies and shattered driftwood, with the incredulous stares on the surrounding faces of the hunting party's mounted riders having shown their astonishment that anyone could have survived such a storm. Tenderly wrapping her in his own cloak, the priest had lifted her onto his pony and taken her into Ferdra's fortress where, after a few days of being well treated and cared for by slave women, she had suddenly found herself cast into her gloomy cell by the red-haired chieftain the day following Gerant's attempted coup. As to the reason for her confinement, she still had no idea.

Ferdra's eyes now left her, and reminding the guard of his responsibility, he drew the shutter back to leave her alone with her sad reminiscence.

Pulling the damp blanket tightly around her trembling shoulders, the pensive Delancia once more found herself recalling the savage fighting in Iscal when every hope she had ever dared to long for had been so cruelly destroyed. She was now utterly convinced that she would never again set eyes upon her secret lover Vescala. But even if she did, would he still love her if he knew of the horrifying assault upon her? Once more powering through her glacial emotions came the ever-distinct remembrance of her appalling rape ordeal in the ship's hold at the degrading hands of her Roman abductors. In her constant torment, she repeatedly kept asking herself why such an inhuman violation had happened to her. However, in her mental and physical isolation − and with her innocence lost forever − the month of the robin was now drawing ominously closer to the tragic, unwary Delancia.

Chapter Twelve

From the valley's western approach Gerant's pale blue eyes scowled across to the ominous-looking fur-clad warriors standing guard on the fort's high parapets; his clean-shaven features clearly, projecting the many intricate wolf-headed tattoos imprinted over his sunken jaws. He cursed to himself when thinking back to the night of the uprising when, along with his followers, they had failed in their attempt to overthrow the king and rescue the 'bride of the sun' whom Ferdra was now holding hostage; otherwise, the stalemate between the warring factions would have been resolved long before the snows had come. Only his priestly advisors were now preventing him from launching an all-out assault on the fort with Ferdra having warned that, if attacked, he would have no hesitation in putting his hostage to the sword.

But how much longer must it be before his hated stepbrother's long reign of terror was finally terminated, he wondered impatiently having promised his followers that even if they were forced into waiting until the spring thaw, his despised step-brother would find no way of escaping the retribution long overdue him. Suddenly from behind him the voice of one of his men rang out in anticipation.

"Look, see, the reinforcements are coming," the man bellowed as Gerant turned to see the barely visible columns of men, carts, and animals scrambling down a deep fissure in the mountainside. Lumbering up through the snow to meet them, he released a confident smile, sensing that Ferdra's days were at last numbered. With the introductory formalities soon completed a jubilant Trestania decided to erect her camp close to Gerant's, whose main force lay garrisoned at the eastern end of the valley. The local peasants were then ordered by Gerant, to assist their southern allies. This they did enthusiastically with their sagging morale having been raised by the welcome sight of so many well-equipped warriors. But it was still a considerable task owing to the deep snow first having to be shovelled clear before the tents could be erected.

Throughout Gerant's camp, everything lay in short supply, particularly fuel. Peat was normally the fuel used in these mountainous regions, but being impossible to cut and dry out in such conditions and owing to the scarcity of woodlands, supplies of timber were constantly having to be carried in manually from long distances by his men. Gerant had some six hundred men, women, and children under his command, with Vescala surprised that so many people could have survived for so long in such harsh conditions. Indeed, the more he looked around the campsite, the more he admired them in having adapted so well under cruel circumstances that more than exemplified their courage and undoubted determination to rid their land of a tyrant.

It was almost nightfall by the time their own camp was finally completed, and standing staring contemptuously towards the grey walls of the fortress's stonework − fused together not only by fire but in blood as well − he listened intently to the local peasants as they told of their king's belligerent temperament that far exceeded any atrocity that he himself, had witnessed over the past year. Fortunately, he was now in a position to visualise the exact layout of the fort's interior, having slowly extracted the information from the locals. This he had achieved, with some difficulty, owing to the dialectical differences between them. However, he was fortunate in knowing just enough of their language, to communicate reasonably fluently with them. If nothing else, he could thank his former masters in Anglesey for his tuition in various languages, he thought smugly.

He now reckoned that in all probability Delancia was being held captive in the royal palace, although no one knew for certain. Momentarily, he cowered within himself on thinking of Ferdra and the mass blood-letting that must ensue before Delancia could be rescued, but sensing a presence behind him he turned to see Ravala's vulpine warrior still closely observing his every movement. As for Ravala's sudden disappearance, had continued to perplex him, for ever since their arrival he had seen no sign of his former adversary.

The following day it snowed heavily, only ceasing with the coming of nightfall, but as he sat inside the little tent he shared with four others, nothing could disperse the shadows of doubt now sweeping over his troubled mind. Owing to the cramped conditions inside the tent, he found sleep virtually impossible with every scheme he conceived to rescue Delancia becoming, after a time, almost ludicrous. Eventually, he fell into a light slumber, but on awakening, the first rays of the dawn brought to him a surge of optimism, for outside a more temperate climate had replaced the severe cold that froze and weakened the hardiest of souls. Breakfast comprised of a handful of corn along with a portion of reindeer meat that they washed down with a bowl of thin vegetable gruel that did little to alleviate everyone's gnawing hunger pangs. However, after eating, and leaving the tent, he hoped to have at least a chance to speak to Brenas only to be suddenly confronted by Durada who was accompanied by one of Gerant's blue-robed priests.

"Good morning, Vescala," Durada said, greeting him cheerfully. And although somewhat suspicious of Durada's over-friendly tone, he acknowledged both men with a smile and a curt bow.

"Listen carefully," Durada then said as his voice turned serious. "By order of the high priestess you have been chosen to embark on a very important mission! You are to take two of our most trusted slaves and along with a local guide you will travel to a small settlement lying just over a day's journey from here. There, you will contact an old wise man by the name of Roldun – who like our brothers belongs to the wolf tribe. When you find him, you are to bring him here to us as soon as is humanly possible."

Showing no emotion Vescala nodded, all the time wondering why he was being sent on the mission instead of one of the local priests who were familiar with the countryside.

"What about the attack, sir? After all, it's going to take me at least three days to get this man back here."

"No," Durada retorted with a shake of his head. "No attack is possible until Roldun arrives. This man of theirs is a renowned seer! And owing to certain ill-omens having been ascertained by the high priestess, she first seeks consultation with him before taking any decision to launch the attack."

"Ill-omens, sir?" Vescala enquired, curious to know more.

"Well, some recent planetary configurations, have inexplicably appeared out of their cosmic positions. These have convinced Trestania that, although the gods are undoubtedly with us, the timing of the assault must be determined exactly in order to keep the bloodshed on our side to a minimum. All she seeks to this end is a secondary opinion," Durada replied reassuringly, having detected Vescala's doubt.

"When am I expected to leave, sir?" Vescala asked, glancing suspiciously at his plausible master.

"Right away! I've arranged everything. The guide will take you there and back. Now collect your cloak and weapons. You will find the slaves and ponies awaiting you behind Gerant's tent... I wish you luck and hope to see you again in some three days from now."

Durada and the other priest then turned sharply from the scene to walk away leaving a badly frightened Vescala to re-enter the tent and begin collecting his belongings.

Feeling uneasy, he then made his way towards Gerant's tent, which lay apart from the others. But reaching the point of departure, he was immediately greeted by Brenas and the other two members of the party, one of whom was Ogmar, the slave who had so enjoyed butchering the Roman centurion back home, with the other being an ill-clad child no older than ten years of age.

"Ogmar, you and the guide take the pack pony and ride on ahead. We will follow behind," Vescala gruffly commanded the man before mounting the pony standing beside Brenas. Both Ogmar and the little guide immediately obeyed his order, and setting off towards the east with their ponies struggling to force a way through the deep, crisp snow, both soon found the blinding glare emanating from the now sun-struck snow painful to their eyes. Remaining silent, Vescala let them ride a good bit ahead before he again spoke.

"Tell me, Brenas, who informed you of this mission?"

"The high priestess, sir. She said it was very important, although she didn't elaborate as to why."

"Then why are you unarmed while Ogmar is armed to the teeth?"

"Trestania said it wasn't necessary, sir. I must confess I did wonder about that…I just assumed it was because he is looked upon as a more trusted slave than me." Brenas replied through a perplexed scowl.

"I could be mistaken, Brenas, but I suspect this is a mission I'm not expected to return from. I fear I'm being led to my death at the hands of Ravala and his henchmen," Vescala declared gravely. As both men, at Vescala's instigation urged their ponies forward, he then explained to the surprised slave that ever since leaving the Southlands, he had suspected that Trestania knew of his illicit love for Delancia, as well as telling him the reason Durada had given him as to the purpose of the mission.

"You see, Brenas, I don't believe for one moment Durada's story concerning the planets. Ever since we entered these highlands the night sky has been overcast and starless. Anyway, I never did take astrological predictions seriously."

"If they are aware of your love for Delancia then why ride into their trap?" a bemused Brenas then asked.

"Where can I run to? It would not take Ravala very long to track me down in these conditions," Vescala snapped apprehensively. There now existed a prolonged silence between them but turning to see that the camp was out of sight, Brenas pulled his mount up, as did Vescala.

"Sir, if they have decreed your death, I will help you all I can to defeat their objective!" The slave exclaimed, bracing his broad shoulders. "Anyway, they must have been aware of our friendship. It wouldn't surprise me if they also had me marked down to die as well. I've lived under their oppression long enough. If we are ambushed, I promise you to take at least one of them with me…I just hope to the gods it will be that bastard Ravala."

Looking relieved at the slave's more than welcome offer of support, Vescala drew his dagger from its sheath and handed it over to him by the blade.

"Thank you, Brenas. Here, take this and conceal it beneath your cloak. Who knows, between us we may yet extricate ourselves from this situation."

By noon they had travelled well beyond the valley, with both men pleasantly surprised to see the mountains give way to a more level terrain rendering them an unobstructed view of the landscape ahead.

"Sir, this is hardly an ambush country. It could be that our mission is genuine," Brenas stated. Vescala nonetheless remained dubious.

"Perhaps, but as of tonight we take turns sleeping. From now on we trust only each other," he replied warily.

Continuing on their way, both men remained constantly alert for any sign of treachery, and by the late afternoon, Vescala decided to recall the other two, who by now were a good way ahead of them. On questioning the young guide, he was informed that the settlement was still a good half-day ride away, and with the dark cloak of the winter's night quickly descending, he thought it best to make camp until the following morning. By now it was so cold that after erecting the small tent they hurriedly prepared and lit a charcoal fire inside it with the little fuel the guide had brought on the pack pony. A grateful Vescala thanked the child for the warm meal he soon made them, for although meagre, it was more than welcome. After eating, the four of them sat around the fire's mellow glow, constantly alarmed by the threatening howls of the distant wolves that perpetually shattered the brooding silence.

Vescala had previously decided that Brenas would take the first watch, and it wasn't long before the other three were fast asleep. However, after only a short time Brenas found it difficult to keep his eyes open in the tepid atmosphere. Eventually, he too fell into a light but uneasy slumber only to suddenly awaken on hearing a remote choking sound that brought to him an immediate sense of danger. Opening his heavy eyelids, his hand instinctively slipped beneath his cloak to reach for the dagger, and with his fingers digging into the hilt with claw-like tension, he discerned in the dim light the kneeling figure of Ogmar attempting to strangle the prostrate Vescala. Silently removing the weapon, and now on his knees, with one lightning stroke, he plunged the sharp blade deep into the side of Ogmar's broad neck. Speedily withdrawing the weapon, he frantically lashed out with his other hand to punch the groaning slave into the fire; an action that sent a thick cloud of sparks and ash up into the air. Now desperate to finish off his enemy, Brenas once more plunged the dagger into Ogmar's neck as the shocked and gasping Vescala raised himself up on his knees to begin dragging the child, who had been sleeping at his feet, out through the tent's entrance. Seeing that Ogmar was now dead, a spluttering Brenas crawled outside only to see in the bright moonlight that the child too was already dead; his woollen jacket saturated across the chest in the warm blood that had poured out from his fatal heart wound. As the two men sat trembling on the freezing snow trying to collect their senses, Vescala suddenly became aware of a sharp pain in his breastbone. Untying the front of his cloak he looked down to see a small patch of blood seeping through his fur jacket. However, after pulling the jacket, and his linen shirt up he was grateful to discover that he was suffering from no more than a small surface wound.

"You must have moved just as the bastard stabbed you, sir," Brenas panted, and grateful to be alive, Vescala sighed heavily before glancing pitifully down at the child's body.

"So, Durada was lying! I was right all along in assuming that he was using this mission as a pretence to have me killed."

"No, sir, the three of us! But the bastards might at least have let the child live. What threat was he to anyone? Ah! If only I had remained awake," Brenas angrily exclaimed, screwing up his face in disgust at his negligence.

"No, Brenas, don't blame yourself. You just saved my life. Trestania and Durada are the child's true murderers. Ogmar was merely acting under their orders. I do not doubt that on his return to the camp he was told to inform the others that the three of us accidentally perished by falling into a crevice or some other such fanciful tale." Still trembling with shock Vescala paused to wipe away the blood trickling out from his wound. "Anyway, we best get back inside. It would be madness to freeze to death after this."

Dragging Ogmar's body outside the tent they rekindled the fire, and after this was done Vescala dressed his wound as best as he could, only to find that by this time his throat was painfully swollen as a result of Ogmar's powerful stranglehold.

"Where do we go from here, sir?" Brenas asked, furious at Durada's mendacity as Vescala punched his fist into the ground.

"I don't know. Somehow, I have to rescue Delancia. As for yourself, Brenas, as far as I'm concerned, you're now a free man. If you wish to go elsewhere and make a new life for yourself, you're at liberty to do so. You can take two of the ponies and Ogmar's weapons with you."

"Thank you, sir, but if it's all the same to you I'd rather stay and help you in your quest. Let's face it, under the present circumstances two swords are better than one," the former slave replied unhesitatingly as Vescala smiled.

"I'm more than grateful for your help, Brenas. But please, never again address me as either sir or master."

Relieved to be facing the future hazards together, the two men smiled warmly at one another. Suddenly the frightened whining of the ponies tethered outside broke the night's silence, and quickly grabbing their weapons, they scrambled back outside, only to be horrified on seeing a starving pack of some dozen or so grey wolves silently encircling the tent; the animals' distinct yellow eyes conveying the desire by with which they viewed their intended meal.

"Vescala, untie the ponies," the quick thinking Brenas screamed out as he began hacking with Ogmar's sword at one of the legs of his sprawling corpse. Desperately hurling the now severed limb with all his strength behind the wolves the snarling pack immediately ran back to fight among themselves in their eagerness to devour the still-warm flesh. After frantically mounting the terrified ponies they headed back towards the valley, with Vescala clutching tightly onto the reins of the three other ponies. Fortunately, the wolves didn't follow; their voracious hunger being more than satisfied by the two corpses left behind and now in the process of being savagely stripped of their flesh.

Having attained a safe distance between themselves and the pack, the two men pulled their mounts up, exhausted but relieved that once more they had brushed shoulders with death and survived intact. But how soon must it be before they fell prey to either Ravala and his warriors or the jaws of the ever-hungry wolves, each of them fearfully wondered.

With the nightscape standing bleak and motionless, they remained ever alert as they slowly continued on back towards the valley. However, as daybreak approached Vescala suddenly spotted what appeared to be a cave high up on the mountainside, and with the fortress still out of sight, they readily agreed that they had little alternative but to scale the steep slope leading up to the shelter.

After experiencing considerable difficulty in struggling up with the ponies, they eventually reached the refuge, only to be astonished on discovering what was not only a deserted cave but also an apparent place of worship. Neither man had ever seen anything like it as all around the walls of the deep, high-domed cavern stood roughly carved stone idols. To Vescala they appeared to be guarding a long stone sacrificial altar situated in the centre of the broad chamber, where a few small animal bones lay scattered over its blood-encrusted top. In the dim light, his alert eyes were suddenly attracted to the cavern's walls where, below the unlit torches resting in their conical iron cressets, were many brightly coloured paintings of unnatural-looking, wolf-headed deities. Moving warily towards the rear of the chamber they came upon a deep recess in the wall containing a stockpile of wood alongside a row of clay and bronze urns. This discovery caused Brenas to suggest, that they make a fire, but being daylight now Vescala was uncertain, worrying in case any escaping smoke might be seen from the fortress. However, Brenas allayed his fears, reckoning that the slight breeze, blowing up outside would soon disperse any smoke. Anyway, they had little choice, with both men, by now visibly wincing from the numbing cold.

They quickly lit two fires, a small one near the entrance to deter predators and a larger one at the back of the chamber to heat themselves and cook upon. Taking the remaining provisions from the pack pony, Vescala calculated that if they were careful then their existing food should last them for three full days. After that they would be forced into killing one of the ponies.

In the comparative comfort of the cavern, they first fed the ponies before sitting down to eat and warm themselves.

Meanwhile, outside, the sky had begun to darken, with masses of heavy, grey clouds gathering low in the heavens, and soon a fresh snowfall, blown by an icy wind, was billowing around the entrance. In the gloom, and safe in the knowledge that not even Gerant's priests would come up to the place in such atrocious conditions, Vescala decided to risk lighting some of the torches. However, after finishing eating, their exhaustive state saw the two men quickly drop off into a deep sleep on the dry, earthen floor

Chapter Thirteen

With the storm outside still raging and the fires almost extinguished, Vescala awoke to find himself shivering with the cold, but with fuel plentiful, he had no qualms in quickly replenishing both fires with a generous amount of wood. Sauntering back to the rear of the chamber, his idle curiosity saw him remove one of the urn lids only to shudder upon finding it full of the dull yellow ash that he knew to be the remains of cremated bones.

Estimating the time at somewhere around mid-afternoon and wandering back to the cave's entrance, he could still see nothing owing to the fury of the blizzard outside. It was with a feeling of lassitude that he returned to where Brenas lay fast asleep, and crouching down beside the now crackling fire, his despondent eyes stared through the smoky atmosphere towards the haunting surrealism of the wall paintings. Sitting down, he closed his eyes to silently pray for a safe deliverance far from the dangers they were yet to confront. But how were they going to rescue Delancia? He wondered apprehensively, with the question now tormenting him. Suddenly a shuffling sound coming from the entrance saw his startled eyes widen, and leaping to his feet he grabbed his spear and instinctively raising it, perceived what seemed to be a phantom figure come stumbling past the stone altar. The stooping figure then slumped to its knees with the clinging snow from its black, tattered cloak cascading across the floor

"Brenas!" he yelled out, stepping forward to stand over the figure; his spear ready to strike. With his sword now held rigidly in his right hand, Brenas first emitted a grunt before jumping to his feet only to see Vescala crouch cautiously down and begin to uncover the figure's hooded features. However, both men were astonished to see that the intruder was no more than an elderly woman whose leathery, tattooed-featured face stared fearfully up at them.

"Who are you?" Vescala asked, but saying nothing, the woman's terrified eyes darted from one man to the other as she stared up at them. Seeing her acute fear, Vescala laid his spear down before helping her over to the fire at the rear of the chamber.

Meanwhile, Brenas had dashed over to the entrance where he could see no more than an arm's length in front of him. Such was the severity of the raging blizzard that it looked to him as if a solid sheet of ice was now separating them from the outside world.

"We have no intention of harming you. But why on earth have you come up here in such a storm?" Vescala enquired, gently placing her trembling, ice-cold hands into his own.

"Sanctuary," came the feeble reply from her twitching lips. "They slaughtered us as they would animals!" she then exclaimed, pulling her hands free from Vescala's.

"Who slaughtered who?" Vescala asked, staring at her contorted features in a puzzled manner.

"Evil slaughtered us – evil," she replied in a voice trembling in terror. Vescala then calmly repeated everything she had said with Brenas unable to fully comprehend her dialect.

"Alright, take your time and go on," he said, once more placing his hands into hers.

"It was just before dawn when your warriors entered mine and the other tents to massacre everyone where they slept. My daughters, their husbands and my grandchildren were all put to the sword. I had been sleeping beneath a large bearskin and that was the reason I survived. After they left our tent, I looked out to see them and Ferdra's warriors systematically butcher all those attempting to flee."

As she paused to sob Vescala informed Brenas of what had occurred, and staring hard at one another, each man was horrified at the implications in her words.

"The one known as Trestania then spoke of a sacrifice to an Andraste!" she then exclaimed, composing herself.

"Yes, that's our goddess of war. Please go on," Vescala remarked grimly.

"Gerant and the priests who were taken alive were then beheaded; this was done by Ferdra and one known as Ravala: I don't know if any others escaped, but I waited until they all went back into the fortress before coming up here."

With the flickering flames of the firelight emphasising the grief in her tragic features, the old woman broke down in a seizure of hysterical weeping. Releasing her hands and standing erect, Vescala threw back the hood of his cloak, and removing the novitiate headband, angrily cast it into the fire; his wild eyes cursing its evil as it was consumed in the flames.

"So that was the reason for Ravala's disappearance," he shouted aloud, shaking his head in dismay. "I've been blind, Brenas: I should have guessed that Trestania would have sought a pact with Ferdra...It's perfectly logical for moral cripples like them to cling together."

"But these men were her brother priests. I mean to turn so treacherously against her own kind..." Brenas remarked in disbelief, knowing only too well the fanatical bonds that fused the priesthoods together.

"No, Brenas, as I explained to you before, their priesthood is strictly a tribal affair. In theological matters, there was little compatibility between theirs and the likes of our own. Now being an anarchic grouping, they were weak. But with Gerant's forces also weak, Trestania saw the opportunity to send Ravala secretly into the fortress in order to strike an agreement with Ferdra, whose own forces were strong and intact. That way both benefited: Ferdra remaining undisputed king and she in turn receiving a hopefully unharmed Delancia."

"Surely the other tribes in these lands must rise against Ferdra for this despicable action?"

"No, each tribe along with their priests are virtually a law until themselves — they will do nothing! The question I now ask myself is what can only two of us do against such supreme exponents of evil as Ferdra and Trestania unquestionably are?"

"Vescala, I think we should leave Delancia's rescue until we return to the Southlands; that way we'll be free of the snows. We can track them all the way back and then wait for an opportune time."

"No, Brenas, I want her free from those evil bastards now…I don't know what she's been through over these last few months — all I know is that I have to rescue her now."

"Fair enough, Vescala: If Ravala can enter the fortress secretly then by the gods we can emulate him," Brenas snarled through a determined grimace, angrily plunging the tip of his sword into the hard earth. "Once inside, and after we've found Delancia, we burn everything that stands. Now Trestania doubtless thinks that we are already dead, and when Ogmar fails to return she will know something has gone far wrong. She will almost certainly then have Delancia too well protected for us to mount a successful rescue attempt. So, providing the storm abates, I think we have little choice but to strike tonight."

"I agree. It won't be easy, Brenas, but after their treachery, all I seek is Delancia and vengeance," Vescala declared sombrely as Brenas slowly extricated the sword.

With the old woman having fallen into a restless slumber, the time dragged slowly by, but by the late afternoon, the murderous storm had, at last, subsided, with the snow eventually ceasing altogether. When she awoke the three of them shared a solemn meal together, with Vescala asking her to refresh his memory as to the layout of the fortress's interior. For once inside, one mistake would almost certainly cost them their lives. After telling the old woman to remain in the cave for at least the next few days, they then decided to take four of the ponies, leaving the other behind in order that she might eventually make her escape to some nearby village.

Although both men were undeniably afraid, each found himself fired by a determination to avenge the loss of so many innocent lives. However, on taking their leave of the old woman, Vescala regretted that they were unable to leave her no more than the pony and a few handfuls of their precious food.

The heavy layers of cloud had begun to disperse as they made their way down the treacherous mountainside. But with darkness now rapidly falling, the fresh snowfall caused them great difficulty in manoeuvring the ponies, and although still bitterly cold, by the time they reached the bottom of the steep incline both men found themselves sweating profusely from their exertions.

The previous day, Vescala had noticed a line of towering rocks lying not too far from where Gerant's camp lay situated, and it was in that direction that they began laboriously trekking through the deep virgin snow. On reaching the rocks, which granted them a perfect hiding place, they could clearly view the fortress where, just as they had hoped, no guards were now posted on the ramparts. There they waited patiently until the late evening before moving on towards what was now the final resting place of Gerant and his ill-fated followers.

Reaching the deserted camp, they immediately harnessed the ponies at the rear of Gerant's tent, the only one left standing. Through the crisp evening air, a fine mist began to descend, partially obscuring the full moon. Even so, they could easily discern all around them the shapes of the many solidified corpses lying half-submerged in the sterile snow. Both men shuddered on imagining the terrible panic the poor wretches must have suffered after discovering treachery was upon them. Suddenly from the direction of the fortress sounds of revelry came floating through the still night air.

"The bastards celebrate," Brenas said in disgust.

"Yes, but that may be to our advantage," Vescala hinted; his keen eyes darting around the remains of the devastated camp. "Look, Brenas, with the exception of the ponies and weapons it appears as if they've never bothered taking anything else back into the fortress. We must find one of the ladders I saw being made the other day. I'll search for one if you try and find some food."

Brenas agreed and, after separating, Vescala stealthily worked his way between the rows of torn-down tents and mangled bodies. However, it wasn't long before he spotted one of the heavy ladders protruding through the snow, and after a struggle to pull it free, he returned to the back of the tent, dragging it behind him.

Meanwhile, Brenas had been fortunate in finding some straw for the ponies and a little food, most of which he placed into the saddlebag on the pack pony. After feeding the animals and then themselves, they waited patiently until the noise from the fort abated. In the meantime, they finalised their plans, with Vescala proposing that they scale the eastern wall; this being the nearest to them, and from what he had been told it was where the fort's livestock were stabled.

It was well after midnight before the fort fell totally silent, and with their swords and daggers tucked beneath their cloaks, the two men carried the long ladder between them. As they headed across the open moor to reach the fortress's high, icicle-bedecked walls, the sweeping snow drifts came up practically to their waists, and after battling their way through the hard-packed snow it was only after exerting their utmost strength that they succeeded in erecting the cumbersome, unsteady ladder up against the wall. With his heart pounding, Vescala was first to climb up, and crouching low on the wide rampart, he was relieved to see no signs of any human life on the other side although directly below him a few isolated sheep lay sheltered against the side of the wall. After Brenas joined him, they then crawled on all fours along the icy rampart and soon came upon a slippery stone staircase that took them to the ground. Drawing their swords and remaining ever alert, they kept close to the cover of the wall and speedily headed towards the northern sector where the main storage buildings lay. Finding their target with ease, Vescala whispered to Brenas to give him a reasonable amount of time before setting the buildings alight. Skipping past the rows of dwelling houses, he immediately made for the royal palace, which he knew to be positioned in the centre of the fort. Gliding over the snow with the silence of a lynx, he kept praying that the palace was indeed the place where Delancia was being held. As it was, he had given himself only a short time in which to make good her rescue before the alarm was sure to be raised.

All around him, everything lay deathly still, but on reaching the long wooden building, ringed by tall, wolf-headed totem poles, he came to an abrupt halt on spotting one lone guard lounging outside the building's front entrance. With a sense of extreme caution, he weaved his way round to the back of the building where the courtyard lay only for his heart to sink on finding that there was no rear entrance to the building, only two shuttered windows securely barred from the inside. Momentarily hesitant, he knew that it was now or never, and creeping along with his back to the wall he stole up to the unsuspecting guard who stood leaning heavily onto his spear. With his sword ready in his trembling hand, the desperate Vescala suddenly ran the last few paces and, muffling the man's mouth with his free hand, succeeded in drawing the weapon's sharp blade across his throat. The merciless cut was deep enough to be instantly fatal, and with the guard's blood spurting out all over the snow, he had to hold onto the jerking body until it was quite still before dragging it to the back of the courtyard. It was the first time he had ever killed a fellow human being, and struggling hard to compose himself he entered the palace only to find a long corridor leading him into a spacious hall. Through the dim and almost spectral glow from the tallow lamps hanging from the roof, he was just able to make out Durada lying sprawled out alongside many of the others in a drunken stupor across the fur-covered floor. Treading carefully between the spread-eagled bodies, he made his way towards the sleeping apartments that he knew to be situated at the back of the hall. The labyrinth of rooms, lay separated from one another by trellis partitions, with each entrance being covered by a heavy fur drape. Warily checking each occupied room in turn, his dejection, on finding no trace of Delancia, clearly showed on his face. However, just as he was about to leave, he spotted yet another room at the end of a narrow corridor. Reaching it, he drew back the drape only to be stunned on seeing Trestania lying sleeping in the arms of her bed companion: a man who, from the detailed description given to him by the peasants, he knew to be King Ferdra. He was sorely tempted to run his bloodstained sword through the two of them. But now, frantically wondering as to Delancia's whereabouts a sudden panic seized him, and grabbing a small urn of tallow oil that he found lying outside the room, he returned to the entrance to pour the highly flammable liquid all over the corridor floor. But where was Delancia? He screamed inwardly! Was it possible that Trestania, knowing of their forbidden love, had placed her in the prison hut as a punishment, he wondered nervously. Fortunately, he knew the hut's location, and disregarding whether, or not he was now seen, he ran over to where it lay between two storage buildings. Finding it unguarded, he raised the locking bar from over the door and throwing it down onto the snow quickly hauled back the creaking door.

"Delancia," he whispered nervously towards the dark silhouetted figure slumped on a stool in the far corner. "Delancia, it's me, Vescala."

But no sooner had he uttered the words than she suddenly leapt to her feet, and rushing over to him she fell weeping into his outstretched arms. Breathing a deep sigh of relief Vescala took hold of her head to gently force it back and in the dim light once more stared lovelorn into her sunken, haunting eyes.

"Surely, I am in a dream?" she asked; her husky voice carrying a lilting beauty.

"It's no dream, Delancia, but we must hurry from here," he replied as she coiled her frail arms tightly around his neck, with pearly tears of unashamed joy tumbling down her pale happy face. "Delancia, I love you more than life but we must hurry. I've got ponies waiting outside the fort."

"But Trestania and the others?" she then asked; a sudden terror now prominent in her eyes.

"Don't worry about them. Come on; let's go!" he exclaimed and grabbing hold of her icy hand, and leading her outside they ran off in the direction of the ladder. However, on passing the palace entrance, Vescala felt a surge of supremacy tearing through him, and momentarily stopping to grab one of the torches from its cresset on the wall, he cast it to the floor of the entrance causing the entire corridor to quickly erupt into an inferno. Now smiling, without any trace of remorse for those trapped inside, they then retraced his steps to run headlong back to the stone staircase where Brenas stood waiting; the slave by now having torched the main granary and some half a dozen other buildings.

Owing to Delancia's weak condition Vescala had to place her over his shoulder to get her down the ladder. But with the three of them safely reaching ground level, Brenas pulled the ladder free from the wall and desperately struggling back through the deep snowdrifts, it wasn't long before they reached the ponies. After a quick search inside Gerant's tent, Vescala found a discarded fur cloak, which he placed over the shivering Delancia's shoulders. By now a heavy mist had begun to descend, and sitting astride the ponies they could just make out the hazy smoke and flames beginning to leap up from inside the fortress. At Vescala's instigation, they turned their mounts to drive them eastwards towards the coast, with each of them praying that their long years of subjugation were finally over. Although Vescala was well aware that many dangers lay ahead of them, a mysterious contentment had now encapsulated his spirit. Somehow, he sensed that all his hopes and dreams were about to be realised.

Chapter Fourteen

Throughout the cold, miserable night they rode as fast as was permissible, with the ponies often hampered by the treacherous snowdrifts. Due to this and the swirling mists they often lost their sense of direction, but by the time the first rays of the dawn had swept over the desolate landscape, the mist had begun to disperse.

Coming upon the partially submerged and cleanly picked bones of Ogmar and the child guide, Vescala dismounted, but after a thorough search he was dismayed on finding no trace of the tent that he reckoned must have been blown away in the previous day's storm. However, as they continued on their way towards the coast the terrain gradually became easier to negotiate, with both riders and animals alike appreciating the more level ground. But with their own and the ponies' resilience having been stretched to the limit by the long night's ride, they decided that they must stop to rest and eat. And as Vescala and Delancia huddled close together, the three of them prayed that the fires in the fortress would have prevented an immediate search party being sent out after them; everyone being well aware, that if either Trestania or Durada had somehow survived then they would hunt them forever, regardless of any danger that they themselves might personally incur. Their rest had to be a brief one though, and below a broiling grey sky, they remounted, with each of them hoping for a fresh snowfall in order to cover their tell-tale tracks. The main problem now uppermost in Vescala's mind was the fact that none of them had any knowledge concerning the land's geopolitical layout. He had no reason to suppose that any other tribes in the area would be friendly; indeed, he thought it more than likely that, if they were to seek shelter from any of them, then they might well be kidnapped and held to ransom or even worse.

From time to time, they passed by a few isolated homesteads from which they kept their distance, but by midmorning, they were forced to come to a halt on seeing the white wastelands yielding to the long, rugged eastern coastline where a dark grey, unfriendly looking sea now effectively barred their way.

"There's nowhere to run. Even now a search party might be stalking us," Vescala said pessimistically as his apprehensive eyes roamed across the hostile, booming surf towards the murky horizon. "I'm afraid there's only one logical option left open to us, and that's to get hold of a raft capable of transporting us over to the European shores."

However, he knew full well that, like his own people, the Picts were only skilled at constructing small rafts that seldom sailed beyond the sight of land.

"We have no experience of seamanship. Even if we had, where do we find such a vessel in this wilderness?" Brenas asked, looking dismayed.

"There has to be a fishing village somewhere nearby," Vescala replied, sensing that Brenas had already guessed that he was about to propose separating. But with each passing moment the vast expanse of water stretching out before them appeared increasingly unwelcoming, and shivering nervously, Vescala was fully aware that contemplating such a sea journey and actually undertaking it were two entirely different propositions.

"Now, Brenas, this is my plan. Delancia and I will ride north as you ride south. If by nightfall neither of us has found a suitable raft, then we turn back and meet up here again by noon tomorrow. On the other hand, if you are successful then start sailing north to meet us; likewise, if we get a raft we will sail south and pick you up. Look, see how the tides in its flood! If we ride out to the water and make our way along its edge, our tracks will be covered. Any search party that might be trailing us won't know in which direction we've gone."

"If a search party does track us as far as here, it's bound to split up in order to resume the search. Doing it your way may well see us all captured," Brenas argued, disliking the idea of separating. His preference was to stay together, hoping that by riding flat out toward the south they might eventually elude a search party.

"Look, Brenas, we have no choice," Vescala snarled impatiently. "I don't like the thought of separating any more than you do. But doing it my way we have two chances of getting a raft quickly. Let's face it, we know nothing of these lands. The sea is our only route to true safety, and even if we don't or can't attempt the crossing over to Europe, at least with a raft we can remain safely offshore," Vescala said, convinced that his plan, although fragile, was the only one that would give them any hope of eventual success, and with Delancia wholeheartedly supporting the idea, Brenas could only offer a grudging nod of agreement.

The three of them then dismounted, and after feeding the ponies they shared a last meal together, before dividing their dwindling provisions. Brenas insisted that they take the spare pony and, after wishing each other good fortune, he remounted to gallop off into the breeze along the flat sands just up from the foaming onrushing waters. The two lovers watched him sadly, each wondering if they would ever see him again. But to Vescala there was little time for sentimentality, and remounting their animals and, with Vescala grabbing the reins of the pack pony, they began riding north.

At first, they found riding along the water's edge to be much easier for themselves and their animals. However, by the late afternoon, the coastline had altered into a truly alien landscape with treacherous, jagged rock formations rising all around them. The small areas of sand they were now encountering lay packed with deadly patches of quicksand that at one stage saw them struggle desperately to free Delancia's trapped pony. With the slippery ground becoming almost impossible to negotiate, Vescala decided that they had no alternative but to follow the coastline from further inland. Leaving the strengthening wind of the shore to take refuge behind a thick clump of snow-engarlanded bushes they again shared a sparse meal, and huddling close together, even the unremitting weather alongside the misery of the cruel terrain failed to diminish the flame of love burning from deep within each of them.

After finishing their meal, they again rode north, but with the ground now rising steeply ahead, their pace became much slower. Eventually, they reached the top of the incline only to be disappointed on sighting a long line of towering cliffs stretching out before them towards the horizon. As yet, they had been disappointed to see no signs of any human habitation, although Vescala was certainly relieved to see no sign of the search party that he anticipated might be on their trail. By the time twilight was descending, they had passed by the cliffs to once more reach level ground where they immediately headed for the now unobstructed shoreline only to see the flood tide rolling in with massive white-crested waves thundering in all along the beach. Both of them prayed that Brenas had enjoyed better luck than they had experienced. But even if they were fortunate enough to find a raft, they were well- aware that they would be incapable of surviving for very long in such a turbulent sea.

Soon the beach had once more become rock-infested. It was dark now and rounding a nearby headland they were delighted to suddenly come upon a tiny stone-built house lying sheltered beneath a shrub-studded cliff. But by the time they reached the abode they were near to exhaustion, and after dismounting, Vescala first drew his sword before lifting the wooden latch and then kicking the door of the house in. He was relieved to find the place deserted, although stinking of mildew, and spotting a small mound of twigs and freshly picked animal bones lying neatly stacked in one corner of the abode's only room, he concluded that it must have been occupied only recently. Now shivering violently with the cold, Delancia slumped down onto the flat stone bench that comprised the only furniture in the place leaving Vescala, whose hands were almost dead with numbness, to struggle with his flints to light the small tallow lamp hanging from the low timber ceiling. After lighting a fire with the twigs, he returned outside to feed the ponies with the little hay left in the saddle packs. Although fully aware of the threat from roaming wolf packs, he had no alternative but to tether the hardy animals to a nearby bush, for even with only two people inside the abode seemed overcrowded. Taking the food and cooking utensils from the pack pony, he returned inside, and it wasn't long before they were sharing their first warm meal since absconding. But having eaten, and with the room now warm, Vescala placed his arm around Delancia as they nestled close together, oblivious to the raging gale that constantly rattled the barred door.

"Do we go back in the morning?" she asked; her liquid eyes, although heavy with fatigue, sparkling in the dim light.

"Yes. I don't think it would be in our interests to go on."

"Supposing Brenas has likewise been unsuccessful?"

Detecting a hint of fear in her whispered question, he stroked her anxious face comfortingly.

"Try not to worry," he murmured reassuringly. "Once we're reunited with Brenas, we'll soon find somewhere safe to live. Even if it's only a cave, we can take refuge there until the spring." Tilting his face to hers, Vescala then embraced her in a long passionate kiss that seemed to free them from the insecurity of their unenviable predicament. But drawing her lips away Delancia repeatedly kissed his unkempt beard.

"When I was abducted by the Romans and then imprisoned by Ferdra I never thought I'd see you again...I thought the gods were punishing me for having fallen in love with you," she said sombrely as Vescala gently eased her away to stare into her shining eyes.

"No, my love, only men and women are capable of such cruelty. But tell me, why did Trestania leave you imprisoned?"

"When she and the others entered the fortress, I was taken to the palace to be questioned by her. The first thing she asked me about was you. In my fear, I told her of our chance meeting on the cliff tops, and of our plan to elope. She then laughed aloud, merrily informing me that on the night of my abduction, you had run away from the fighting, only to be captured and executed for your cowardice. She and the priest known as Durada then interrogated me at length. After that ordeal, she appeared pleased, and speaking to me in a kindly manner, she then informed me that, for the sake of my soul and the well-being of the southern tribes, I had to completely erase you from my mind. All she appeared interested in was whether or not my virginity had remained intact over these past terrible months. She obviously hadn't believed me at first when I told her that no man had ever made physical love to me." Delancia paused, too ashamed to tell Vescala the truth. "Anyway, she then ordered me back to the prison hut until the following morning, and where I was to pray to the gods to forgive me for foolishly having become infatuated with you. Vescala, I did pray – but for death! The misery and degradation of these past months were bad enough, but the thought of living without hope was unbearable. You were the only hope I ever dared to harbour! And when she said you were dead...then to see you standing in the doorway...I....I." As she broke down sobbing, Vescala tenderly kissed the warm tears tumbling down her pale cheeks.

"Beloved Delancia," he whispered, drawing back. "In its search for fulfilment perhaps a love as indestructible as ours can overcome even the cruellest twists of fate. Over these last few months, I too experienced hell! When I thought you dead, I was like a man in constant darkness, stumbling along a path leading to nowhere. But let's forget the past; we have each other and that's all that matters."

Suddenly Delancia's eyes darted down to the fire. "If they were aware of our love, as Trestania told me, why didn't they kill you long ago? And why go to all this trouble to rescue me; a mere priestess?"

With a carefree smile on his face, Vescala gently took hold of the nape of her neck to pull her back to him until their noses touched.

"I spoke your name in a dream," he whispered. "Unfortunately, I was overheard by my master; that's how they knew about us. As for having me killed, well one of Trestania's slaves certainly tried. Luckily for me, Brenas thwarted him. Trestania also knew that to rescue you might cause great bloodshed; but there again, maybe she only undertook the mission to satisfy her fundamental sadism," Vescala remarked, deliberately lying. He didn't wish Delancia to know the terrible truth regarding her own destiny, and pressing his lips to hers he sensed a love that even in his dreams he could never have imagined. Suddenly Delancia pulled herself free from his passionate clinch.

"What was that?" she whispered as her startled eyes darted towards the door. But smiling sympathetically at her fear, Vescala grabbed her to pull her back to him.

"Relax, it's only the sound of the wind," he said assuredly.

"No, I heard a noise and it wasn't the wind," she said convincingly, and sensing her obvious alarm, he grabbed his sword and crossed the room to slowly unbar the door. However, no sooner had he raised the locking bar when the force of the gale suddenly flung the door wide open to instantly, extinguish the lamp. Staggering back into the fire, Delancia's harsh scream momentarily confounded him, and with his heart now pounding, his immediate sense of danger saw him rush outside only to meet the piercing howl of a wolf rising above the wind.

"Close and bar the door, Delancia," he yelled, turning to see her first hesitate before obeying his command, heading towards the terrified ponies, he struggled on through the snow only to see the full might of the wolf pack now attacking the animals.

Moving relentlessly forward, his flailing sword slashed and cut into the pack until the snow around him lay blood-spattered. But his desperate assault to protect the ponies was futile, and with three of the snarling wolves now turning on him, he found himself up against almost impossible odds as they forced him to retreat further and further from the house until it was out of sight. Now facing near certain death, an exhausted Vescala fought as he had never done before, and after a long, fearsome struggle he eventually succeeded in killing all three animals. By this time, he knew that the ponies would be dead, and forcing his sweat-sodden body on, it seemed to him to be an eternity before he at last sighted the gloomy outline of the hut reappearing. Struggling on to reach its safety, he knew that for his loved one and himself, there was now no possible escape. For ahead of him the glowing torchlights of the mounted search party were rushing along the beach to confront him.

With the ponies' dead, and the remainder of the wolf pack vanishing into the night, he reached the door hearing only the sound of the inclement wind. Falling and lying exhausted, he could do no more than scrape weakly at its rough-hewn surface with his bloodstained fingertips. Making a frantic effort he attempted to call Delancia's name, but it was to no avail; his white, bloodless lips being incapable of uttering any comprehensible sound. And with his entire body now immobilized in exhaustion, he looked up to see the indomitable, black-hooded figure of Trestania staring down at him from astride her pony.

"Ah, my dear Vescala, if ever a man crawled headlong into hell-fire, believe me you certainly have!" she exclaimed; a sneer lacing her tongue and a grisly smile prominent on her pale features. Gasping for breath, Vescala could only shake his head in revulsion, as she then summoned two of the warriors.

"Bring the girl out to me," she commanded, and quickly dismounting, the warriors kicked Vescala aside before forcing the door open as Durada rode up to Trestania's side.

"You, prepare a pony for the sinless one," he shouted to another warrior as the distraught Delancia was then dragged outside.

"Where is the slave, Brenas?" Trestania demanded, frowning down at her.

"I don't know, Highness, he ran away from us," the trembling Delancia answered, glancing pitifully down at the immobile Vescala.

"In what direction did he go?"

"W…west I…I…think," she stammered out in a reply that was far from convincing.

"I shouldn't worry, Highness," Durada said interrupting. "Ravala will soon find him. It's very foolish of you to try and save such a worthless life, Delancia. We already assumed that he travelled south alone." Suddenly Durada turned his attention to Vescala. "As for you, young man, by the grave dereliction of your holy vows you have jeopardised the soul of this sacred girl." Pausing, he glanced over to Trestania. "Highness, I fear that he may have corrupt…"

"That remains to be seen," Trestania snapped, effectively curtailing his words. But lying in the snow, Vescala was still incapable of speaking as his sombre eyes wandered up to Delancia's, thankful that death, no matter how cruel, must soon unite them forever.

Trestania dismounted, and with a wry smile on her lips led Delancia back into the hut where by now a slave had rekindled both the fire and the lamp. Behind the closed door, she was once more interrogated by the high priestess. Meanwhile, Durada ordered that Vescala be bound and blindfolded. However, after only a short time the two women returned outside with a now jovial high priestess immediately helping Delancia onto a spare pony before remounting her own pony. She then commanded the warriors around her to fall into a column behind Delancia, Durada and herself before screaming her praises to the sun god and ordering the party south and home. With his wrists firmly tied in front of him with a rope bound from around the neck of the warrior's pony ahead of him, the blindfolded Vescala found himself dragged along at the rear of the column.

As the party carefully worked its way back along the treacherous clifftops, Trestania decided to press on through the night and come the approaching dawn they had once more reached the long flat coastline. By this time the wind had subsided, and with the sun's rays skirting a golden horizon, they were soon reunited with Ravala and the rest of the army. He and his men had failed to find Brenas, although he was able to inform Trestania that the slave had bartered his pony and sword in a nearby village for a small fishing raft. However, Trestania appeared unconcerned at the news. Smiling contentedly, she knew Brenas to be an inexperienced seaman and that eventually he would be forced into returning to dry land, where in all probability he would be sacrificed to one of the Pictish gods.

As they proceeded along the beach where the sea's now calm waters splashed gently around the ponies' hooves no one noticed the tiny one-mast raft sailing not far offshore. Brenas, whose eyes were as sharp as any hawks, stood erect on the unsteady craft, utterly dejected on spotting the long columns moving slowly along the shoreline. He could barely distinguish Delancia's hooded figure but there was no mistaking the miserable, stumbling wretch being dragged along at the rear of the columns. Lonely, afraid, and shivering violently with the cold, he pulled his cloak around his ears and somewhat nervously cursed the gods for their treachery. With only a little of his food left, and facing the prospect of certain death should he return to land, he knew he had no alternative but to set sail eastwards in an attempt, to reach the far-flung European shores. However, on raising the tiny leather sail, the slave experienced a terrifying isolation and with it a sense of betrayal that seemed to penetrate his very soul.

Chapter Fifteen

As the journey back to the Southlands continued, Trestania often insisted on the army riding on through the night. After five days had elapsed, she and Delancia, being escorted by Ravala and some fifty of his warriors, suddenly left the main force to ride south at a gallop.

With Durada now left in sole command of the remaining army, they eventually stole well away from the snow-bound wilderness. However, as a result, the constant friction from the ropes binding him, Vescala's heavily chapped wrists grew increasingly painful, and behind his sightless eyes, it now seemed to him as if he had been walking for an eternity. By now his feet were swollen and bloodied; his boots having been so badly worn that only the upper parts of his legs received any protection from the moorland bracken and russet heather the party frequently encountered. With his ragged clothing permanently damp it clung to his tortured body like a second skin. For at no time was he ever allowed any shelter from the elements; his roof being the sky and his walls the forever-ravaging winds and rain. No one ever spoke as much as a word to him, with his only human contact being when he was meagrely fed by what he presumed to be slaves. But even throughout his meals a silent vigilance was always maintained. At times his enforced blindness, along with his physical suffering, became so acute that he would lapse into unconsciousness, only to be dragged bodily over the rugged terrain. There were times when he could roughly estimate their progress by the distinct smell of the pine forests they often entered into. But when lying alone during their infrequent rest breaks, the sharpest of sounds, like an unfettered bird chirping happily high in some treetop, would see him immersed into a period of self-pity where he would bitterly regret ever having been born. The little sleep he was permitted brought to him the only respite from his misery, but even in sleep his tormented nightmares saw him relive the horrors of his recent past. Sometimes he would awake, disturbed and trembling, only to know the hell of a silence that seemed to be devouring what fragile sanity he had somehow managed to retain.

As they advanced south they again breached the great forests where his feet would shuffle through deep tracts of rustling skeletal leaves. On such occasions, he would imagine his own decaying bones lying scattered across some alien forest floor, although, in his distress, he sensed that his worthless life would in all probability end within the blazing fury of a wicker image. The only prayers he now ever muttered begged for his beleaguered soul to be speedily released from its earthly existence to find a lasting consummation in the hereafter with an immortal Delancia.

One day, after an unusually long sleep, he was rudely awakened by a rough hand tugging at his long, mud-caked hair. After being fed and then forced onto his feet he was again made to walk, only this time it was much quieter than in the past. For now, he was aware of only a few ponies trotting ahead of him instead of the incessant clatter that had been created by the whole army. After a while, he was stopped, and for the first time since leaving the stone house, the rope was cut from his swollen wrists. Suddenly the blindfold was wrenched off his head, with the savage glare from the high sun forcing him to his knees in excruciating agony. However, his hands were prevented from protecting his eyes by the two warriors on either side of him who immediately pulled him back onto his feet to hold his arms rigid. Now blinking rapidly, his streaming eyes slowly began to focus on the wide clearing stretching out before him and which was surrounded by ancient yew trees.

"Welcome home, Vescala."

He peered hatefully towards the motionless figure of Trestania who now stood before him with the vivid blue of her penetrating eyes burning into his own.

"Strip him," she commanded the warriors, who immediately began to pull and tear at his tattered clothing until he stood naked. Although his body was horrifically cut and bruised, Trestania, who had now been joined by Durada, showed no compassion whatsoever at his injuries.

"You have a new home, Vescala!" Durada exclaimed contemptuously. "At least until such time as the high priestess has decided what's to be done with you. I pray you will find it to your satisfaction."

Trestania now beckoned to one of the warriors who promptly handed Vescala the knotted end of a long, thick rope. He was then pushed towards a deep circular shaft that had been dug out from the earth behind him. Grasping tightly onto the rope the two warriors began to lower him down into the pit whereon reaching the flat-stoned bottom he nervously looked around before staring up in disbelief at the faces of Trestania and Durada silhouetted against the distant sky.

As the rope snaked slowly back upwards, the warriors quickly dragged a heavy iron grille, like some cold embracing cobweb, over the top of the pit to enclose him in partial darkness. He could see that all around him there was nothing bar the level floor and the sheer, circular earthen walls stretching the height of three men above him. And with the width of the floor more than the length of his own outstretched body, he knew that any escape attempt was inconceivable. In the dim light filtering down into the dank-smelling chamber, he stared in horror at the many open, weeping wounds covering his lacerated body. Few sounds breached the chamber's grim atmosphere, and desperate to attain some warmth he crouched down low into a foetal position, with his vacant eyes occasionally staring up to the remoteness of the of the distant world so far above. Time crawled slowly by, but as darkness approached a small hatch in the centre of the grille cover was suddenly flung open with two drinking vessels lowered down to him on a thin rope; one containing water and the other a thin lukewarm gruel of oatmeal and goat's milk. On finishing the sparse meal, he watched both vessels disappear up towards the surface, and with the hatch above clanging shut, its eerie echoing lingered endlessly in his mind until sleep brought to him a restless peace.

On awakening, he found the cold so intense that he was forced to rise and move his aching body around the chamber in an attempt to ease the icy numbness that he now felt had penetrated deep into his very bone marrow. As morning broke, he ate another sparse meal lowered down to him; knowing only too well that these harsh, inhuman conditions must soon terminate his suffering. Almost every moment of his naked isolation was spent in wondering if his beloved Delancia was still alive and if she was, then what had become of her? Her face was etched into every facet of his mind. And yet, no matter how hard he tried, he could at no time recall each precious detail of its euphoric beauty. Sometimes he would forget which of her eyes was sapphire blue and which one was aquamarine. It now seemed to him as if an evil shadow hung between his memory of her and her overpowering and loving reality.

The morning of the fifth day of his confinement saw the grille above removed. At first the sun's strong rays forced him to shut his eyes, but on feeling the end of a thick rope brushing lightly against his shoulder, he slowly reopened them.

"Tie the rope around your waist and hang on," came the shouted command from an unknown face peering down at him from the edge of the pit. Momentarily hesitant, Vescala half-suspected death to be awaiting him on the surface, but composing himself, he did as he was ordered and allowed himself to be painfully raised up whereon reaching ground level, he was immediately helped over the edge before being forced onto his feet by the two brawny warriors who had raised him.

The tepid heat emanating from the red winter sun brought instant warmth to his trembling frame, and peering around the clearing he suddenly glimpsed Durada coming towards him with an armed slave in attendance. As Durada marched up to face him the priest first grinned at his emaciated condition before turning to the slave.

"Get him over to the shelter and tidy him up," he commanded the slave through a sneer. Vescala could hardly believe that this was the once kindly benefactor, who not so long ago, he had looked upon almost as a father. Aided by the slave, he was then taken over to where a canvas sheet was draped between two branches of a yew tree, and where below this an iron cauldron filled with hot water hung suspended over a charcoal fire. He was then handed a rag by the slave with Durada telling him to wash himself thoroughly. After this was done, the slave soothed his open wounds with herbal ointment before bandaging his mutilated wrists and feet. Vescala was surprised at such treatment, especially when the slave began to trim his long hair and beard with a sharp knife. However, as Durada handed him a long white robe and a pair of flimsy leather sandals, he began to realise just what was going on.

"It's been decided that you are to be granted a fair trial. I sincerely hope that you will conduct yourself with the dignity expected from a novitiate," the priest said, staring into Vescala's stony gaze.

"Why bother with such pretentious nonsense?" Vescala asked through a forced smile. "There can be but one verdict and you know as well as I do that it's already been reached. All that remains is for Trestania to decide how best to degrade me in my execution."

"No!" Durada exclaimed angrily, "I said a fair trial, and I meant it. One of the trinity of high priests will be in attendance.

You would be wise to repent before him. That way you might yet escape death. Now here, put this headband on."

Taking hold of the novitiate headband Durada offered him, Vescala cursed as he flung it at the priest's feet.

"The robe and sandals I will wear, but I will gladly die before I ever again don your blood-drenched status symbol," he shouted defiantly as Durada stood shaking his head. "Very well, Vescala: I assure you that you do yourself no good whatsoever by taking such an arrogant, unreasonable attitude. In the past, neither priest nor novitiate has ever received capital punishment. Believe me, lad, unless you quickly control your foolish ways you will undoubtedly become the first!" Durada exclaimed in a firm uncompromising tone, only for Vescala to laugh cheekily at the threat.

"There's little of my body left to burn. Anyway, I don't believe for one moment that you who masquerade as mortal gods will ever succeed in destroying my spirit. Now, I suggest you go straight to hell...master," he said contemptuously spitting at the stunned Durada's feet. Turning away from him, the priest's face burned with rage as he commanded the two warriors to. "Bring the fool," before heading along the track leading from the clearing into the forest.

After dressing into the robe and sandals, Vescala's hands were immediately bound behind his back with cord, and with a black hood suddenly placed over his head the slave and warriors pushed him in Durada's direction.

It was well into the afternoon when they reached the village where his trial was to be held. The court building itself, being roofless, was almost identical in shape and size to the one in which he had attended the trials earlier in the year. By now the benches inside were crammed full with some two hundred priests in attendance and entering into the building, he could clearly hear the excited murmurings of the crowd as he was led through the spectators towards the raised wooden pedestal in the centre of the arena. He was then made to stand on it before being untied and having the hood removed. However, it took a few moments for his vision to focus properly, whereupon he immediately detected directly in front of him the imposing figure of the high priest, sitting upright on an even higher pedestal than that of Trestania and the nine druids seated below him. The eyes of the white-robed and long-bearded high priest remained keenly fixed on the haggard features of the accused, and looking around, he saw that every druid now wore white robes; the exception being Trestania who wore her customary black attire.

As the high priest shouted for the trial to commence, a mortifying fear suddenly crept over his entire being with a marked silence quickly falling around the expectant benches as the eldest of the nine priests rose to his feet to stare confidently up at the accused.

"Vescala, kinsman of the tribal lands of the Durotriges, you are charged by us with the forcible abduction and attempted rape of the sacred woman known by the holy name of Delancia. In accordance with our legal code, I have to ask you how you plead to this first charge," the man asked in a loud, officious voice. But knowing that he had nothing to lose, Vescala spat to the ground before replying.

"I happen to love this young mortal woman with all my heart and soul!" he exclaimed sincerely. "She's no more sacred in the eyes of your so-called sun god than any other mortal woman. As a child, she was in all probability abandoned beneath an oak tree by some poverty-stricken peasant girl driven to despair by the soul-destroying bondage that the peasants are forced to live under; conditions that you self-appointed guardians of our morality encourage. To charge a man for no more than love is, to my mind, the greatest heresy of them all!" Vescala screamed the words at the prosecutor only for his outburst to draw astonished gasps from the spectators.

"I asked you for a plea, not an insult," the prosecutor snapped back angrily as Vescala stood grinning scornfully down at him as the man turned to look up for support from the high priest, whose dark, unresponsive eyes never left Vescala's. But the high priest maintained a dignified silence.

"Very well," the prosecutor said through a light sigh as, once again, he turned to face the accused. "Now the second charge against you is that you and your co-aggressor, a former trustee slave named Brenas, whom we now know to be dead, were responsible for the murders of twenty-one people in the arson assault that you carried out in the Caledonian tribal lands. I'm sorry to inform the spectators that these victims included four of our own warriors as well as King Ferdra, chieftain of the wolf tribe. How do you plead to this charge?"

Vescala shuddered outwardly at the man's words, and although shocked by the news of the slave's death, he felt a glow of pride surging through his weakly frame. If Brenas and he had achieved nothing else with their lives, they had at least rid the earth of a true tyrant! He thought retributively.

"Well then am I not to be congratulated for my actions? After all, by killing that bastard Ferdra, Brenas and I did mankind a great service," he shouted out, caring nothing for the looks of disgust on the faces around him. But solemnly shaking his head, the prosecutor continued.

"The third charge against you is that, again by means of arson, you did attempt to murder the high priestess and a prominent member of the inner council of druids, namely Durada. Also, you did attempt to murder some two hundred warriors and slaves of the Atrebate tribe, one of whom included the illustrious warlord Ravala. Again, I ask you to plead."

Smiling impudently down at Trestania, Vescala refused as the prosecutor turned despairingly to the high priest.

"Your Holiness, there are many lesser charges of heresy and theft which I can bring against the accused. To pursue them would be time-consuming: I move that we continue only with the charges stipulated."

Remaining impassive the high priest nodded his approval. At the instigation of the prosecutor, Ruadi and Straval were then brought into the courtroom and told to stand with their backs to the high priest and face the accused. In turn, they related their evidence as Vescala − who was denied an opportunity to cross-examine the witnesses − exploded with rage at the blatantly fabricated litany of lies being voiced against him only for his protestations to be drowned out by the derisory outbursts directed at him from an increasingly hostile audience. Finally, it was the turn of Durada and the voluble Trestania to give their evidence, with Vescala violently angering the high priestess when he laughed aloud at her absurd accusation, that he and Brenas had killed Ogmar and the child guide. However, he was warily surprised when she placed great emphasis on the court on the fact that 'the blessed one,' as she referred to Delancia, had not been physically molested.

By the late afternoon, the testimony of all the witnesses was complete, and as the prosecuting druid took his seat alongside Trestania an expectant hush fell over the proceedings. All eyes now looked up in reverence to the high priest, who momentarily glanced around him before his sparkling eyes finally settled on Vescala's.

"You have listened to the evidence against you, young man!" he exclaimed in a deep voice that boomed around the arena. "If what I have heard is only half-true then I can only say that I am astounded. Nonetheless, the high priestess has entitled you to a defence. Now, if you so desire, you may relate to me your own version of this sorrowful tale."

Everyone's eyes switched to Vescala, who braced himself. Acknowledging the high priest with a nod, and nervous as he undoubtedly was, he addressed his audience loudly and eloquently, beginning from the time when the two priests had come to take him from his mother's house. As he spoke, his confidence seemed to grow and omitting nothing, he then went on to tell of how he had released the distressed woman whose refusal to remarry had caused her to be banished from all tribal contact. He then went on to speak of his loathing of slavery and human sacrifice and of his desire to see a more just and equal society. However, the encircling crowds gasped aloud when he told of his uncontrollable love for Delancia. But then when recounting how Trestania and Durada had ordered Ogmar to murder him and that he had come upon the high priestess sharing Ferdra's bed, a near riot broke out with some of the priests nearest to him attempting to drag him off the pedestal.

With shouts of "Execute him" now being emitted from most lips, Vescala stood calm and unconcerned, but quickly restoring order Trestania nodded at him to resume. But declining to say anymore, he stood staring nonchalantly around the sea of faces feeling satisfied within himself that he had told the truth.

Above the courtroom, the open sky had begun to darken with a few bright stars becoming visible through the cold air. Beckoning to the slaves, Trestania then ordered that the torches lying in their cressets along the walls be lit. After this was done all eyes once again turned to gaze upon the high priest, whose long, snow-white hair and beard, in the glare of the torchlights, brought to his countenance an almost spiritual appearance.

"As you have recounted, Vescala, at the time you ran from your abductors you were a mere child when coming upon the most sacred of trees," he said almost casually. "At the time there were many among us, including myself, who thought that you might have been the 'chosen one,' who is eventually destined to free our faith from the bonds of Roman tyranny and once more establish its true authority throughout the enslaved lands of Europe. How misguided we all were, young man. Have I changed so much over these last twelve years that you fail to recognise one of your so-called abductors?" he shouted haughtily, now pointing his finger at Vescala whose shoulders jerked back in bewilderment. But as his eyes scanned the priest's fearsome stare, it was with a macabre sense of intuition that he remembered the face and all the hell that seemed to be represented in its aged lineaments.

"How ungrateful you truly are Vescala. Did you never think that were it not for the priesthood, you would almost certainly have shared the communal grave of your family who were so tragically taken in the plague that decimated your tribe."

Vescala winced at the high priest's authoritarian statement, and drawing his eyes from the priest's, he glanced down sensing a fleeting shame.

"If ever a man condemned himself by allowing his soul to be poisoned by evil, then surely you have done so," the high priest commented, only this time in a mocking tone. "Now you have the conceited audacity to talk to us about equality among men. But did we not treat you as an equal? Indeed, the munificent Durada even took you under his wing to give you the additional benefit of his personal tuition. You're also quick to blame us for the grim poverty of the peasant masses. We are not responsible for that scenario. Have you learned nothing from us? Surely, you must know that when a man dies, he is judged by the gods on the life he has lived while on the earth. If he was a poor man but had led a good worthwhile existence then when reincarnated the gods will elevate him to a higher position within the social structure. On the other hand, if he has committed great evil like you yourself have admittedly done, then in his next life, he must endure the pain of servitude and deprivation. Such is the will of the gods, young man; all nature is eternal resurrection; it cannot and never will be altered!"

"Damn the will of your perverse gods," a now angry Vescala shouted, with his curse drawing yells of indignation from the spectators. But remaining unruffled the high priest resumed.

"A criminal adventurer such as you are, Vescala, would, if given half a chance, sow indescribable chaos throughout our lands. You will never realise that ambition! Now your lust, murders, and lies, which have been directed against our most holy and revered of persons, have brought shame upon us all.

But even although your heresy is beyond all human comprehension, we can still be merciful to one of our own." Suddenly the high priest paused, only to resume in an imploring manner. "If, even at this late stage, you are prepared to sincerely repent for your sins, then you may yet save your soul. If not, then by your own stubbornness and the self-destructive forces within you, you must suffer the consequences. Think very carefully before making your decision."

Bearing a conceited smile on his face, Vescala first glanced around him before again directing his eyes towards the high priest.

"You people are no more than a semi-secret society who rule the masses as a law unto yourselves," he said spitefully. "You care nothing for the liberty or dignity of your fellow men and women. As for the demonic forces you so blindly worship as gods: I believe in them as much as I believe those surrounding me to be 'the shadows of the sun' whom you so arrogantly entitle yourselves to. You ask me to repent – but for what? The only crimes I ever committed were to have devoutly loved a mortal woman and to have tried to treat our less fortunate humans with respect. Some inner logic now tells me that there are no gods, but if there should be then there can only be one true god: a god of love and mercy! Totally unlike your evil demons, who in their existence stand idly by watching the rich aristocracy and priesthood feed on the slaves and peasants like the bloated maggots who devour their way through a decomposing corpse."

His speech was now drowned out by angry protests from the spectators, and soon a slow vociferous chant of "Burn him!" resounded throughout the arena, but with her face now rouged with pounding veins, an irate Trestania leapt to her feet to demand silence. With the chanting immediately ceasing, Vescala, who had remained unmoved by the threat, was permitted to continue.

"A priesthood should be at the vanguard of any just society; indeed, a true priesthood should bear the armour, sword, and shield of the nation's social conscience. Whether you sacrifice Delancia and myself or millions of innocents in the future, mankind will find no lasting peace until a truly caring and compassionate priesthood attempt to exorcise the destructive elements that rule the souls of you self-ordained hypocrites. You are not, and never will be, such a priesthood."

"Enough, Vescala," the high priest demanded, unable to hide his discomposure at the arrant madness voiced by such a once-promising novitiate. "By your actions and words, you have condemned yourself; I now command that the council of jurors rise to give their verdicts."

However, an embittered Vescala stood shaking his head at what was no more than a formality, as each juror, including his prosecutor, stood to declare the accused's guilt on all three charges. As each verdict was announced, it was met by wild cheering from the excited crowd. With the pronouncement of the last judgment; Trestania ascended the few wooden steps up to the high priest to embark on a long inaudible conversation with him. Returning to her former position, she then stood staring up at the accused with a strange, almost maternal sympathy now prominent on her face.

"As always in such tragic circumstances it is my sad duty to pronounce the punishment to fit the crime," she said softly. However, as she spoke a chilling evil seemed to fill the arena. "We have all heard the accused speak of his hatred of slavery. Well, let me remind the young fool that less than ten percent of the population of these islands are held in bondage, and those who are damned well deserve to be!"

Throughout the arena there was a ripple of agreeable applause at her words.

"He dares to chide us regarding the so-called downtrodden peasantry. Tell me, my proud Vescala, is it not a fact that when one of their children falls ill, do we not treat and care for it as equally as we would the child of a king? You also spoke of a social conscience. I'm afraid it's a statement you haven't yet begun to understand. For, if you did, you would surely know that we are a predominately agricultural-based society whose people are dictated against not only by a harsh climate but also by an army of diseases which perpetually ravage the crops and animals needed for our very survival. Tell me, Vescala, is it, not we druids who organise the seasonal planting of the crops and who are responsible for the conservation of the forests and animal, bird, and plant life? Who else but we druids have the knowledge to cure the countless maladies that all too frequently threaten so many with the hell of famine and starvation – a knowledge built on a foundation of centuries of failure and human suffering? Whether you accept it or not, Vescala, we, the administrators of the law, the theologians, the philosophers, the physicians, are and always will be the backbone of our great society; we druids whom you have had the audacity to so callously denigrate." Trestania was interrupted by spontaneous applause from the spectators. "And now, gentlemen." As silence fell, she now addressed her words to the audience. "All present have heard the defamatory allegations made against our most stalwart of priests, including myself. Gentlemen, enlighten me. If I was supposedly sharing Ferdra's bed, how on earth am I here today in such exalted company when he was burned to death?"

Everyone laughed as all eyes turned to stare towards the flummoxed Vescala who, like the others, wasn't to know that it had been Ravala who had rescued both the high priestess and Durada.

"Gentlemen, I have heard with great sadness the cries to burn the accused resounding around this arena," she said with the laughter subsiding as her expression altered into one of amazement. "Do you suppose for one moment that I, the highest ranking of all priestesses, could even contemplate burning one of our own kind? No, gentlemen. None of our own has ever faced the fires! We cannot burn one who has taken the final vows! And this surely is a young man who is more to be pitied for the black insanity that snares his mal-contented spirit than to be burned as one of the common peoples. No god would welcome such a sacrifice! For this fatuous nineteen-year-old, who pretends to be a champion of universal emancipation, longs only for martyrdom, and that I will ensure he never receives."

There was an insincere pretence in her tone, and lowering his head Vescala became afraid of her intentions. Looking around the arena Trestania's furious eyes searched purposefully into all those meeting her own. Suddenly her long, trembling finger was directed menacingly toward the spectators who could see by her altered expression the threat she engendered.

"Even in a trial as secret as this one, there's always a danger that his outrageous ideological beliefs of equality might reach the ears of the ignorant masses and in turn create a dangerous insurrection. Your silence regarding this trial will be a lifelong one – you have been warned!" she screamed, spitting her words through gritted teeth. Lowering her arm, she continued, only this time in a relaxed mode. "After conferring with His Holiness: I have decided to spare the wretch's life," she said calmly. Vescala trembled at her words as a rising crescendo of disgruntled murmurings rose from the benches. But Trestania resumed, totally unconcerned at the objectors who quickly fell silent.

"This young fool longed for a mistress and I will grant him one. But a mistress far surpassing his wildest fantasies. Gentlemen: I was aware all along of his unnatural infatuation for our blessed Delancia and therefore took the step of having his movements carefully monitored. But this new love in his life goes by no mortal name, for she is known as 'death in life.' When he longs for death, and there's no doubt in my mind that he does, he will not find it easily. We will watch over him like guardian hawks as he lives naked and isolated in the pit that will incarcerate him until the time when death mercifully releases him. When hunger afflicts him, we will feed him – meagrely. When he grows cold, we will grant him warmth – just. If he should fall sick, and he will, we will cure him. No one will ever again speak as much as one word to him. If he should dare to even contemplate either escape or suicide, he will be forcibly prevented. In his naked seclusion, he will undoubtedly live far longer than most of us present. But as the long days and months evolve into years, he will experience the presence of an immutable loneliness and with it an agony that far outstrips the pain of burning. All outsiders who knew of him will be informed that he died from natural causes. Gentlemen, to we druids there never has been and never will be heroes among dissidents!" Trestania paused to direct her bland expression towards Vescala whose dejection clearly showed over his grimacing features. "Now, as you are all aware this very night heralds in the month of the robin – the end of the fourteenth month which delivers us into a new year. But tonight is even more unique; it being in our holy calendar cycle the time when the sun god accepts from us his spiritual bride – the woman whom the guilty one so vehemently lusted after I think it only fitting that he be made to attend the sacrifice to witness with his own eyes the legitimate demand of our beloved god. I further decree that an epic poem be composed in honour of the noble Ravala's role in the 'blessed one's' rescue. And now, gentlemen, with this trial at an end let the warriors enter to remove this self-appointed and false messiah of the so-called enslaved and impoverished masses!"

Trestania's words were met by uproarious applause from the benches. But looking tearfully up at the darkening magenta sky, a disbelieving Vescala could find no prayer to alleviate the numbing despondency now wracking his body and soul. Re-entering the arena, the warriors passed through the joyous throng to once again bind and hood him. After being dragged back through the jeering crowds Vescala could hardly believe his fate, and stumbling out through the doorway, he was then kicked and pushed towards a secluded hut lying at the far end of the deserted village.

With the warriors remaining to guard him, some time elapsed before a haggard slave woman brought the three of them a warm meal. However, the now-unhooded Vescala's refusal to eat was met with a savage beating that made it relatively easy for one of the warriors to forcibly thrust the food down his throat.

Although now only partially conscious, he suddenly became aware of being taken from the hut and led along a path where a long procession of torch-bearing and chanting peasants headed towards the nearby forest. By now total darkness had fallen, and fighting to regain his full senses, he found the encompassing noise to be almost unbearable. On reaching the forest's edge the peasants, who were barred from going near the most venerable of shrines, parted before them to reveal a long turf-ridged pathway ahead. The warriors then handed him over to two waiting priests who immediately removed the sandals and bandages from his feet. Holding on to his still-bound wrists, they then led him through an avenue of tall trees now standing against the star-strewn sky like dark, lifeless veins.

Now fully alert, Vescala glimpsed a full moon shimmering through the continuous lacework of branches, but at the sight of a lone snowy owl gliding below the branches on silent wings, he came to an abrupt halt only to be physically jerked forward by the priests. He could feel the soles of his naked and still badly swollen feet scrape painfully against the hard pebbles below him, reminding him of his childhood experience, and as a grey spectre of midwinter frost swept over the forest floor, he instinctively knew that this was the identical pathway he had so desperately travelled then. It wasn't long before they came upon the circular grass mound, where the four paths met and where a huge bonfire now stood blazing in its centre. Almost immediately, torch-bearing druids in their hundreds, began gathering from the eastern and western routes. Quickly organising themselves into columns three abreast, they then began to move slowly along the northern track, with the procession headed by an aged precentor who led them in humming a melody that filtered hauntingly through the vapid air.

With his bound wrists having been checked by his priestly guards, the three of them joined the others at the rear of the procession. But such was the pain in his swollen feet, by the time the sacred glade came into view he was near to collapsing. After being partially carried through the avenue of carved totems, he was then forced to kneel on the frost-matted grass close to the knoll where the statuesque oak tree stood.

All around the sacred glade, from the high branches of the surrounding trees, white canvas drapes hung limply down in the freezing air; each of them decorated with the symbols of various deities. Now entrapped within the web of an almost nightmarish atmosphere, he stared towards the straight lines of some five hundred or so priests and priestesses who stood facing the sacred tree, noting that, like their male counterparts, the priestesses now wore pure white robes and headbands. To the accompaniment of an unseen and solitary pounding drumbeat, the entire congregation joined in singing a slow, melodious song whose lyrics were dedicated in praise of the sun god. With the repetitive lyrics growing increasingly louder, he suddenly found his bruised mouth being gagged with a strip of linen by one of his guards while the other again checked that the bonds binding his wrists were secure. As this was being done an elderly torch-bearing priest stepped forward to ignite a thin line of fire that quickly spread in a circle around the knoll' With the ring of pale-yellow flames leaping up no more than a body's length away from him, Vescala sensed that these flames were intended to destroy any evil spirits that might be lurking near to the tree itself. Now staring up at the sacred tree, he saw that it stood exactly as he remembered it from his childhood, and with the cessation of the drumbeat the priestesses alone were left to gently hum a passive melody that, in his trepidation, he somehow knew to be the song of death.

A freezing ground mist crept stealthily over the frost-tainted grass, as throughout the sacrificial site coloured crimson incense now burned everywhere. Like some troubled, meandering spirit its sacrosanct smoke floated steadily upwards until it encapsulated the moon's silver sheen in a blood-red veil. But with the hollow rhythm of the drumbeat starting up again, the expectant congregation fell deathly silent. Suddenly glancing over to his right, he saw coming towards him from the far end of the glade, the exalted figure of a white-robed Trestania, whose flame-red hair cascaded over her shoulders like rivulets of fresh blood. Directly behind her came one of the trinity of high priests whom he recognised as the presiding judge at his trial; his silver hair now adorned with a white-horned ox-hide that hung down to cover his white-robed shoulders. Behind the high priest walked the crimson-robed, golden-masked arch-druid, flanked by two masked, torch-bearing slaves. Momentarily shivering, Vescala now felt as if his soul had been frozen in time. The very appearance of the arch-druid was far more terrifying than anything he had previously known; the inanimate, burnished golden mask with its narrow slits for eyes seemed to represent the centuries-old evil of all the tyrannical despots who had been and who he sensed were still to visit mankind.

In his distress, he was at first almost unwilling to acknowledge the naked figure gliding listlessly behind the arch-druid, and desperately fighting to set himself free, his horrified eyes conveyed the anguish he felt at her sight. However, the more he struggled the more the priests standing over him pressed down on his shoulders with an iron grip.

With an almost pleasant smile, Trestania turned to acknowledge the fifty or so priestesses behind her with a short bow before she too joined the other high priests. By now they had entered in to the fiery circle along with Delancia, who was immediately led by the two slaves up to the tree. She was then turned to face the high priest before being manacled by her wrists and ankles to the heavy bronze chains nailed into the tree's broad emblazoned trunk. With her arms stretched taut above her shaven head, Vescala could see that, apart from the sacred crown of mistletoe, the only other attire she wore was a short black cord tied around her swan-white neck to show her mortal inferiority before the oncoming presence of the divine sun god. He could faintly sense the sweet aroma from the holy vervain oil that had been smeared all over her beautiful body and which caused it to glow erotically in the surrounding flames. However, on spotting the small circular tattoo, representing the sun god, and etched into her right breast, he drew his eyes up to hers only to see that they were glazed and devoid of any emotional response as she stared ahead oblivious to either compassion or understanding. Reckoning that she had been heavily sedated the terror-stricken Vescala watched as the garish Trestania slowly removed from the white sash around her waist a small but razor sharp, golden-handled sickle. As the pounding drumbeat accelerated, she passed it to the arch-druid who, after consecrating the weapon with a short whispered prayer, returned it into Trestania's outstretched palms. She in turn placed it into the strong hand of a statuesque slave whose face was hidden behind a grotesque leather mask shaped in the form of a badger's head. As the man walked slowly towards his unsuspecting victim, Trestania suddenly turned sideways, and with the drum pounding ever faster, her fiery eyes glanced down to Vescala, who was again frantically fighting to struggle free from his guards. But by the time he had succeeded in getting onto his feet, the slave had raised the weapon high above his head only to bring it down and savagely embed it deep into Delancia's side, where he drew its pitiless blade over her abdomen in a horizontal cut.

Delancia's agonized scream lingered on the onerous air for what seemed to Vescala to be an eternity. As her stricken eyes pierced into his, the slave twice more raised and brought the weapon down again to hack and tear into his victim's now convulsing body. Horrified at the sight of the seething mass of entrails now pouring out from her gaping wounds, Vescala slumped to his knees only to see them cascade down her twitching legs and form into a heap around her twisted feet. Averting his disbelieving eyes, he again glanced up, only this time to clearly see her writhing lips attempt to utter what he thought to be his name before her pallid head fell forward, with the sacred crown of mistletoe tumbling past her tortured dangling corpse to come to rest on the heavily blood-stained earth.

With the drumbeat pounding ever louder all hands, including those of the hierarchy, were raised towards the heavens as a great cry of thanksgiving rose up from everyone's lips to acknowledge the sunlight now beginning to infiltrate the colourless unmourning sky. Physically and spiritually devastated, Vescala drew his tear-filled eyes away from his beloved's degraded mortal form hardly believing what had taken place. It seemed to him as if it were only yesterday that he had stood before the very same tree thankful for his safe deliverance. Suddenly, his half-shut eyes discerned an adder sliding ominously out from its winter nest of stones and leaf mould between the gnarled roots of the tree. In the disordered turmoil of his mind, he now tried desperately to reason within himself, knowing that to sight a serpent during any sacrificial ceremony was considered by the druids to be an omen portending a future disaster.

With an inhuman smile masking her face, Trestania once more turned to look down at him but seeing the dread covering his bloodless features, she followed his transfixed eyes, to likewise spot the adder now sliding among the entrails. Falling back through the ring of fire, the high priestess screamed hysterically as her bulging eyes turned towards the arch-druid who, with the other high priest, was also staggering back through the flames. For, between its sharp, white fangs, the serpent now held the distinct form of a tiny blood-drenched human foetus!

The fearful mutterings of the congregation filled the still air as the sound of the drumbeat ceased. And as word of the horror spread, everyone suddenly began running in a panic-stricken swarm into the bleakness of the surrounding forestry leaving an almost-demented Vescala all alone with the petrified high priests, who could only stand impotently watching as the serpent devoured the infant child. To those remaining, it seemed like an endless torment before the serpent finally left the corpse to return to its lair, leaving them to ponder fearfully over the dreadful implications the ceremony held.

Eventually, the forest's silent trees became immersed in the sun's newborn rays, and as the high priests stumbled blindly away from the sacred glade, two living men were left all alone.

Not far behind Vescala, and standing by himself on the very spot where he had so calmly witnessed the grotesque ritual, Straval stared up at Delancia's remains. With his features unwavering, he glanced coldly down to stare hard and long at his one-time confidant. However, unlike his fellow priests, he understood neither fear nor sense of foreboding, and with a grim expression of fulfilment flitting over his features, he casually walked into the forest leaving an emotionally shattered Vescala all alone with the butchered remains of his tragic, unfulfilled love.

Chapter Sixteen

With the fresh leaves and blossoms bursting forth from the surrounding trees, Lascal sat down to listen intently to the spring songs of the encircling mistle-thrushes. It was the first peaceful moment he had experienced for some time, and with the forest aglow in a frenzy of colour, the young man lay wearily back on the lush grass feeling content that he had, at last, succeeded in eluding Ravala's soldiers who, for the past three days, had so ruthlessly hunted him. Putting the recent danger to the back of his mind, he stared placidly up at the cloudless sky and smiled, happy in the knowledge that he would soon be reunited with his lovely wife and the rest of the commune; providing they hadn't been forced into moving their campsite yet again, he thought suffering a twinge of anxiety. After a short but pleasant rest, he rose to his feet and placed the sword held ready in his hand back into the leather scabbard hanging from his broad flaxen belt.

Remaining ever alert, he resumed walking north with his keen hazel eyes constantly scanning the forestry for any threat that might appear. As he walked, he chuckled to himself on imagining the relieved expressions on his relatives' faces when he strolled back into their distant camp, with the vision of his young wife Silena looming uppermost in his thoughts. Now into his seventeenth year, Lascal was a tall, sturdily built individual, independent of mind and with a swarthy complexion masking his chiselled good looks with the long black hair cascading down and over his broad shoulders giving him an almost regal appearance. However, of all his fine attributes, his greatest was his undeniable courage; a courage that in recent times had been put to the test more and more frequently against the enemies of his commune and which included the entire druid priesthood.

A sparsely wooded hill now stretched up before him, and climbing up to its summit, he scanned the deep wooded valley far below. His thoughts returned to the night of the attack when he and his two accomplices had been forced to separate, having been surprised by Ravala's well-planned ambush. But with the distinction of being the fleetest runner among them, he had taken it upon himself to head south alone, before eventually succeeding in drawing the pursuing warriors and their hunting dogs away from the other two.

At the time, he was being pursued, he had often thought that his end was near, but the narrow river he was fortunate enough to have encountered was to prove a merciful ally. Following its shallow waters, he had periodically crossed over from one bank to the other until the well-trained dogs had finally lost all track of his scent. He had then doubled back through the forest in an attempt, to meet up with his accomplices but as yet had found no sign of them and he could only hope that they had made their way safely back to the commune's encampment. Suddenly throwing his head back, Lascal laughed aloud when recalling the bungling ineptitude so often shown by the warriors whom Ravala deployed to exterminate his father's rebellious commune. Ravala's men must have numbered over fifty strong, he reckoned, and yet to have seen them in such confused disarray when he and his accomplices had separated was almost inconceivable. For on making their way to the orchard fields that they had been ordered to destroy, it had been the noise created by one of Ravala's warriors' ponies that had alerted them to the ambush. Even so, it had been a long arduous chase, he reflected in a serious vein, and he was well-aware that the commune would have to show more discretion in the manner by which they struck at their selected targets. For in his obsessive quest to destroy the commune, Ravala had now began to employ their own guerrilla tactics against them.

Throughout the country, it was a well-known fact that the commune's guerrillas were a major thorn in Ravala's side, with the arch-druid himself having granted him a free hand in order to eradicate them. But over many years the bellicose Ravala had failed to accomplish this. As a result, his entire life was now dedicated to that fateful day when he would personally witness the commune's total destruction.

Running down through the tall ferns infesting the steep hillside, Lascal's hair flowed with each step, gleaming like the lustre on a raven's wing. And as he ran, he prayed that the day would soon come when his small commune would find a peaceful existence far from the danger forever threatening them, for ever since his earliest recollections, he and many of the others had known no existence other than a nomadic one.

Reaching the basin of the valley he came to a startled halt on seeing ahead of him a huge brown bear trundling lazily through the trees. Silently he drew his sword but, completely ignoring his presence, the creature passed harmlessly by, leaving him more than relieved to re-sheath the weapon and resume on his way through the dense woodland.

Although weary and hungry, his nimble feet skipped lightly over the thick undergrowth, and by noon he had covered such a good distance that he decided to rest on the grassy verge of a small pond where a family of otters swam undisturbed on its far banks. Saturated in warm sweat, he removed his uncomfortable linen jacket and trousers to hang them up to dry on a branch of a nearby tree with the cool air soon drying his naked body as he gathered edible fungi and roots for a welcome meal.

After eating, and with his sword unsheathed and by his side, he lay hidden among some thick vegetation by the edge of the pond, and in the serene atmosphere, his heavy eyelids quickly fell to take him into a deep and much-needed sleep.

By the time he awoke, the sun had slunk well below the dark leafy treetops, with the pond's motionless surface reflecting the mottled pink sky above. For a little while he was content to lie in such peaceful surroundings. But the sudden fluttering of a lone bird coming from the alder bushes behind him saw him clasp tightly onto the hilt of his sword and, leaping to his feet, he stepped forward. Peering suspiciously into the gloomy ever-threatening forestry, his alert eyes perceived no danger, and strolling over to where his clothing now hung dry, he first dressed before washing his face in the pond's cool waters.

Now invigorated, he continued on his journey before breaking into a fast sprint, stopping only when coming upon an ancient, abandoned quarry that stretched out a good distance ahead of him. Crouching down on the grassy ridge of an overhanging cliff, he spotted through the twilight gloom four of Ravala's warriors camped directly below him; one of their savage hounds glowering menacingly up in his direction. However, in the knowledge that even more warriors might be in the vicinity, he decided to press on through the night. Straightening up, he once again ran off in a northerly direction and, aided by the luminescence of a full moon, soon forgot the dangers that the forest held at night.

With the cold air of the onrushing dawn enveloping him, he was now so exhausted that he had no alternative but to stop and rest. Once more his clothing was drenched in humid sweat, and slumping down against the gnarled trunk of a massive yew tree, he neither bothered to strip to dry off nor to take the precaution of removing his sword from its scabbard. Soon it was bright and sunny and, for a while longer, he sat listening to the sleep inducing tapping of a distant woodpecker. Feeling hungry, he was just about to rise and search for food when he suddenly caught a shadowy figure in the corner of his left eye and diving instinctively to his right, he just succeeded in eluding the powerfully flung spear that whistled past his cowering head. Panic-stricken, and with no idea where the assailant had come from, he desperately stumbled into an upright position, at the same time somehow managing to draw his sword as his warrior opponent ran at him carrying a long-handled battle-axe in one hand and a hunting net poised to enmesh him in the other.

Panting with the unexpected shock, he crouched low to avoid the weighted net swung clumsily at him by the screaming warrior. But the parrying sword stroke he released failed to strike its target, allowing his opponent time to bring the axe across and sink it deep into the top of his left arm, with the blow shattering the bone and causing it to protrude sharply from the torn, ragged flesh. Oblivious to the pain, he staggered to one side and ducked just as the axe once again cut through the air, only this time well above his head. But the ferocious power of the poorly timed blow momentarily unbalanced the cumbersome warrior, granting Lascal enough leeway to speedily lunge and thrust his sword up to embed it deep into the man's broad fleshy diaphragm. Shuddering with the sharp pain, the warrior instantly released the axe to fall heavily backward to the ground, and with his attacker's gaping eyes now stupefied in shock, Lascal's thrashing sword sank mercilessly into the man's unprotected head until he lay quite still. Stumbling backward a searing pain now shot down his badly injured arm, and slumping to his knees he repeatedly cursed himself for his arrogant indifference, knowing only too well that, had he been more alert when resting, such a wound could so easily have been avoided.

Glancing fearfully down at the gory mess, he flung his sword down before laboriously crawling over to the dead man to tear a strip of linen from his torn jacket. Struggling to retain his composure he somehow managed to tie a makeshift tourniquet around the deep gash; thus, preventing any further loss of blood. However, the pain he was now suffering forced him to retch and vomit up what little food remained in his stomach.

Trembling and perspiring heavily from his exertions, he quickly gathered and re-sheathed his sword, and slowly rising to his feet once more began to make his way through the forest. He hadn't travelled far though when he suddenly came upon a long dirt track running north to south and seeing that it would be much easier to walk on rather than through the undergrowth, he decided to follow its northern route. His pace was much slower than it had been, and although his pain had eased a little, it was the paralysis in the fingers of his left hand that began to give him cause for concern. He now sensed that, unless help was soon forthcoming, then either gangrene might set in, and with it, death, or he could at best face the prospect of carrying a withered arm around with him for the rest of his life. Such thoughts terrified him, and warily drawing his sword, and keeping it at the ready, he continued along the seemingly endless path, now fully alert to any danger.

The sun was high as the path led him into a wide clearing pockmarked with small rocks. Although uncertain, he proceeded on, with the absence of oak trees among the surrounding forestry proving to him that the glade was not one of the religious sanctuaries that his father and others of the commune's elders had so often warned him to avoid. Reaching the centre of the glade, he suddenly came to a halt when noticing a rusting circular iron grille covering what appeared to be a wide hole in the ground. Momentarily puzzled, his eyes were then drawn to a long thick rope, coiled up close to the grille, with one end of the rope tied to a wooden stake embedded into the earth. Spinning round, he cautiously scanned the immediate area only to see that nothing stirred, and throwing his sword down, his curiosity impelled him to tug at the heavy grille with his good arm until it slowly began to move. Soon the hole lay partially uncovered and staring down into the black dankness of the pit, Lascal could hardly believe his eyes. In the dim light far below him, he could just make out the naked figure of a crouching man, whose forearm covered his eyes to protect them from the brilliance of the sun's glare.

"Who are you? Why are you imprisoned in such a place?" he asked, but as his voice echoed eerily downwards, the poor figure below made no attempt to reply. Now rising onto his feet, Vescala drew his arm away to shield his eyes with his long, bony fingers. But as Lascal deliberated over the man, he suddenly recalled his father telling him of how the druids sometimes incarcerate their prisoners in such a manner. Spontaneously grabbing hold of the rope, he flung it down to him.

"Grab the end and climb up! I'll help you as much as I can," he shouted down, only for Vescala to just stand as if mesmerised by the order. "Look, you must hurry, now try and climb up," he pleaded, and drawing his hand from his eyes, Vescala first peered at the rope's frayed end before tremulously clutching at it.

As he began the struggle to raise himself, Lascal wondered if the warrior he had just killed had perhaps been some kind of guardian employed to ensure the man's captivity. Slowly and painfully Vescala's skeletal arms and legs strained to pull his emaciated frame up the sheer, slime covered wall confronting him as, bit by bit, Lascal helped him by keeping a strain on the rope with his good arm.

It seemed an eternity before Vescala's black-nailed fingertips clutched at the long grass overlapping the perimeter of the wide pit. And with both men panting and perspiring heavily from their efforts, Lascal released the rope and grabbed hold of the prisoner's long hair to pull him over the edge. As the gasping Vescala staggered onto his unsteady legs, Lascal stood horrified that any human being could have degenerated into such a wasted form. For a few brief moments, he was forced into drawing his eyes away from the man's debauched nakedness; with every bone in his body gruesomely protruding from his yellowish, anaemic looking skin that bore the weal marks of a cruel torture.

"Who are you? How long have you been detained like this?" he asked in a voice ringing with compassion. But ignoring him and making no reply, Vescala swept his dark, hollow eyes around the glade to absorb the long-forgotten beauty of the bountiful surrounding greenery.

"Who are you…you must have a name?" he again asked, only for his question to again go unanswered as Vescala's tearful eyes rose towards the infinite blue heavens. Searching beyond the man's mud-streaked face and long hair and beard, Lascal found it impossible to determine his age, and sensing the horror of the prisoner's long confinement, he felt even more conviction that all the injustices his commune had been fighting to put right were fully legitimate. In the past, he had often wondered about the tales of druidical savagery so frequently related to him around the campfires by his father and the other commune elders. There were times when he had concerns about some of their stories; reckoning them to have been exaggerated, but staring pitifully at the slavering, sub-human wretch, now muttering incoherently towards the sky, he no longer doubted their authenticity. He was now convinced, as never before, that the priesthood was indeed far more evil than any tales relating to their black practices could ever convey. With a heavy heart, he wondered just how many other unfortunates were confined under similar barbaric conditions.

Suddenly Vescala drew back; his penetrating eyes transfixed on the blood saturated bandage so crudely wrapped around Lascal's wound.

"Don't be afraid: I injured my arm in a fight. Now look, I'm going to take you with me," Lascal said calmly. "The commune I belong to has for many years been waging a guerrilla war against the same enemy who have so maltreated and degraded you. Please believe me when I say you have nothing to fear," he said reassuringly as his suspicious eyes darted around the clearing, where everything lay still and silent, with only the branches of the surrounding trees appearing to bow as if acknowledging the universal brutality so reminiscent of mankind! Looking more relaxed, Vescala's cracked and discoloured lips opened as if attempting to speak, only to close again without having uttered any sound. Lascal smiled in the belief that he had gained the man's confidence.

"Come on, let's go," he said picking up the sword before walking briskly towards the northern end of the clearing whereon reaching the cover of the trees, he turned to see Vescala still standing beside the pit he had grown to know so intimately.

"Either come now or remain there forever!" he snarled impatiently; his features now contorted by the discomfort he was suffering. But just as he was about to turn to re-enter the forest, Vescala's pathetic figure began to lope sluggishly towards him.

The track continued to run north, but Lascal was taking no chances. Reckoning that in the event of a search party being sent out to find Vescala, it would be wiser if they travelled deeper into the forest. However, after leaving the track their progress became painfully slow, with the badly suffering Lascal often having to stop and help his companion who was struggling to walk any reasonable distance without stopping to rest.

It was early in the afternoon when they came upon a wide fast-flowing river, and with the tough, angular features of his face now chalk-white from his excruciating pain, Lascal collapsed to the ground; his perspiration-lashed body shivering uncontrollably as his mind fought to stave off the unconsciousness now threatening him. His glazed eyes now saw only a blurred reality, although he was capable of discerning the resinous taste of a small, sturdy twig being thrust between his teeth. For a brief moment, his eyes suddenly cleared to see his companion carefully unravel the soiled bandage from around his gaping and now heavily congealed wound. After taking the bandage down to the river's edge and thoroughly rinsing it out, Vescala returned to wash the wound clean. But, as he began picking the slivers of shattered bone from the open flesh with his long, cracked fingernails, the blinding pain caused Lascal to pass out.

The resetting of the bone proved a difficult task, and on achieving it, Vescala first tore part of the bandage into long thin strips before leaving Lascal to go deep into the forest. After a short time, he returned, carrying with him a handful of comfrey roots and cobwebs. Using Lascal's sword, he then crushed the roots against a flat stone until they had coagulated into a thick paste before placing the cobwebs over the open flesh and then gently smearing the paste over the wound before rebandaging it. He then went over to a lime tree, and then using the sword, cut off a long thin branch that he chopped into three splints. Laying them out the full length of the arm, he quickly tied them into position with the remaining strips of linen.

Lascal came to, feeling groggy, but the first thing to strike him was the fact that he could feel very little pain. Raising his head to look down at his arm, he was stunned to see it so expertly treated, and he was more than relieved to once more, feel the life in the fingers of his hand. Struggling onto his feet, he was surprised to see his companion busily roasting a squirrel over a glowing fire. But Vescala, who had his back to him, never heard Lascal coming up to him.

"I can't thank you enough for what you've done for me, stranger. But I would be even more grateful if I could address you by your name," he said in a controlled, trembling voice, only for his words to be met with silence from Vescala, who kneeling by the fire, split the roasted squirrel he had trapped in two with the sword before handing one of the portions up to him. Seeing no response to his words, Lascal took the food and walking unsteadily back over to the riverbank to eat left his companion to his own thoughts. After eating, but still tired and weak, his desire was to stay put until the morning. However, his instinct told him otherwise, and slowly rising to his feet, he went back over to where Vescala sat staring into space.

"I know you must be tired, but I'm afraid we have no alternative but to leave right away," he said almost apologetically. But once again making no reply, Vescala rose and, with a reluctant nod of agreement, handed the sword back to Lascal.

The river confronting them proved to be mercifully shallow, with the fast-flowing waters only coming up to their thighs, and crossing over with little difficulty they resumed their journey north. As night fell a languid moon painted the forest silver, making it easier for them to stealthily progress towards the site of the commune's encampment. However, to both men, it seemed a lifetime before a mauve-coloured dawn sky replaced the moonlight with the sun's rejuvenating rays. By now they were both physically exhausted, and sensing that they would collapse if they were to continue, Lascal decided that they must sleep, albeit for only a short time.

A thicket of long ferns provided them with a safe refuge, and after a restful sleep, it was Vescala, who was first to awaken. It was warm and sunny now as his eyes transfixed themselves intently on the numerous life forms surrounding him. The rich colours along with the invigorating scent of the blossoms, appeared to carry in their essence an ethereal ecstasy, bringing to him memories of a past that for so long he had denied himself. And with his lungs eagerly consuming the warm humid air, his alert eyes continued to absorb the beautiful forms of the encapsulating scenery for some time before the still weak Lascal eventually awoke.

At his instigation, they immediately resumed their journey; stopping only for a short time to kill, cook and eat an injured fawn that they were fortunate enough to discover hiding in the long grass. It was mid-afternoon when they reached the ancient yew tree where Lascal had expected to find one of the commune's lookouts posted. However, on searching the immediate area he was disappointed to find no one around, and turning to Vescala his eyes conveyed his concern.

"It may be, that my people have been forced to transfer their camp to a safer site. It must mean that there's an enemy force in the vicinity. Let's hope they won't be too difficult to find," he said with a distinct apprehension in his voice as once more they pressed on, only to soon reach the outskirts of the settlement that had lain situated atop the summit of a densely wooded hill. Scaling the steep slope, Lascal fervently prayed that his loved ones weren't lying massacred up at the top. But on reaching the summit he emitted a prolonged sigh of relief when finding no sign of life or indeed anything that might have suggested that the place had recently been inhabited. Convinced that his people had made a peaceful departure, and hadn't been the victims of some surprise attack, he began a search of the small clearing where the camp had been. Eventually, he discovered the pre-arranged sign he was hoping his father had left in the event of the commune's departure. A small white pebble lay in the centre of a patch of grassless earth, and picking it up, he was delighted to see a tiny white feather whose sharp quill pointed to the east. He grinned widely, knowing that it was in the opposite direction to the quill in which they had travelled. After explaining the situation to Vescala, the two men descended the hill and, although still very weary, resumed their journey following a westerly route.

As time passed by the savage conditions underfoot began to sap their remaining strength, but with the deepening twilight of the overcast sky beginning to engulf the endless network of trees, the sudden shout of "Lascal" coming from the shadows behind them saw both startled men spin round. Drawing his sword Lascal pointed it towards the tall figure now emerging from the gloomy trees.

"Put it down, man. Don't you recognise my voice?" the oncoming figure yelled at him.

"Is that you, Aldrun?" Lascal asked, peering furtively at the man's silhouette: Aldrun being one of his father's closest advisors.

"None other," came the reply, and emitting a whoop of delight, Lascal replaced his weapon. "I'm sorry, Lascal, we waited for you as long as we possibly could," Aldrun said through a beaming grin as he walked up to the relieved youth. "Unfortunately, we had a report of a large enemy force nearby so we had no alternative but to move."

"Yes, I reckoned that would be the case. Tell me, how is everyone? My wife, has she missed me?" Lascal asked as Aldrun glanced warily at Vescala.

"Missed you – no one has ever seen a woman so smitten with despair."

But the broad grin on Aldrun's heavily stubbled features quickly turned to a suspicious look as he first glanced down to the splints enmeshing Lascal's arm and then again over to Vescala.

"What happened to your arm?" he asked; his eyes never leaving Vescala. Lascal then explained all that had occurred since the night of the ambush. Placing his arm on Lascal's shoulder, Aldrun turned him away from Vescala.

"Well, firstly, the other two made it back safely," he said in a whisper. "But this stranger you rescued – it could be that he's one of Ravala's many spies. How do you know he can be trusted? After all, you don't know his name, tribe, or indeed what crimes he may have committed."

"He's no spy, Aldrun; take a look at the state he's in," Lascal said tersely, turning to point at Vescala.

"Aye, he looks about as much use to us as a shroud would be in paradise," Aldrun quipped insensitively. Drawing his sword, he went over and pointed its sharp tip directly at Vescala's scrawny throat, "All right, name yourself and your tribe," he sternly demanded as Vescala's wide eyes stared in bewilderment at Lascal. "Where did you learn to treat a wound in such a fashion? Only the druids have these skills," he commented, prodding the tip of the sword against Vescala's throat, and forcing him to stagger timidly back. "Come on, answer! How long were you held in captivity and why?"

"Leave him alone," Lascal insisted. "Can't you see, Aldrun, that this man is no more than yet another victim of their tyranny?"

Now feeling a little sympathy towards the cowering figure before him, Aldrun lowered the sword and replaced it in its scabbard. "Let's hope your judgment's right, Lascal, but tomorrow we will make him talk one way or another. When he does your father will have the final decision as to his fate."

Removing his long cloak Aldrun ordered Vescala to put it on before leading them through the forest.

Total darkness had fallen by the time they reached the settlement, where everyone, with the exception of the camp guards, had retired for the night, and leaving the other two, Lascal was only too happy to enter his own family's tent and surprise the moping Silena.

Aldrun then escorted Vescala to his own tent, and after lighting the tallow lamp and then taking his cloak back, he gave the stranger some of his spare clothing along with a little food before leaving him to rest for the night. However, prior to re-entering the forest to resume his own guard duty, he commanded the camp guards to watch the new arrival very carefully.

Having eaten the succulent cold beef, Vescala then dressed for the first time since his trial. Lying down on the mat of rushes that served as Aldrun's bed, he looked around the small hide tent before extinguishing the flame that burned with a sweet smell of incense in the clay dish at his side. Warm and comfortable for the first time in many years, he closed his heavy eyelids only to feel his embittered soul stir as his mind attempted to understand the amazing events of the past two days. Soon a true sleep fell upon him, blessed in a reposed peace by the universal hand of love that guides for eternity the inspirational truth of what was now to Vescala a truly embryonic freedom.

Chapter Seventeen

The broad, slanted deerskin tent stretched taut above their heads granted the leader of the commune's family ample protection against the rain teeming down outside. Meanwhile, inside, Lascal's mother, with her baby daughter strapped to her back, sat in front of the fire eating in quick snatches from the hind leg of a roasted squirrel.

"Mother, I've already explained to you that I'm convinced that this man is not one of Ravala's spies. Wait till you see him! The man's wasted body bears the scars of a long, sadistic oppression," Lascal remarked convincingly, only for his mother Elliana, her features troubled to merely shrug at his words. Holding onto his injured arm, he then stepped past the fire and over to the tent's open entrance where staring aimlessly at the early morning downpour, he tried to imagine the atrocious conditions that must have prevailed in the deep pit.

"You certainly seem to have convinced yourself that this stranger can be trusted. I'm not so sure one as young as you can determine that," she then replied in a chastising manner as Lascal sighed.

"Yes, I have to admit that for any individual to have survived for even a short time in such a place is difficult to believe…I have the impression that this man had been imprisoned for years."

"Yes, and that fact alone aroused my suspicions," Elliana exclaimed. "You don't know what crimes he may have committed. Anyway, your father will interrogate him thoroughly when he returns. If he's satisfied that this man is yet another innocent victim of druid injustice, we will welcome him into the commune with open arms," she said as Lascal suddenly spotted a rain-sodden and weary looking Aldrun loping towards the tent.

"Silena, prepare a meal for Aldrun, he looks as if he needs it," he commanded, turning to his wife who sat by her mother-in-law's side. Putting down her plate, Silena quickly ladled a generous helping of warm stew and gravy from the cauldron over the fire into a wooden bowl. As Aldrun entered the tent Lascal helped him off with his cloak.

"I'll be dammed glad when my stint of guard duty is over; that bastard thunder god must have pissed a flash flood last night," Aldrun commented, grabbing the welcome meal from Silena's outstretched arms, and sitting down beside Elliana, he greedily shovelled the food into his mouth with his fingers, leaving Silena to resume her own meal.

"You should be grateful, Aldrun; the bastard might have shit," Lascal quipped cheerfully. As everyone laughed, the noise awoke Elliana's infant who on unstrapping the child from the harness on her back, then loosened the ties on the front of her dress to begin breastfeeding her.

"Have you checked on our new addition yet, Aldrun?" she enquired.

"No, not yet, but I took the precaution of having him closely guarded."

"What's your opinion of him?"

"Well, your son seems to think he's genuine enough…I'm not so sure though; his expertise in treating Lascal's wound aroused my suspicions. As you know Elliana it's normally only the druids who have such skills. He certainly looks as if he's been through hell though. Nonetheless, I feel we have to be cautious. Ravala's too cunning to underestimate. It's not improbable that this man could be one of his undercover agents."

"Yes, I agree, Lascal would do well to remember the way Ravala tortured and then beheaded his elder brother."

Aldrun nodded in agreement, but having finished her breakfast Silena put her plate down and joined Lascal, who placed his good arm around her slender waist.

"If my husband trusts this stranger, then so do I," she remarked haughtily as Lascal gently kissed the side of her head.

"When is my father expected to return?" he then asked Aldrun.

"Today or tomorrow; at the moment he's meeting our informant. We can only hope he's managed to obtain some news regarding Ravala's movements. Let's face it; we don't want to shift camp again, especially in this damned weather."

"Why don't they leave us alone? How can two hundred poverty-stricken and ill-equipped peasants be any threat to them?" a dewy-eyed Elliana asked, looking down at her child.

"They will never leave us in peace!" Aldrun exclaimed venomously. "As long as just one member of this commune remains alive, he will remain a threat to the recalcitrant druids and their bloodthirsty masters. I'm afraid we're doomed to live in a state of impermanence until such time as there is a full-scale national rebellion against their evil ways," he said, staring wildly into his now-empty bowl. Like every other member of the commune, Aldrun had good reason to despise the priesthood, with the memory of his slain wife and child still as fresh in his mind as if they had died only yesterday.

"Anyway, thanks for the meal. I'll leave you now and hopefully snatch some sleep," he said, rising to his feet and handing the empty bowl back to Silena.

"Hold on, Aldrun," Lascal said, going over to a pile of dry clothing. "Here, you can borrow my cloak: Silena can dry yours by the fire. I'll bring it along to you later."

Donning the cloak, Aldrun thanked him as Lascal watched sadly from the entrance as he began running towards his own tent, which lay apart from the others.

"I think he hates the druids more than the rest of us put together," Silena remarked, and laying the bowl down she spread the wet cloak out in front of the fire.

"He has every reason to hate them," Lascal replied sternly. "Some years, ago his wife tragically gave birth to a mentally retarded child; the malady going undetected until the child was into his third summer. When the priestesses came to take him, his wife naturally enough refused to surrender him to what she knew would be a sacrificial death. Aldrun, who had been away on a hunting trip, returned home to be informed that both of them had been burned alive in the monstrous wicker images they erect to celebrate the arrival of the spring season."

"How did the druids discover the child's condition?" Silena asked.

"Apparently one of his wife's former suitors told them, whether through spite or jealousy, I don't know. Anyway, on hearing of his family's fate, Aldrun killed the man responsible and then the first two priests he laid his hands on. Afterward, he escaped into the forest to eventually join up with us."

"How can anyone even contemplate taking the life of such a child and justify the crime in the name of some god?" a horrified Silena then asked.

"Simple! To the druids, such a child is imperfect, with the deformity seen as a reflection of tribal behaviour. As an act of appeasement to their gods, he or she must be sacrificed. The same insane law also applies to the animal and plant kingdoms; indeed, according to the druids, nothing must be eaten or even touched if it is in any way unclean. By that, I include physical imperfection. Still, we all know that this law doesn't apply to their ruling classes, Ravala's living proof of that," Lascal added through a sneer, and for a little while longer he sat talking to his mother, leaving Silena to clean the breakfast dishes.

By mid-morning the rain had ceased, and taking his leave of the two women, Lascal grabbed Aldrun's now dry cloak. Leaving the tent, he headed through the long, wet grass towards Aldrun's abode. However, he was only halfway there when he was forced to stop and explain to the many delighted well-wishers who surrounded him how he had managed to elude Ravala's warriors. Eventually managing to get away from the throng, he approached the tent where a lone guard stood maintaining a silent vigil.

"Did the newcomer give you any trouble through the night?" he enquired, walking up to the man.

"No, none, he slept right through until Aldrun returned. I was told to remain at my post while Aldrun slept. It's great seeing you back, Lascal," the guard replied, offering him his handshake. Reciprocating the gesture, Lascal then entered the tent to find Aldrun lying fast asleep on the mat of rushes, while a now fully clothed Vescala sat beside the small charcoal fire supping from a bowlful of warm broth. Vescala's appearance was much tidier now and although the clothing hung loosely on his thin body, it was the transformation in his facial features that took Lascal by surprise, with the man having washed and trimmed his long hair and beard. Even so, his pale, sunken features appeared to Lascal to emphasise an acute loneliness lurking behind his dark, piercing eyes. Staring down at him he wondered as to what mysteries lay in his past.

"Now listen carefully to me, stranger!" he exclaimed forcefully. "If you are to remain here with us, we have to know who you are and what crime you committed, if indeed you committed any crime. I must warn you that you are regarded as a possible spy, and should you fail to satisfy my father as to your true identity, there's no way I can guarantee your safety."

Staring up at Lascal, Vescala gave a feeble nod as his lips broke into a narrow grimace, but still, he made no attempt to break his silence.

"Why are you so reluctant to talk? We only wish to be your friends," Lascal said, pointing to Aldrun. "Over many years, we in this commune have also experienced great suffering; indeed, take the man who lies sleeping and who fed and clothed you. The druids burnt his wife and child alive! Believe me, there are numerous other examples of their evil among us," Lascal said; his voice pleading for a response.

But finishing the broth, Vescala remained silent as his solemn eyes lowered to stare into the hot embers of the blood-red fire. Lascal sighed dejectedly, and after some time had elapsed in which neither man spoke, Aldrun awoke. Aldrun was an abrasive character aged around thirty-five years, tall and powerfully developed with craggy pock-marked facial features that seemed to emphasise the pain of his intensely felt loneliness. Over the passing years since the deaths of his wife and child – whom he had worshipped – a terminal hatred had grown in his soul, leaving him with an insatiable appetite to inflict vengeance against the druids or anyone even remotely associated with them. This he more than exploited when taking part in the commune's incessant guerrilla raids against the authorities. Rubbing his stubby fingers through his thick mane of long black hair, he somewhat reluctantly raised himself from his bed and stumbling wearily over to the suspended water bucket he splashed his face thoroughly as if trying to cleanse himself from the horrors that forever haunted his nightmares. "What time is it, Lascal?" he asked, drying himself on a hanging rag.

"It's a little before noon; you haven't slept very long."

"No, I haven't had a decent sleep since…" Aldrun's reply tapered off into a confused mumbling. Sensing his distress Lascal changed the subject and sat down by the fire.

"Did my father say how long we might expect to be staying here?"

"No, but he should have a good idea when he returns," Aldrun answered ambiguously. "This army that is searching for us, Lascal, apparently it now stands over four hundred strong and rumour has it that these numbers are to be increased. If only we could raise a similar number. Think about it; we could then meet our enemy and defeat them in open conflict. Once successful, the peasants would flock to us in their thousands instead of the handful of escapee slaves and so-called criminals who comprise our present commune. Let's be honest, as things stand, burning crops and granaries and stealing what food and clothing we need to survive has only succeeded in ostracising us from the peasant masses. I'll tell you this Lascal, some of these fools actually believe our raids to be the work of evil spirits who manifest themselves into human form in order to punish them for failing to show total obedience to the druids. No, I feel we must begin striking at the viper's throat rather than prick at its tail. If we started to assassinate tribal kings and members of the inner council of druids instead of unimportant nobles and local priests, then and only then will the peasants begin to show any respect for our cause."

"I disagree, Aldrun," Lascal said with a shake of his head. "My father's well aware that the highest placed in our lands are too well protected. As we are at the moment, we would never get near enough to scare them, never mind assassinate them."

Aldrun sat down by the fire, undaunted by Lascal's outright rejection of his proposals.

"I have the greatest respect for your father, Lascal, but I think that even he, brave as he undoubtedly is, senses that in the long term our cause is futile. No, if we are to overthrow these bastards, then we must do as I've suggested. I feel it might be wiser if we were to split the commune and operate in smaller well-dispersed units; that way we could hide a damn sight easier and cover a far wider area. Think about it, Lascal. At the moment we have some…" Aldrun was about to say that they had seventy capable fighting men but, suspicious of Vescala, he bit his tongue. But now looking thoroughly bored, Lascal stared down into the fire having too often in the past listened to Aldrun's persistent disagreements over his father's tactics.

"My father would never agree with you Aldrun; anyway, we're not alone in our struggle. Although we may be the largest single group of dissidents, there are others; this we know from the reports given to us by our informants."

Suddenly their conversation was interrupted as the guard came rushing in through the entrance.

"Lascal, your fathers just returned. He wants the three of you to report to his tent right away," the man stated. Lascal and Aldrun immediately jumped to their feet, and after helping the unsteady Vescala up they left the tent, only to have to force their way through the inquisitive crowd who had gathered to obtain a glimpse of the new arrival.

Meanwhile, Silena and Elliana – with her child once more strapped to her back – had already left the main tent, having been ordered out to allow the interrogation to take place. Leaving the guard outside to contend with the crowd, the three men entered the tent with Lascal quickly pulling the bearskin cover back over the entrance. However, to the astounded Brenas, who stood by the fire, it was as if a phantom had suddenly appeared. Staggering back, his stunned eyes could hardly believe the presence of the tragic figure now standing before him. Suddenly Vescala jerked forward.

"Ca…can it really be you, Brenas? O…or am I consigned to spend eternity in a land of the living dead?" Vescala's hoarse voice cried out in disbelief, leaving the flummoxed Lascal and Aldrun utterly confounded at his words. But after quickly composing himself by drawing in a deep breath, Brenas rushed over to the gaunt Vescala, and with his tear-filled eyes reflecting a true sorrow, he placed his hands firmly on his old friend's bony shoulders.

"Yes, Vescala it's me," he proclaimed in a whisper. But almost numbed by the shock confrontation, Vescala slumped to his knees and wept.

"I've spent an eternity in a living hell, Brenas. How is it that you stand before me when I was told of your death so long ago?" he asked, recalling the terrible events of a past that had so nearly destroyed both their destinies.

"Father, this surely can't be the novitiate druid?" Lascal enquired meekly, as he and Aldrun then helped Vescala back onto his feet.

"Yes, son, and it's fifteen years since I last saw him being dragged along the Caledonian shoreline. Ever since that day, I've lived with the shame that I failed to help him in the time of his greatest need."

"How could any man have possibly survived for so long in the conditions he was forced to endure?" Lascal asked, noticing the remorse now prominent on his father's features. But wiping the tears from his eyes, Brenas smiled at Vescala.

"Yes, Lascal, your mother told me about the pit. But you have heard me speak of this man on many occasions and believe me, all that I said of him was true. He's living proof of man's struggle for a just, honest, and decent society."

"And to think I suspected him of being one of Ravala's spies," Aldrun said through a wry smile, chiding himself at his mistrusting nature.

"Ravala!" Vescala yelled; his wide eyes blazing angrily at the mention of the name.

"Yes, your old adversary," Brenas remarked, frowning. "Except now he's a far more cunning enemy than he ever was in the past. But for the moment we don't have to worry about him; we have too much to discuss. Come and be seated by the fire: Lascal, go and fetch your mother and tell her and everyone you meet of this remarkable reunion," he commanded, unable to disguise his pleasure as he and Aldrun then helped Vescala over to sit him down on the log by the fire. Although mentally disoriented, Vescala suddenly experienced an exhilarating happiness bursting into his soul, for to be among friends when for so many years he had known only a vehement hostility was almost unbearable.

"Tell me, my old friend, what became of the virtuous Delancia?" Brenas asked sympathetically. But the question saw Vescala shudder violently as his eyes clouded over, and staring deep into the blazing fire he saw in its flames a barrier within his mind; a sinister, dark psychological blockage that somehow refused to allow him to acknowledge certain events in his past.

"She died, Brenas," he answered in a soft whisper. "She died: I cannot recall when, where, or how. All I know is…she died."

Noticing the apparent distress on his face, Brenas sighed and bowed his head.

"When we separated all those long years ago, I had, after a time, managed to obtain a small raft on which I put to sea. From offshore I well remember seeing you being dragged along the beach. I was on my way to pick you and Delancia up. Had I returned to shore I might have succeeded in rescuing at least yourself. To put it bluntly, I was afraid! In all humility I now ask for your forgiveness," Brenas pleaded, and for the first time since his rescue, Vescala smiled.

"Ease your conscience, Brenas. If you remember, the unwise decision to separate was entirely mine," he declared warmly. "There is nothing to forgive. At the time no man could have done more to help Delancia and myself than you did; indeed, you risked your life on more than one occasion. Perhaps a fate was decreed for us that we never understood either then or even now."

"Did they keep you in the pit all the time?"

"Yes, mostly," Vescala replied, reflecting on the fact that he was now thirty-four years old. For over his dark oppressive years, he had lost all track of time. "Oh, but the druids saw to it that I was kept closer to death than life. You see the priesthood never kills one of its initiated. To the best of my knowledge, I was removed from the pit on only four occasions, and then only because I was desperately ill. After recovering, I always returned to it. At the very beginning, after the druids had tried and sentenced me, I attempted suicide either by strangling myself with the winter clothing I had been given or by eating the slime clinging to the pit's dank walls. But whenever I tried to end it all the tiniest of golden wrens would uncannily fly into my prison through the gaps in the grille separating me from the outside world. As the long weary years slowly elapsed, its timely appearance, alongside the distant and inspirational bird songs floating down to me from the surrounding forestry became my sole friend and comforter. Even now, I find it all very strange simply because my lone companion is, owing to its size and great wisdom, classified by the druids as being sacred. It was as if death itself had somehow mysteriously refused to acknowledge my existence."

"Indeed, death did, Vescala!" an amazed Brenas exclaimed. "You see, the day Lascal rescued you just happened to be the first day of the month of the golden wren! But your existence over these long punishing years must have been a true hell?"

"It was, Brenas; indeed, hell would be paradise in comparison. But tell me, what became of you over my dark fruitless years of confinement?"

Warming his hands by the fire, Brenas momentarily hesitated to tell his own story. Although he had changed little over the interceding years, Vescala noticed a few wrinkles around his eyes along with the scattered grey streaks in his sleek hair where before there had been none.

"When I saw what I then considered to be your hopeless position, I raised the raft's sail and set course for Europe. To this day I've no idea how long I remained at sea. But every terror a man could experience followed me, as I was swept along in conditions so savage that I frequently prayed for a merciful death. I survived by feeding on an injured seabird that I was lucky enough to catch when it landed on the raft, and by cupping in my hands and drinking the plentiful supply of rainwater that fell. One day, when I was close to death from cold and hunger, I spotted on the horizon what I was later to discover, to be the long, dark coastline of the Germanic provinces. In my exhausted condition, I somehow managed to beach the raft before collapsing among some rocks up from the shore. The following day, I was found by an elderly farmer and his wife who occupied a small homestead just inland and then fed, nursed, and sheltered me. After regaining my strength, I remained with them for well over a year, working for my keep by tending to their animals and helping them in their fields. Over many months, I was soon to obtain a fluent knowledge of the Germanic tongue and, during that long, hot summer's windless days, I was to experience, for the first time in my life, the true meaning of liberty. In the period of time that I lived alongside these kind people, I was never once questioned about my past or where I had come from; indeed, they treated me almost like a son. Even when I met one of their holy men, he made no mention of my facial scar. These were happy times for me Vescala, but as there is peace, so there exists war! One cold autumn morning, the old man informed me that all able-bodied men were to report to the nearest township to make preparations to defend the land against an imminent Roman invasion." Brenas paused, and as the memory of that time swept into his mind, his eyes narrowed to momentarily shrink into his head. Vescala, however, was enthralled by his story and urged him to continue.

"I suppose, I could have absconded, but I felt duty bound to repay them for the wonderful hospitality they had shown me and so I went. I was then armed with a shield, sword, and spear, and along with some five hundred or so others, who comprised our small army, we marched for five days before entering into a dense conifer forest where we met the Romans in open conflict. As you no doubt can imagine, Vescala, it was a bloody massacre. Our leaders had told us that to engage them in forest conditions would suit us more than them. But I'm afraid compared, to theirs, our battle expertise was non-existent, and although the opposing forces were evenly matched numerically as well as in terms of courage. They seemed to have three men to every one of ours. However, I was one of the lucky ones and was taken prisoner alongside a few of the others who had survived the battle. After a few months held in captivity, we were then marched overland in a gruelling journey, to the mighty city of imperial Rome itself. I can assure you, Vescala, when we entered Rome and witnessed such vast, ornately constructed stone buildings and monuments, it was an experience that no man could ever forget. Although I detested the Romans themselves, I had to admire the human ingenuity that had conceived, organised, and erected such a supreme citadel. But then, standing in the forum alongside my fellow prisoners, I looked down at the chains binding my wrists and ankles, recalling your words that all such empires are built on greed, extortion, and injustice! We were then sold off as slaves, with each of us having had placed around his neck a clay tablet bearing his master's insignia. For the second time in my life, I was to experience the insidious process of spiritual deterioration!

Later on, we were transported to the coast, and shipped over the sea to a silver mine situated in southern Spain. There, we were put to work underground hewing the ore from the rock with no more than a blunt pickaxe and shovel for tools. Our guards were true tormentors, ever eager to use their lashes on our backs, and in the murderous time I spent in that hellish place, I must have seen hundreds drop dead from overwork and starvation. Our lives were easily expendable; the average life expectancy being little more than a year with fresh batches of slaves being brought in every few months to maintain productivity and thus ensure the merchants' profits.

One day by good fortune, four of us accidentally tunnelled our way through to an old abandoned mineshaft. We succeeded in keeping our discovery from the guards by refilling the entrance to the shaft, and after deciding to escape it took us many days before we found an opportune moment. When we again broke through to the disused shaft the draught from the inrushing air extinguished our lamps, leaving us in total darkness. The shaft itself was low and narrow, and crawling along on our hands and knees we began to grope our way toward the source of the fresh air. We hadn't gone far though, when the passageway dipped sharply, leading us into deep water that came up to our chests. But even that, alongside the fearsome blackness, failed to deter us as we floundered and groped our way along in a claustrophobic terror where it seemed as if time itself had ceased to exist. Two of the others in the group came from the Rhinelands, with the other member coming from Greece. However, as the shaft began to rise, and just as we reached dry ground, the Greek collapsed and died from his exertions. Sadly, we had no alternative but to leave him behind in that terrible place with the three of us then proceeding on until eventually the ground in front of us began to rise quite steeply. Believe me, Vescala, when I first glimpsed that tiny pinpoint of light ahead of us, I think it was the finest moment of my life! As we struggled on upwards towards that shimmering glimmer of freedom, I swore, and reaffirm it now, that never again would I be enslaved to any man or system. Tired and hungry, we first had to widen the tiny opening with our bare hands before we succeeded in breaking through to the grassy surface. Our next objective was to seek a safe refuge, which we found in a forest not far from our point of escape. There, we managed to remove our bronze manacles by laboriously striking at them with sharp granite rocks. Afterward, we travelled only at night, living off the land, and some six months later, and after many narrow escapes from the authorities, eventually reached Gaul where the three of us separated. The other two wanted me to go back with them to the northern part of the Rhinelands, which was still free from Roman occupation, but for some inexplicable reason, I decided to return to my native land. By the time I had made the channel crossing over from Gaul on the crude raft that I constructed, I had been away for just over five years. However, there I was a tribeless renegade wanted by my own authorities and never envisaging for a moment that one day I would be the leader of a guerrilla force. Anyway, for a few months afterward, I remained as a recluse, hiding in the great forests, until one day ten years ago I came upon a small group of people who, like myself, were classified as social outcasts. Among these people who at that time numbered a mere twenty-eight strong, was a woman named Elliana. With the passing months, we were to fall in love, and ever since have lived as husband and wife." Suddenly Brenas paused, and bearing a contented smile, he rose to his feet. "But it may be, my old friend, that you know her!" he exclaimed, pointing to the tent's now open entrance where Elliana stood beside her son Lascal and his wife. Turning his head to the entrance, Vescala rose slowly only to be astonished to set eyes upon the enchanting woman whom he had rescued when, as a young novitiate priest, he had returned from the sacred island.

For a few moments, Elliana likewise stood stunned. Suddenly she dashed over to hold Vescala's thin face in her trembling hands.

"My son told me of a miracle, but a reunion such as this is beyond all understanding," she sang out in an emotional voice, searching pitifully into the eyes of the man who so many years before had undeniably saved her life. Vescala though, could only stare back at her, utterly confounded by the strange manner in which fate had manipulated their lives. Although he found her to be a lot older looking; the hardship of the long years spent in the forest having taken their toll on her former beauty, he once again sensed the purity that appeared to emanate from her radiant eyes. Drawing her hands away, Elliana brushed the droplets of tears from her cheeks, and going over to Brenas she placed her arm around his waist.

"When I first met my husband Brenas, the first act he undertook was to rescue and unite me with my two sons, who you might remember were taken from me."

Vescala nodded as she pointed to Lascal, who stood hugging Silena.

"Lascal is my youngest son and my husband's stepson. Unfortunately, just over a year ago my eldest son was captured and put to death by Ravala; nonetheless, Vescala I owe you so much. Ever since we first met, Brenas and I have often discussed the unknown novitiate priest who had rescued me. Until now, we were never certain if it had been you or some other who had acted so gallantly. My surviving son Lascal and the child I carry on my back are living proof of my eternal gratitude to you."

"Yes, Vescala, my daughter," Brenas declared proudly through a broad grin. Vescala smiled; in the excitement, he had failed to notice the tiny bundle strapped onto Elliana's back.

"How ironic, Lascal, that I should first rescue your mother and then all these years later you should do the same for me. I can find no words to describe...."

As Vescala hesitated over his choice of words, Brenas laughed aloud, and taking hold of a small keg of wine lying in the corner of the tent, he began to fill the drinking vessels quickly produced by Lascal.

"Let's celebrate, old friend, and let's pray that the future is as happy as this incredible reunion. To the future," he toasted, handing one of the cups to Vescala who raised it to each of them in turn.

Seated around the fire, the tent's occupants talked for the rest of the afternoon of the many adventures that had befallen them over Vescala's lost years. However, by the early evening Aldrun, who was as delighted by events as the others, decided it was now time to turn their attention as to Ravala's whereabouts.

"What news from the informant?" he then asked Brenas.

"Well, for the time being, our position looks reasonably secure. Apparently, he's moved southwest at the head of an army now numbering some four hundred strong. As a precaution, I've doubled the camp guard and placed them further from the camp than is normal."

"Good. At least it gives us more time to organise our next attack. Did you obtain any information as to how Ravala succeeded in aborting Lascal's raid?"

"No. Like myself, he reckoned they were spotted by one of Ravala's spies when Lascal foolishly decided to cut across open countryside rather than take the longer route and keep to the forest's edge."

Lascal bowed his head morosely at the rebuke. However, Vescala was now anxious to know everything about the commune's activities.

"This informant, Brenas, how reliable is he?"

"The best…I knew him when he was a peasant farmer and I a trustee slave. He inherited a small homestead on his master's death, which he successfully expanded. He's now one of his village elders and is in an excellent position to monitor Ravala's movements. In doing this for us, and at great risk to his own life I might add, he's saved us on a number of occasions. We're lucky to have such a friend, although I must confess, I would prefer to see some of his kinsmen take up arms against Ravala and his druid paymasters."

"Yes," Vescala agreed, lowering his eyes dolefully. "I suppose that fear alone is Ravala's greatest ally. That's a fact the bastard's sure to revel in. Still, Brenas, ten years is a long time to be running."

"Yes, up until now we've been fortunate in having kept one step ahead of the authorities. One day, though, I fear our luck will run out. If that day ever arrives, we can expect no mercy. I don't suppose they would spare even the youngest of our children," he proclaimed, looking fearfully at his slumbering daughter. Vescala nodded, knowing full well that Ravala would butcher them all without pity.

"Tell me, Brenas, where was Lascal going when he was ambushed?"

"I had sent him south with two others to destroy as many crops as they could. We never despatch more than a squad of four, at least not since the night Lascal's brother and seven others were ambushed and killed. But I'm afraid that particular blunder was a classic example of overconfidence on my part."

"No, you weren't to blame!" Elliana exclaimed, glancing sympathetically at her husband. "Had my son heeded your advice, instead of trying to rescue the slaves constructing the hill fort, he and the others would be alive today."

Seeing his wife's distress, Brenas felt it prudent to change the subject.

"Tell me, Vescala, do you remember the day when we talked of building a seaworthy craft and escaping to a far distant land of peace and plenty?"

Vescala nodded and smiled; it was a dream he had constantly envisioned in the nightmare of the pit.

"You know, Vescala, I have often lain awake at night thinking about that elemental land. If it does exist, I fear it is the only place on earth where our commune could find a truly safe refuge."

"Perhaps, Brenas. Failing that, I think Ireland would be the only other alternative; regrettably, though, even there the druid web exists."

At Vescala's statement, Aldrun's wide eyes showed the hatred of a disturbed mind.

"What the hell's the point in running?" he shouted abrasively. "You must surely know by now, Vescala, that dreams never materialise. Only by swimming upstream against a torrent of druid blood will we ever find the peace and plenty you men speak idly of."

"And how many of us must drown in pools of our own innocent blood?" Everyone was taken aback at the fury in Elliana's question, but undeterred she continued. "My husband has spoken to me many times of the voyage over the great ocean that he and Vescala once hoped to make. I can think of no finer dream to pursue than that. I, for one, am sick and tired of forever running and hiding in the forest's shadows, always having to look over our shoulders. More than anything, all I want, is a small place to call our own. A place – and I don't care where – to raise our child without having to worry every night as to whether or not we will see the dawn of another day. I've heard you before, Aldrun, going on about sending kings and priests to join their ancestors, but remember when one of them dies he is all too easily replaced. But tell me, just how many of our irreplaceable men have to die in order to kill just one king?"

With his pride having been dented by Elliana's scalding words Aldrun threw his cup to the ground and stormed, red-faced out of the tent.

"Yes, it's true that we once discussed such a journey, but we were much younger then and fired with the spirit of adventure," Vescala said softly to Elliana, whose anger quickly subsided.

"Oh, I realise that such a venture is impossible," she replied through a melancholy sigh. "But there are times when Aldrun infuriates me! Revolution and revenge don't interest the majority of us. If that hothead had his way he would lead us into mass slaughter. He's far too full of personal vengeance to see the situation in its true light. You must understand, Vescala, some among us have lived like this for nearly sixteen years. Are we to be expected to go on living like animals for the rest of our lives? No! I would rather give Ireland a try than stay in this country any longer. Even if we were to experience only a few years of true freedom before being discovered, it would be to my mind, almost worth a premature death." Elliana spoke with a powerful despair prevalent in her voice, and raising his eyebrows, Vescala stared thoughtfully at Brenas.

"As I see it, Brenas, it appears as if your commune is afflicted by a dilemma to which you may have no answer," he commented. And as in the past Brenas was more than interested in what his old friend had to say.

"Go on, Vescala."

"It's like this: stay in these islands and you're doomed to hide like bats in daytime, perhaps forever. If, somehow, you were to get over to Ireland you would certainly embrace freedom. But for how long? A day, a month, a year, or two perhaps? But you would be forced to live with the lingering torment that, one day you might be discovered. There again you could always try Roman-occupied Europe where you would doubtless survive. However, going by your own experience, Brenas, it's almost a foregone conclusion that your people would live and die in bondage." Vescala paused as his eyes darted to Elliana: "I appreciate only too well that sixteen years is akin to a life sentence, Elliana. You once told me that there were no gods, however, I can't agree, my years in the pit convinced me otherwise. You must rekindle the glow of belief that I sense still exists in your heart. Oh, I don't mean credence to the inert demons that, through the priesthood's instruction, have devoured our true faith since infancy. I speak of the undeniable hope that our existence is held sacrosanct by the life force that gave us creation – one universal god of love: I firmly believe that men and women are born to create their own destinies, and if you so desire, then the journey to another land may yet become a possibility."

"Excuse my ignorance, Vescala, but to even consider leaving this country is pointless!" Lascal exclaimed. "Fifteen years ago, there were only two of you. Now there are some two hundred of us. I think our people would sooner face the danger they're familiar with than travel into the unknown where the risks are incalculable."

Feeling as if he had spoken out of turn, Vescala grinned. "You're right Lascal; perhaps it's the wine going to my head…I'm not used to it you know," he jokingly retorted as everyone laughed. "However, Lascal, it may well be that the forever-open eye of a man's soul has to see beyond unimagined dimensions if we are to free ourselves from the stagnant scourge of the persecuting injustice that you yourselves have for so long endured." As Vescala paused, there was a lengthy silence between the tent's occupants with Silena rising to replenish the drinking vessels.

"I think I understand your motivation but…"

"No, Lascal, I don't think you do," Vescala replied, blatantly interrupting him. "Now let me relate to you a story. The first time I was ever removed from the pit was when I was close to death while suffering from a raging fever. As I've already stated to your father, my punishment was that I should not die, and so I was taken to the surface to be treated below the surrounding trees. Early one morning, I regained full consciousness only for my eyes to focus on the beautiful sight of a pair of blue tits, perched on a leafy branch above me and teaching one of their young chicks to fly. The sight so inspired me that, when I was returned to my isolation, I composed a small poem, which I entitled simply "Freedom." Vescala then proceeded to recite his poem.

> *"On crooked bough in leafy lair,*
> *Protected by paternal care,*
> *A fledgling in tremulous hope relies,*
> *But courage it timidly denies!*
> *And seeing it falter the parent cries,*
> *Rejecting fears eternal lies,*
> *And wings of fluff attack the skies!"*

"Tell me, Lascal, is this commune not unlike that tiny uncertain fledgling who with one courageous leap obtained forever, its freedom and independence?"

Lascal though remained unimpressed. "My father told me before of this journey the two of you once considered. But how can we even think of such a voyage when we have no vessel large enough to carry our numbers? Supposing we had, who among us has the skill to navigate us to…any destination?" he asked as Vescala stared firmly at him.

"No doubt Brenas told you about the coastal town of Iscal?" he enquired of Lascal, who nodded. "I don't know if trade was ever resumed with the Roman provinces. If it was great merchant galleys were frequently berthed in its harbour."

"Yes, it was," Brenas stated. "When I returned from Gaul, I was to see two of their ships sailing southwest towards our coast. Anyway, it wasn't so long ago, when on one of our raids, we stole some quality wine. As you know, Vescala, such a wine has always had to be imported."

"That's right, Brenas. Well, Lascal, let's assume a ship could be obtained. All you would then require would be seeds, farming equipment, tools, weapons; indeed, enough equipment to create an affluent settlement and to cultivate the crops you would plant in a new territory."

"And what would we eat on such a voyage?" Lascal asked, sounding sarcastic at such a far-fetched discussion.

"Obviously, the ship would have to carry food. Don't forget, your father crossed the North Sea single-handed, and look how he survived. You would get fresh water from the rain, and an ocean the size of the Atlantic must surely, provide you with an ample supply of fresh fish."

"Alright, then who navigates? There must be few seamen, with either the fortitude or stupidity to embark upon such a voyage."

"The man who already navigates such a ship will go anywhere with a dagger at his throat," Vescala replied as Lascal smirked.

"And what become of the slaves who I've heard man the galley oars? Do we use their services?"

"No! You first steal a ship and then sail it round the coast to a predetermined point where you release the slaves before shipping aboard your own people and the supplies."

"So, we merely place these slaves back into a counterfeit existence? The very same miserable existence from which we ourselves, are running?"

"Look!" Vescala exclaimed, growing tired of Lascal's sarcasm. "It's certainly not for me to say whether you should or shouldn't embark on such a venture, but don't you think it might be a good idea to make contingency plans in the event of a dangerous situation arising, a situation that could well see your entire commune annihilated."

Leaning forward, Brenas put his cup down.

"You must admit, Lascal, the idea makes good sense. With such a ship we could go anywhere. Don't forget ten years ago when our guerrilla campaign was first launched, Ravala, who was ordered, by his king to find and destroy us, had only a handful of warriors under his command; now he commands four hundred. With each passing day, the chances of him finding us must be increasing, but with a ship in our possession, no one could ever hunt us. None of the coastal tribes in these islands have ships the size of these Roman galleys. Believe me, son, I've seen them."

"I think the idea's brilliant. After all, what have we to lose?" Elliana commented, only for her son to shrug nonchalantly.

"I, too, am tired of running, mother," Lascal said as his eyes darted back to Vescala. "But like Aldrun, I would sooner stay, and fight for our freedom. Anyway, the whole idea's hypothetical."

"No, Lascal, you're wrong," Brenas said forcefully. "As leader of the commune, I propose to place Vescala's suggestion to steal a ship before the people and let them vote on it."

For a while longer Lascal and Silena, who agreed with everything her husband said, argued with Brenas and Elliana against the idea, only for the disagreement to eventually simmer down leaving each pair convinced that a majority of the people would see their point of view. As Elliana and Silena rose, to begin preparing the evening meal: the three men remained seated.

"Tell me, Brenas, did you ever find out what became of Straval?" Vescala asked, staring thoughtfully into the fire.

"I've no idea...I assume he returned to Anglesey."

"Yes, he will be a full priest by now. No doubt I would have been the same. Do you know what became of the others?" he asked lethargically, with the wine having made him slightly drowsy.

"Durada and Ruadi, no. But around ten years ago, when by chance I was reunited with our present informer, he was to tell me a story regarding a rumour that had apparently been circulating for a long time. I never found out for certain though, but according to him, the rumour contained more than a semblance of truth. The story went that one day some fifteen years ago two young boys from a village north-east of Iscal had been playing on the outskirts of a small wood when they came upon a body hanging by the neck from the branch of a tree. After informing the local priest of their discovery, they were suddenly spirited away by other priests who informed their parents that they were being taken to the sacred island in order to receive educational and religious instruction. Well, just as in your mother's case; both sets of parents, were then paid in silver and warned to remain silent as to their children's discovery. However, someone must have talked for the next thing that happened was that the parents, along with their remaining children, disappeared, never to be seen or heard of again. As you know, Vescala, the druids classify suicide as a mortal sin. To this day my informant is convinced that the person who took her own life was none other than... Trestania!"

Vescala gasped aloud at the shock of this news.

"As I've said, it's doubtful if anyone will ever find out the real truth simply because the druids would never allow it to openly circulate, that their highest ordained priestess had killed herself."

"Yes, you're right, that's something they would have forcibly censored. When did you say all this occurred?"

"Fifteen years ago; they say it happened just after the midwinter ceremonies , in the month of the robin to be precise."

As he began to sense a long-lost memory surfacing from the horrors of his tragic past, Vescala suddenly shuddered. Even now he could only vaguely remember the last time he had seen

Trestania, and that had been at his trial. But his instinct now told him that something terrible had happened after that; a sinister event, that even after all these years, remained locked deep in his mind.

"Let's hope her black soul found some peace," he commented, brushing aside his fears.

"In hell?" Brenas queried through a sneer.

It was then decided between them that until such time as Vescala could get a tent to himself, he would have to share with Aldrun. By this time the evening meal was prepared, but after heartily eating the stew and partaking of a little more wine, Vescala began to feel dizzy. Politely asking his host to accompany him outside to take the fresh air, the two men then walked through the encampment with Brenas more than eager to introduce the new arrival to everyone they came into contact with.

By now the rain clouds had dispersed, and as they strolled through the nearby forest, Brenas spoke at length of the commune's uncertain future: Vescala finding him more than enthusiastic to discuss the possibility of stealing a ship and embarking on the voyage they had schemed about so long ago. However, the more they spoke of it, the more Brenas became determined that his commune would have to free themselves from the drudgery of their nomadic existence.

Low in the clear blue sky the sharp needles of the setting sun were now retreating from the earth, and returning to the settlement both men were now convinced that, with enough faith and luck, the voyage to a new life could become more than a dream; indeed, they were now reconciled to the harsh fact that their dream had somehow to become a reality.

Chapter Eighteen

By the time the month of the golden wren had surrendered to that of the swallow, Vescala had fully adjusted to his new environment, and by the late summer, he appeared a completely different person from the pathetic figure who had emerged from the pit. Gone was his yellow pigmented skin with its natural colour having been restored by the rejuvenating sunlight; this along with the two meals he received daily had quickly seen his thin frame fill out, allowing him to regain his previous strength.

By now he was an integral part of the community, his medical skills, in particular, being greatly appreciated by the impoverished people. But it was Lascal who had most cause to be thankful, for after Vescala had removed the splints and further treated his wound, he had found his arm to be as good as new. Even Brenas now seemed like a new man whereas in the past, he alone had taken all the major decisions regarding the commune's well-being, he now found Vescala's wise advice easing what had, over the long years of running, become an intolerable strain. Nearly everyone liked Vescala, the lone exception being the embittered Aldrun who resolutely refused to place his wholehearted faith in any 'former druid," as he all too frequently described him as being. It was an attitude that often resulted in arguments flaring up between Brenas and himself.

However, the threat of the predatory Ravala was never far from anyone's mind and owing to the close proximity of his army, the commune had been forced into moving their encampment on three separate occasions since Vescala's arrival.

Over the preceding months, Brenas and Vescala had both taken the opportunity to begin discussions with the commune's numbers regarding their ultimate plan of escape. At first, nearly everyone, scoffed at the proposition to steal a ship, but seeing their leader's sincerity many, after a time, began to take the idea seriously. Debating meetings were then held among them in order to discuss the proposal in greater depth and, although Aldrun, Lascal and a few others remained vehemently opposed to the idea, a referendum was then taken among all those over the age of fourteen years, with an overwhelming majority agreeing with Elliana's opinion that as things were, they had little to lose. With the decision to seek a new life having been accepted and ratified, Brenas concluded that, at least for the time being, it would be wiser to abandon all guerrilla raids against the authorities. He also decided to remain sheltered in their present encampment , providing it was safe enough, until after the winter being well aware that any sea journey, even over to Ireland, would have to wait until the following spring. In the meantime, he thought it a good idea to send a small expedition south, to reconnoitre Iscal. Although there were other coastal towns where merchant galleys berthed Iscal, was the one that he and Vescala had been familiar with.

Vescala and Lascal, who had never seen the sea, were the chosen ones to go on the mission, and after a hard night's ride, they eventually reached their destination. It was still early in the morning and, from the high cliffs where Vescala had so long ago, stood alongside his beloved Delancia, they looked down through a fine mist to the deserted town. He could see that little had changed over the past fifteen years; indeed, the empty harbour and the little houses stood almost the same as he remembered them. But recalling the momentous night of the Roman attack, his forlorn eyes scanned the harbour area only to see that the only building never rebuilt was the lodging house where Delancia had stayed prior to her abduction. Suddenly Lascal grabbed him by the shoulder.

"Look, man; look at that!" he exclaimed in astonishment as Vescala turned to see two huge merchant galleys sailing through the mist towards the harbour like two mythological titans, and with his hitherto dejected face lighting up in a radiant smile, he knew with absolute certainty that such a ship could be captured. However, Lascal, who up until now had remained convinced that the whole idea was insane, instantly changed his mind. Never had he imagined men to be capable of building structures as powerful as both the galleys unquestionably were.

"My father often told me of such ships, but I never took them to be this size. Aye, Vescala, maybe your idea is feasible…my only reservation is how do we capture such a vessel?" he asked, overawed at their sight.

"Don't worry about that; we cross that bridge when we come to it," Vescala replied stoically. And with the ships heading for the harbour under their oar power, and having seen all they needed to, both men remounted their ponies to begin their homeward journey.

On their return to the settlement, Brenas was delighted with their information; immediately deciding to resume with their guerrilla raids, only this time with the sole intention of stockpiling as much equipment and food as they could possibly muster. Meanwhile, Vescala was tasked with drawing up a list of requisites they would need to take with them. Tools for carpentry and forging were essential, as were weapons and farming implements such as traction ploughs. Also required, would be looms for weaving; stocks of wool; sieves; querns; kneading boards; beeswax for smelting; flaxen and rawhide ropes, alongside bronze and iron containers of every shape and size. Seeds such as wheat; rye; oats; corn and beans were also classified as essential although he decided against taking any domesticated livestock, owing to the space they would take up on board the ship. However, the list of requisites seemed endless, and throughout the late summer, autumn and winter months carefully executed raids were perpetrated against many distant isolated villages; thus, yielding a growing amount of equipment, which they in turn stockpiled at various points near to the coast.

Brenas now heard from his informant that owing to the severe economic damage that his raids were causing, Ravala's army had been further strengthened, with a fortune in gold and land having been offered by the druids for any information that would lead the authorities to the location of the commune's sanctuary. And even though Ravala's spies were everywhere, Brenas decided that the time had come to throw all caution to the wind, with the series of raids he now embarked upon using up to ten men at a time, rather than the maximum of four he had previously favoured. Three spectacular raids led by Brenas himself were deliberately aimed against the Cantiaci tribe whose lands lay close to the great chalk cliffs overlooking the channel separating Britain from Gaul. This was done in the hope, that Ravala and his cumbersome army would travel east in search of them. For a time, the ruse worked allowing Vescala and Aldrun to lead smaller raids against the northern villages and at the same time seek out a safe haven on the south-west coast in order to stockpile the masses of equipment that by now, they had accumulated.

By the time Ravala had turned his forces back, Vescala had found an ideal location situated to the west of Iscal. The spot itself, being a small, barely accessible cove, lying between two heavily wooded cliffs. Prior to reaching the small strip of beach, a densely reed-infested tract of swampland had first to be negotiated with the entire site being encompassed by a protective forest. The location had been carefully chosen, being virtually impossible for any major force to launch a surprise attack, and having scrutinised the place personally, a satisfied Brenas decided that the time had come to move the entire commune onto the spot.

However, the evacuation of the camp along with the shifting of all the equipment they had previously hidden in their scattered hideaways proved to be a tedious and laborious task that had to be done under cover of darkness and by the time their goal was finally achieved, it was almost the end of winter.

By this time, Brenas had received yet another report from his informant stating that Ravala had split his army into three divisions; the devastating news having been greeted by everyone with a sense of impending doom, especially when they heard that Ravala was further strengthened in having been joined by a highly mobile force comprising of some fifty well-armed charioteers. Elliana and many others now, began to urge Brenas and Vescala that the time had come to leave Britain for good, although both men were well aware there was still much to be done. Once again, Aldrun insisted to the people that rather than run, they should make a final stand against the authorities, explaining to them that by undertaking such an action they would ignite a flame that must inevitably flare into a national revolt. But there were few who even bothered listening to him. No one among them sought martyrdom; indeed, all the people now desired was to find a truly safe refuge far from the reach of Ravala's ever-threatening army.

With the commune's tents having been erected at the edge of the swamp just up from the beach, lookouts were posted to the north, south and east. However, even though the tents were heavily camouflaged with bushes and reeds, Vescala remained concerned that some small offshore fishing vessel might inadvertently spot them, and with each passing day, the feeling of anxiety now prevalent in the camp appeared to him to be increasing.

As wood was in plentiful supply, Brenas ordered that work begin on the construction of the large rafts that would be required to take the people and their equipment over to the ship when and if they acquired one. He knew that it would take some time to build the rafts, and again he proposed to Vescala that he should once more go on a mission to reconnoitre Iscal.

After being away for over a day, Vescala returned just as the dawn was breaking over a dull sky, and finding Brenas up and about in his tent he reported to him that there were now three merchant galleys lying berthed in the harbour. However, just as he was about to leave for his own tent, they heard a shout coming from the swamp, and dashing outside, they spotted one of the lookouts running towards them carrying in his arms what appeared to be a half-naked boy.

"The child brings grave news, Brenas," the lookout said, laying the exhausted child on the sand. "Alright, lad, tell these men what you told me."

Vescala and Brenas, who had now been joined by others who had heard the commotion, then kneeled beside the youngster, who was around eight years of age. But they could see by his ragged clothing and the flaming red weal's, covering his naked legs that he must have been running through rough terrain for some considerable time.

"Don't be afraid, son; tell us what's happened," Brenas said stroking the child's mop of muddy hair reassuringly.

"Four days ago, Ravala entered our village," the child croaked staring up at Brenas through heavy eyes. "My grandfather was taken away and tortured. Before he died, he told my mother where one known as Brenas was to be found. She then told me to get to him and warn him that Ravala was on his way."

Drawing in a deep breath through clenched teeth, Brenas glanced at Vescala whose face conveyed his apprehension.

"I am Brenas, son. Now is there anything else?"

"Yes, I overheard Ravala issuing his orders. He said he would be staying in our village overnight. He then sent messengers to the north and west to tell his commanders to join him as soon as possible. But they should still be a good way off…I was travelling through the night as well as the day…I've had no sleep and have only eaten the bread my mother gave me."

Brenas sighed, admiring the courage that had seen one so young make such a murderous journey.

"What's your name, son?"

"Tymaron."

"How did you get here, Tymaron?"

"By pony, but I lost her in the swamp and covered the rest on foot."

"Did your grandfather say if he gave Ravala our exact location?"

"I don't know. My mother said Ravala knew you were camped on the shore near Iscal."

Looking downhearted both men stood up.

"His grandfather was my informer. He obviously, talked under interrogation. We'll have to move fast" Brenas remarked in a voice carrying a sharp edge to it. Once again, he knelt by the child's side. "Your grandfather's great courage runs through your blood, Tymaron. I'll get someone to feed you. Afterwards, you can get some sleep," he said, and rising up, he ordered one of the women to look after the child before turning to a tense Vescala, who spoke with a sense of urgency. "One of us has to remain here to organise things. If you like I'll take Aldrun, Lascal and three others and return immediately to Iscal."

"Will six of you be enough? You reckoned it would take at least twenty men, to capture a ship."

"Yes, I know, but you may well need the extra men to defend this place until we return. If we leave now, we can reach Iscal by nightfall. We must get a ship tonight and have her here, no later than noon tomorrow. Any time after may well be too late."

"Fair enough," Brenas commented, trying to sound optimistic. "I'll make certain all the equipment is ready to be ferried aboard the moment you arrive. If we make an immediate start, it shouldn't take us long to complete the last two rafts, but remember, the closer inshore you can bring the ship the better."

"Yes, the tide should be high by the time we get back. Our main enemy now is time itself. Oh, one thing, Brenas, have someone on the beach with a brightly coloured sheet, just in case we sail past the cove. Failing that make some landmark…It might be difficult spotting your exact location from out there."

"I'll do that. Now let me wish you luck," Brenas said, and shaking hands, the two men stood grim-faced. By now most of the people were up and about, and as they separated, Brenas began issuing his orders, leaving Vescala to marshal around him those he had chosen to go with him.

Gathering their cloaks, arms, and a little food, the small party quickly headed through the swamp and up to the woodland, to where the ponies were tethered and watched over by one of the lookouts. Vescala had also brought along a grappling hook tied to the end of a length of rope, however, having slept little the previous night he now felt desperately tired. And as they mounted their steeds, he was fraught with anxiety; convinced that their failure to procure a ship would see a brutal massacre of those they were leaving behind.

Once beyond the forest, they rode flat out, stopping only for a short time, to eat and rest their ponies. Continuing on their way with the twilight descending around them, they came upon a small coppice situated not far from the town. After dismounting, they first chased the ponies off before making their way over the heathland to the western cliffs where crouching low and peering through the gloom, Vescala breathed a sigh of relief. For he had been proved wrong in assuming that it would take some time to unload the cargoes, with only one of the single mast vessels now lying moored in the harbour next to the quayside.

Down in the town itself, everything lay deathly still and waiting patiently for total darkness to descend, the time dragged slowly by, with each man's thoughts tainted with dread as they pondered over the bloodshed that might ensue. The sky was moonless and the weather calm as Vescala at last gave the order to begin the descent, and with their swords at the ready, the six cloaked figures moved warily down the cliff's steep slopes. By means of the grappling hook they found it relatively easy to scale the stockade at the bottom, and with everyone safely over they silently made their way through the darkness towards the cover of the storage buildings lying in front of the narrow quayside. From the town behind them, a few sporadic bursts of revelry swept through the motionless air although Vescala could see no visible signs of life as he stealthily led them towards the front of the buildings. Now ahead of the others, and rounding the corner, the sudden sounds of muffled voices saw him raise an arm to signal to the others to halt. Remaining alert he proceeded on alone, stopping abruptly on spotting two armed guards standing with their backs to him among the unmoving shadows close to the ships bow. Stealing nimbly back to the others he grabbed Aldrun by the arm.

"There are two guards. If the rest of you stay put Aldrun and I will take care of them," he whispered, and using the shadows for cover they stole up to completely surprise the men, who put up no resistance against the powerful sword blows that tore into them. Seeing them lying dead at his feet, Vescala and Aldrun signalled to the others to join them before silently making their way in single file up the gangplank and onto the deserted deck where he led them to the open hatchway close to the ship's stern. Suddenly, from below the deck, came the noise of laughter.

"Now listen. It doesn't sound as if there are many aboard," Vescala whispered tremulously. "Most of them should be whoring it up in the town, but take no chances. Once below we'll try to rush them. If the navigator is aboard, I don't want him killed. Remember to strike only to wound, and only then if you have to!"

"Suppose he isn't?" Lascal enquired.

"Then we use what crewmen there are. They at least will be able to get us out into the open sea. After that, we'll just have to take it from there."

Everyone nodded in agreement as the cautious Vescala, with his blood-stained sword at the ready, began leading them down the dark steps that would hopefully take them to where the crew's quarters lay situated. At the bottom of the staircase a long, dimly lit gangway stretched out before them, but after searching the tiny cabins branching out on either side of them, they found them all to be empty. Suddenly from a room at the far end of the passage a few muffled voices erupted. Moving towards the sound, and standing back the impetuous Vescala quickly kicked the door in, with the four men drinking wine in the cramped cabin jumping to their feet in amazement. However, before they had time to gather their senses, each of them found the point of a sword up against their throats.

"Apart from the galley slaves who else is aboard?" Vescala demanded in his broken Latin, at the same time prodding the tip of his sword gently into the throat of the small man standing trembling before him.

"No one! The captain and the crew are up in the town drinking. We four are the watch," the dark-skinned man replied.

"Good. Is the ship's navigator with them?"

"No, you're speaking to him, but who are you? We are no more than a trading vessel that came to your shores in peace."

Turning to Lascal a jubilant Vescala couldn't believe his luck.

"This man's the navigator!" he exclaimed as Lascal and the others whooped with joy. Turning to face the man, Vescala lowered his sword to firmly push its tip against his chest. "From now on I'll be issuing your orders. Your three companions, I take it they're just ordinary crewmen?"

"Yes."

"Right, I want the four of you up onto the deck where you will take the ship out of the harbour and set sail on a western course. Do you understand?"

"Yes, but where are we going?" the man enquired, looking puzzled at the command.

"Don't ask questions. Do as I say otherwise, I will have no alternative but to kill you."

The navigator visibly trembled at the threat as Vescala lowered his sword and ordered everyone up to the deck where, the crewmen quickly raised the anchor, leaving Aldrun and the others to begin untying the vessel's ropes from its moorings.

"What country do you belong to?" Vescala then asked the navigator who stood at the ship's stern.

"We are all Spaniards in the employment of a powerful Roman merchant. Your act of piracy might well constitute an act of war against Imperial Rome!"

"I don't give a damn for Imperial Rome. Now order your men to lower the sail."

"I can't; the ship will first have to clear the harbour. We have to use the oars to achieve that," the man retorted acridly.

"Alright, you and I will go below the deck and order the galley slaves to…."

"No! I must stay at the helm. Take one of the crewmen. He'll know what to do."

Vescala eyed the man suspiciously, but having no knowledge of seamanship, he was forced to call Aldrun over.

"Aldrun, watch this little bastard like a hawk. If there is any treachery, wound him, but whatever you do don't kill him," he commanded. Along with Lascal and one of the crewmen they returned below the deck with the crewman leading them to the lower deck where the galley slaves sat chained two apiece to the oars.

There were ten oars on either side of the vessel, making some forty slaves in all; their semi-naked and brutalised bodies reminding Vescala of his own terrible ordeal. Strolling along the gangway separating the chained groups, he glanced uneasily into their murmuring eyes that, even more than the deep lash marks on their backs and shoulders, seemed to represent an age-old misery. Walking back to Lascal and the Spaniard he turned to address the slaves.

"If you men put your backs into it and work hard over the next few days, I promise you that when we reach the country known as Ireland you will all be set free," he declared, with some of the slaves smiling at his statement while others merely grimaced in bewilderment as Vescala then turned to Lascal.

"This crewman is needed down here. It must be to beat the timing of the oars on the drum beside you," he said, pointing his sword at the drum. "Now watch him. If he gives you any trouble, you know what to do."

Lascal acknowledged the command with a nod as Vescala returned up to the deck. Meanwhile, back on the shore, everything lay still and silent, and with Vescala shouting the navigator's orders down to the Spanish crewman, the others quickly finished untying the ship's moorings. After only a short time, they cleared the harbour area with no difficulty, as the ship slowly slipped out unseen into a calm open sea. At the navigator's command to his men, the ship's wide leather sail was quickly lowered, and with a slight breeze now aiding them it wasn't long before the lights of Iscal were left far behind them. To Vescala and the others, it was a strange experience to be surrounded by the gently stirring waters nonetheless, everyone was delighted to have taken the ship so easily. Standing by the side of the navigator at the helm, he then told him to steer the ship under its maximum oar power but to keep her as close to the shore as was possible.

With an ever-strengthening breeze behind them, they made good progress throughout the night, but come the dawn the navigator had become increasingly agitated at the repetitive order to stay inshore, persistently pleading with Vescala to let him steer the ship clear of the possible hidden reefs and sandbanks of a coastline that neither he nor his companions were at all familiar with. However, Vescala remained uninterested in the man's complaints, for, owing to the now-murky weather, he was far more concerned in case, they failed to recognise that particular part of the coastline where the commune anxiously awaited their arrival.

As the ship continued to cut speedily through the water; by noon Vescala was growing increasingly apprehensive. The coastline now appeared uniform with the appearance of many wooded cliffs and coves making it virtually impossible for him to determine which one might be their target. The thought began to trouble him that Ravala may well have struck, in the time they had been away. But with the sea spray now beginning to lash the deck it was Aldrun – standing by the deck rail on the ship's starboard side – who suddenly, emitted a yell when spotting the bright red sheet being waved from the shore. He was immediately joined by Vescala who likewise shouted triumphantly on seeing the tiny dot-like people scampering all along the distant sands. Rushing back to the navigator he ordered him to turn the ship towards the beach and to steer her as close to it as he safely could. The man then commanded his crewmen to raise the sail, telling Vescala to inform those below deck to have the slaves pull at the oars at their minimum rate. At the same time, Aldrun helped with the raising of the sail leaving one of the crewmen to begin plumbing the waters depth.

"Five fathoms," came the man's shout, whereupon the navigator swung the tiller and slowly the ship began to ease her way towards the shore. With the navigator listening intently to the numbers being called, Vescala occupied himself in examining the small rowing boat strapped to the deck beside the mast. However, at the cry of two fathoms, the Spaniard shouted to Vescala that they must drop anchor.

"No, we must get closer in," Vescala insisted.

"We can't; the tide will soon be on the ebb. If we go in any further, we may run her aground…as it is, we're too close for comfort," the man barked nervously. Glancing towards the shore Vescala could now clearly see the loaded rafts lying moored all along the beach.

"Alright. If you drop the anchor, I'll shout below to stop the oars," Vescala said, having no alternative but to agree to the man's demand.

With this done, he and Aldrun, made an immediate start on untying the rowing boat, and after some difficulty, they and the crewmen succeeded in lowering it over the ship's side. Leaving Aldrun in command, Vescala then commandeered one of the crewmen, and using the rope ladder flung over the side by the navigator, the two men quickly clambered down into the vessel. However, owing to the gathering wind the sea was now quite choppy, forcing the Spaniard at the oars to use all his strength in rowing towards the beach. By now the rafts carrying the equipment had begun to move towards the ship; the sturdily constructed vessels being guided by two men apiece, who pushed and directed them by means of long poles that they simultaneously plunged into the seabed. Passing them by, Vescala shouted his encouragement before leaping from the rowing boat to splash ashore where he was met by a relieved Brenas who had dashed over to greet him.

"Well done, man! Is there any chance of getting the ship closer in?" he asked through a beaming smile.

"No chance! As it is, the tide will soon be receding. Unless we hurry, we may well have to move her even further out. Now the rowing boat is big enough to take four adults at a time, so I suggest, we start shipping the elderly and children over on it."

"Alright; I think we can spare one of the rafts for the womenfolk. It should take at least ten at a time." "Good…has there been any sign of Ravala?"

"No, not yet. Let's hope it stays that way."

The beach now lay littered with masses of equipment, with more still being retrieved from the camouflaged storage points. But all around them pandemonium had broken loose and leaving Brenas to oversee the loading of the rafts, Vescala quickly restored order among the excited throng who had congregated around the rowing boat with the children. After telling the Spanish crewman to row the most elderly and the youngest children over to the ship and then to keep returning for the others, he then ordered, that any women, capable, should attempt to swim out to the vessel. Silena and those of the younger women who were strong swimmers immediately plunged into the freezing waters, leaving, the vast majority of them to form an orderly line to await their turn on the rafts. Altogether there were six rafts in use, including the one to be used by the women, and with a semblance of order having been restored things began to get moving. But with the vast amount of equipment still to be moved off the beach, and with time now racing by, both Vescala and Brenas began to realise that the evacuation would take much longer than they had anticipated. They were, however, more than relieved on seeing that the long poles had succeeded in getting the first of the rafts right up alongside the ship's hull.

*   *   *   *   *

Exhausted by his effort in returning to the main force, the advance scout collapsed in a heap at Ravala's feet.

"Well, what news?" Ravala demanded gruffly. Frantically panting for breath, the man looked up at him.

"Sir, they've somehow commandeered a Roman merchant ship. It is lying anchored in the bay beyond the swamp. They've built rafts and have already started to move their people and provisions towards it…although they have much to do yet."

Gritting his teeth Ravala immediately sprang into his chariot.

"The freebooters have been sighted!" he screamed at his surrounding army who had been enjoying a short rest in the forest's glade. "If we reach the bastards in time, I promise you that every man present will be rewarded in silver. If any among you is fortunate enough to kill the one known as Brenas, he will be rewarded with gold and land. But I warn you, failure to

252

procure the complete annihilation of these rebels will result in one in ten of you dying." Ravala paused to stare coldly at his men. "By my hand! Now I want you through that swamp in double quick time."

At the threat, his men quickly jumped to their feet for they could see in their leader's deranged eyes that he more than meant what he had said.

Soon the chariot's drivers were whipping frantically at their teams of ponies, forcing them towards the marshlands and leaving the foot soldiers to run behind them. But it wasn't long before the chariot wheels became stuck fast in the patches of boggy ground lying at the boundary of the marsh, and with Ravala cursing ferociously at the drivers for their inability to overcome the murderous terrain, he knew that he had no alternative but to order the army to progress on foot.

Leading them forward, he now prayed to every conceivable god that his long years of searching would soon be avenged in the massacre of those who had eluded him for so long. In the past there had been many occasions when he had come so close to discovering their whereabouts, only for fate to have treated him cruelly. Indeed, such had been his humiliation at his inability to destroy the rebel band that a few years ago he had put one of his four wives to death for having dared chide him about it. Now he scowled sadistically as he thought of the slave, Brenas, having spent many a sleepless night wondering as to the identity of the rebel leader who had so cunningly kept one step ahead of him. But thanks to the description extracted from the old man he had brutalised back in the village; he knew it had to be the same slave who he remembered from way back.

By now Ravala was just ahead of the rest of his army, and loping forward he now had to hack with his sword to clear a pathway though the densely packed reeds in front of him. Not far behind him came his second in command, his young nephew Crezala, who took great pride in emulating his uncle's violent nature.

As dusk began to fall the decimated army of some eighty strong at last reached the end of the swamp; the deadly patches of quicksand having taken a heavy toll on their original numbers. But it was an exuberant Ravala who was first to spot the five men on the beach, still occupied in loading the provisions onto the two rafts remaining on the shore, and now inflamed with a desire to kill and ritually behead his enemies, he ran forward well ahead of the others, screaming as he went.

By this time all the women and children, along with the vast majority of the men and equipment, were aboard the lurching galley, and with the tide on the ebb, Lascal – who was aboard the rowing boat and which was just about to hit the beach – suddenly yelled out on spotting Ravala running down towards them.

"Leave everything and get into the boat," Brenas screamed out to the others on sighting Ravala, and with the exception of Vescala, they began wading out to the rowing boat, now in the process of being turned towards the galley by its Spanish oarsman. Running back, Brenas tried to grab the irate Vescala but, brushing him aside, and with vengeance burning in his hateful stare, Vescala unsheathed his sword to calmly begin walking to attack his breast-plated enemy. However, as the two men approached one another, Ravala suddenly stumbled to a halt, and with every nerve in his body now quivering uncontrollably his startled eyes stared awe-struck at the sight of the avenging figure coming upon him: a man who for so many years he had assumed dead.

By now, Brenas had quickly picked up a discarded spear from the beach, and with a now-composed Ravala again rushing towards Vescala, he immediately launched the weapon only to see it plunge directly through Ravala's broad stocky throat. Instantly dropping his sword and shield, both Ravala's hands clutched desperately onto the shaft of the spear as he staggered back a few paces before his huge frame crashed heavily down to the ribbed sea sand; his terrified eyes never leaving Vescala's until the life force had slipped from them forever.

"Come on, let's go," Brenas pleaded as Vescala dropped his sword, and running back, the two men dived headlong into the sea, just in time to narrowly avoiding the volley of spears now being hurled at them by Ravala's onrushing warriors. With the weapons continuing to whistle past them, they were forced into swimming a short way out to the rowing boat where grabbing onto its stern they were soon pulled safely out of range, with none of the missiles having found a target. Reaching the galley, Aldrun flung a rope down to Lascal, shouting at him to tie it to the prow of the vessel. The men then scrambled up the rope ladders dangling down from the ship's rail where they collapsed onto the crowded deck, with each of them now shivering uncontrollably from the cold. However, they were soon back on their feet, and as Aldrun and one of the other crewmen busied themselves in raising the anchor, Vescala gave a hand with the halyards to lower the sail before ordering the navigator to get the oars moving to their maximum rate. This was quickly done, but just as everyone was about to breathe a sigh of relief the ship shuddered violently as it stuck fast on a reef directly below her hull. With the ship now stranded, a tense Vescala noticed through the twilight gloom that one of the rafts they had left behind was beginning to move ominously towards them carrying six of Ravala's warriors who as soon as they came within range began to release fire arrows towards the stranded vessel. Almost hysterical with rage, Vescala screamed at the navigator to do something, but the frightened man could only stand shrugging his shoulders, muttering that there were too many people and too much equipment on board.

Seeing that the other raft was now heading towards them, pandemonium erupted, and screaming at the top of his voice, Vescala ordered all the women and children to get below the deck. However, as the panic-stricken people began to move in one mass towards the hatch the ship suddenly groaned and tilted, and with the oars continuing to strike furiously into the water she slowly began to slither off the reef. Soon the oars had pulled her free as everyone cheered heartily. But as the navigator steered her in a westerly direction the two by now-waterlogged rafts were close enough for the fire arrows to find their mark on the ship's stern. Tying a rope around his waist, Aldrun ordered some of the men to hold onto it before climbing over the ship's rail, where after a tenacious struggle, he succeeded in pulling the arrows free, only to drop them harmlessly into the sea. With a salt-laden breeze now aiding them it wasn't long before they had sailed well out of firing range, and with everyone now laughing and jeering at the fading sight of the outwitted remnants of the army now strung out all along the beach, Aldrun clambered back up onto the deck to be informed by Vescala of Ravala's death.

Now fully comprehending that they had finally escaped after their long years of running and hiding, Brenas and Elliana, along with many of the others, broke down and wept in each other's arms. They now had a ship capable of transporting them anywhere they chose to go and with the exception of a few cuts and bruises, the people were all but unharmed. It seemed too good to be true.

Meanwhile, back on the shore a grief-stricken Crezala knelt beside the prostrate body of his beloved uncle, and freeing the spear from his throat to cast it aside, he then removed Ravala's breastplate. As was the custom, he drew his dagger to thrust its blade deep into his kinsman's still heart whereupon withdrawing the weapon, he licked the blade clean of blood before rising to address the encircling warriors.

"See how the vermin sail towards Ireland," he shouted menacingly as his trembling hand pointed the dagger towards the fleeing galley. "By the blood of my beloved kinsman, I swear to the gods that regardless of how long it takes, I will pursue them. And when I catch up with them , and I will , I will stain the ocean in their unholy blood!"

After ordering each of the men to emulate his action with their own daggers, Crezala commanded that Ravala's body be carried back inshore. With his spear held in one hand and his circular bronze shield drawn tight to his chest, Crezala, dangerous, resolute, and sworn to avenge, stood alone glaring hatefully towards the vessel now sailing into the deepening purple twilight.

Chapter Nineteen

Once out to the safety of the open sea they raised the rowing boat and strapped it back down onto the deck. The atmosphere on board remained one of total euphoria, and with the weather favourable it took them only nine days to reach the rugged and beautiful coast of south-eastern Ireland. However, these days could hardly be described as uneventful, with Vescala having used the time to convince most of the people that their future lay not in Ireland but in the land that he believed lay much further to the west. He was fully backed in his assertion by Brenas, Elliana, and even Lascal only for the dejected Aldrun to once again raise his voice in dissent. Subsequently, it was decided by Brenas that all the adults aboard should hold a meeting on the deck at noon to decide once and for all where their future lay.

It was still early in the morning and, with the ship dangerously overcrowded, Brenas decided that the time had come to release the galley slaves, in order, to fulfill Vescala's promise to them. Having dropped anchor close to a deserted headland, it took them some time to unfetter the slaves from their chains but before being rowed over in batches to the narrow strip of beach on the mainland, each of the men were given some linen from the ship's unloaded cargo, a few arms and the little food that could be spared.

The sky was clear with a light breeze skipping over the ocean's surface, and leaning over the ship's rail, Vescala watched intently as the white foam of the waves gently dissolved into the distant band of golden sands. He regretted the fact that the slaves had to go, but even if they were taken back into captivity, he was certain that their lives on dry land had to be a far better one than the drab existence they had known. He turned to see Brenas and Aldrun at his side and soon all the commune's adults had gathered before the three of them. Nearly everyone knew the position of Vescala and Brenas, but not so of Aldrun's stance, and with the open palm of his outstretched hand, a serious-looking Brenas gesticulated to Aldrun to address the audience.

"I, for one, have no intention of going any further west than Ireland, regardless of any vote taken at this meeting!" he exclaimed conclusively. "I've already discussed the situation with some of you. Like myself, many of you have formulated the opinion, that it would be wiser to stay in Ireland than attempt to tackle the unknown dangers that the Atlantic must surely hold. Personally; I think the whole idea is insane. No one has ever attempted such a journey! Let's be honest; it's highly improbable that this land Vescala speaks of ever existed."

"How many of you wish to leave?" a stern-looking Brenas asked; glancing speculatively at Aldrun, but feeling bitterly disappointed at his one-time close associate's obstinacy.

"Up until this moment some thirty-five. What we want, is to be put ashore, on one of the uninhabited islands that Vescala assures us lie further along the coast."

"And just how long do you hope to survive there?" Brenas asked as Aldrun smiled contemptuously at Vescala.

"A damned sight longer than you will…I believe that this former druid is leading you all into certain death!"

"What about Ravala's death? How long do you think it will be before his friends and soldiers hunt you down like animals?" Vescala retorted, angrily unable to hide his contempt at Aldrun's jibe.

"That's a risk we're prepared to take. Now I feel it's only fair that we be allowed to have
our share of the equipment and provisions which we all gathered over the past months."

Disheartened by Aldrun's decision, Vescala shook his head as Brenas stared in disgust at him before turning his attention to the others.

"Many years ago, I swore that never again would I live in bondage. What I said, I meant!" he shouted at the top of his voice. "But if Aldrun wishes to leave then so be it; he's more than welcome to his share of the spoils. As far as his followers are concerned, I beg you to put your faith in Vescala's knowledge and reconsider your decisions…I truly believe him when he says there's a land beyond Ireland."

The debate among them continued for some time longer. However, after a great deal of persuasive talking from either side, a vote was eventually taken which, much to Vescala's disgust, transpired in only two of Aldrun's followers having changed their minds in electing to remain with the majority. Including Aldrun, it now meant, that thirty-four members of the commune would be leaving: twelve men: twelve women, and nine children. And with everyone now dispersing to attend to their various duties, Vescala turned to Brenas.

"Aldrun must be mad. What chance will these children have?" he asked tersely as Brenas raised his eyebrows in a sardonic manner.

"It's their children and it's their decision Vescala: I don't see that we can do any more to make them change their minds."

Brenas then left him to help some of the others, who were busy raising the rowing boat, leaving Vescala to lean over the ship's rail and ponder the magnitude of his responsibility. He well recalled his old master telling him of the land that he was convinced lay beyond the mighty Atlantic − a land that had stirred his imagination since the early days of his education. Even allowing for his rebellious attitude against the priesthood and through the long years of his imprisonment, he was never to forget the wise old master's words. It's strange he now thought somewhat forlornly, how a man may forget many things in his lifetime and yet never forget those who taught him. For a few moments of nagging uncertainty, he now wondered if perhaps Aldrun was right, and cupping his face in his hands, he momentarily felt like a blinded crab in shallow rocky waters, desperately seeking shelter from a gathering storm above. However, the sudden sound of the wind-whipped sail blew his doubts away, and turning, he saw the little navigator standing by his shoulder.

"Where do we go from here?" the man enquired as Vescala eyed him uneasily.

"What's your name, Spaniard?"

"Mondena."

"Well, Mondena, we first travel west, to where a cluster of uninhabited islands lie, and there some of our people along with your fellow crewmen will be put ashore. Afterwards, we sail to the extreme western point of Ireland and over the next month will remain inshore where you will educate and discipline our people in the art of seamanship. With me acting as interpreter, you will teach us how to use the oars to their maximum efficiency, and when and how to raise and lower the sail; indeed, all about the ship and the sea, until we are expert. Failure to comply with my demands will result in all our deaths – including yours! You see, Mondena, at the end of that month we will again sail west, only to then keep on sailing until we eventually reach land."

"But nothing lies beyond Ireland!" Mondena exclaimed with his dark eyes showing acute terror. "The ocean out there is uncharted. Everyone knows that where the Atlantic ends so does the world. You have no right to abduct me like this...I have a wife and children back home."

"Yes, Mondena. You've done well for yourself, I've no doubt, that back home you have some very nice property to go with your wife and children...I don't suppose for one moment that it's ever bothered you that your affluence is founded on centuries of human misery! Nor do I suppose that your conscience has ever been troubled by the constant flogging your galley slaves endured over their long years of brutalising captivity?"

The Spaniard looked flummoxed at the statement.

"I was only obeying orders. You can't blame me for that."

"I was only obeying orders! History's most infamous words," Vescala snapped, and staring disdainfully down at Mondena and feeling no sympathy for his plight, he drew his dagger to place its tip under his chin. "Never forget, you little bastard, that like us you belong to the Celtic race…I'm sure you would rather be among kinsmen than shackled physically and spiritually to your Roman masters."

"This ship will never tackle the tempestuous Atlantic. She'll break up in one severe storm."

"She seems strong enough to me," Vescala retorted before removing the dagger, much to the relief of the cringing Spaniard.

"No, Vescala! I beg you not to embark on this madness. To a man the sea can be an enchanting mistress, but have you any idea of just how savage a mistress she can suddenly transform into?"

"No," Vescala admitted, turning to stare down into the clear, shallow waters of the bay. "But I do know this, Mondena: on this ship we have the women to equal her beauty and the men and motivation to tame your savage enchantress."

"Never!" Mondena yelled, but spinning round, an angry Vescala grabbed and pushed him over towards the tiller. There was no way he could risk the navigator escaping and so he subsequently ordered two of the others to first gag him and then tie him to it. After then conferring with Brenas, they decided to raise the anchor, and once under full sail, the ship slipped smoothly along, with the mute Mondena having been told to keep her as near as was safely possible to the rugged coastline. However, with both the men and women now manning the oars, but devoid of the expertise of the galley slaves, their speed was severely curtailed.

It took another five days before they reached the islands Vescala had learned of while studying under the druids. And, after a lengthy discussion with his group, Aldrun happily informed Brenas that they had decided to settle on a small but heavily wooded island lying a good distance out from the mainland.

It was early in the morning when the ship dropped anchor close to the island's deserted beach. With a heavy heart, Brenas once again attempted to dissuade Aldrun from leaving. But adamantly, refusing to even reconsider his decision, work immediately began on rowing over all the equipment that he and his followers were entitled to take.

It took nearly two days, to row everything over to the shore, where by now, the group had set up a temporary camp, and with the rowing boat returning for the last time, Brenas stood by the mast staring at the small party on the beach. He was deeply saddened that he and Aldrun had parted under such unhappy circumstances. But like Vescala, he too was now suffering from the occasional bout of misgivings as to whether, or not they were doing the right thing in risking so many lives on such a venture. And yet, he reckoned assuredly, their unenviable position was one in which there could be no question of compromise. Their mission would end in one of two ways; either complete success or total failure. But on hearing Vescala's shouted command to raise the rowing boat for the last time, the all-inspiring and eternal flame of one word seemed to burn ever stronger in his mind – freedom!

Soon the ship was under full sail, and as she glided over the water towards the open sea, Aldrun and all those left behind on the shore waved and shouted their encouragement to the few who had remained up on deck.

It was another five days before they reached the most south-westerly point of Ireland. Once there it was with a stern resolve that Vescala, Brenas, and Mondena went about the task of organising the others into a well-disciplined and highly trained unit that they hoped would be more than a match for the intemperate conditions they must face in the near future. Using a rota system devised by Vescala, all capable men and women, and all but the youngest of the children, took their turn in learning how to manipulate the oars to their maximum efficiency. Mondena had placed great emphasis on the danger of fire breaking out on board the vessel, with the women who were responsible for the cooking told that full buckets of water must, at all times be kept within easy reach of the two cooking stoves situated in the galley's spacious kitchen below the deck.

Vescala estimated that they had enough food stockpiled to last them for some three months at sea and although food and water supplies were adequate, enough for the time being, small hunting parties were sent across to the mainland to obtain fresh meat to last them for the thirty- days they required to train and adapt themselves to life at sea. He was however well- aware that their water stocks wouldn't last forever and worried in case the weather should remain clear and dry, he ordered that buckets must at all times be left on deck to catch the rainwater when it fell. Lascal's fishing lines soon added to their food stocks with a healthy catch of herring and mackerel. But young Tymaron who had been helping him, complained bitterly when on hauling up one of the lines he was stung on the hand by a jellyfish caught on the hook. Having lived inland all his young life, it was the first time the child had ever seen such a creature.

Their thirty-day training period flew by, and on a bright sunny day, they slipped anchor and sailed west to begin the long voyage into the unknown. By nightfall, they could no longer see the green Irish coastline, and come the following daybreak everyone on board began to sense for the first time the fearsome isolation that the surrounding slate-grey ocean brought upon them. By noon heavy rain swept over the calm sea as up on deck, Vescala felt more inspiration than fear as he viewed the endless expanse of ocean with the ship, now under full sail and oar power, sliding smoothly over the ocean's rain-flecked surface. As was normal, most of the people remained below the deck for the best part of the day, but with the rain ceasing they came off their shifts on the oars to come up to the deck in their numbers in order to stretch their legs and partake of the fresh air. Like everyone else, Elliana had to take her turn at the oars, but somehow, she still found the time to supervise the two wholesome meals issued daily; this over and above looking after her child and organising games for the other children, whose boundless energy could in no way be stifled even by living in the intolerably cramped conditions below the deck.

Even so, morale among the people had never been better. By now both Vescala and Brenas had been taught enough about steering the ship to relieve the morose Spaniard, whose depression appeared to have deepened over the past month. As a result, Vescala, had the man watched at all times…even when asleep.

For another twenty idyllic days, the weather held steady but early one morning, from beneath a tarnished grey sky, a ferocious storm suddenly broke loose, and with the storm's fury quickly growing in its intensity, panic began to spread throughout the vessel. At Mondena's instigation, the sail was lowered; likewise, he called for the oars to be drawn in and all hatches and portholes to be securely battened down. It was then agreed between Vescala and Brenas that everyone with the exception of Vescala and Mondena should remain below the deck. But a helpless Vescala could only stand beside the helm watching the mountainous sea whipping and hurling the craft around as if it were no more than a tiny strip of driftwood. Beneath his sodden clothing he could feel his very blood freeze in terror; never having imagined that the ocean, so peaceful one moment, could so quickly erupt into such a devastating maelstrom.

As he and the Spaniard struggled to prevent the ship from being submerged, below the deck seasickness had begun to afflict nearly everyone, with their plight not helped by the unhygienic conditions they were now forced to endure. However, with the cruel day slowly passing into an even more alarming night, no lamps were lit for fear of fire, and in the tomb-like blackness below the deck the only sounds to breach the roar of the wind-driven waves and the groaning timbers were the pleas of whispering mothers, desperately trying to reassure their whimpering children that all would be well.

Come dawn, the storm had finally abated and Brenas, who like most of the others had found sleep impossible, unbolted the hatch, and clambering aloft found Vescala and Mondena still at the helm, with both men utterly exhausted and visibly suffering from exposure. Shouting down to Lascal to lend a hand, they then helped them below the deck with Brenas calling on Elliana to get them something warm to eat and ensure they rested. However, on returning to the deck with Lascal and some of the others, he was delighted, to see that no damage had been done to either the mast or the rigging. On taking over the tiller, he ordered that the sail be raised, but owing to the exhausted condition most of the people were now in, he decided against utilising the oars at the same time telling Lascal to issue wine from the hold and to be distributed in generous helpings which brought to everyone a cheerful respite from the suffering that had so nearly brought them to disaster.

The sea remained choppy for the rest of the day but by twilight, the wind had ceased with the vessel gently rolling ever westwards. Having eaten and rested, Vescala and Mondena returned to the deck where Vescala immediately told the Spaniard to relieve Brenas, who joined him at the ship's prow. Both men were overjoyed to have mastered such atrocious conditions, and standing quietly, they observed the great sinking red sun paint the ocean's surface in vermilion and turquoise hues that shimmered below the faintly flickering stars of early evening. Scanning the limitless heavens Vescala, like the Spaniard, calculated their westerly direction by the position of the stars, and after a short discussion with Brenas, they decided against using the oars for the time being in to allow everyone to obtain a good night's rest.

The following morning, Vescala relieved the Spaniard, and hoping to make up for lost time, he ordered that the oars be manned and struck up to their maximum rowing power. With a forceful westerly wind now springing up the ship soon made good speed. And from the stern of the vessel, Lascal once again lowered his baited fishing lines only to quickly see the deck strewn with a writhing mound of silver herring that the womenfolk immediately gutted, salted, and stored in barrels down in the hold.

As the days passed, squalls remained frequent although none had the severity of the first storm and no land had yet been sighted, after thirty-five days on the open sea, morale aboard the vessel remained surprisingly high. The only dissenting voice to be heard was the persistent grumbling of the navigator. But Vescala never bothered translating anything he said to any of the others. Indeed, the only time he ever addressed the man was to remind him to keep steering the ship on a westward course.

For the next few days, they ploughed on through a thick bank of fog that completely obscured their view. But as the fog, slowly dispersed, Vescala – now beginning to sense a growing apprehension among some in the commune – prayed that land would soon be sighted. However, with the coming of clear visibility still nothing was to be seen, and gazing wearily at the never-ending ocean stretching ominously ahead of them, his confidence waned as he wondered, if perhaps he was as insane as the Spaniard now repeatedly claimed. Suddenly he recalled the druid legend that told of the madness befalling anyone who dared seek any life other than that decreed to him by the gods. For the first time, he wondered, whether it might be wiser to return to Ireland rather than continue to advance into the unknown.

"Thirty-eight days and all you have to show is endless water," Mondena proclaimed from the helm as Vescala turned angrily from the deck rail to face him.

"Listen, we've probably travelled further than most men would ever have dared to and in conditions that would have seen the bravest of Roman gladiators cringe in terror," he replied calmly.

"That's as may be, but you must see by now that no land lies out here," Mondena said disconsolately. "To go any further is pointless. Your people will only mutiny! Believe me one more severe storm will see them throw you and the one named Brenas overboard!"

"Never," Vescala scoffed through a brusque laugh. "I don't believe for one moment they would ever do that. Our people have put their implicit faith in our judgment. Anyway, if a majority of them were to decide that they wanted to go back, neither Brenas nor myself would make any attempt to prevent them," Vescala stated as the scowling Spaniard then spat at his feet, an action that saw Vescala grab him by the throat. But the unexpected and excited shout of "Land ahead" saw him release the man as he turned to see a jubilant Lascal rushing towards him.

"Look, Vescala, land!" Lascal screamed out, pointing southwest. Having been occupied with his fishing lines, he had suddenly spotted the three tiny specks just visible on the horizon through a haze of fine drizzle. Grabbing hold of Vescala, who likewise spotted the islands, the two men jumped and yelled for joy, with the resulting commotion bringing a startled Brenas and a few of the others up onto the deck. But with everyone's hopes now soaring, Mondena began to shout and scream that they had reached the very ends of the earth, and what they were actually seeing were some of the pillars that held up the four corners of the sky. However, once the initial excitement had subsided, Brenas dashed back down below the deck where after informing those manning the oars of the discovery, he then ordered them, with tears in his laughing eyes, to row as they had never done before. Returning to the now crowded deck, he, like the others, watched the ship cut speedily through the water towards the land. But owing to the state of terror that Mondena was now in, Vescala had been forced to take control of the tiller only for the euphoria they were experiencing to prove short-lived. For they were now close enough, to see that the islands were no more than three gigantic icebergs whose very bulk and structure astounded them. No one up on deck could fail to show on their dejected faces the bitter disappointment they felt, and, as the ship slipped slowly between the gleaming towers of ice, Vescala cursed to himself, on seeing ahead of them nothing but the all-too-familiar sight of the vast, unfriendly ocean.

"Alright, everyone back to work," Brenas shouted and for the first time since leaving Ireland he detected concerned expressions on the faces of those surrounding him. Sluggishly, obeying him, many of them began to wonder if Vescala's advice was as trustworthy as they had first been led into believing. Miserable, and looking downhearted, an anxious Brenas strolled over to the helm where Vescala stood alongside the equally unhappy Lascal and Mondena.

"Elliana was just saying to me yesterday that she reckons some of them to be growing impatient!" he exclaimed bluntly as Vescala drew in a deep, mournful breath.

"Has anyone actually mentioned going back?" he asked.

"A few have hinted at it…I fear, that unless we find land soon, they might insist on it."

"I honestly wouldn't blame them, Brenas. But they must remember that to return will take us at least another thirty-eight days. On the other hand, if we continue, we may discover land tomorrow or the day after. If we explain that to them it might help to alleviate their misgivings."

Lascal shook his head. "You say it might be tomorrow or the next day. Supposing we never find this land?" he asked as Vescala rubbed thoughtfully at his forehead.

"I never said it would be easy, Lascal. Nothing worthwhile achieving in this world ever is − is it?" he asked as Lascal nodded wistfully before returning to where the young Tymaron was baiting the fishing lines, leaving Vescala to turn to Brenas.

"If the people should become too restless, Brenas, then we must go back, but it would be a tragedy after what we've come through. We'll just have to keep their faith in us from sinking any lower."

Mumbling in agreement Brenas took his leave to return below deck, leaving Vescala alone with Mondena. The glum Vescala then turned to look back at the immense cliffs of the icebergs they were now moving speedily, away from. Suddenly laughing aloud, he spun round to face the Spaniard.

"Well then…so much for your pillars holding up the sky," he quipped sarcastically. But making no reply to the remark, even the torrential rain now pouring down couldn't hide the embarrassment covering Mondena's face.

Chapter Twenty

The days seemed to grow ever longer as the increasing sense of isolation began to play on everyone's nerves. This resulted in the smallest of trivialities, sparking off feuds, which grew in intensity with sometimes entire families bickering and fighting among themselves, making discipline difficult to maintain. Even Vescala grew more and more cynical as the desolation of the vast ocean gnawed ever deeper into his once-assured confidence. Squalls now blew up with an insufferable regularity, buffeting the ever-groaning ship's timbers in a continuous barrage of waves that threatened to swallow the vessel forever. By this time, they had spent fifty days on the open sea, with still no sign of any land, and among the people, a lethargic misery had now replaced the once-convivial atmosphere that they had experienced for so long. The monotony of their work allocations, alongside the harsh and claustrophobic conditions they had to endure, caused many among them to complain more and more bitterly as both Brenas and Vescala began to sense that their popularity had slumped to a dangerously low point. Elliana would often rebuke the malcontents for their constant grumbling as a spineless bunch who hadn't the courage to go on. However, her somewhat unfair verbal attacks did nothing to forestall the growing sense of anarchy that appeared to be lurking in every corner of the unhappy vessel.

Come the morning of their fifty-first day at sea the weather at last improved. It was a warm, bright sunny day as Brenas and Vescala, who stood conversing by the mast, turned to see the elderly and nervous-looking figure of Endvar standing before them, a little in front of ten of the other men.

"We have heard a rumour, Brenas, that our food rations are to be drastically cut. Is it true?" Endvar asked placidly as

Brenas glanced at Vescala who stood warily eyeing up the others.

"Yes, Endvar: I'm afraid it is. We have no alternative; our food stocks are dwindling much faster than we anticipated," he replied, staring into the old man's eyes.

"Then we must insist the ship be turned around and set on a course back to Ireland!" Endvar exclaimed, in an uncompromising manner and although neither he nor any of his accomplices were armed, both men were left in no doubt as to the legitimacy of the demand.

"Now just hold on," Brenas retorted sternly. "We all democratically agreed to undertake this journey knowing full well the hardships we would have to face. If you remember, Endvar, there was no one at the time more enthusiastic than yourself."

"Yes, that's as maybe, Brenas," Endvar replied as his gaunt features broke into an embarrassed grimace. "But we expected to find land long before now. No, I'm afraid that as much as we respect you, we, and I speak for the vast majority, have decided that we've come far enough. We now insist that we turn back."

Hearing the shouts of approval coming from Endvar's supporters, a grim disappointment showed on Vescala's salt-burned features.

"And how long do you think we'll last in Ireland? Providing we ever reach Ireland again," he asked calmly in order not to antagonise the others. But Endvar's mood turned to anger.

"Then, Vescala, you leave us no choice but to place you in irons! As far as I'm concerned, we've listened to you long enough. Even an imbecile can see there is no land out here. I'm sorry, Vescala, but our people have lost faith in your mad beliefs." He yelled, biting his lip on recalling the fact that it had only been a few months since Vescala had cured his young grandson of the fever that had so nearly ended his life. Suddenly Brenas pushed the old man in the chest, causing him to fall back into the arms of his followers.

"Listen, and listen well!" he shouted angrily. "Maybe I should have told you before but Elliana and I didn't, in order to prevent panic. The truth is that most of our remaining food stocks in the hold have perished. We only have enough to last us for another five days."

By now Endvar had struggled back up and was standing with Brenas in a nose-to-nose confrontation.

"You're lying," he yelled, shaking with temper.

"No, Endvar, I can take you down to the hold and show you."

Suddenly Vescala spotted a strange, distant shape hovering low in the sky, and indicating to the others with his pointing finger everyone turned to look southwest from where the dark, fluttering form was approaching the ship.

As they watched the giant bird coming closer, a sudden terror gripped all those on the deck, with the exception of Mondena, who had seen such a bird before. Although Vescala hadn't, he knew by the shape of the huge black and white bird's curved yellow beak that their visitor was no more than a harmless albatross.

"Land has to be near," he muttered, unable to control his excitement. "This is an omen of incredibly good fortune. Our intruder is an albatross; a bird I learned about while studying under the druids. The fact that it's here undoubtedly proves that land has to be nearby."

For a few moments, Endvar stood uncertain. But as the great bird landed on the ship's prow, he nodded in sullen agreement at Vescala, and beckoning to the others to follow, they withdrew to return below the deck.

The news of the bird's unexpected arrival boosted everyone's confidence, and for four contented days, it remained undisturbed among them. However, even after such a time no sign of land was forthcoming. By now their food rations had been restricted to one meal a day, and with fish in scarce supply floating seaweed became their only other food source. But as a bank of thick fog drifted towards them, the great bird suddenly flew south to vanish into the mist. Once again, the optimism that had prevailed amongst them quickly turned to despair.

Two miserable days slowly elapsed as the fog held the ship in a bleak, malevolent shroud, but, when eventually dispersing, a dull morning sun was to show yet again the discouraging view of a landless, lifeless sea. The eyes of nearly everyone on board now appeared to Vescala to stare at him with a stifling hatred. For the moment, no one had again mentioned going back; nonetheless, he was in no doubt, as to the imprecations, some of them were longing to utter aloud.

As they continued west the weather, once more took a turn for the worse, and with their food situation becoming ever more critical; Brenas ordered that the sacks of seeds that they had intended to cultivate in their new homeland, were to be opened and distributed amongst them. Unfortunately, only a few of the sacks had escaped the blight and the ship's rats that had so effectively destroyed their other food stocks. Vescala now found himself assaulted by a conscience that constantly derided him for having so selfishly deluded a once proud and defiant people who now went about their chores trapped within a morbid delirium.

As the weather rapidly deteriorated the ship's sturdy oaken structure was suddenly bombarded by thunderous spasms of waves that repeatedly threatened to rip her apart. It now appeared to all those on board as if they had breached the very centre of the ocean's heartbeat. Even more alarming to Vescala was the fact that a serious outbreak of dysentery was afflicting more than half of them as between his stints at the helm and the little sleep he was managing to obtain, he struggled on humanely aiding and comforting the undernourished sick. However, even in the sanctity of his stolen sleep he could in no way escape the heart-rending screams of those who continually pleaded for a merciful deliverance.

By their sixtieth day at sea the storm had broken, bringing a golden sun to look down on the stricken vessel that, by now, had become a floating sepulchre. Exhausted, and struggling onto his unsteady legs, Vescala laboriously ascended the steps leading to the deck whereon unbolting the hatch, he found the exhausted Mondena still by his station at the helm. Owing to the sick condition of Brenas, and his own attendance to the suffering commune over the period-of- time that the storm had lasted, the little Spaniard had been relieved on only three occasions. Staggering over to lean onto the ship's rail, he could only admire the man's resilience. But now staring at the sombre vastness of the ocean, that alongside the sky seemed to swim depressingly around him, he became impervious to the mournful cries, rising from below the deck as in his mind, his tormented soul, screamed to be released from the tomb of his desiccated flesh. Next to join him up on deck was a grief-stricken Elliana, and as her slow shuffling feet moved her towards him, he turned to see her clutching tightly against her heaving bosom the pale, lifeless body of her small daughter. Behind her came an embittered Brenas who bowed his head gravely, frantically trying to find the comforting words that might help alleviate her agonised sobbing.

By mid-morning, the ship's beleaguered survivors had carried aloft and strewn the deck with some twenty rotting corpses, including ten children. And with the sunlight turning the ocean's surface into a frenzy of undulating flames, a heartbroken Brenas, issued the order to cast the bodies over the side. It was a heart-rendering task, and when done, he could only stand watching by the ship's rail as the tiny body of his only child bobbed gently up and down just below the surface of the burning waters. As he stood weeping, he cursed his stupidity in embarking on such a reckless enterprise; now convinced that they had reached the very ends of the earth, and tenderly holding onto the hapless Elliana, he sensed that they too must soon suffer a similar fate.

By now it was mid-afternoon, and with an utterly despondent Vescala having taken over at the helm to grant Mondena a well-deserved rest, Lascal, who was at the ship's prow, suddenly yelled out, on spotting the dark fin of a huge fish darting around the floating bodies. Rushing below the deck to fetch a bow and some arrows along with a long thin rope, he quickly returned to tie the rope onto the quill of an arrow before releasing the weapon only to see it strike deep into the creature's great oval-shaped head. As the shark vanished into a swirl of seething water, Lascal tied the rope around the deck rail and, with everyone's eyes scanning the ocean for a lengthy period-of-time. The white belly of the fish was eventually spotted floating on the surface. With all hands now hauling on the rope, the bulky carcass was slowly dragged alongside the hull but, by the time they had finally accomplished the task of manoeuvring the slippery carcass onto the deck, it was early evening. In a feverish haste, they started cutting up the fish, with the oily steaks quickly shared out and eaten raw. It was the first decent meal any of them had taken in four days, and having eaten their fill, the remains of the shark were quickly salted and stored below the deck.

The following day some of the shark meat was used to bait the fishing lines; this resulting in a healthy catch of a variety of fish. However, as their food situation became less acute, the ship was suddenly becalmed with everyone aboard, now increasingly concerned regarding the chronic shortage of fresh water. For nowhere in the sultry, windless sky was there any sign of clouds. Brenas now took the opportunity to inform Vescala that, after having conferred with the others, he had decided to attempt to return to Ireland and, for the first time between them, the two men exchanged angry words.

A much happier atmosphere was now prevalent throughout the ship, but the feeling among the people towards Vescala was now one of bitter resentment. Whenever he attempted to talk to any of them, he was acknowledged by silent, hate-filled stares, the people only addressing him when conversation was absolutely essential. As for the ebullient Mondena, he did frequently speak to him, but then only to chide him for his insane dream that had resulted in so much suffering and death. His words deeply wounded the heavy-eyed and distressed Vescala, who now found himself almost as emotionally isolated as he had been in the remoteness of the pit.

With the vessel turned, toward the east, another ten parched days elapsed for those on board. But with no wind in the sail and the weather remaining oppressively hot, the ship moved on by its oar power alone with morale among the people by now having sunk to an all-time low. The late afternoon of their seventy-second day at sea saw the sky begin to take on an ominous appearance, with a thick cumulous of cloud; having suddenly been swept in from the north by a strengthening wind. Vescala had by now taken over the tiller from Brenas, with the ship bowling along for a while under a full sail but, by midnight the gathering storm had broken loose, only this time with an intensity that none on board – including Mondena – had ever seen or imagined. With the sail raised, and the oars drawn in, all hatches were closed, leaving Vescala to stand alone at the helm watching in awe the incessant lightning flashing across the sky like some celestial claw. And, as the seething waves climbed higher than even the 'Mountains of the Wolf' had stretched he heard in the thunder's eruptions, the terrifying roar of destruction.

As the rain-lashed night passed slowly by, he was constantly threatened with being swept overboard by the churning surf, now flooding the deck. Suddenly the sharp noise of splitting timber rose above the storm's hellish roar, and leaping just in time, he fell flat out across the flooded deck to avoid the shattered mast that came crashing down directly over the tiller. In his panic it was more instinct than anything else that saw him grab and cling with all his strength to the ship's rail, now being repeatedly lashed and submerged in the tempestuous waters. Fortunately, Brenas had heard the mast falling, and tying a rope around his waist, he shouted to Lascal to hold onto it before clambering up the steps to the hatch whereon unbolting it, he was drenched in an instant by an avalanche of water cascading across the sloping deck. Struggling out through the hatch, he had to fight with all his strength against the driving wind and rain before reaching the shattered mast where he searched through the darkness for any sign of Vescala. But as the ship lurched violently on the heaving ocean, he suddenly spotted him and succeeded in reaching him just as another giant wave had almost plucked him off the rail. Panting for breath, the two men slithered back over the deck, and after a determined struggle eventually reached the hatch and relative safety. The exhausted Brenas immediately bundled the semi-conscious Vescala into Lascal's arms, who on carrying him down the steps left Brenas to close the hatch and shut out the storm's unrelenting fury.

Abandoning Vescala to fend for himself in one of the bleak cabins, Lascal returned to where his desperately sick wife lay. But below the deck, there was to be no respite from the storm's tyranny as the days now passed by in an ever-growing despair. However, with the food and water once more rationed to a minimum, and owing to the severe dysentery afflicting nearly everyone; few of the people were capable of eating anyway.

Lying isolated from the others Vescala, in his trance-like solitude, at long last began to recall, the events of that terrible night so long ago when the ill-fated Delancia had been murdered; with the mental barrier that for sixteen long years had kept the dark facts locked deep in his mind inexplicably vanishing. Lying drenched in freezing perspiration, he began to relive in vivid detail the monstrous sin perpetrated against her by the assassin priesthood. In the dank blackness of his morbid entombment, his gaping eyes desperately searched around for some comfort. But with his imagination going berserk he once more found himself staring into Trestania's demented eyes, only this time she took the form of a phantom high priestess whose ghoulish black-hooded head now hovered above his outstretched body. In the embalming darkness, and with her hollow shrieking laughter ringing in his ears, his mind now suffered the persecution of a past horror that more than equalled his present plight. Suddenly a voice erupted in his head, obliterating even the sound of Trestania's ghostly laughter and the unceasing roar of the wind and waves outside.

"Remove them both to his 'death-in-life' and there let them lie in their depraved harmony," the voice had commanded. Outside the tomb of his quaking flesh, Vescala now found himself looking upon the sacrificial clearing to see Delancia's body being un-manacled from the sacred tree. Only now could he recognise the voice that had spoken with such dreadful authority as belonging to the duplicitous Straval. Slaves had then dragged the body of Delancia along with himself back through the forest where on reaching the pit, he had first been stripped naked before being pushed over the edge. For the remainder of that eventful day and the following night, he had lain unconscious. However, in the dim light of the spreading dawn, he had awoken into a freezing, silent world only to see Delancia's butchered corpse placed directly opposite him! For every sickening moment of that terrible day, he had glanced periodically into her wide, lifeless eyes. It was a retribution that none, but the blackest of minds could have conceived and enacted. At the end of that horrific day, the grille above had been removed, with Straval's voice then ordering the slaves to. "Raise her up and burn her remains!"

Vescala's tortured screams now rose above the storm's deafening howl, but as his ravings continued no one ventured forth to help him. By now there was no one on board capable of helping anyone other than themselves; they were now a people resigned to death.

With the storm continuing in its furious intensity the last of their food and water dwindled away until nothing remained. But by the morning of their eightieth day at sea the storm had at last subsided, and by the late afternoon, the equatorial sun-gilded ocean had settled into a pacified expanse.

It was an exhausted Lascal who was first to rise onto his unsteady legs and tentatively climbing the stairs leading up to the deck, he unbolted the hatch. Raising it he found himself temporarily blinded by the fierce sunlight now powering its way down into the hold. Shielding his eyes with his arm, he stumbled up onto the deck only for his unbelievable shout of "Land" to force a stunned weary Brenas up to join him.

Although unable to understand the statement, an expectant Mondena then helped Vescala to his feet before leading him up to the deck where Brenas and Lascal stood; their arms supporting one another, among the shattered wood and rigging strewn out all around them.

"Look, Vescala, land," Brenas croaked through parched lips as his bulging eyes stared towards the ascending greenery of the land stretching out before them on the ship's starboard side. But Vescala could only stare incongruously ahead, and fraught with sadness, a gentle runnel of tears trickled slowly down his pale face; knowing that below his feet many more lay dead.

With his cracked lips trembling, Mondena viewed the destruction on deck, and although the small rowing boat had remained intact, it was a miracle that any ship could have survived such a storm he concluded.

Soon the deck was crowded with the lice-infested survivors who had struggled up from the unsanitary conditions in the hold; their dehydrated bodies now, covered in weeping sores. On sighting the new land, many openly wept and fell to their knees in thanksgiving; save for one desperate young mother who, with her stick-thin arms, raised her small dead son toward the land as if somehow hoping that it would regenerate the life back into him. It was with a sense of compunction that Vescala stared towards the mysterious land, only to mutter, "So the old master was right," but then only in a suppressed whisper heard by no one. Slowly, he turned to look around at all those who had survived the ordeal, but as he did so it appeared as if all the recent intense hatred directed towards him had vanished. With a flock of squawking gulls hovering above them, the stricken vessel rolled gently on the translucent blue waters as the incoming tide swept her ever closer toward the silver sands that melted into the densely vegetated hills dominating the eastern horizon.

Chapter Twenty-One

After safely anchoring the ship, they untied and lowered the rowing boat with Vescala, Brenas and Lascal quickly boarding her. Being by far the strongest, Lascal took the oars although it took him some time before he succeeded in beaching the vessel, and with the tide just into its flood they were forced to walk a good distance before their feet sank into the scorching white sands of a long-deserted beach. As their eyes absorbed the supremely, beautiful scenery spreading out before them it was Vescala, who noticed the little stream tumbling down into the sea from the verdant plains ahead of them. Water meant life! And at his behest, the three of them promptly headed towards the stream where after slaking their terrible thirsts, they sat for a short time to rest below the burning sun.

It was Vescala who was the first to rise and staring up at an unknown species of encircling gulls, he proposed to Brenas that the three of them conduct an immediate search for food. With the others readily agreeing, they began to search for edible crustaceans among the many rock pools littering the coastline. However, owing to the now intense heat they first had to shed their jackets before starting to pluck handfuls of the alien molluscs that clung in thick shoals to the rocks. These they flung into their spread-eagled jackets until between them they had gathered up a huge pile, and caring not as to whether the molluscs were safe to eat, they proceeded to break them open with large pebbles before sucking and chewing on the raw, salty flesh they yielded.

With their ravenous hunger satisfied they continued to gather the rich harvest for the others. Brenas now suggested to Lascal that he return to the rowing boat to begin bringing the others ashore; a task he enthusiastically undertook. But by the time everyone had come ashore and with their hunger and thirst fully satisfied, the sun had dipped to touch the horizon, leaving a wine-red tropical sky to look down over the weary survivors who, after two guards had been posted, slept out along the length of the beach.

The following day, after everyone had again eaten, Brenas ordered that the bodies still aboard the ship were to be brought ashore and given a decent burial in the rich earth up from the beach. It took nearly all day to accomplish the task and, as he watched the burials taking place, Vescala with an infelicitous look in his sunken eyes felt relieved that no recriminations were being voiced against him for the disastrous voyage that had claimed so many innocent lives. But nothing could pacify the cruel denunciation in his mind, that his selfishness had been responsible for such a tragedy. He now calculated that, from the two hundred and thirty commune members who had originally set out from Britain, only one hundred and fifty-six shared in the historic experience of having discovered what he prayed was indeed a virgin territory.

Over the next few days, everyone was employed in the gathering and preparation of food, now comprising of seaweed, shellfish, and the few seagulls and fish they were managing to catch. But by their sixth day on the beach, and with everyone's strength improving, it was decided among them that, having seen no sign of any other human life, the time had come to despatch an armed party into the country's interior in order to explore it in greater depth and to seek out the more nourishing game. They also decided to make a start on unloading some of the ship's cargo, and being the most senior among them, Endvar was left to supervise this task.

Shortly before the dawn of their seventh day ashore, a heavily armed Vescala, along with Brenas, Lascal and two others, left the main group sleeping on the beach. At first the land stretching out before them lay flat, although covered in waist-high grass, and with a sanguine sun beginning to rise serenely above the horizon behind them, the alert party ventured forward into the ever-brightening floriferous landscape.

By midmorning, they had entered in to the woodland whose strange twisting trees and bushes grew increasingly dense as the ground below them rose to meet the base of the towering hills ahead. As they advanced, each man was constantly amazed at encountering the great variety of brightly plumaged alien bird life, alongside the multitudes of the many bejewelled insects, who endlessly disturbed the still, humid air. By this time the jungle was alive with unnatural sounds that seemed to be coming at the now heavily perspiring group from all directions. Wonderfully sculptured exotic trees and plants now encapsulated them, and the deeper they penetrated the steaming, tangled undergrowth, the more the mystical greenery began to afflict everyone with a sense of timelessness. To an inspired Vescala, here was a paradise, opulent in its beauteous life forms and unchallenged, it appeared, by man's destructive hand. However, they were still physically weak from their long immolation in the ship's hold, and at Vescala's intimation, they took a short rest to eat the little food they had brought along and drink from the narrow brook cascading down the increasingly steep hillside. As yet they had seen no animal life, and for a short time, they talked excitedly about what they might discover over the summit of the precipitous slopes. But at the sight of a tiny yellow-patterned frog making a tremendous leap from one massive plant leaf onto another, Vescala rose to his feet to be quickly followed by the others.

Resuming their ascent, the men's thin linen jackets and trousers were once more quickly sodden in sweat. Below their now painful feet the creeper-strewn ground grew steadily steeper, and this, alongside the constant insect bites they were having to endure, was beginning to cause them acute discomfort. But every time anyone stopped to gather up his strength the steadfast Vescala shouted encouragingly at them to keep going. Suddenly the ever-alert Lascal launched his spear towards a small furry creature he spotted skipping through the high treetops, and with the weapon striking its target, both animal and spear came crashing down through the thick foliage to fall to the ground ahead of them. After a short search, it was Brenas who found the creature.

"What in the name of the gods is it?" he asked in astonishment, unwilling to touch the ugly-looking animal, who's black, hair-covered body showed certain human characteristics. Stepping forward, Vescala first pulled the spearhead free from the dead animal before picking it up and closely examining its carcass; at the same time, recalling an incident from his childhood.

"It's alright: I think it's a monkey," he said to the others who now surrounded him.

"What the hell's a monkey?" Brenas asked, surprised at Vescala's coolness.

"One day, when I was a child on Anglesey, we were given a lecture by an elderly priest who had returned from a long exploratory mission overseas, that over a ten-year period had taken him to many of the world's far distant countries. Afterward, the priest removed from around his waist a thick leather belt, into which, was etched, many forms of the foreign animals he had encountered on his travels. At the end of the lecture, we were told to sketch the various animals in the dirt and memorise each of their names. Although all this happened when I was no more than ten years old, I'm delighted to say that I can still recall most of them – including the monkey."

"Is it poisonous to eat?" Brenas enquired through a subtle smile.

"No, I shouldn't think so. From what I remember the old druid, certainly made no mention of any of the beasts drawn on his belt being poisonous. However, he did emphasise, that owing to their size and ferocity, some of them, were extremely dangerous."

"Did he tell you which country the monkey was associated with?" Lascal asked as Vescala shrugged.

"He probably did, but I don't recall it. Anyway, from now on we'll have to be careful."

Handing the monkey back to Lascal, Vescala turned away, with none among them having suspected that he had lied to them. Slinging the quarry over his shoulder, Lascal led them forward as they resumed the stiff upward climb, but it wasn't long before they found themselves having to hack a pathway with their swords through the suffocating foliage. At the sight of a luminous blue and green butterfly hovering just above his head, Vescala came to a halt staring in wonderment at the intelligence that had conceived such an unimaginable creation. But almost simultaneously, Lascal yelled out in disgust, for nestling snugly on a sprawling yellow leaf lay the biggest, most horrendous-looking spider any of them had ever seen.

With the sun now beating mercilessly down through the treetops, they stole ever higher and deeper into the unseemly wilderness and, as they advanced, the cackling and screeching sounds coming from the jungle's interior began to play increasingly on everyone's nerves. There were times when it appeared as if they had penetrated the very heart of hell itself! For below their feet, the pristine moss, enmeshing the jungle floor, was alive with giant centipedes, spiders, ants, and every other type of creeping insect the human mind could ever have imagined. Sluggishly they pressed on but reaching a tree-infested plateau, Lascal suddenly stopped, and with his heart clamouring against his chest, he turned to the others, pointing to a gigantic diamond-patterned snake whose thick, slithering body was coiled around a lichen-covered tree trunk. For a few moments, they stopped to stare fearfully, in awe at it before continuing upwards only to eventually come upon a small pool lying between the roots of a huge thorn-studded tree that once again amazed everyone. Here they drank and rested, with Lascal more than eager to skin and roast the monkey, but with mid-afternoon approaching, Vescala and Brenas disagreed deciding that there was no time. As they advanced, they spotted many more species of monkey flitting through the trees, which, by now, were growing thinner on the ground. However, with the air cooler and the terrain rising even more steeply they soon found themselves, having to make frequent stops to rest their weary limbs.

By the late afternoon, an enthusiastic shout from Lascal – who had reached the summit some way ahead of the others – saw them struggle up towards him. On reaching him the sight that they met, was so overwhelming that they could only stand and gaze in disbelief at the luxuriant scenery spreading out before them. Even in their most fanciful of dreams, none of them had dared to imagine the existence of such a place. For directly below them a vista of rolling jungle swept down to the sheltered, green plains of a long, fertile valley, where cutting through its centre and snaking gently along until it ran into a small lake at the far end lay a clear, blue stream whose sparkling waters slaked the thirst of a vast, sprawling herd of an unknown species of fawn-coloured deer.

"Gentlemen…providing it's safe, might I suggest that here among this superb scenery that we create our new homeland?" Vescala proclaimed emotionally, wiping the web of sweat from his face. And sensing that their long years of running and hardship were finally over, the others said nothing as each man met his words with a tearful nod.

With their spirits strengthened but their stomachs empty, they readily agreed to try and kill some of the vast game herd. After descending slowly down the tree-studded hillside they reached the basin of the valley and cautiously began to make their way over the plain's springy turf towards their prey. As they stealthily advanced, a sweet heavily scented breeze kept them on the windward side of the unsuspecting animals just long enough for their spears to bring down two of the creatures before the remaining herd bounded off in great leaps to disappear into the safety of the surrounding trees. Yelling with joy the five of them then ran over to stare down at the bulky carcasses, where two carved horns protruded proudly from each long, elegant head.

"These animals are probably antelopes," Vescala declared, strolling around one of them. "They are related to the deer we had back home. Anyway, it is getting late… I think it would be best, if we got the carcasses over and back down the hill."

"I agree," Brenas replied. "There should be enough meat here to feed everyone for a few days…I can't wait to see the other's faces when they see this place."

"I disagree, father," Lascal said as his eyes scanned the valley. "I think it would be better if you and Vescala remained here to explore the place in depth. The three of us are perfectly capable of taking the carcasses back. It'll be much easier travelling back downhill. We will return sometime tomorrow with the others. By then you should have found a suitable site for us to make a start in the building of a temporary stockade."

"An admirable suggestion," Vescala said. "But I must insist that you leave us a morsel of meat to eat. Oh, another thing, Lascal, take the monkey with you. After you have shown it to the others, tell them you had the personal honour of killing Ravala's twin brother."

Everyone laughed heartily at the quip, and with a large portion of meat having been cut from one of the animal's haunches, the two men stood on the steep banks of the stream watching the other three heading back up the valley's steep slopes with their cumbersome loads slung across their shoulders. From the surrounding jungle came what sounded like a thousand differing bird songs, and observing that the air was now almost free from the swarming insects that had caused them so much annoyance, Vescala turned to the pensive Brenas who stood scanning the glorious landscape.

"I'll say this, Brenas, we're both good for a few years yet. Here in this valley, I honestly believe we can create a free and equal society, the likes of which even the Greek democrats would have envied. My only regret is that so many didn't survive to share this day with us."

Recalling with dismay his tragic daughter, Brenas raised his eyebrows and sighed, "Yes, the inspirational beauty of this place has rekindled the hope for the future that I had forsaken. Let's pray, that when the others see it, they too, will feel the same as we do."

Knowing that they had to find a suitable site in which to make a temporary camp, they returned to the outskirts of the jungle to collect firewood that they carried up to the base of an overhanging cliff; a spot that granted them an excellent view of the surrounding terrain. After lighting a small fire, they soon skinned and roasted the meat and having satisfied their ravenous hunger, they made their way along the jungle's perimeter, which stretched out, all along the entire length of the valley, on both sides of the hills. However, they had walked only halfway when Vescala spotted below him a long and relatively flat plateau close to the stream. After going down to the spot both men readily agreed that the plateau's steep incline would form a natural defensive rampart and that, when built, the stockade would grant them a commanding view of the entire valley.

By now, they had already found building materials: such as wood, and stone in abundance along with clay from the edge of the stream. But, on reviewing their situation, just one problem remained insurmountable in their minds; the fact that they had no seeds, by which, to take advantage of the rich, red earth that the stooping Vescala was now running through his fingers. As of yet, they had seen no sign of any animals that might be domesticated, although this fact didn't cause them too much concern. With the stream and the ocean doubtless providing them with a rich yield in fish and wildfowl, they were confident that the commune could, if necessary, survive and prosper purely from hunting.

Wiping the fertile earth from his fingers onto his trousers, Vescala stood staring up towards the clear, blue sky, uncertain as to whether the seasonal cycles in this land would be similar or entirely different to those back in Britain. He suggested to Brenas that, just as a precautionary measure, it would be wise to make preparations in the event of a severe winter emerging later in the year.

By the time they had walked around the entire valley, the sun had begun to slink into a chasm of deep, crimson-tinted cloud, and with the surrounding trees and bushes now filtering into blackness they returned, tired and hungry, to the encampment where they immediately rekindled the fire and reheated some of the roasted meat. After devouring their meal, they gathered enough wood to keep the fire maintained through the night, and choosing to take the first watch Vescala, sat upright, leaving Brenas to fall into a deep, comforting sleep. And with the final setting of the sun, the great arching sky above stormed into life in a white fire of glittering starlight that shone in unison with a full moon, hanging, suspended from a solitary gossamer cloud.

To Vescala, the valley's beauty now carried an air of enchantment the likes of which he had only ever experienced in the all-too-brief company of his long-departed Delancia. And with her memory resurfacing in his mind, the long years of his imprisoned agony flooded into his emotions like some black deluge. In his momentary despair, he failed to notice that, from out of the moon-struck trees on the valley's far side a group of animals had begun to make their way down to the banks of the stream. The stream itself was shallow enough for them to cross over easily and suddenly spotting the danger, he grabbed the spear by his side and raised himself into a crouching position. But the dozen or so animals, none of whom he recognised from the old druid's belt, were content to drink from the waters, before, making their way to the far end of the valley. Relieved, he again slumped down into a seated position, only this time his eyes were more alert as various animals, again none recognisable to him, began to emerge from the jungle.

As the time went by, the sounds of the night seemed to grow sharper and more menacing. Suddenly the thought occurred to him that great monstrous creatures might well inhabit this corner of the earth, just as they had done in prehistoric times. It was with a sense of dismay that he recalled the massive fossilised skeleton uncovered on Anglesey when drainage ditches were being dug and shivering violently as a sharp chill crept into the air, the remainder of his watch was spent in trying to ease his imaginary delusions. He estimated the time by the path of the moon, and seeing it directly over where the stockade was to be erected, he woke Brenas. After warning him about the animals, he lay wearily back to rest his head on the cold, soft grass to quickly lapse into a well-deserved slumber.

He awoke feeling refreshed to see Brenas busily reheating the last of the meat over the fire. Above him, the sky was a translucent blue that illuminated the valley in an even more splendid array of colour than on the previous day, and being warm and sunny now, he stood up to watch the antelope on the other side of the stream peacefully basking and grazing; oblivious to the presence of the new predators intending to colonise their rightful domain.

"The others should get here shortly. I'm willing to wager they left at first light," Brenas said through a happy smile.

"Yes, I only hope some of the elderly don't find the journey up too exhausting," Vescala replied, stifling a yawn. Handing a healthy portion of the meat over to him Brenas sat by the fire with his contented eyes lazily scanning the landscape. For a while longer they discussed the future. But after Vescala had finished eating they decided to make a start on planning the structure of the stockade and the layout of the buildings within that would be required to see the commune live in security and relative comfort.

Taking their weapons with them they strolled down to the stream, where a flock of pink flamingos strutted peacefully in its clear waters. After washing themselves, they returned to the site of the planned stockade where it was quickly agreed between them that, once the circular stockade's high wooden walls were built, one spacious communal hut would have to be erected within them to provide temporary living accommodation before concentrating on the building of each family unit's huts. With these completed and occupied the communal hut could then be utilised as a storage area for weapons, farming implements, and general requisites until they could organise and erect proper storage buildings. They were also aware that they would have to embark immediately on digging out a number of underground storage pits for their food and pelts, and with their conversation growing more excitable, each man envisaged in his mind's eye the affluent, peaceful settlement they hoped would soon rise to dominate the unspoiled landscape.

"Tell me, Vescala, do you think any other people inhabit this territory?" Brenas suddenly asked.

"I don't know, Brenas. If we should come into contact with any other of our fellow mortals, it could be that we will discover a race of people so far in advance of the Romans that even their technological achievements will appear primitive in comparison."

"Yes, but the Romans regard us as being non-thinking barbarians. How will an even more advanced civilisation look upon us?"

"After the hell we've been through lately, we can only hope our fortune has turned, for the better. But let's not be too premature in our optimism indeed if anything, we may find that as the years go by our greatest enemy might be ourselves! Anyway, all this is pure conjecture. There may well be others! But if by chance any survivors from the original Atlantis did find their way here, it's not improbable that the wheel of fate has turned full circle. Indeed, they might well have degenerated into a sub-stone-age culture."

"Then where do you think we are?" Brenas asked through a puzzled frown, beginning to wonder if Vescala knew more about this land than he was admitting to. But there was no time for his question to be answered as a sudden, distant cry saw them turn to see many running figures rushing down from the jungle towards them, and although still a good way off, the joy in their trailing voices was clearly evident through the stifling air.

It was young Tymaron who was first to reach them only to throw himself upon Vescala, who almost wept on seeing the ragged remnants of the scattered commune members racing towards him with everyone glancing around in wonderment at the incredible beauty of what was to be their new homeland. With the antelope dispersing all around them, Elliana, whose face shone as radiantly as a new-born star, ran up to Brenas, and hugging him tight, she immediately insisted that their new homeland be referred to as 'Freedom Valley,' a proposal met by stentorian shouts of approval from the others. Soon they had all congregated around Brenas and Vescala but glancing around, Brenas could see no sign of Lascal. Elliana was quick to inform him that he, along with a few of the other men, had decided to remain on the shore to make a start on unloading some of the ship's cargo. However, at Lascal's command, some easily transportable equipment such as axes and tools had been brought up with the main group.

Having rested, and after the initial excitement had died down, Brenas ordered work to begin on felling a patch of the jungle's trees which he intended to use in the building of the stockade's defensive walls. A small, stocky-built former slave named Calvas then volunteered to lead a hunting party, and though, both Brenas and Vescala agreed to the proposal, they felt it prudent to advise him against travelling too deep into the jungle's interior. After a short discussion with Vescala, Brenas then gathered everyone around him, to make them fully aware of the vast work output that would be required over the next few months. It then took some time for Elliana and himself to allocate the people to their various tasks, such as who would hunt, cook, and who would fell the trees. Soon after, everyone set about their tasks, with the exception of the aloof Mondena, who stood with his back to the others; the Spaniard being unwilling to participate in the euphoria affecting everyone else. Spotting him, Vescala strolled over to where he stared down at the ground.

"There's no way back, Mondena! You would be as well to accept that fact," he said in a tone that showed a sympathetic understanding of the man's unhappy isolation.

Spinning round, Mondena's eyes conveyed a curious look.

"Tell me, Vescala, what do you intend to do with the ship?"

"When we find out for certain that these lands are safe to inhabit, then we are hoping to beach her and break her up – the wood will come in useful."

"Vescala, I might as well tell you now…I've no intention of remaining here. My knowledge of the sea brought you and your people this far. To be perfectly honest with you I now feel you owe me a favour."

"Alright, Mondena, name it?" Vescala demanded, taken aback at the man's adamant stance.

"What I want is to be given a little wood from the ship and to be granted the use of enough tools to enable me to build a small stable boat that I hope will carry me back home to Spain."

"Mondena, you once accused me of embarking on a suicidal mission. Well, now I accuse you. Believe me; I'm truly sorry for your sad predicament. But don't you think it would be wiser to stay here and carve out a new life for yourself rather than attempt to cross that hellish ocean alone?"

"No!" Mondena exclaimed emphatically. "Now I've grown to admire and respect you and your people. When you kidnapped me, you had nothing to lose! As you told me yourself, you faced death wherever you went. But here in this place – beautiful as it is – I too have nothing to live for. All I ask is to be given the material and tools that will allow me to return to my wife and children. My father and his father before him were expert boat builders. When I was young, they taught me enough of their craft to enable me to build the small boat I'll require." Mondena flexed his muscles and stared hard at Vescala. "I'm going, Vescala, even supposing I have to swim all the way back."

"Alright," Vescala snapped, sensing that nothing he could say would dissuade the determined Spaniard. "We can no longer keep you against your will. But first, I'll have to speak to Brenas, although I don't visualise him raising any objection to your request. Hopefully, we should be able to beach the ship in a few months from now; indeed, as soon as we've completed the stockade and communal hut. You must appreciate, that there are many women and children among us whose safety is paramount. When we can guarantee their security, I don't think anyone will object to you being granted permission to leave if you so desire."

"Then I'll help you to build your village!" Mondena exclaimed, smiling for the first time in a long time.

For the remainder of the day tree after tree fell before the swinging axes, and after being trimmed of their branches they were manually dragged over to the plateau where they were stockpiled. By the early evening, the hunting party had returned bringing a healthy supply of antelope and monkeys, with the animals being quickly skinned and cooked just in time to greet Lascal and his group, who were suddenly spotted struggling towards the camp with their burdens of provisions strapped onto their weary, aching backs. A great cheer then went up from everyone to greet the nine men, with Vescala delighted on being handed a string of wild runner beans by Lascal, who had come upon them growing in the jungle. Earlier on, one of the men had also discovered a cluster of giant mushrooms while helping to fell the trees. And as they sat around the bright campfires listening to the merry singing of the surviving women and children, everyone began to grow increasingly optimistic over a future that only a few days before had appeared to have been lost forever.

Chapter Twenty-two

Having taken a few days off from work, in order to explore the surrounding countryside in greater depth, Vescala, and Brenas travelled well beyond the valley only to be delighted on their return to inform the others that they had found no sign whatsoever of any other human inhabitants.

By the end of their first month of colonisation, the stockade's defensive walls lay complete, leaving only the portcullis to be placed into position. Meanwhile, inside the compound, work had already started on the erection of what was to be the main communal building. The apparently inexhaustible array of wildlife continued, to astound everyone, with new species being discovered every time hunting parties were despatched. Subsequently, a variety of the smaller monkeys and a larger form of the British field mouse were captured and caged. These were then experimented upon by Vescala to determine which of the rich abundance of larger fruit, berries, roots, herbs, and other plants were safe for human consumption. By carefully observing the varieties they ate and which they rejected, he was able to build up a mental dossier of which types of plant life were to be avoided. After this task was done everyone – including the youngest children had to then memorise every significant detail of the offending species. Their food situation was also helped by the discovery, of a type of wild grain along with the black bread made from seaweed gathered and strenuously carried up from the shore. Large quantities of high-grade honey were to be found everywhere. And after much experimentation with yeast substitutes, they were soon capable of producing a plentiful supply of quality mead.

By now, Vescala had undertaken yet another survey of the surrounding countryside, this time alone, and once again reported back, that he had found no sign of any human life. As a result of this, the galley had been beached, with most of its wood being stripped and carried up from the shore and recycled in the building of the family huts. Just as Vescala had previously intimated to Mondena, no opposition from Brenas and the other committee members was raised over his request to leave; consequently, most of the Spaniard's time was now spent on the shore, slowly shaping his carefully designed craft.

With work well advanced on the spacious huts that would house the individual family groups, outside the stockade, just below the plateau, many small rectangular fields had been staked out. These were allotted to each family unit, with wild grain, beans, and a variety of fruit-yielding bushes now planted in their respective plots.

In order to obtain a more democratic form of government than the one-man system that had ruled the commune for so long, Brenas, at Vescala's instigation, decided to put to the people his intention to elect a five-man governing committee who would be responsible for the day-to-day running of the settlement. With everyone readily agreed to this proposition, a vote was quickly organised and counted ending in the resulting committee comprising of Vescala, Brenas, Endvar, Calvas, and an exuberant Lascal who, given his young age, was highly honoured to have been chosen. Owing to the people's magnificent dedication in the creation of the settlement, the committee's first decision was to announce three days of rest and celebration; a decision greatly appreciated by everyone, as it would be their first decent period of relaxation since their disembarkation from the ship.

By the time late summer arrived the stockade and communal hut had been completed, with Mondena finishing his work on the craft that would hopefully take him home.

Sometimes when fishing offshore in the small rowing boat – all that remained of the galley – Lascal would sit and admire the lonesome Spaniard's dedication to his family. But like everyone else in the commune, even Lascal, adventurous as he was, held out little hope for the man's eventual success.

For another month, Mondena dogmatically persevered in his task until at last his boat lay complete, and early one morning, having laboured on through the night, he stood back with a sense of achievement to admire his handiwork. Although not much bigger than the ship's rowing boat, his craft was sturdily built, with a small and ingeniously designed collapsible mast, having been constructed in its centre. Having situated the storage area for fresh water and food supplies into a compartment at the stern of the open vessel, in severe weather a thick, resin-coated leather tarpaulin could be quickly hauled over the vessel's entire length, and once tied down would hopefully render the boat unsinkable. In fair weather the covering could be stored in yet another compartment Mondena had built into the boat's bow. Although small in structure, his vessel was designed for durability and speed, and he remained confident that, given enough luck, he could expect to land on Spanish soil within forty days.

Turning his attention toward a troop of baboons feeding on shrimp and crustaceans among the rock pools further along the shore, Mondena's smug smile showed man's heartless nature at its worst. How alike were his kidnappers to these half-witted creatures, he thought retributively? Ever since that fateful day when they had sailed out from Ireland Vescala had persistently ordered him to maintain a westerly course. However, at every available opportunity he had turned the ship southeast with his ultimate intention being to steer her to an isolated part of southern Spain. It had been so simple for him to deceive Vescala and the others. And although the frequent storms had blown them well off his planned course, he remained convinced that they had generally maintained a south-easterly direction and that the land on which he stood was none other than the western coast of an as-yet-unexplored part of the dark, mysterious continent of Africa. He was more than familiar with the North African coastline, having sailed in that region, of the world on many occasions. However, the south of the continent, although known to exist, remained a total mystery even to the Romans. His instinct told him, that if he followed the coastline in a northerly direction, he must eventually reach the 'Gibraltarian Pillars of Hercules,' and once past them Spain and home. Leaving the vessel fully prepared for the sea journey, he began the trip back to the valley, happy in the knowledge that the following morning would see him on his way.

That night Elliana and some of the other women had organised a surprise farewell party for the little Spaniard in order to allow everyone an opportunity to wish him a last farewell. The party was held in the smoke-laden atmosphere of the communal hut, with the centerpiece of the banquet being a huge antelope roasting on a spit at the far end of the packed hall. Owing to the language barrier; Mondena had seldom directly communicated with anyone apart from Vescala nonetheless, the depth of the feeling in which they held him surprised him. As everyone took their turn in shaking his hand and wishing him success, some were close to tears with each man and woman well aware that, were it not for the Spaniard's expert seamanship, they would probably never have survived to set foot on the earthly paradise of which they were now the undisputed masters.

Suddenly Vescala stepped up onto one of the benches laid out all along the four walls.

"Let's drink to Mondena and pray that he will soon be reunited with his loved ones," he shouted out, raising his cup of mead. Everyone else then joined him in the toast before embarking on the singing and dancing, leaving the two men to drink alone at the back of the hall.

"I'll say this, Vescala, if my family were here with me, I should have been quite happy to remain among you. But without them, I could never have been happy – such is my love for them," he declared as Vescala smiled and stepped back down, to the floor.

"When you do eventually get home, Mondena, you could always return with them," he proposed. But sweeping his long black hair back from his perspiring brow, Mondena shook his head at the suggestion.

"No, no way. When I reach Spain, I'll be more than happy to spend the rest of my days on dry land. But tell me, Vescala, do you never miss your loved ones back home?"

"No, I have no family...I'm afraid providence has treated me somewhat unkindly as far as family life is concerned." As Vescala spoke Mondena noticed the vacant loneliness filling his eyes. Although he had no love for the man, he now felt a certain sympathy towards his abductor.

"Still, who can say what the future holds?" Vescala then said, cheerfully.

"That's true. I did notice in recent times the amorous glances passing between you and that daughter of Calvas...what's her name?"

"Arlesia. Yes, I must confess over these last few months I have developed a strong desire towards her. To be perfectly honest, I'm still trying to pluck up enough courage to ask her father for her hand in marriage."

"Oh, I'm sure your request would be granted. It would be good for your commune to begin expanding. I can think of no better environment in which to bring up a large family."

Both men smiled agreeably as they walked through the noisy dancing throng to replenish their cups. But, as the warm evening wore on, Vescala found himself more and more, in the welcome company of Arlesia, who was a sprightly, young girl now into her fourteenth summer with bright cheerful hazel eyes that mirrored her more-than-pleasant personality. Back in Britain, he had paid no particular attention to her, but ever since her mother had been one of the first to die aboard the ship, her prominence had become increasingly apparent to him. He had found himself admiring not only her graceful physical beauty but also the strong self-discipline she showed as she undertook her responsibilities with a driving enthusiasm. Indeed, she had been an inspiration to many older than her. The long age gap between them mattered little to him. It had always been customary for an older man to take a young bride, especially if his existing spouse had failed to produce a son in the marriage. Anyway, it had been the druidical law for centuries that if a man could afford to maintain two, three, or even four wives then he was perfectly entitled to do so.

One of the first acts the committee had endorsed was the decision to retain the Celtic laws appertaining to marriage. However, the stalwart Elliana had insisted that no woman should ever be trapped into a marriage she opposed and that no man be permitted to take more than one wife. As to her first amendment, the committee was, in unanimous agreement with her with each man being well- aware of the unhappiness which that particular -event, had brought into her own life. But as to her other amendment, there had been much discussion and deliberation among the five men before it too was accepted, the principal reason being, that there simply just weren't enough women for any man to have more than one wife.

Unlike life back in the old country where women were normally treated as mere chattels, they were now allowed to attend and speak at the committee meetings which were held on the first day of every month. And although disbarred from any free vote that the committee might call on the men to take, it was generally agreed among everyone that the women had been granted a far greater emancipation than even a priestess or indeed a noblewoman would ever expect to receive back in Britain.

After Mondena was gone the commune would number one hundred and fifty-five, comprising fifty-one men, and fifty-five women, of whom thirty-four were of childbearing age and thirty-nine children whose sexes were almost equally divided.

The committee had previously discussed in depth the problem of interbreeding occurring among them. It was to prevent this that Vescala had been chosen to undertake an extensive exploratory mission, firstly along the coast and then inland in an attempt, to seek out and contact any peaceful civilisation that might exist in what so far was found to be an uninhabited territory. The idea for such a venture had been proposed by Vescala himself, who had placed great emphasis, on the grave danger that long-term interbreeding could have within such a small communal environment.

As the evening advanced the singing and dancing grew even more boisterous with Elliana inadvertently announcing to some of the women standing beside her that her daughter-in-law Silena was pregnant. The news spread like wildfire, reaching the ears of a stunned Silena who hadn't even informed her husband of the happy event. But she was nowhere near as surprised as the drunken Lascal who suddenly found himself swamped by groups of well-wishers. After congratulating him, Vescala then entered into a conversation with Mondena: proposing to him that, as he himself, was leaving in the morning, it might be a good idea if they were to travel down to the shore together; explaining to the little Spaniard that he could help him launch his boat into the water. Mondena readily agreed, being grateful that someone was seeing him off on what was going to be a long and dangerous voyage.

Vescala had decided that after leaving Mondena, he would first, follow the southern coastline before turning inland to travel east. He had informed the others that his travels would take him at least three months, and as there was still so much work to be done within the compound of the stockade, he had stated a preference to travel alone. Although the others had agreed, Brenas had voiced his reservations regarding the unknown dangers that a man might face in travelling alone through alien terrain, particularly on foot. But Vescala had discounted such fears, reckoning that he had personally come through enough danger in the past that had to be at least the equivalent of anything he may confront in the near future. Suddenly the obese figure of Calvas staggered over to where Vescala and Mondena were now seated; he was about to wish them luck on their various missions. However, on seeing the intoxicated condition the man was in, Vescala saw his opportunity; a fact that didn't go unnoticed by Mondena who nudged him in the ribs with his elbow.

"Calvas, I should like to have a word with you in private," Vescala said, rising to his feet. With a puzzled expression masking his bloated, ruddy features, Calvas escorted him through the dancing throng and out the door where the warm night air was now alive with the sounds of the wild coming from the nearby jungle. Turning to face Calvas, Vescala drew in a deep breath.

"I don't know if you ever noticed, Calvas, but my feelings towards your daughter Arlesia have recently developed into more than just friendship. With your permission, I should like to take her hand in marriage," Vescala said, nervously clearing his throat whilst awaiting a reply from a stunned and wide-eyed Calvas, who was elated at the thought of his only daughter marrying a man of such stature as Vescala.

"You, of all people, have more than my blessing and most certainly my permission to ask her…you do her, her brother and myself a great honour," the grinning Calvas replied, placing his strong hand on Vescala's shoulder. "But there's one small snag," he then muttered, removing his hand and his smile gone. "I regret that I am unable to provide you with a suitable dowry."

Both men laughed aloud at the jest with such a requirement under druidical law having, at Vescala's instigation, been waived aside in their new homeland.

"Tell me, Vescala, how do you think Arlesia will react to your proposal?"

"Believe me, Calvas, I'm not at all sure."

"Well, son, I've seen the look in her eyes when she's been in your company. I think you'll find her more than happy to accept your proposal. If you wish, I'll send her out to you. After all, there's no time like the present to begin planning for the future."

"I agree. Now's as good a time as any to ask her," Vescala replied as the beaming Calvas then re-entered the noisy hut leaving him alone to gaze up at the ethereal beauty of the star-strewn sky.

"You desire to speak to me, Vescala?" Arlesia asked in a trembling voice as she slowly walked from the open doorway towards him. Drawing his eyes from the sky it took him a few moments to escape the hypnotic effect that the glittering starlight held over his mind. Glancing down to the timid figure standing before him, he could not help but compare her physical attributes to those of his tragic Delancia. Perhaps this was the reason as to why he had felt so attracted to her in the first instance, he wondered sadly. And although he did feel a genuine love for the young girl it was a tepid love, devoid of the intense passion he had experienced and still felt even after all these years for his lost Delancia. For a moment he felt ashamed of himself, being well aware, that his spiritually impotent love was in reality no more for him than a means of creating an heir.

"Arlesia," he whispered tenderly, staring into her dark, innocent eyes, "I've taken the liberty of asking your father for his permission to have you as my wife. He has consented, and all I require to make me the happiest man alive is for you to likewise agree."

"Yes," she declared. But the speed of her reply took Vescala by surprise and stretching up onto her tiptoes she flung her arms around his neck to bring her moist lips up to his. Quickly breaking away from his cool embrace her head dropped to rest against his chest.

"When will we marry? Please say it will be soon…I'll bear you many sons," she said softly as Vescala held her tight and smiled at her innocent charm.

"We will marry as soon as I return from my mission," he replied as Arlesia's petite face looked up at him, showing her disappointment. "Come on, cheer up. I may not be gone as long as I've anticipated. Even if I am, the time will soon pass."

"But it's such a long time; why not let someone else go?" she asked petulantly, coiling her slender arms around his waist, and smothering his face with her kisses.

For a while longer they embraced only for Vescala to suddenly break free from the clinch and, placing an arm around her slim waist, he led her back towards the entrance of the hut.

"No, my love. I'm afraid it has to be me who goes but don't fret…I have every intention of returning safely. Now let's go in and announce our betrothal."

After they re-entered the hut, their good news was met with another round of merriment that lasted until well after midnight. Soon afterward everyone lay fast asleep around the hall with Arlesia lying peacefully coupled to Vescala who remained awake, gently stroking her long black hair with his fingers. In his heart, he knew that he would find only a modicum of happiness with his future child bride, but his mind was troubled by other matters, indeed more troubled than it had been for a long, long time.

He found himself capable of sleeping only in snatches and come the first light of daybreak he rose and, leaving Arlesia's side, joined Mondena who was already up and eating leftover scraps from the previous night's feasting. Both men had finalised their preparations the day before, and as Vescala joined him in breakfasting they exchanged few words; each man now feeling apprehensive regarding their different missions. Mondena had been permitted to take with him as much food as his vessel could carry, along with a sword, dagger and the tools that would allow him to carry out any essential repairs that he might be required to make to the boat while at sea. As for Vescala, he would travel light carrying only a sword, a spear, and a small rucksack containing enough food to last him a few days. After that, he would be forced into living off the shore and the land.

By the time they had finished eating, the blazing sun was above the horizon and with everyone else still fast asleep they quietly gathered their equipment. They then made their way, across to the portcullis, which was immediately raised for them by the lone sentry, who wished them luck. Both men acknowledged his kindness with a handshake before proceeding at a brisk pace, over the plain towards the tranquil, jungle-enmeshed hills. They were all alone now, save for a majestic flock of white ibis that stood fishing and preening themselves in the stream. Crossing over the water they entered into the humid jungle where they quickly found themselves covered in an uncomfortable film of sticky sweat. With the sounds of the wild floating eerily around them they soon travelled over and down the steep hillside to head for the long ribbon of aquamarine ocean stretching out ahead of them. Reaching the deserted beach Mondena proudly showed Vescala his boat, which lay sheltered between two large rocks not far up from the high tide mark.

"As you can see, Vescala, the tide is just on the ebb," he said, pointing to a pile of wooden rollers stacked by the vessel's bow. "Using these rollers, I made to act as a slipway, it won't take us long to launch her."

Vescala nodded, and putting down his spear and rucksack he took up an armful of the rollers to begin laying them out and down towards the water, leaving Mondena, who was whistling a merry tune, to place his weapons and provisions into the boat. By the time Mondena had finished filling the water tank with freshwater taken from a nearby stream, Vescala had laid out the last of the rollers. With everything now prepared both men took up their positions on either side of the vessel to begin pushing her towards the sea whereon the small but heavy craft was hauled slowly along until its bow kissed the water's edge. But with both men now perspiring heavily in the stifling air the vessel momentarily stuck fast, and they had to give her one final push before she slid speedily along the last roller, resulting in the two of them falling headlong into the cool, refreshing water.

Aided by Lascal, the Spaniard had given the boat a trial run some days previously. But on seeing her once again floating on the receding tide, a jubilant Mondena stood knee- deep in the water and, raising his arms high into the air, shouted his praises to one of his gods. As Vescala stood up Mondena splashed over to offer him his handshake.

"I may be travelling alone, Vescala, but I want you to know that you and your people will always be in my thoughts."

Vigorously shaking the Spaniard's hand Vescala could feel the tension mounting in his head.

"May your gods go with you, Mondena – wherever you travel," he said, and releasing his hand and stepping back he ushered the Spaniard to go aboard. However, as Mondena, whose back was now to him, began to clamber aboard, Vescala quickly unsheathed his sword, and with one swift stroke sent its sharp blade crashing deep into the back of his unsuspecting victim's head. Clutching onto his bloodied thatch with both hands Mondena emitted a high-pitched squeal, before stumbling and staggering back through the water where he turned around, aghast, only to see Vescala recoil backward. But inspired by the evil necessity of his murderous intent, Vescala bounded forward, to again bring the flailing weapon down, only this time into the Spaniard's forehead. Mondena's legs instantly buckled and almost gave way under the blow's impact, and although he somehow managed to stay on his feet, he screamed wildly as his gaping eyes stared in stunned disbelief at the blood-lust in the eyes of the man who, only the night before, he had taken pity on. With the blood now pumping in torrents through his fingers to discolour the shallow waters surrounding him, he ploughed desperately back to reach the scorching sands and began to stagger erratically away from his executioner. But there was to be no escape with Vescala immediately pursuing him and with yet another ferocious blow he once more launched the sword down onto the back of the fleeing Spaniard's head. This time it sank in even deeper, severing four of the terror-stricken man's fingers and, as Vescala released the sword's hilt Mondena stumbled for a few more paces with the ruthless iron now embedded deep into his expiring brain. But looking upwards, he collapsed onto his knees, with his blood-streaked eyes meeting for the last time the hyacinth blue sky and falling forward onto his face, his fingerless arm convulsed for a few sickening moments before his body lay motionless over the blood-saturated sand. As Vescala lunged forward to extricate the sword from the gaping wound, a chilling horror flooded into his soul, and falling to his knees he tried hard within himself to justify such a despicable action. How could he of all people have so brutally prevented such a harmless little man from seeking a re-unification with his loved ones? He wondered fearfully. And yet what choice did he have? If Mondena had succeeded in returning to Roman-occupied Spain, it would only have been a matter of time before he would have talked about his experiences to others. Words that would almost certainly have reached Roman ears, and once Rome knew of the existence, of a rich and uninhabited land she would have speedily despatched her armies to invade and swallow into her already vast empire what was probably the only earthly paradise the commune was ever likely to find. No, he now thought coldly if one small galley could master the fury of the Atlantic, then thousands could, and with their superb technology, the Romans would have undoubtedly have built even greater ships by which to transport their colonists to begin afresh a new era of barbaric inequality.

For some time, he had suspected Mondena of having deceived them, with the old druid explorer having spoken of an African continent lying to the south of Spain. It had been from that particular continent that he had seen most of the animals etched into his belt. Vescala would never know for certain though, and although his decision to kill Mondena had been a painful one, he could never have allowed one man to jeopardise the lives of so many others.

His intention had been to tie Mondena's body down into the boat and, using the small rowing boat lying berthed a little further along the beach, take it to beyond the low tide mark and there sink it. But with the world strangely silent around him and with even the waters lapping the shore appearing to be creating no sound, he suddenly felt a terrible panic seize him.

Pale and trembling, he rose to his feet and dragged the corpse back up the beach to where the boat had originally been moored. Using his bare hands, he scooped out the sand from between the rocks for what would be Mondena's final resting place. By the time he had finished digging the shallow grave, he was panting for breath, and after tipping the corpse into the grave, he returned to the beach to retrieve the missing fingers where finding them with no difficulty he kicked over the soiled sand until no traces of blood were to be seen before returning to the grave to place the fingers into it. As he began refilling it, he shuddered as some sweat from his perspiring brow fell to splash over Mondena's blood-drenched face. However, the grisly task was soon completed; witnessed only by the mute elements, and with the ebb tide now taking the boat out to sea, he stood erect breathing a sigh of relief on reckoning that no one back in the settlement would ever know the true fate that had befallen the Spaniard.

Gathering up his weapons and rucksack, he was just about to leave the scene to head south when his eyes inexplicably darted down to the sand covering the grave. For a moment he stood petrified, thinking that the sand had moved. But just as he was cursing his imagination for playing tricks, his eyes were again drawn back to the spot and this time there was no doubt in his mind that the sand had moved…indeed, was still moving! With neither movement in the still air, nor breath in the interred corpse, the white shifting sands continued to heave and swirl as if some abnormal life force had entered the sanctity of the grave itself. Now imprisoned in his terror, Vescala stepped back! And with his entire body numbed with shock, his eyes remained transfixed on the grave where, one by one, each of the severed fingers was breaking through the sand's surface to begin groping towards his feet. Filled with self-loathing and disgust, and feeling as if trapped within some outlandish nightmare, he turned to flee south along the deserted beach. With his spear almost glued to his hand, he had to force his sluggish limbs with all his strength through the energy-sapping sands. But as he ran, never daring to look back, nowhere did it seem possible to escape the torrid screaming now emanating from the direction of the grave; a screaming that would haunt his conscience for the rest of his life.

Chapter Twenty-three

On approaching the beach, a badly shaken Lascal momentarily stepped back, for jutting out from between the two guano-splashed rocks, a skeletal arm and part of a human skull were now clearly visible. Suddenly it struck him that the remains were indeed human and not some animal's as he had first suspected. Kneeling, by the side of the grave, he carefully swept away the thin veil of sand covering the remains until the entire length of the corpse was evident. The deep clefts in the skull caused him to shudder, but with the body's clothing having remained almost intact, he shook his head in disbelief, with there being, no doubt in his mind as to whom it had once adorned. Pushing the dry, straggly hair to one side he closely examined the massive wounds that had been inflicted on the back and front of Mondena's head; all the time wondering as to what had happened. Gradually, he turned his curious eyes away from the remains to scan the ocean's calm waters where only a few gulls soared and swooped in their never-ending quest for food. Was it possible that Mondena had set sail only to have been blown back onto the shore by a storm, or had some animal savaged and killed him prior to his departure? Indeed, had Vescala quarrelled with Mondena and then killed him? He thought frowning gloomily anxious to know the answer, recalling that young Tymaron and himself had been fishing offshore only a few days after Mondena had supposedly set sail, and all that they had seen then were the slipway rollers leading down to the sea. Anyway, it was obvious that the body had been deliberately interred, and now utterly bemused, he rose to his feet only to grimace on thinking that Vescala might well have shared a similar fate. Suddenly, he heard his name being called, and walking back around the rocks he saw the tiny figure of Tymaron running along the water's edge coming in his direction.

"Lascal, come and see. I've found a boat," his voice sang out in its childish innocence, and not wishing the child to see the gruesome remains, he ran over to meet him.

"There's a boat lying on its side high up on the beach round the headland. It looks like the one the Spaniard built," Tymaron panted out, pointing to the northern headland.

"Alright lad, show me."

As the two of them ran back along the beach, Lascal was even more baffled than before. In the three months since the two men had left the settlement, Tymaron and himself had often fished in that area, and at no time had they ever sighted any vessel. Rounding the headland, his scowling eyes remained cautious as he stopped to walk around the boat that, just as Tymaron had said, lay on its side a good distance up from the high-water mark. Once again, his perplexed eyes stared towards the gulls skimming low above the ocean's surface, wondering if perhaps they were the only ones who might know the answer to the deepening mystery. Turning to view the vessel two questions began to trouble him. What had happened to the boat in the time since Mondena's death? And if Vescala had indeed taken the boat, what had become of him?

On closely inspecting the marooned vessel, he saw that the leather tarpaulin that had been tied to its side was gone with the undamaged mast still lying tied from the bow to the stern just as Tymaron and himself had last seen it the day before Mondena's departure.

Up-righting the vessel, he then checked the food stocks only to find, that they had long perished. But after forcing open the sealed wooden tank containing the water supply with his dagger, he became convinced that neither man had ever set out to sea, with the water remaining untouched. Suddenly the terrifying thought occurred to him that both men had indeed launched the vessel only to have been attacked and killed by aliens.

"How did it get back here, Lascal?" Tymaron asked, interrupting his thoughts.

"Don't ask questions…get back to the rowing boat and make a start on salting and storing the fish we caught earlier on."

"It is the Spaniard's boat, isn't it?"

"Look, do as you're told…I'll answer your questions later," Lascal snapped. Seeing his rising anger Tymaron left before receiving a cuff over his ear. But with the thought of natives existing in their new homeland striking more than a note of anxiety into him, Lascal again pondered over what might have happened. Examining the hull of the boat, he was baffled by its lack of barnacles, having expected the hull to have been encrusted in them after so long at sea, just as the Roman galley's hull had been when they had beached her to scrap her.

Leaving the vessel, he returned around the headland to rejoin Tymaron, who, by now, had almost finished packing the morning's catch from the rowing boat into the small wooden barrel lying by its side. Ordering the child to gather a sack full of whelks after completing his chore, he returned to the partially exhumed corpse.

Pulling the skeletal remains free from the sand, he noticed that four fingers were missing from one hand, and carefully scrutinising it, he could only surmise by the clean cuts on the bones that Mondena must have used it to fend off a blow to his head from either a sword or axe. First checking that Tymaron was well out of sight, he quickly dragged the remains up to the graveyard where they had interred all those who had perished aboard the galley. Using his sword he hastily dug out a shallow grave from the soft earth. After re-burying the remains, he returned to the beach where he began prodding the sand over a wide area with his spear in the event of Vescala having been interred in a similar manner only to come upon some of the slipway rollers lying buried just below the sand's surface.

Recalling that two nights previously there had been a violent tropical storm, he was almost certain that it had been the driving winds, that were, responsible for uncovering the grave and perhaps tossing the boat so high up onto the shore. Even so, he still found it hard to believe that the body had gone undetected for so long, for over the past three months he had frequently berthed the rowing boat in the sheltered spot between the rocks. Although seeming preposterous, it suddenly crossed his mind that Vescala might have done the killing. In that case, what puzzled him was why he should have then buried the body in such a conspicuous place. After all, Vescala was well aware, that the rowing boat was usually berthed in that spot and with that knowledge must have known that at some time there had to be a good chance of the corpse being uncovered by the boat's keel as it was dragged up the beach and berthed between the rocks. But what could have motivated Vescala into taking such an action? The bewildered Lascal now kept asking himself. The committee had fully discussed the possibility of Mondena eventually reaching Spain, and then talking to others of their discovery. But they had all agreed unanimously that such an event was highly improbable, with each of them, including Vescala, convinced that the little Spaniard would perish at sea.

For a while longer he continued to search for another grave but finding nothing he returned along the beach to where the rowing boat lay. Sitting on the boat's side his mind kept turning over all the relevant facts of what was, indeed, an intriguing mystery. However, after a time, the thought that Vescala, of all people, was capable of slaughtering a man in such savagery became almost inconceivable; nonetheless, he now felt duty-bound to challenge him over the matter if and when he ever returned.

Looking around, he could see no sign of Tymaron, and ambling, slowly around the headland he spotted him prying around Mondena's boat.

"I told you to gather whelks," he shouted, walking up behind the child who immediately spun round.

"I did! There's a whole sack-full lying beside the boat," Tymaron replied, impudently parodying Lascal's deep voice. Looking down at the child's mischievous face, Lascal broke into a grin.

"Sorry, kid; I didn't see them."

"Is it the Spaniard's boat?"

"Yes, son. We must assume he was swept overboard. The storm the other night flung the boat back up onto the beach. Maybe he was trying to find his way back to us," Lascal concluded.

"He must have been a brave man."

"Aye, son, that he was. Anyway, we'll have to be getting back to the stockade. If you return to the rowing boat I'll join you shortly."

Lascal then waited until the child was out of sight before emptying the boat's water tank, and gathering up the remains of the rotted food he threw it into the sea. After this was done, he re-joined Tymaron who helped him to haul the rowing boat back up the beach and berth her between the rocks. Strapping the barrel of fish onto his back, and with Tymaron carrying the sack of whelks, they began the long uphill climb back to the valley.

It was late in the afternoon by the time they reached their goal, but nearing the stockade Lascal's suspicion regarding Vescala was still troubling him when, from the rampart, the guard's voice rang out.

"Vescala's back, he arrived this morning shortly after you two left."

Unstrapping the barrel, and dropping it as he ran, Lascal sped through the raised portcullis towards the communal building where Vescala, who appeared none the worse for wear, stood with his arm around Arlesia in conversation with Brenas and

Calvas. Suddenly spotting Lascal, Vescala let go of Arlesia and rushed over to meet him.

"Great to see you, Lascal," he said holding out his hand, but stopping in his tracks Lascal failed to reciprocate the greeting.

"I'm glad you made it back, Vescala! All be it in one piece!" he proclaimed with a sneer writhing on his lips; a sneer that momentarily confounded Vescala, who expected him like the others to have been delighted at his safe homecoming.

"Tymaron discovered the Spaniard's boat on the shore this morning, not far from where he set sail!" Lascal exclaimed acridly. However, as Vescala stood rigid at the news his heavily tanned features betrayed no emotion.

"Then the little fool must have perished at sea. He should have taken my advice and stayed with us. Was there any sign of his body?"

"No, none," Lascal answered, managing to disguise his anger at Vescala's callousness, and staring into Vescala's cold, unwavering eyes, he sensed that the returning traveller knew the full truth about the affair. The two men then found themselves joined by the others who had overheard their conversation.

"That's indeed bad news, son," Brenas remarked sympathetically. "We had all hoped he might have made it. As Vescala said, he should have listened to his advice. Anyway, Arlesia and Vescala are to be married tomorrow with Calvas promising us a feast we're unlikely to forget."

"Yes, Lascal. Let's not forget that life goes on," Vescala commented only for Lascal, whose disgust showed on his face, to turn on his heels and storm away, leaving the others surprised at his behaviour. But with a wry grimace on his face, the unperturbed Vescala shook his head.

"It must have been upsetting for him to have found the boat. He did like Mondena: I for one can well understand his feelings."

The others agreed with his statement, the exception being Arlesia, who ardently snuggled closer to him. Like her future husband, she cared nothing for the unfortunate Spaniard; they had each other and as far as she was concerned, nothing else mattered. Brenas then resumed the conversation they had been holding before Lascal's appearance.

"As you were saying, Vescala you reckon the territory to be uninhabited?"

"Yes, as far as I could see the country is ours. Even so we must show caution; after all, there was a great deal of territory I was unable to cover. Personally, I feel that if we are to create the radical society we so often discussed, Brenas, then just as a precautionary measure it might be wiser if we strengthen our present defences. In this little kingdom, we have all the natural resources men and women, could ever desire. To be perfectly honest, I see no point in implanting the commune outside this valley, although in years to come I can find no objection to making the occasional exploratory mission into the surrounding terrain."

Once again, the others agreed as the smiling Vescala bent to kiss the top of Arlesia's head. As he did so Brenas and Calvas burst out laughing at the sight of little Tymaron stumbling towards them carrying in his outstretched arms the sack of whelks on top of the heavy barrel of fish.

The following morning was dull and overcast, and in anticipation of the coming celebrations everyone had risen earlier than usual with Elliana immediately setting about the task of supervising the preparations for the wedding banquet.

The ceremony was held in the communal hut at noon, witnessed by Brenas, Elliana, Calvas, Silena, and the morose Lascal. Being the eldest commune member, it was Endvar who conducted the simple ceremony that comprised of an exchange of bracelets and vows dealing with love and faithfulness. As the happy floral-bedecked couple left the building the cheering crowds outside showered them in brightly coloured petals.

Meanwhile, on the long rows of hewn-out logs that had been converted into makeshift tables, a magnificent selection of dishes lay spread out, ranging from simple sweetmeats to lobster smothered in a specially created seaweed sauce. jugged antelope, fruit, and vegetable salads, along with a more-than-ample supply of mead to wash it all down, had also been provided; all this having been done at short notice by Elliana and the other women.

After the speechmaking was over the feasting and dancing began in earnest with everyone having given the customary wedding presents. Two large nuggets of gold, accidentally discovered in the stream by the young Chevada, made a more-than-fitting gift for the lovely Arlesia, who looked resplendent in her pale blue wedding gown. However, the finest gift of all was made by the other committee members, who presented the newlyweds with the first of the newly completed family huts.

By the late afternoon the sun had at last emerged through the cloud, and with the noisy atmosphere from the proceedings now infiltrating the entire sun-drenched valley, Silena, who was now into her fifth month of pregnancy, suddenly keeled over in a faint. Taking her up in his arms, Lascal carried her into the cooler air of the communal hut, at the same time calling for Vescala who, after briefly examining her, was able to reassure him that she was suffering from no more than over-excitement and a little too much to drink.

"Let her sleep; she'll be all right once she's rested," he said smiling as Elliana then burst in through the door.

"Is she alright?" she enquired of Vescala, who cheerfully reassured her that there was nothing to worry about. "Thank heavens for that. She was just saying earlier, how she's chosen a name for the son she's going to bear."

"Oh! She mentioned nothing to me, but I'm only the child's father!" Lascal exclaimed mockingly with Elliana laughing at her son's pretended indifference.

"She's going to call him Cramon, after her grandfather who, according to Calvas, had been a gallant warrior who died in battle."

"Yes, I've heard her mention him," Lascal said as his mother knelt-down, to comfort the now partially conscious Silena. At Vescala's instigation, the two men decided to leave the hut to re-join the festivities, but on making their way over to the others, Lascal sensed that the time had come to confront Vescala with the truth.

"Hold on a moment, Vescala," he asked, stopping as Vescala turned to face him. "Vescala, you have done much good for my family and myself, and If I am mistaken in what I am about to say I will apologise unreservedly. Yesterday morning, I discovered Mondena's remains. I've since come to the conclusion that you killed him. What I find hard to understand is how such a man of compassion, as you unquestionably are, could butcher in cold blood a man as insignificant as the little Spaniard?" Lascal said, staring directly into Vescala's powerful gaze. Having braced himself at the revelation Vescala scowled at him.

"Listen and listen well, Lascal! At the time of the sacrificial burnings, I witnessed more human suffering in one day than I hope you will ever see in a lifetime. In the course of my life, I've seen my entire family destroyed by plague, my one-time best friend converted into a religious maniac, and the finest love of any man's life debauched at the hands of a murderous priesthood. I've stood trial for crimes I never committed only to then spend nearly half my living years entombed in hell. As to your question…I had to kill him and bitterly regret having to do so. I honestly believe it was for the good of us all. I knew Mondena better than anyone, being the only one who could communicate fluently with him. There was no doubt in my mind that he would have talked to his Roman masters regarding this place had he made it back to Spain. The fact that the committee thought it safe to let him go was irrelevant; the man was determined to leave, no matter what was decided. There again, maybe the truth is that I killed him to satisfy my own selfishness. Let's be honest, this is probably my last chance of finding any long-term happiness…I just wasn't prepared to see one man jeopardise that unfulfilled ambition." As Vescala paused, his scowling features turned to sadness. "Tell me, Lascal, have you ever known the anguish a remorseful conscience brings? Do you have any idea what it's like to be afraid of the simple desire known as sleep? To lie awake at night, terrified, in case you see again the faces that perpetually haunt your recurring nightmares; the worst of all being Mondena's screaming, blood-drenched features!"

Lascal grimaced awkwardly, sympathising at Vescala's plight.

"Two nights ago, a severe storm uncovered his remains. I re-buried them in the graveyard up from the beach."

"Does anyone else know?"

"No…Tymaron had been fishing with me, but I made certain, the kid saw nothing. If it's any consolation, I give you my word, that you and I will be the only ones ever to know the truth."

"Thank you, Lascal. If the others were ever to discover what I had done my stature in their eyes would be severely diminished. It would be impossible for me to maintain my position on the committee. Although I don't feel any absolution, there is a certain relief in sharing such a sin with another. Even so, those few moments of frenzied savagery will stalk me forever!"

"I'm sorry for having approached you about it, Vescala: I can now understand your motivation. I just had to be sure; after all his killing could have been the work of natives."

"Well as far as natives go, there are none! Over these last three months, I explored the lands to the north, east, and south of us without finding any sign of human life. However, I did discover many other species of animal life such as elephants, giraffes, rhinoceros, and hippopotamus." Vescala then stopped to smile at the bewildered look on Lascal's face; he never having heard of such creatures. "I'll say this, Lascal, this truly is a beautiful country, but beauty can often mask the deadliest of predators. That's why at our next committee meeting I will recommend, as I did to Brenas, that we remain here in this valley and go no further afield."

"What about the danger from interbreeding?"

"Our moral discipline will ensure that no incestuous relationships will occur…we'll be alright," Vescala answered confidently. As the two men strolled back to re-join the celebrations Lascal felt better in having learned the truth of the affair.

The singing and dancing carried on until well into the evening and with Arlesia retiring to their hut to prepare herself for her husband, Vescala found himself in the company of Brenas and some of the other men who were chiding him regarding the pleasurable night lying ahead of him.

"I trust you won't require an aphrodisiac?" the jovial Brenas enquired of him.

"No, the finest aphrodisiac is human imagination," Vescala merrily replied as everyone laughed. "But I'll say this, Brenas, aphrodisiac or not, it's that damned long since I participated in intercourse, I fear I've forgotten how to do it anyway."

Again, Brenas and the others laughed at his light-hearted quip before leaving him to join his young bride. Entering the hut, his eyes showed his desire as he stared down at the supine body of the naked Arlesia, who lay seductively across the antelope skins scattered across the middle of the floor. However, as he stepped towards her, he was harbouring in his mind a far greater secret than even his cruel slaying of Mondena.

After he had run terror-stricken from the graveside, he had travelled south for some twenty days. It had then been by pure chance that he had accidentally stumbled upon the 'others,' a native race of primordial barbarians with skin as black as a moonless night; the old druid explorer having spoken to his class of a dark-skinned race of African people. Vescala was now convinced that Mondena had indeed deluded him and that the commune was almost certainly entrenched somewhere on the African continent. The interlopers were not alone and never would be! And as he spent the night in lovemaking, Vescala, as well as the other settlers, had completely overlooked the fact that this very night would, in the druidical calendar, herald in the month of the cuckoo!

Chapter Twenty-four

For eighteen contented years, the commune lived undisturbed, and in that blissful period they inflated their numbers and prospered in an affluent lifestyle that back in Britain would have been unimaginable. Back in the old country, the infant mortality rate had been one survival from every three children born. But here, given a far superior standard of living alongside a life-enhancing climate, three out of every four of their newborn children survived, with such children delivered into an environment filled with the hope of a glorious future. Over the years, as the commune's prosperity had flourished, there were few men and women anywhere, on earth fortunate enough to have experienced such a dynasty of harmony and peace. For with the coming of each fresh dawn the valley had breathed into their souls the true meaning of freedom.

However, one fateful morning early in the nineteenth year since the founding of the settlement, their good fortune was suddenly destabilised as a plague of locusts, swarming in their countless millions, attacked and devoured their carefully nurtured crops along with vast tracts of the surrounding countryside's vegetation. It was to be a shattering blow! But over the following two years worse was to follow, with blight having destroyed most of their new crops. Even the stream in the past, a valuable food source, now yielded fish covered in a fungus that rendered them inedible. As a consequence of these natural catastrophes, an air of disenchantment had grown among the people. Vescala, now into his fifty-fourth year, explained to them that such disasters were no more than a phase in nature's cycle, and for a time, the malcontents among them were satisfied with his interpretation of the calamities. But when the once-abundant game reserves began, to steadily depreciate; the people began to grow, increasingly apprehensive. Once again, Vescala tried to reassure them that the depopulation of the animal life was partially a man-created phenomenon precipitated by excessive hunting, primarily in the pursuit of sport and pleasure. However, many spurned his explanations, especially the younger commune members who preferred to believe that the valley's guardian spirit had now deserted them.

More than anything else, Vescala blamed himself for their current predicament. He recognised that it was he who had been responsible for the tuition that had sadly seen the younger generation grow up and develop ideas that flaunted the strict legislation agreed upon by everyone when they had first arrived in the valley so many carefree years before. Equality and freedom of expression had now become rampantly abused with the subsequent indiscipline having seen the people's morality slowly degenerate. They were now faced with a crumbling legal and moral framework only loosely based on Vescala's own philosophy and which had resulted in the younger generation openly flaunting the marriage laws; with promiscuity flourishing and incestuous relationships having become an all too common an occurrence.

By this time the commune's numbers had swollen to two hundred and ten, with many of the founding members having passed away, including Endvar, Calvas, and the virtuous Elliana, who had died from a stroke some four years previously. The now-adult Chevada and Tymaron had replaced Endvar and Calvas on the committee, now forced by public opinion into calling an emergency meeting in the communal hut. Cramon and Chevada, being the recognised leaders of the large rebellious faction, had demanded the meeting, with Lascal and Silena's eldest son in overall command of the malcontents.

It was early in the morning when the people began streaming into the hut where Vescala sat alongside Brenas, Lascal, and Tymaron who had taken their places beside him on the bench behind the table at the far end of the room. The other benches, set out in rows in front of them, were soon filled to capacity, with Vescala noticing that Chevada had elected to remain with Cramon: the two of them having positioned themselves behind the crowds near to the door.

By now it was stifling hot, and on the crammed benches most of the people were fanning themselves with small sprigs cut from the tinder-dry scrub lying outside the stockade. Nearly everyone in the village over the age of fourteen was in attendance as Vescala stood to call the meeting to order. However, no sooner had he done so than from the back of the hall Cramon demanded to speak, and hearing the howls of agreement from his many supporters, Vescala eyed him with unease. Cramon had developed into a giant of a man with a well-structured physique not dissimilar to the build of his old adversary, Ravala, and with his long black hair emphasising his wide brown eyes set deep into their puffy sockets, there were times – particularly when his temper was enraged – when he took on an almost demonic appearance. Although only into his nineteenth year, he was not without a persuasive personality that more than matched his massive frame. Over these past two years, he had succeeded in turning not only his two younger brothers against his father but also his mother Silena, who looked upon her eldest son as being a born leader. Lascal, now thirty-eight years old, sat beside Vescala feeling a bitter sense of frustration. He had persistently appealed to his wayward son to show more responsibility in his objective that he and his followers be allowed to leave the valley and travel east to seek a more meaningful and prosperous existence. But all his pleading had been in vain, with Cramon remaining stubbornly adamant that his course was the only one that in the long term would save the commune from a slow annihilation.

"Very well, Cramon, say what you must," Vescala shouted out, and sitting down he wondered how two such decent people as Lascal and Silena could ever have produced such a despicable caricature of a human being as their arrogant son unquestionably was. From the back of the hall, Cramon addressed his audience who had turned on the benches to face him.

"We, the overwhelming majority, have demanded this meeting in one final attempt to convince our elected committee that the only choice lying ahead of us is to leave this valley," he shouted out bombastically, pointing his finger at the four committee members who sat with their heads bowed. "Enlighten us, gentlemen? Is it your blindness or simple cowardice that motivates your persistent refusals to submit to our legitimate demand? Let's be honest our small society is slowly stagnating. And although every year sees an expansion in our numbers, you still insist on telling us that the only realistic life for us, in what you admit to be a vast territory, is for everyone to remain shackled to a dull, repetitive existence within the boundaries of this damned forsaken valley. We've even heard from Vescala's senile lips, only recently I must add, that the country is infested by a race of black-skinned barbarians whom no one else among us has ever seen or even found any trace of." Cramon's derisory tone brought tumultuous applause from the benches but as the noise abated, he resumed in a determined voice. "The glorious pioneering spirit that first brought you elders to these shores lies dormant within us, the younger generation. I feel it's only just that I once more plead with you to support the journey which we intend to undertake…albeit with or without your permission. Over these last two years, we have seen crop failures on a disastrous scale as all around us the dry soil lies dressed in a mantle of shrivelled grass. As for the stream providing us with sustenance, it did at one time, but no longer. Even the once-abundant game herds have dwindled alarmingly; indeed, were it not for the ocean still providing us with a rich harvest of food we would now be facing imminent famine. Now it's for you on the committee, with the exception of Chevada I must add, to face the hard facts that this valley, the only homeland that many of us have ever known , is in the process of dying and that those trapped in it are slowly tumbling into an abyss of self-destruction. I now ask you; do you honestly believe that our present existence, the very one you created for us, has fulfilled the dreams you once hoped would materialise? Gentlemen, the answer must be no!" As Cramon paused the hall was filled with murmurings of approval at his words. But fixing his eyes firmly on Vescala's, he continued. "You, Vescala, taught me many things over the years and I will always be grateful to you for that. However, owing to your intransigence over the last two years I'm afraid we've come to the parting of the ways. It is now I, who have the vast majority of the people behind me, and it's my avowed intention to release them from the spell-binding chains of broken promises that you have so deluded them with and to lead them away from this spiritually reclusive bondage!"

Cramon raised his arms to acknowledge the rapturous applause now coming, from the benches. But rising to his feet, Vescala's beseeching eyes searched around the sea of faces for support, only to be met by a torrent of heckling.

"It's only good manners to allow your committee the democratic right of reply," he said, addressing them in a loud but calm voice. For this wasn't the first time in his life that he had faced such a hostile reception. Even so, he had never thought he'd see the day when he would be so badly treated by his own people. Soon the clamour of antagonism being directed at him subsided, and from behind the table he pointed his wavering finger reprovingly at the now seated Cramon.

"As you have all observed, Lascal's eldest son is hardly renowned for showing courtesy towards your elected committee…but so be it, Cramon. Over these last two years we have listened to your incessant complaints until I am personally sick to death of hearing them. If you and the others are hell-bent on leaving, then sadly, I am powerless to prevent you. All I can do now is plead once more with you to wait at least another few months until after the rainy season before embarking on a quest that might well lead you into disaster."

"What rainy season? We've hardly had any rain for nigh on twelve months!" One of Cramon's disgruntled supporters shouted out. Vescala knew only too well that he couldn't deny the claim but on suddenly recalling an experience from his childhood, he placed his hands flat on the table and leaning forward impressed himself onto his audience.

"Let me tell you a true story. When I was a child there lived in my village an old woman who, from the moment of her birth to the time of her death, never once passed beyond the fields surrounding our village stockade. On that tiny strip of god's creation, she was to remain for some sixty years. Throughout her childhood, then into marriage, childbirth, and old age, she lived content to raise her large family in complete ignorance and isolation from the outside world. I remember her only vaguely, but I do recall my mother telling me how envious people were of her placid, loving nature. Whenever anyone in the village was in trouble or required help, she was always willing to comfort and advise. Now over the course of her long life, that woman must have experienced the good as well as the bad times. I know that recently things here have been bad but the rains will come again. Those among you who would so easily sacrifice all the years of suffering that went into the creation of our beloved settlement would do well to keep that old woman in mind. Unlike your scheming empire builders, Cramon and Chevada, who seek power through material possession, she sought neither. Inside her confined world, she discovered something almost unique – a spiritual tranquillity that I believe we too will find, but only if we stay here and remain united. I can well understand your impatience and frustration at the events of the past two years, but don't forget we had seventeen years of plenty before the sad circumstances of the last two. No, the good times will return, you must believe me!" Vescala proclaimed emotionally knowing in his heart, that it was impossible to repudiate Cramon's claims. Sweeping his straggling grey hair back from his creased forehead, he looked despairingly around only to see the disdainful expressions on the sea of faces before him that were enough to convince him that he had finally lost all credence, with the majority of people now well and truly ensnared in the web of discontentment that had been so cunningly spun by Cramon.

"Vescala, your cheap philosophy is as dead as the old woman you spoke of!" Cramon shouted out indecorously to roars of laughter from the benches. "I have stringently organised everything, and I can now inform the committee that we will be making our departure sooner rather than later. I've no doubt some among you will wish to remain here and continue to suffer the misery of the past two years. However, if you should change your mind, you will be more than welcome to come with us. As things stand there are now two hundred and four men, women, and children who have confirmed their loyalty to our cause. By my calculations that leaves only six prepared to stay, although I hope to see these numbers depleted. Gentlemen, that's all I have to say!"

"Think again, Cramon. You're leading these people into a dangerous, unexplored territory!" Vescala screamed imploringly. But as he sat back down his plea went unheeded, indeed almost unheard, as the cheering crowds streamed back outside carrying aloft the jubilant Cramon and Chevada.

With a solitary tear sliding down his aged face a forlorn Brenas turned to stare into Lascal's expressionless eyes.

"All we fought and suffered for disintegrating before our very eyes. It's all so meaningless. I'm glad your mother never lived to see what's become of her grandson," he remarked almost in a whisper. But before Lascal could reply Vescala cut in.

"No, Brenas! Had it not been Cramon and Chevada who instigated the dissension, it would have been some of the others. Don't forget, when we were their age, the world was a challenge. It wasn't enough to remain in one designated spot and timidly accept the rules and regulations laid down to us by our elders. No, I'm afraid the generation gap between us appears unbridgeable…I wouldn't mind so much if all they were seeking was a more prosperous yield from the earth, but I fear the aberrant Cramon is only interested in power."

There was a long silence between the four men; now the hall's sole occupants.

"I still think Cramon and the other young hotheads had it far too easy," Brenas suddenly commented, interrupting the continuous cheering infiltrating into the hall from outside. "I mean what do they know of tyranny and slavery? They couldn't even begin to contemplate what some of us went through to get where we are today."

"Yes, I know," Vescala said through a resigned sigh. "Everything we taught them seems to have been largely ignored or forgotten. At least we have the consolation of having shown them the true meaning of social equality. If nothing else we gave them a way of life, that back in the old country would have been unimaginable. I'm afraid all we can do now is pray that this insane venture of theirs will open the young one's eyes to life's innumerable hardships. Hopefully, after a period of privation and suffering, they will be glad to return to the security of the valley."

"No, Vescala, I know my son too well," Lascal said disagreeing. "He's too proud to ever return and admit he was wrong. No…I fear what we witnessed this sad day is the obliteration of our little society. When people are given peace and prosperity for so long, it's heartbreaking to find that only two years of not-too-severe hardship can induce such a despairing dissatisfaction. But what I find most hard to accept is that the leader of the dissenters is my own son! A man whose monumental ego could be leading us into a chaotic destruction."

"It's not all his fault," Brenas disagreed. "That bastard Chevada had a lot to do with it. In fact, the lad was all right until they became friends. That bastard has a lot to answer for."

"Well, that may or may not be the case, Brenas." Tymaron, now a tall twenty-seven-year-old, spoke out with conviction. "However, I don't think we can blame all our misfortunes on either individuals or the quirks of nature. Perhaps at the very start of our colonisation we created a future built on the fantasy that we had discovered the ultimate terrestrial paradise. I must be honest for nigh on seventeen years it certainly appeared that way. But to my way of thinking the first mistake was made when the original committee decided to sever most of the cultural bonds, we had grown up to accept back in the old country, leaving us virtually devoid of history, tradition, or indeed any meaningful religion. Then came the greatest mistake – to have treated all men as equals. I'm afraid it was a doctrine that over the years was selfishly abused. No man can ever be the equal of another we are created as independent, free-thinking individuals, and are destined to remain that way until the day we die. As a result, the ambitious had to carry the idle and ill-disciplined, whose complacency eventually eroded the strong one's instinctive desire to strive towards a progressive advancement. Over and above that, our all-too-easily obtained affluence led to a debilitating apathy among us, which in turn accounted for the slow erosion of our moral discipline. Maybe the strictly enforced moral code of the druid had its good points!"

Vescala winced angrily at Tymaron's views but this was no time for any theological debate with the shouting from outside now echoing repetitively in each man's lonely thoughts as they silently reflected upon the demise of a lifestyle they sensed was about to disappear forever. Staring towards the doorway, Vescala shook the tears from his eyes as he remembered Elliana. Perhaps it was as well that death had spared her the ignominy of seeing the disintegration of the commune, he thought sadly. But what was to become of the picturesque village and who, indeed if any, would want to remain as he himself had chosen to do. Suddenly Lascal cleared his throat with Vescala having already guessed what he was about to say.

"I'm sorry, Vescala…I would like to stay but I've no alternative but to go with my son. As you know, Silena and his brothers are in agreement with almost everything he says."

"There's no need to apologise, Lascal," Vescala retorted through a sympathetic smile. "If he was my son, I would probably do the same. I don't know if any of you are aware of it but my own wife has also decided to leave. Let's be honest, it's common knowledge that my marriage was over a long time ago."

With the other three maintaining a dignified silence, Vescala clasped his hands together and cast his mind back to the day when he had taken the young Arlesia as his bride. For the first ten years of the marriage, they had been as happy as any couple could have reasonably expected to have been. But over these latter years his wife had certainly succeeded in making him look a fool, he thought, feeling a twinge of bitterness towards her. She had openly boasted to everyone about her long-standing love affair with Chevada. It was an admission that had severely damaged his reputation in the eyes of the others. Even so, he held no real hatred towards her. Perhaps the wide age gap between them had been one reason for her infidelity; there again, if their stillborn son had survived maybe the bond between them might have been strengthened instead of weakened. Still, he should have foreseen that the youth who had presented her with the gold nuggets on their wedding day was destined to become more than a mere friend, he thought remorsefully. Although now into the autumn of his life span, the memory of his first love, Delancia, still haunted him. He had never loved Arlesia as he should have. No woman could ever have replaced Delancia in his affections. Somehow, he sensed that the time would come when he would again embrace

Delancia's spiritual existence. But only by fulfilling his own destiny would he ever be delivered towards that immeasurable moment.

"I too must leave, old friend," Brenas declared, breaking Vescala's train of thought. "Believe me, I would rather stay although I still hope to be able to influence Cramon and get him to change his mind. But I made a vow to Elliana before she died that, no matter what happened in the future, the family would always stick together."

"No, father," Lascal said, disagreeing. "You're now over sixty years old. Surely it would be wiser to remain here than risk such a journey."

"I've made my decision, Lascal: I had hoped to be buried beside your mother when my time came but I made her a promise and I intend to keep it."

"That's a brave decision, Brenas," Vescala stated, knowing that Brenas had never been the same man since Elliana's death.

"Well, I for one, will not be going on a search for some mythical paradise that I know doesn't exist. Nor will I stay here!" Tymaron suddenly exclaimed, breaking into the conversation with the others glancing at each other through puzzled expressions. "Don't get me wrong, every moment I've spent here has been a revelation. Had the others elected to stay I too would have been content to remain. Somehow though, I've always felt that my life in this valley has been no more than a passing phase in my life. Let's be honest, Cramon's motivation is based purely on his own selfish desire to seek personal glory. I for one have no intention of following such a man. But I can certainly do nothing with my life by staying here."

"Then where will you go?" Vescala enquired.

"Back to Britain!"

"And how the hell's that to be achieved?" he asked, throwing Tymaron a severe look.

"Simple…I'm young and strong and I intend using the boat Mondena built. Lascal will agree that I've kept it well maintained over the years; indeed, it's as good as the day he completed it."

"Yes, but you don't have the seamanship skills Mondena had. Anyway, he didn't make it back…did he?" Vescala retorted sarcastically.

"Maybe so, but it's no more dangerous a mission than the others are about to undertake," Tymaron snarled; his handsome clean-shaven features breaking into a scowl. "Be honest, Vescala, you must know in your heart that we can never return to the social stability we had before. That fact has been staring us in the face for two years now. Then there's always the threat from those natives you once encountered. I wonder just how long it will be before Cramon's colonising force, and that's what it is, will equal any Roman or druid outrage? No, the decent standards originated and imposed by the founding committee have long been forgotten. I very much doubt if we shall ever see them return."

Lascal was irked at Tymaron's words and it showed on his weather-beaten face.

"I think your ideas drastic, to say the least!" he exclaimed, shaking his head. "Like the others, I'm only going owing to the sad circumstances we now find ourselves in, but one day I hope to return. Regarding the natives, well what you say is pure conjecture. Even Vescala will admit that none of our scouting expeditions has ever found one shred of evidence that these barbarians might inhabit our particular region. As for my son, I know he's headstrong but I can't see him ignoring the bitter lessons we learned back in the old country."

"I'm not so sure about that, Lascal," Vescala remarked. "After all, he only heard the stories handed down to him by us. I hate to say this to you but I don't think for one moment that he either believed us or even cared!"

Sighing deeply, Lascal bowed his head in shame. He knew Vescala had spoken the truth and inwardly prayed that one day Cramon would redeem himself in the eyes of the other three. However, Vescala now turned his attention back to Tymaron.

"What you said about never returning to our former stability may well prove prophetic, but I for one am staying in the hope that the majority will eventually return. But for the love of me, I don't see any point in trying to get back to the old country. You certainly won't be any better off there than you are here."

"I disagree…I feel we are in the wrong place at the wrong time. I was only a child when we left the old country, but I do recall Aldrun: I think he was right in wanting to stay and fight for his freedom."

"You're an ungrateful wretch! Were it not for us you would never have known the meaning of the word freedom!" Lascal shouted angrily. But Tymaron made no reply to the taunt; knowing that had it not been for his own heroic action as a child none of them would be alive today.

Suddenly the imposing figures of Cramon and Chevada appeared in the doorway. And as the four men stared at them, they swaggered up to the table to stand pompously before the committee members with Cramon tightly gripping the hilt of the bone-handled knife protruding from his broad belt.

"Some thirty days ago I sent two scouts from here to explore the country to the east of us. Providing they return bearing good news we will uproot the settlement and leave in two months from now," he declared, staring almost contemptuously down at Vescala. "By then all our preparations should be finalised. I now inform this defunct committee that I have been elected the people's undisputed leader and have been granted absolute authority over all those prepared to seek a happier and more prosperous existence."

"In other words' you're a bloody dictator," Tymaron muttered. But bending over to place both his fists on the table,

Cramon grinned scornfully down at him; his thick lips parting to show two rows of stained and displaced teeth.

"Watch your tongue, Tymaron! You're no match for me and you know it," he snapped as Tymaron lowered his eyes, aware that he could never defeat Cramon in any physical combat.

"Now if any of you wish to come with us, you must be prepared to accept my commands unreservedly. Anyone breaking my laws can expect no mercy, blood relation or not!" Cramon then exclaimed.

"You're no dictator, Cramon: you've elevated yourself to the position of a god," Vescala commented with a derisive chuckle. Now standing at his full height, Cramon glanced wildly at him.

"Your wife seems to share your opinion, Vescala. At least that's the impression I formed when she and I shared the same bed two nights ago," he retorted through a sneer as Chevada laughed with Vescala's face betraying no emotion.

"Well, well, Chevada, your new master steals your mistress. Let's hope he never takes a fancy to you," he quipped and ceasing laughing, Chevada's upper lip trembled in anger. "As for you, Cramon, you and Arlesia are well matched; her promiscuity is as rampant as your recklessness!"

"You have the mind of a simpleton, Vescala," the grinning Cramon replied, only for Vescala to smirk at the insult, but not so Brenas who jumped to his feet.

"That's enough, Cramon! Childish insults like that hardly become our new leader. After all, we expect a 'god' to act with dignity." his derogatory remark struck hard at Cramon whose blazing eyes darted spitefully at his grandfather. However, Brenas sat back down, unconcerned at the hatred being directed towards him, and after only a few moments Cramon's temper subsided.

"Alright," he muttered in a composed voice. "With the exception, of you four, only Endvar's sick wife and the crippled half-wit Cetra are staying. I must know if you are remaining with them or coming with us so kindly make up your minds."

"Your father and I will be joining you," Brenas replied. "Vescala and Tymaron have decided to remain here. I just hope that the totalitarian power you've received will be used wisely. To be perfectly honest with you, I don't see these broad shoulders of yours carrying such a responsibility. But if at any time in the future you should seek counsel your father and I will be only too glad to advise you."

Cramon merely acknowledged the kind offer with a grunt as he and Chevada turned to march back out of the hall, leaving Lascal to turn to Vescala.

"I must apologise to you, Vescala, for my son's ignorance. It was bad enough in the past when he cunningly used Arlesia's adulterous association with Chevada to publicly humiliate you – words fail me as to this recent behaviour."

"Think nothing of it, Lascal; it takes more than a few ill-chosen words to upset me. I suppose he'll be wanting to take most of the equipment with him?"

"No," Lascal replied grimly. "We will make damned certain the four of you are left well provided for. I intend to get him to leave a good stockpile of food and equipment behind in the event of us having to return in an emergency. I don't think even he's ridiculous enough to risk losing everything in the swamps and jungle we must inevitably encounter."

"So be it! And now, gentlemen, I suppose the time has come to rescind what I fear has been the last of our meetings," the unhappy Vescala declared with a hollow ring to his words. The four men then rose simultaneously from the table to make their way silently between the crudely built benches that so often in the past had held their attentive audiences.

Meanwhile, outside, the crowds had dispersed into small huddled groups; none of whom took the slightest notice of the four men as they stepped out into the warm sunshine. On parting company with the others, Vescala immediately made his way over to the hut where the late Endvar's wife lay seriously ill. Entering the solemn atmosphere of the dimly lit room he knelt down beside the frail old woman's bed of rushes only to see her face contorted in a deathly grimace. Closing the lids of her lifeless eyes, he wept bitterly. For while all the recent dissension and hatred was being voiced, she in her wasting illness had been ignored and left to die alone. To Vescala her death epitomised the end of an epic adventure.

Chapter Twenty-five

The following morning just after daybreak, Vescala and Tymaron carried the old woman's shrouded corpse on the long journey to the communal graveyard up from the beach where they interred her alongside her husband. By the time they had finished shovelling the last of the earth over her grave, the sun was high in the sky, and with their shovels slung over their shoulders, they strolled casually in the warm mid-day air back down to the beach to sit and rest on the sand. After some time had elapsed, it was Tymaron, who broke the silence between them.

"Let's hope they again found the happiness they shared for so long on earth. It's merciful she didn't live to see what's become of us."

"Aye, lad, I don't think she was ever aware of recent events. After all, it was a long illness. I only wish I could have done more to have eased her dreadful pain."

Tymaron lay back, his thoughts overtaken by the dangerous voyage he would soon venture upon, leaving Vescala to watch the waves gently lapping the shore. Suddenly Vescala became overwhelmed by an urge to confess to the young man about Mondena's murder – a crime that even after all these long years still haunted him. But as he did so the bright-eyed Tymaron listened attentively enough, although seemingly unsurprised by the confession.

"You know it's strange, even as a child I felt there was more to the story than Lascal originally told me. I wonder why he tried to discourage me yesterday?"

"Because he thinks a lot of you, Tymaron. He just doesn't want to see you die young. If you insist on making this voyage believe me you will," Vescala declared sullenly; his face reflecting his disapproval as he stared thoughtfully at the ocean.

"I'm glad you told me the truth about Mondena; it gives me a little more confidence in tackling the sea alone. I must say Lascal's been a great friend in keeping such a secret for so long."

"Yes, it's a pity his eldest son will never be half the man he is. Still, the man who seeks greatness must forever be humbled. Let's hope that he who fired the imaginations of the others will in time, be found out for what he's been to the commune – an intellectually blind and destructive hemorrhage," Vescala stated acrimoniously. A long period of silence then existed between them, before they rose to begin the arduous journey back to the stockade.

On the way back, Vescala tried to convince Tymaron that his intention to return to Britain was insane. But the young man remained aloof to his pleas, and by the time they had reached the valley, his disinterest had turned to anger.

"Look, Vescala, nothing you say now or in the future is going to dissuade me. Let's leave it at that!"

"Then wait at least six months. Who knows, the others might return. I know things look bleak at the moment, but I still feel that, given time, we might salvage some, if not all, the stability we enjoyed before."

Almost bored by Vescala's persistence Tymaron nodded in a resigned agreement.

"Alright, I'll give it three months, but only on the condition that you come with me should the others fail to return."

"If you must go back then go! But don't ask me to accompany you. There's no reason on earth for me to return to the old country," an adamant Vescala retorted. Sensing, that that it was pointless to go on arguing, Tymaron shrugged his shoulders and began moving downhill in the direction of the stockade, closely followed by an irritated Vescala.

It was early in the afternoon when they reached the raised portcullis where Brenas met them, with grave concern clouding his eyes.

"Bad news, Vescala, I'm afraid young Cetra seems to have disappeared!" he exclaimed in a chilling voice.

"How is that possible?" Vescala enquired, knowing how severely handicapped the child was.

"Apparently when you left this morning, he was seen hirpling towards the portcullis. I'm afraid that, after letting you two out, the guard had to answer a call of nature and forgot to lower it. It looks as if he tried to follow you."

"Has a search party been organised?" Vescala asked as his troubled eyes wandered over to the jungle.

"Yes, Lascal and ten volunteers have been out searching all morning. One of the women spotted him from her doorway early on. But reckoning that the portcullis would be closed she thought nothing of it. It wasn't until Silena went looking for him to give him his breakfast that he was found to be missing."

"Well, we certainly didn't see him," Vescala stipulated, glancing anxiously at Tymaron. "He must have headed for the jungle hoping to find me and then got lost. I can't see him getting far on his own. After we've eaten, Tymaron and I will join the search."

The search for the handicapped child lasted three full days, with the shallow stream, the lake, and the surrounding jungle, including the area leading to the shore, having been thoroughly scoured with no clues as to Cetra's fate to be found.

For the first time in many months, it began to rain, and with Vescala and Tymaron soaked through and exhausted, they returned to their hut where they were met, by Cramon.

"I've ordered the search to be aborted!" he exclaimed abruptly. "We just don't have enough time to go on looking for him. We must assume he was taken, by an animal."

His words struck hard into Vescala, who knew that he had no option but to agree.

"Very well, Cramon, but we two will go on looking."

"Fair enough. As you can appreciate, I can't spare the men."

"Cramon, only a few months ago every man, woman, and child would have been out searching for him. How times have changed."

But unwilling to become involved in an argument, Cramon diplomatically ignored the caustic remark and returned to supervise the building of the wooden carts that they would take on their journey.

As the days passed by the two men continued their search, only to find no clues that might resolve the mystery. Eventually, a downhearted Vescala had no alternative but to discontinue the search. More than anyone else, he was deeply saddened by the loss of the child, having cared for him ever since his mother's death some two years previously, and as they returned to the stockade, he felt a depressing sense of injustice that such a helpless child should have died terrorised in the hungry jaws of some wild animal.

The two-month period allotted to prepare for the journey flew by with nearly everyone inside the stockade fully employed in the final preparations for the long trek they would undertake. Meanwhile, the scouts had returned, having travelled eastwards into the interior and much further than Vescala had ever gone. Their report to Cramon was that great fertile plains lay some sixty days march away; this being the time they estimated it would take the entire commune to reach the area. Throughout their travels, the scouts had found no apparent signs of human life, although at one stage, in their journey, they had come upon a huge tree trunk bridging a deep river. At the time the discovery had bewildered them. However, Cramon merely scoffed at the suggestion that men might have placed it there, reckoning that in all probability it had been carried downstream when the river was in flood. It seemed a perfectly reasonable explanation that neither the scouts nor any of the others - with exception of Vescala, disputed. The men had also encountered many vast herds of game such as gazelle, zebra, antelope, and wildebeest; indeed, so vast were the herds that they were almost afraid to report their discoveries in case they were accused of exaggerating their claims. They also reported that the numerous streams and rivers they had come upon had shown no sign of the fish in them being diseased. However, they were careful to emphasise that the trek would be extremely hazardous, owing to the dense jungle and treacherous swamplands they would first have to overcome before reaching the fertile plains.

Cramon was delighted to hear all this, instantly referring to the new territory as the 'plains of gold. But listening to their report, Vescala sneered regarding the authenticity of their claims, and in front of everyone he accused both scouts and Cramon of deliberately inciting the people into a nomadic existence that must inevitably lead to their destruction. Once again, he warned them that savages inhabited these lands. However, his warning was to no avail; he was merely laughed at, with Cramon accusing him of wallowing in a pique over the fact that he had lost control of the people. And as the days went by no one paid the slightest attention to the man the little children now called the 'crazy prophet,' with even the attitudes of Brenas and Lascal beginning to soften. For the more the trek was planned and discussed, the more each man found himself admiring the courageous spirit of adventure that by now even the youngest children were voicing.

On the eve of their departure, any opposition that might have materialised against Cramon's leadership had effectively ceased, as throughout the settlement a calm sense of destiny now appeared to hold everyone in its grip.

Vescala was a little surprised that the drunken celebrations he had been anticipating didn't materialise, and strolling through the settlement in the twilight gloom he sensed an almost unearthly silence dwelling among the households. Some twenty stockpiled carts lay close to the portcullis, and spotting Brenas checking one of them, he went over to join him only to be acknowledged with a curt smile.

"Think again, man, there's hardly one among us who wouldn't be glad of your company" Brenas stated as his eyes caught Vescala's.

"No, you have a new authority now," Vescala replied, scratching at his greying beard. "Anyway, I'm quite content to spend my remaining years as the caretaker of this most intricately designed and enchanting valley."

"Suppose we never return, Vescala? It seems such a pity that our long friendship should end like this," Brenas remarked; a crestfallen expression covering his graceful, wizened features.

"One day we will be re-united Brenas – albeit in an ethereal existence," Vescala replied assuredly.

"I hope so. All through the years of hardship my happiest were spent with Elliana. How I miss her and long to be with her again."

"You will old friend…you will," Vescala replied sympathetically, knowing that the old slave's health was rapidly failing and that it would be nothing short of a miracle if he made it to the end of the journey. But neither man felt it fitting to dwell on sadness, and shaking hands in an act of unpremeditated brotherhood, they silently parted with each man returning to his hut to await the morning.

Come the dawn a disturbing breeze rustled eerily through the tinder dry grass outside the raised portcullis. Meanwhile, inside the stockade everyone had risen early. And after breakfasting it was a heavily armed Cramon who stood issuing his final orders to all those gathered around the long column of loaded carts which would be drawn by the wild oxen that over the years they had succeeded in domesticating. Hoping to motivate the others Cramon had placed his own family, now including his mistress Arlesia, at the head of the column. And with two scouts having been sent on ahead, the morning sun rose into a clear sky as Cramon cheerfully raised his spear and shouted the command for the column to advance.

To the downhearted Vescala, who stood to the side of the portcullis beside Tymaron, it was almost unbearable listening to the whiplashes and rumblings of the metal-rimmed wooden wheels trundling past him. And, although the oxen were powerful animals, it seemed to him to be an impossible task to drag such heavy, cumbersome vehicles over such a vast, restless untamed territory. As the small groups passed him by, he acknowledged every individual with a nod, with the sadness in his eyes directed primarily on the small children who trudged merrily along behind the noisy carts. But at the sight of a tiny child toddling behind the last vehicle, he sensed in his heart that he would never see any of them again. More than anything, he desired to shout his good wishes to them, but somehow his quivering jaw failed to respond to his emotions, and as tears tumbled from his trembling eyelashes to slink into his beard the carts clattered away with only Brenas having turned around to wave him a last farewell. And as a lone dark cloud slipped over the face of the high luminous sun, a solemn shadow suddenly immersed the entire valley.

"Well, that's it then!" Tymaron exclaimed concisely. "Don't waste your tears on them, Vescala. Let them discover for themselves the futility of the venture into which they're so recklessly embarking."

"If nothing else I had to admire Cramon's organisational capabilities," Vescala replied, wiping the tears from his eyes on the sleeve of his jacket. "And although some of his decisions were incredibly misjudged, I have to admit to being surprised at the depth of his spiritual discipline. What a tragedy that there was never any element of compromise between us."

"I would forget all about that squalid ambitionist! Start concentrating on the day when we return to Britain."

"Don't make me laugh, Tymaron: I can assure you I'll be here for the rest of my days," Vescala replied tersely. At his instigation, they untied the portcullis rope, and after lowering it Tymaron went about his business, leaving Vescala to ascend the wooden ladder leading up to the rampart of the stockade where he watched the new pioneers make their way slowly towards the hills at the far eastern end of the valley. However, by noon they were out of sight, and descending the ladder, he returned to his hut to prepare a meal for the two of them.

All too soon the days became months, with Tymaron spending more and more time on the shore practicing in the boat for the day when he would set sail for Britain. By now he had almost disassociated himself from Vescala, often staying away for days on end; this annoying Vescala who constantly worried for his safety. As for Vescala, in recent times he had begun to suffer from bouts of agonising pain in the leg he had broken as a young man, and he now only left the stockade to go for water and hunt, mostly for small game that was easily trapped.

The following month was to bring a period of consistent rainfall; the first in almost two years, that rapidly transformed the valley into something like its original state. After only a few days the yellow-tainted grass had transformed into a panorama of rich greenery with the listless jungle now enhancing the spectacular landscape by flowering into a vibrant myriad of colour. By the end of their second month alone, Tymaron spotted a small herd of antelope grazing at the eastern end of the valley, and soon afterward Vescala discovered that the fungus afflicting the fish in the stream had vanished. It was just as Vescala had predicted, with the valley having taken on a new lease of life. As the days elapsed, he now prayed fervently that the others would soon return to once more farm the network of now-overgrown fields outside the stockade and hunt the herds of game now increasing daily in their numbers.

With Tymaron having returned from the shore, early one evening the two of them sat outside Vescala's hut enjoying succulent wild pig meat sizzling on the spit above the charcoal fire. It was warm and humid, with massive banks of dark grey clouds having rolled across the sky for most of the day. Even the static air seeming alive in the atmosphere of the gathering storm, but with the first blinding flash of forked lightning splitting the heavens, both men grabbed the remaining food to quickly take shelter in the hut. Now standing by the open doorway, Tymaron watched in awe the inspired elements dancing high in the stratosphere.

"I wonder where the others are now?" he asked, turning to face Vescala who was seated on a pile of animal skins in the centre of the room.

"I don't know. One thing's for certain, they'll get damned wet this night."

No sooner had he replied than a sudden crescendo of thunder shook the walls with a ferocity that threatened to bring them crashing down around Vescala, who jumped with fright.

"Tell me?" Tymaron asked, unable to stifle a smile at Vescala's fear. "If the others fail to return before I leave, what will you do? Let's face it, with your leg deteriorating you're going to find it increasingly difficult to hunt for your living."

"I'll get by, lad…I always have," Vescala remarked with an air of independence before reclining on his elbow to stare vacantly towards the doorway where outside the now pelting rain had begun to extinguish the fire.

"You're crazy, man…crazy," Tymaron said scornfully.

"Yes, perhaps I am…I have the feeling I'm in excellent company."

Tymaron laughed above the thunder's roar at the retort. But Vescala looked solemn, having felt for some time that they had been growing apart.

"Did you remember to lower the portcullis when you returned?" he then asked, unwilling to get involved in any argument.

"No, damn it, I forgot all about it," Tymaron replied, screwing up his face at his forgetfulness.

"Well, you best wait until the rain lets up," Vescala said shaking his head. It wasn't the first time recently that Tymaron had failed to close the entrance after Vescala had left it open for him. Leaving the doorway, Tymaron joined him for a time on the pile of skins. However, sensing that the teeming rain wasn't going to let up, he began looking around for his thick hide cloak. Finding it he slung it over his head, all the time cursing the fact that he had to venture out in such foul weather. Leaving his sullen companion, he at first almost timidly stepped out into the settlement's ghostly atmosphere before running through the saturating downpour and over towards the portcullis. Now soaked to the skin, he was just about to untie the rope to lower it when, through the hazy sheets of rain, his eyes spotted something lying outside on the muddy pathway. At first, he took it to be no more than a few pieces of discarded linen. But splashing through the gathering pools of water, he stopped dead in his tracks as his bulging eyes comprehended the horrific sight lying before him. Momentarily, a sudden seizure of shock held his mind in an evil grip. But then, discarding his cloak, he turned to run back through the portcullis and over to the hut.

"What's wrong, son; what's happened?" Vescala asked, rising to his feet, and alarmed by the terrified expression on the young man's face. But Tymaron, who stood in the doorway panting for breath, said nothing, and entering the hut, he beckoned Vescala to follow him by violently pulling at his jacket. After releasing himself from the frantic tugging, Vescala managed to grab a sword before Tymaron succeeded in pulling him outside and dragging him through the portcullis and over to the sight that had so horrified him. Unwilling to go closer, the dumbstruck Tymaron stood pointing to the horror as Vescala's alert eyes first scanned the rain-shrouded hills and jungle before cautiously making his way over to the spot.

At first, he too could hardly believe his eyes, but after a few moments had crawled by the initial impact of the discovery saw him slump to his knees. Wiping the teeming rain from his stunned features, he first glanced back to Tymaron before his eyes once again met young Cetra's dismembered remains; his heart thundering on seeing the severed malformed arms and legs lying to either side of the pigeon-chested torso. Above the neck lay the child's decapitated head, with the brain having been removed and which now rested grotesquely beside the head on a tuft of flattened grass. In their terror, neither man spoke. They knew well enough whose body it was, but why, each now asked himself, should the bloodless corpse first be dissected and then so carefully arranged?

"One thing's for certain, no animal was responsible for this," Vescala declared in a soft voice shaking with emotion. Joining him, Tymaron glanced back to the stockade, morbidly wondering if perhaps those responsible for such debauchery were now lying in wait for them, recalling that the portcullis had remained open since at least the late afternoon; that being the time when he had returned from the shore and there had certainly been no sign of anybody then.

"How long has he been dead?" he enquired of Vescala who was examining the remains.

"Not long; as you can see the limbs are still pliable," he replied, pausing to shake his head and at the same time trying to gather his senses. Gently handling one of the child's arms, he estimated that he had died earlier that morning. Suddenly the thought struck him that the previous night had been the first night of the full moon.

"Do you think the natives were responsible?" Tymaron asked, but ignoring his question, Vescala's attention was now concentrated on the head lying on its side beside the undamaged brain where he immediately noted that a large section of the cranium had been cut and removed. But the method by which it had been achieved astonished him, with the neat incisions clearly showing that a high degree of anatomical skill had been deployed. Leaving the head, his eyes then glanced over to where the child's torso lay, and turning it over onto its side, he shuddered on seeing the gaping hole in its back where the heart, as he suspected, had been removed.

"Well, Tymaron, there's no doubt in my mind that this is the work of some kind of priesthood…I imagine they probably poisoned or asphyxiated him before removing the heart."

"But what's become of the heart?" Tymaron asked as his pallid features twitched nervously.

"I don't know. We must assume it was used in some sacrificial rite. It was known to the druids that certain primitive races first remove the victim's heart before interring it into the earth as an appeasement to their fertility goddess."

Suddenly grabbing hold of Vescala, Tymaron pulled him to his feet.

"Listen to me, Vescala!" he yelled angrily. "We must leave, it's all over. The only alternative is to end up like that poor little beggar. Now let's gather our weapons and get down to the boat."

"What about the others? Do we leave them to suffer Cetra's fate?"

"Yes, damn it! What choice do we have? As it is they may already be dead. At least we still have a chance, albeit a slim one. Look, Vescala, we are placed on this earth for only a short span of time and I for one have no intention of leaving it prematurely. Now come on, let's go."

"All right we go! But not before nightfall, and only after we've given Cetra a decent burial," Vescala snapped, staring down at the child's pitiful remains. Perhaps it was a sudden fear of death or an inherent sense of destiny that had been the prime factor in his decision. And although in the far past he had sought death, he now desired to live; all the time feeling a momentary shame at the thought of not at least attempting to contact Brenas and the others.

Carrying the child's remains back through the gateway they immediately lowered the portcullis. Vescala then obtained a shovel from a nearby storage hut, and hastily burying the body, he left Tymaron to make a search of the other huts to ensure that no intruders had entered the settlement while the portcullis had remained open. However, save for themselves the village remained deserted.

It was late in the evening by the time they had completed their tasks, and with the rain having ceased, a solitary ray from the receding sun forced its way through the dispersing clouds. Both men were now soaking wet, and after changing into dry clothing they hurriedly gathered the arms and the sack full of fresh food they would take with them. Fortunately, little food was required – with Tymaron having kept the well-stocked boat in a constant state of readiness, and for the remainder of the evening they sat in the hut to await the black African night.

As Vescala lay back on the lion skins a glum Tymaron sat by the open door.

"I well remember the day when Cetra was born," Vescala said, breaking the lingering silence between them as his voice echoed around the room. "It was apparent even then that he would never be normal, although I must confess that the word normal when applied to, we humans conjure up the most amusing comparisons. Anyway, at the time, I had hoped that his powerful heartbeat would herald in the true meaning of the freedom we were seeking. After all, he was the first surviving handicapped child to be born into the commune. Naturally enough, I thought his presence would be beneficial to the social equality most of us desired. Unfortunately, after his mother died nearly everyone rejected him. What I now find ironic is that such a tragic child should be the first of us to die at the hands of the very pagan morality many of us struggled for so long to escape."

"Why wait four months before killing him?" a confused Tymaron then asked.

"It's difficult to say. I suspect that ever since the day when we first came to these shores our every movement has been observed. When Cetra disappeared, he was probably looking for me. Perhaps he got lost when wandering into the jungle trying to find his way to the shore or maybe he was kidnapped the moment he set foot in the place. Let's face it, he was an affectionate child who would have gone quietly along with anyone who paid him the slightest attention. Now if you think back to the day when he disappeared you will recall that a great deal of activity had been taking place both inside as well as outside the stockade. What I'm referring to was the construction of so many carts. Place that fact alongside the extensive scouting mission Cramon had sent out and there you have the semblance of a motive."

"But how?" Tymaron asked not understanding.

"Look at it this way: supposing twenty years ago the natives of this land saw us coming to their shores from across the ocean. Can you imagine what effect the sight of such a huge ship must have had on an ignorant and superstitious mind? You see, Tymaron, these people may have regarded our intrusion into their territory not as an invading force but as the coming of white-skinned gods. Of course, I could be wrong in my assumption. They may not have been aware of our existence until we had been long established in the valley, although I don't think so. Now let's suppose that they regard this valley as a holy place. How then do you think that a black-skinned race of barbarians would have felt on seeing a fair-skinned race of aliens coming to their shores from across the gigantic spasm of water we call the Atlantic: a people whose technology was far superior to theirs? They've probably watched and studied us for years. When they saw us preparing to leave, they naturally wondered why. Perhaps through no more than sheer curiosity they then decided to kidnap one of us when the first opportunity arose. Now when they discovered Cetra to be so tragically afflicted they would have known for certain that we were neither gods nor indeed godly emissaries. As we know, physically and mentally deformed people are to be found in every race throughout Europe, so why not among the natives here as well?"

"It's a good theory, Vescala, but it falls down on at least one point: gods or even their emissaries are not supposed to die. In the time we've spent here, we buried enough dead…they must have noticed that!"

"Alright, then let's suppose they cremate their dead. Maybe in their religious beliefs burial is as alien to them as cremation is to us."

"Yes, but you once told me that the druids sometimes cremate their dead."

"That's true, but only at a time of sacrifice to appease a god or to eradicate plague as in the case of my own family. But at all other times earthly internment was practised. Anyway, that's as maybe. Now let's assume their priests or wise men saw in our coming to their lands the hope of some undertaking lying in their ancient beliefs. Perhaps a leadership emanating from us would eventually have led them to a superior level of existence, just as I had hoped so long ago that the survivors of Atlantis might have done for us. However, now that they suspect that we've embarked on a policy of colonialism then they will almost certainly kill the others — but for the time being, I don't think they'll harm us."

"Why not?" the surprised Tymaron asked.

"If I'm right, and I imagine I am, I should reckon it highly unlikely that they will want to offend their gods by spilling human blood within what may be a consecrated place. Back in the old country, even the highest-ranking druids could only draw human blood within a consecrated site, but then only on specific dates. It may well be that these people hold similar beliefs."

"You mean as long as we stay here, we're safe?"

"Yes. On the other hand, if we leave then they might kill us!"

"Then how do we leave undetected? Let's face it, it's a long way to the shore. And why haven't they killed me already? I made enough trips to the shore over the last few months."

"To your last question…I don't know. As far as escaping goes, we'll just have to risk it!" he exclaimed as his alert eyes stared out the door to where the darkness was swiftly descending. But in the deathly silence of the hut, each man now sensed a creeping apprehension engulfing him.

"So, you were right all along, Vescala. Had the others stayed their safety was virtually secured. But tell me, what were those natives like? You never really went into much detail before," Tymaron asked, wiping the clammy palms of his hands on his trousers. Sighing heavily, Vescala recalled the day so long ago when he had murdered Mondena.

"After killing Mondena, I travelled south following the coastline. One day I decided to head inland in search of game; up until then, I had survived by eating shellfish and trapping sea birds. Entering into the jungle, and after unsuccessfully hunting for some time, I spotted from beyond the trees ahead of me a thin wisp of smoke rising high into the still air. With a sense of extreme caution, I made my way towards it, only to come upon a long deep valley where, nestling at the bottom, lay some twenty or so crudely erected bee-hive-shaped huts. They were small in size and appeared to be constructed from branches covered over in animal pelts. You can imagine my surprise at making such a discovery, and for a while, I stood astounded. But suddenly from the entrance of one of the dwellings there emerged a black-skinned and totally naked woman who came out to gather some nearby wood that she used to rekindle the fire burning in the centre of the village. But no sooner had she returned into her hut than I heard a great deal of shouting, and from the cover of the trees on the far side of the valley a mass of running men rushed out and headed down towards the settlement. There must have been at least a hundred of them, again all black-skinned, with each man wielding a short wooden club and what looked to me to be a stone-headed spear. The carnage that followed was swift and decisive with every male in the village dragged from the huts before being bludgeoned to death with blows from the clubs. After the men had been killed the screaming women, young and old alike, were quickly herded together like cattle before being moved to the far end of the village. Their children, regardless of sex or age, were then hauled from their mother's arms and held by their ankles, only to be swung high into the air and have their heads smashed open against the nearest rocks. I was standing a good distance from where this was happening but unable to detect any physical differences between the opposing factions; indeed, they all looked alike, with each of them being slight of stature with black skin and black woolly hair. There didn't appear to be any leader among the attacking force, and I found their aggression to be totally dissimilar to the technique of warfare back in Britain, where there is always a nobleman warrior along with his second-in-command, who throughout any conflict keeps to one side of the affray to supervise and shout out their tactical commands. In our warfare, it was customary to ransack and then burn a captured village, but this didn't happen with these people. All they seemed to want were the unfortunate women. I got the impression that the aggressors had been well-briefed beforehand, perhaps by a king or priesthood. However, the entire action took only a short time to accomplish, and all I could do was stand and watch as they vanished back into the jungle with their hapless captives. At the time I was naturally horrified at the implications my discovery had. After all, if there were primitive barbarians to the south of our settlement it was highly probable there would be others to the north and east. As you know, over the years I made numerous penetrating searches of the countryside and although I never again sighted the natives, I did on two occasions stumble upon human tracks alongside the remains of man-made fires. But not wishing to instil a sense of neurosis in the others, I kept the secret to myself for some seventeen years. It was only when Cramon and Chevada began their dissension that I was forced into speaking out about my discovery. Oh,

Brenas and Lascal certainly believed me. But not the rest, as you know. Maybe I was wrong and should have told everyone at the time. There again perhaps it's as you said before, that we are in the wrong place at the wrong time."

"When did you first suspect we were being watched?"

"I had my suspicions from the moment I discovered the natives. But the decisive factor was when you found Mondena's boat washed up three months after I killed him. There's no way that boat ended up there by itself. I think the natives, why I've no idea, put it there. Now there is poor Cetra: I suppose that has to be the final confirmation. Anyway, none of it matters anymore; it's time to go!" Vescala concluded firmly, and rising to their feet they gathered up their weapons and food to step out into the darkness where only a few stars twinkled faintly through the obscuring cloud that fortunately for them effectively hid the moon.

Nervously and silently, they made their way through the rows of empty abodes that had once witnessed so much happiness. Soon they reached the portcullis, where Vescala suggested that they smear their clothing, hands, and faces in mud to camouflage themselves. With this done, Tymaron slowly raised the portcullis just enough to allow them to slip underneath. Crawling along on their stomachs they then made their way through the long, wet grass, finally reaching the steep banks leading down to the swollen stream. The sounds coming out of the nearby jungle now screamed out through the black night air and, after slithering down the bank to the water's edge, both men felt relieved on having reached what they reckoned to be a relatively safe spot. Crouching low they then followed the stream westwards until they reached the point where its banks levelled off with the ground. Crossing the water, and again crawling along on their stomachs, they made their way in an upward direction towards the dark but increasingly sinister-looking jungle. At last, they reached the cover of the trees where panting and perspiring heavily from their exertions, they crouched down low behind some bushes to take a short rest and to look down for the last time at the valley that for so long had been their home. By now a few small animals had begun to emerge from the trees to go down and drink from the stream. Suddenly Tymaron's keen eyes spotted something moving near the stockade.

"Look, see, by the portcullis," he whispered, pointing through the gloom where Vescala was just able to make out a dark shape prowling around it. But he reckoned it to be no more than an animal although Tymaron, whose eyes were much sharper, was convinced that the lone figure was human. With the very air itself now appearing to stand like an oppressive veil between them and the home they would never know again, they rose, and turning, crept stealthily through the dense, humid jungle, with each man constantly aware of hidden eyes that seemed to be lurking before and behind their every footstep.

A swift rustling of the bushes caused by some disturbed creature saw them come to an abrupt halt and raise their spears to strike, but nothing was forthcoming, and with Tymaron having to aid Vescala, owing to his infirm leg, they fled on through the seemingly endless night with their greatest enemy continuing to be their own fears and delusions.

Close to exhaustion they at last escaped the jungle's suffocating terror. However, on reaching the deserted beach they stumbled over to where the boat lay berthed with Tymaron immediately beginning to lay out the rollers, leaving Vescala to place the food and weapons into it. The two men then had to summon up their remaining strength in order to launch her, and quickly clambering aboard, it was the re-doubtable Tymaron who grabbed the oars, and with an almost supernatural burst of desperation rowed feverishly until reaching deep water where almost breathless, he stopped to stare hard at Vescala who was seated by the boats' stern.

"They could have killed us at any time! Why let us go?" he gasped, hardly daring to believe they had made it.

"I don't know! Perhaps they failed to spot our escape or maybe they had other reasons…I just don't know," a perplexed Vescala replied, turning to look back at the long, dark deserted African coastline.

Meanwhile, back at the stockade, the portcullis had been re-lowered to the ground, and in the eerie atmosphere of the communal hut, the tattered and emaciated figure of Arlesia lay spread-eagled across the floor. It was broad daylight now, and sluggishly raising herself into a standing position she stared towards the open doorway; her wild, staring eyes showing the insanity into which her mind was almost totally consumed. And with her ragged dress almost non-existent alongside her matted filthy hair, her once radiant facial features now showed the reality of a premature aging.

For a few moments, she stumbled around the hall before again collapsing onto her knees, only to scream aloud as the many open wounds covering her body caused her a terrible agony. In her rancour, she began to recall the ill-fated journey, and sobbing bitterly a cold remorse stole into her soul as her mind travelled back to the time when she had left the stockade alongside her lover Cramon. It had all seemed so promising at the time, she thought as tears streamed down her face, and as the days had passed by her future had looked so secure, with even Brenas having to grudgingly praise Cramon for his resolute ability in commanding the people. Indeed, Cramon had certainly been a changed man, never happier than when helping others overcome the many difficulties experienced on the trek.

Over the first twenty days, everything had gone relatively smoothly. But early one morning the discovery that a young girl had disappeared in the night had caused many among them to question the wisdom in going any further. A search party had been quickly organised to find her, and for two days they remained in the midst of a dense jungle while the searchers combed a wide surrounding area. But just as in Cetra's case no trace of the little girl was to be found. At first, her distraught parents had refused to go on. However, when the stalwart Cramon insisted that they must, Lascal had openly objected, only for Silena to accuse him in front of everyone, of cowardice; her humiliating taunt forcing Lascal to reluctantly agree with his son.

As they pressed on everything had again gone well. But during their thirty-fifth night away from the stockade a mother, father, and their three children suddenly vanished, only this time from within the very heart of the campsite itself. That very night, Cramon had personally assigned the two camp guards but when the discovery was made the next morning the guards were as baffled as everyone else, for during the night they had seen and heard nothing. However, the strange disappearances had little effect on Cramon, who was quick to tell the others that the family had in all probability deserted him in order to make their way back to 'that old fool, Vescala,' in spite of the fact, that none of the family's possessions had been taken.

At Cramon's insistence that they keep on advancing a premonition of dread struck into the hearts of the majority with a division of opinion splitting the commune right down the middle. After a heated argument between Cramon and Lascal, it was decided that the two factions should separate, with Cramon's followers continuing to advance and Lascal and Brenas returning to the stockade with the others. Although Lascal had been infuriated at his wife electing to remain with her eldest son and his followers, Cramon remained unconcerned at the rift in his own family. As far as he was concerned, he was well rid of those whom he suspected had been incapable of making such a journey in the first place.

By then they had reached the edge of the jungle only to come upon a long ravine stretching out before them. It had been midday when the two parties had separated, with Cramon leading his group, numbering eighty-eight, along the ravine while Lascal and Brenas proceeded back through the jungle at the head of the others. But passing through the ravine had proved more difficult than Cramon had anticipated, with the carts continually getting stuck fast in the waterlogged vegetation at the base of the soaring perpendicular cliffs. And as the blue twilight descended around them, he issued the order to set up camp just as the advance scouts returned to report the sighting of a vast swamp some two days journey ahead.

That night had been peaceful enough, but with the coming of the dawn Cramon, who had been the first to rise, ordered that they move out of the ravine before breakfasting. Perhaps it was the menacing atmosphere of their mysterious surroundings that had so agitated him into giving such a strange command or maybe a premonition. But it was the last order he was ever to issue, and just as everyone was preparing to move out a destructive fall of massive rocks launched by unseen hands hailed down on them from the cliff tops high above. Cramon's warning scream of 'Avalanche' was stifled abruptly as his body crumpled beneath a huge, jagged rock, killing him instantly. Arlesia, who had been close to him, had managed to leap clear just in time, only to then stumble into a deep fissure in the cliff face where striking her head on a rock face, she was immediately rendered unconscious. Later she had come to, shocked and dazed, and having struggled to regain her senses the vague awareness of many voices speaking in an alien tongue had seen her cautiously rise to stare out from beyond the huge rock almost covering her refuge. But all she could see were mangled bodies lying dead among the scattered rocks. Having waited until the voices had gone, she fought free from the fissure, only to be physically sick with fear as she had searched in vain for survivors. But everyone lay dead, with those who hadn't died beneath the rock fall having had their skulls clubbed open.

Only in the mystery of her nightmares had she previously experienced such a fearful loneliness, and running through the blood and gore she had then fled back along the ravine before collapsing from exhaustion at the jungle's edge. In the morning, she resumed her desperate flight, struggling and stumbling along towards the stockade, but with her mind swimming in terror her every step brought a growing apprehension that her very movements were being observed.

As the long insecure days had passed, she survived by eating just enough wild fruit to sustain her diminishing strength. But somehow her returning love for Vescala spurred her on, and bitterly regretting her infidelities, she swore that when eventually reaching the stockade she would go down on her bended knees to beg his forgiveness.

There were times when she had wandered as aimlessly as a windblown seed, but on the first night of a new moon, she had come upon a clearing where through it wound the stream that her intuition had told her would lead her back to the valley. Stopping to rest, she had been about to search for a suitable tree in which to spend the night when the moon suddenly vanished behind a cloud. In the almost impenetrable gloom, she eventually found one with a great gnarled trunk, and guided by touch alone, she ascended one of the long creepers hanging down from its branches; the jagged scrub engulfing the trunk of the tree painfully cutting into her arms and legs. With the moonlight reappearing, her hand had then brushed against something soft but clammy, and turning, she came face to face with the ghastly decomposing head of Brenas, whose still body hung suspended by its neck from yet another creeper. At the sight of his sunken lifeless eyes, she slithered back down the creeper to crash heavily down to the dank earth. In her horror, she had risen only to see hanging from all the surrounding trees the corpses of all those who had left Cramon. Feeling as if some invisible claw had torn through her soul, she had then aroused the jungle's unseen inhabitants with her demented screaming, and with her eyes transfixed on the mutilated corpses illuminated in the bright moonlight, she suddenly found herself surrounded by the haunting screeching sounds pouring back out from the jungle's interior.

As she fled from the clearing, her partially clad body fell incessantly among the jungle's tortuous webs of slashing scrub and thorn bushes. However, oblivious to pain, only her subconscious desire to survive had fortified her faltering steps as she moved ever closer to the valley and he within the stockade who would absolve her from the sin that had so corrupted her. Crawling beneath the partially opened portcullis she had sensed, even before searching the huts, that like all the others Vescala, too, was gone forever.

With her dementia now accelerating, the lonely Arlesia wept hysterically, and tearing at her long, filthy hair she scoured her face and body with her long, black nails until her act of self-mutilation destroyed forever the beauty that so long ago had captivated Vescala. In her fearful destitution she rose slowly, and taking hold of one of the torches from the wall she quickly lit it with her flints before running outside. Momentarily, she stood gesticulating at the surrounding sun-struck huts, whose lime-washed walls appeared in her madness to stand as imaginary druid priests condemning her for her sins. Screaming as she staggered along, she in turn ignited each of the thatched roofs before carrying the torch flames to the walls of the stockade itself. Soon a tempest of consumptive fire and streaming black smoke rose towards the clear heavens, and running back into the communal hut, she first set fire to its roof before entering the room to violently cast the torch among the benches lying stacked against the walls. With a mental firestorm now incinerating her mind, Arlesia stood laughing uncontrollably as her red-rimmed eyes stared wildly towards the choking smoke billowing around the doorway, and as the flames grew in their intensity her repeated cries of 'Vescala' echoed ferociously throughout the hut. Meanwhile, in the mystical jungle surrounding the valley, ever-watchful eyes stared in awe at the destruction of the stockade and the village within, and by noon all that remained of the once-idyllic settlement were a few charred, smoking logs lying among the piles of white ash being gently carried along on a sweet-scented breeze.

The fallen Arlesia, who as a young child had only briefly known the druid priesthood, died a victim of her own, early childhood morality. Back in her true homeland of Britain the druidical punishment for adultery was death by burning!

Chapter Twenty-six

"Come on, old fellow, wake up! You've been dreaming again come on," Tymaron's imploring voice whispered so as not to awaken the others. Vescala, now into the winter of his age, lay back on the perspiration-drenched straw bed below him, and grunting aloud he acknowledged the voice that had broken his nightmare; a repetitive horror that would nightly resurrect his past as it swept through his mind like some dark celestial breeze.

"Is that you, Tymaron?" he asked in a voice hoarse from shouting and staring up at the shadowy figure leaning over him.

"Yes, it's me. That's the last six nights you've woken everyone with your shouting. I fear the only hope the rest of us have of getting a good night's sleep is to send you back across the ocean," Tymaron replied, emitting a coarse laugh. Now raising himself to recline on one elbow, Vescala wiped the torrents of sweat cascading down his almost hairless head with his long bony fingers.

"You've no idea what it's like, son. They keep coming back to me. It's as if they're still alive but living in some purgatorial netherworld."

"Who keeps coming back?"

"The dead…the dead of the past."

"It's only your imagination. No one can harm you here," Tymaron muttered through a sigh. Although he sympathised with Vescala's plight, there was a definite impatience in his voice but just as he was about to return to his own sleeping quarters, Vescala suddenly grabbed his naked arm.

"How long has it been?" he asked morosely as Tymaron wrenched his arm free.

"Eight years. Now forget the past; try to get some sleep."

Alone in the little recess, Vescala slumped back sensing that the dawn must soon arrive to breach the long night's insufferable darkness. In the deathly silence of the hut, his dazed thoughts returned to that fateful morning when they had set sail from the African shore. For many months they had followed a northern route, always sailing within sight of the coast in order to escape the tropical storms they had frequently encountered. However, at no time did they ever attempt to contact the natives who inhabited the frequently sighted coastal villages that dotted the beautiful but treacherous African shoreline.

It took them just over a year to reach the straits of Gibraltar, confirming Vescala's long-held suspicion that Mondena had indeed deluded them. They had then continued to follow the Spanish coastline, only to be involved in a short skirmish with coastal pirates who had sailed out from the shore to intercept them. After Tymaron killed one of them with his spear they were free to resume their journey until they eventually reached the southern coastline of Gaul. At that stage in their voyage, Vescala had proposed that, before returning to Britain, they should first head for Ireland and there try to contact Aldrun and his group, assuming of course that they were still alive.

It was to take them another year to reach the southern Irish island where Aldrun and the others had disembarked so many eventful years before. It was on a cold, frosty morning when they finally landed on the beach, and after making a thorough search of the entire island they were disappointed to find it completely uninhabited. However, they remained on the island for only a day, with Tymaron's discovery of some human bones and two skulls, lying half-submerged in the sand, leaving them in no doubt that Aldrun and his group had almost certainly perished. Leaving the island, they then sailed over to the Irish mainland where they had stayed for two years scraping a meagre existence from the sea and surrounding marshlands and living in a makeshift hut that they had constructed to protect themselves from the elements.

By that time both men had been worn out by their long arduous journey, with neither of them very keen to make the crossing back over to Britain. It had been Vescala who had suggested that they remain in Ireland to begin a new life, and much to his surprise, especially given that he probably had surviving relatives back in Britain, Tymaron agreed.

With the coming of the following spring, they again set off in the boat, sailing north until they came upon a sprawling village lying up from a long sandy bay. Both men had previously agreed to tell anyone enquiring about their identities that they were a father and son in search of Vescala's niece who had been abducted from Britain some two years earlier. Having given themselves false identities, each man would now profess to belong to the large scattered tribe of the Iceni people. They had also decided never to tell anyone about their African experience; both men having sworn to each other that everything that had occurred to them over the past twenty-three years would go with them to the grave.

After landing, they introduced themselves to the village chieftain, and although made welcome they were, for the first few months, treated with a certain distrust by the villagers. Eventually, and after gaining the peoples' trust, Vescala even succeeded in convincing one of the local druid priests who had visited the out-of-the-way village every few months of their sincerity.

The dialectical variations between the locals and themselves were not dissimilar to the language problems Vescala had experienced in the land of the Picts. However, this he quickly overcame, and it had been after successfully curing, by means of his herbal treatment, one of the village elder's children of an eye inflammation that the chieftain had insisted that the two strangers could remain in the village for as long as they desired.

Life in the village was peaceful and productive, and both men had worked hard in the fields to provide for their food and lodgings. But after six months had elapsed, Tymaron was to fall in love with one of the local maidens, and in order not to arouse any suspicions, Vescala decided to leave on the pretext that he was resuming the search for his supposedly kidnapped niece. Before departing though, he had insisted to the chieftain that Tymaron remain behind, at the same time giving his blessing to the young man's by then imminent marriage.

It had been early in the summer when they had eventually parted company, and for the next three years, Vescala travelled throughout the country virtually living as a hermit for most of that time. There were occasions on his travels when he encountered the Irish druids, only to find them every bit as fanatical in their devotions as their British counterparts. He was, however, surprised at the many differences existing between the two religious groups. In the legal sense the Irish druids were in no way as powerful nor did they practice human sacrifice as in Britain; indeed, they were content just to sacrifice animals in their religious ceremonies. Another difference he discovered was that their calendar cycle comprised of twelve lunar months rather than fourteen, with each of the months being associated with the name of a river animal or fish rather than a bird. Nonetheless, he found them to be held in the highest reverence by the Irish people, and nowhere near as feared as the priesthood back in Britain had been.

Although his journey throughout the beautiful, emerald green island had been spiritually rewarding, early in the autumn in the Irish month of the otter he decided to return to the southern village. On the way there, he came upon a small village where a marriage ceremony had just taken place, and having been made welcome by the bride's father, he joined in the feasting and celebrations that continued well into the night. However, when seated with many others around the huge bonfire blazing in the centre of the village, he finally heard of the tragic fate that had befallen Aldrun and his group so many years before. One of the local bards had after a boisterous singsong related a long epic poem telling of how a great British warlord named Ravala had met a courageous death at the hands of escaping brigands. Throughout the recitation, which was constantly interspersed with druidical propaganda, the names of Aldrun and his followers had frequently been mentioned in the most derogatory terms. The poem culminated by describing how the great warrior's nephew, Crezala, and his henchmen, had sailed over from the British mainland only to then bribe a local tribal army with gold and subsequently slaughter Aldrun's little commune who had lived peacefully on the island for a mere one hundred days. At the time Vescala had shown no outward emotion at the confirmation of Aldrun's fate. He knew that such a poem would be related, perhaps for centuries, to countless numbers of unsuspecting listeners who would never know the truth about the incredible heroism and endurance of the people whom the bard had so eloquently denigrated. Later, when alone, he had wept on thinking of the little children of the future who would only hear the distorted lies that all too often masquerade as accurate historical fact.

On his return to the southern village, he was warmly welcomed back. And after explaining to the chieftain that the search for his niece had proved fruitless, he was overjoyed to be told that in the time he had been away, Tymaron had indeed married and had already fathered two healthy sons. Tymaron had been delighted to see him again, and having been gifted a hut and some land as a wedding dowry, he insisted that Vescala live with him and the family he adored. It was a great and continuing consolation to Vescala that the young man had found true happiness, with Vescala being more than content to spend his remaining years in the village where the pace of life languished so peacefully among the striking scenery of the surrounding countryside.

As the latter years had slipped by everything had gone well for him. But with his infirm leg now rapidly deteriorating, his working capabilities had been reduced to performing no more than the most menial chores. As a result of this, he had in recent times become a liability to the family, and over the last few months it was this fact alone that had seen him contemplating whether or not to leave Ireland forever. But with his recurring nightmares causing even more consternation, he finally made up his mind that it would be better to go now.

By this time the sweat on his body had dried, and in the darkness, he slowly eased himself into a seated posture to begin dressing. Raising himself up by means of the long staff he now had to use to get around he finished dressing, and donning his heavy sealskin cloak, left the small but comfortable recess that over the past two years had been his sleeping quarters.

Silently stealing past Tymaron and his lovely wife, who lay sleeping in the far corner of the spacious hut, he reached the door. Turning, he looked down for the last time at the two tiny children lying fast asleep near to the fire in the centre of the room; their curled-up bodies just visible in the faint glow emanating from the fire's dying embers. Trembling with emotion the unhappy Vescala momentarily pondered over his decision, but in his heart, he knew it was pointless in regretting what had to be done. His departure meant one less mouth to feed to a family who, as it was, had to struggle hard to keep themselves. Gently unbarring the door, he stepped out into the dark damp early morning air, and quietly closing it behind him, he hobbled away, with his presence only acknowledged by a few grunts from the pigs and goats in their nearby pens. However, on reaching the entrance to the stockade the young man on guard duty casually lurched up to greet him.

"A bit early for a stroll Vescala," he remarked through a pleasant smile.

"Yes, I can't sleep. I thought I might watch the dawn rise over the bay," Vescala replied as the young man raised the portcullis.

"See you when you get back then," he said cheerfully as Vescala went through the gateway only to hirple badly as he struggled along the muddy pathway leading down to the deserted shore. Passing by the small fields surrounding the village the sharp tang of the invigorating sea air drifted into his nostrils. Soon he reached the shore where the boat built by Mondena lay moored alongside the rickety wooden pier that also harboured a few flimsy coracles bobbing gently on the ocean's calm swell.

Over the past few months, he had secretly kept hidden on the vessel a sword along with some provisions, and limping slowly along the pier the dull tapping of his staff appeared to welcome the piercing light of the dawn now spreading slowly across the heavens. With the air damp and chilly, he was glad to be wearing his sheepskin jacket and two pairs of linen trousers beneath his cloak. But on reaching the end of the pier his unwieldy clothing caused him some difficulty as he descended the small ladder that took him down into the boat. After checking that the provisions were intact, he had no hesitancy in untying the vessel from its mooring before slowly rowing out into the bay's placid waters. However, he had rowed only a short distance when the cry of 'Vescala' breached the still air, and raising the oars, he perceived a half-dressed Tymaron racing along the pier.

"Where are you going, Vescala?" he shouted out after him; with Tymaron having awoken not long before, and after rising to check that Vescala was all right had been astonished to have found him gone.

"It's time to go, Tymaron!" Vescala exclaimed emphatically.

"But this is your home. Please come back, you'll perish out there alone!" Tymaron pleaded, beckoning with his arm for Vescala to return. Unperturbed though, Vescala lowered the dripping oars and, as the boat began to cut through the water, he paid no attention to Tymaron who kept begging him not to go. Soon he had cleared the bay whereon reaching rougher water, he raised the tiny sail before turning the boat south with Tymaron continuing to follow him from the shore; all the time imploring him to return. But it was midmorning before the exhausted Tymaron finally accepted the fact that he was leaving forever, and coming to a halt, his eyes filled with tears as he hoarsely shouted his good wishes to his old comrade before turning back and heading for home.

Although feeling guilt-ridden by the manner in which he had left Tymaron and his family, the continuing good weather helped raise his flagging spirits, and after sailing on through the night the following day saw him once again pass by the island where Aldrun and his group had found so little happiness and where now only a few scattered gulls inhabited the shore.

For another four days, he sailed close to the coast before suddenly turning the vessel southeast to leave Ireland's unspoiled serenity forever. However, now on course for the Southlands of Britain, the weather suddenly deteriorated, and for ten nerve-wracking days and nights, he was all alone with the open sea in all its unmasked fury. At times he was forced into bailing out the swamping waters with his bare hands in order to prevent the vessel from capsizing. But with his sleep taken in short snatches, by the fifteenth night not even the howls from the shrieking wind could prevent him from falling into a deep sleep.

On awakening in the morning, cold, miserable, and with his clothing sodden, he raised his stiff body only for his eyes to once again engage the imposing mist-enshrouded cliffs of his homeland lying silhouetted against the dim red sunlight. With the sea now calm and the damp air motionless, he took the oars to begin rowing as fast as he could to generate some warmth back into his shivering body.

Finding no suitable spot on the rugged coast on which to land, and at the mercy of the treacherous currents, he spent the next few days living in intolerable conditions. Fortunately, he had sufficient food and water left to sustain him, and with a strong southerly breeze springing up he continued eastwards under a full sail for three more days, passing at a distance the sheltered town of Iscal.

Sailing on through the night, and after an intermittent sleep, the morning saw him come upon a long, uninhabited cove where a line of grass-flecked sand dunes rose up to melt into a heavily forested landscape. Dropping the sail, he rowed in an almost leisurely manner towards the shore; witnessed only by a flock of oystercatchers that, on spotting him, scurried away along the silver shingle.

By the time the boat's bow had scraped into the shingle, a radiant sun had broken through the grey cloud, and as his warped hands released the oars, he gathered up his sword and staff and what little was left of his food, which he tucked into the pouch inside his cloak. With his struggle with the sea forever at an end, he clambered over the side of the boat to set foot on his native soil for the first time in thirty eventful years. Abandoning the boat to the ebb tide, he sensed in the surrounding silent atmosphere, a devout malevolence as his impetuous steps took him back into a world that so long ago, he had felt impelled to reject. And yet what inexplicable desire had motivated him into returning, the hooded figure kept asking himself as he slowly ascended the dunes. Vanishing into the cover of the trees, a desperately weary and lonely old man remained unaware that the forever violent month of the red-backed shrike was drawing ominously near!

Chapter Twenty-seven

For two soul-searching days, Vescala took refuge in a small damp cave situated deep in the dense woodlands and whose entrance lay partially hidden by a protective thicket of holly bushes. With his sword by his side, he awoke on the third day shortly after daybreak and quickly re-lit the fire to give him some warmth. As he sat finishing the last of his food, he felt content and at complete ease with the world, and caring nothing for the future, he suddenly extinguished the fire and rising up re-sheathed his sword into the scabbard beneath his cloak. Grabbing his staff, he struggled out through the bushes and into the oppressive gloom of the midmorning air where he stared briefly up at the chill grey colours of the marching clouds lying low in the sky. A gentle spray of rain suddenly struck his wrinkled features and, drawing the hood of his cloak over his head, he walked with the aid of his staff through the woods where following an easterly direction, he emerged from the cover of the trees to see a rugged grassy terrain spreading out before him to the murky horizon. By now it was raining heavily, and for the rest of the morning, he continued on his way until coming upon a track running north to east with fresh hoof-prints from many ponies having turned it into a mass of soft, yielding mud. After deciding to follow the route it wasn't long before he spotted in the distance a barrier lying across the track, comprising of some twenty or so derelict chariots. Reaching the spot, and just as the rain ceased, he strolled through the wreckage only to be puzzled at the irreparable damage that had been done to the vehicles. Although he could see no signs of any discarded weapons, he left the place, concluding that the site must have been the scene of some recent conflict.

Proceeding on his way, by midday the gorse-infested landscape had begun to rise, and, with a torpid sun now forcing its rays through the dull sky, he lowered his hood. Suddenly to his right, he spotted the tall figure of a long-haired young man standing on a small hillock staring over at him.

"Hey, traveller, I've just cooked a hare I trapped. There's more than enough for two, come up and join me," the young man shouted, beckoning with his arm for Vescala to approach him. It was the first person he had seen since his return, and with the invitation appearing friendly enough he left the track to limp up to where the heavily garbed youth was standing. However, on reaching him his smile rapidly turned to a grimace on seeing the triple-coloured headband of the novitiate priest covering his forehead.

"Come on, old man, sit by the fire and get some warmth," the youth said cheerfully before helping him through the long damp grass and over to the charcoal fire where skewered onto a spearhead hung suspended the roasted hare. Thanking his host, Vescala sat down with his eyes never leaving the youth who was around seventeen years old, square-shouldered, and slight in build with kind, brown eyes just visible from behind the long coils of black hair cascading down and over his forehead and which now partially covered his headband.

"Where do you travel to, old man?"

"The nearest town I suppose…I'm just a wanderer," Vescala replied, drawing his eyes from the youth, and staring down greedily at the food.

"These are strange times to be travelling alone. Look I've got some wine in my saddle pack," the youth said before going over to his pony tethered to a nearby gorse bush.

Returning, he brought with him a small goatskin pitcher of wine and one bronze drinking vessel, which he filled and handed to Vescala.

"Here, you look as if you could do with this."

Taking hold of the cup, Vescala sipped from its rim as the youth sat down opposite him. "Where have you come from?" the youth then enquired, but at the question, Vescala gulped the remaining wine down, and with a hint of mistrust in his eyes passed the cup back over to the young man who immediately refilled it for himself.

"Oh, I just got back from Ireland, having spent the last few years with friends I made there a long time ago," he replied as the young novitiate detected his unwillingness to elaborate.

"Forgive my inquisitive nature, old man; my master on Anglesey is forever telling me that my prying mind is at times tantamount to no more than snooping," the young man commented through a cheeky smile. Vescala smirked at his sincerity and what unease he had felt about the novitiate rapidly dissolved.

"What's your name, son?"

"Cerix, and yours?"

"Tell me, Cerix, have you just returned from Anglesey?" he asked, ignoring the youth's question.

"Yes, when I heard of the situation down here, I cut short my studies in order to help get my family north as soon as possible," the downcast Cerix replied.

"What situation are you referring to?"

"Surely you must have heard? Oh, of course, the news might not have reached Ireland yet!" Cerix exclaimed, pausing momentarily to gulp down the last of the wine. "Some twenty days ago, under Emperor Claudius, the legions of Imperial Rome crossed over the Channel from Gaul to begin a full-scale invasion of our south lands; apparently with the intention of absorbing our islands into their Empire."

"What!" Vescala yelled; his eyes almost bursting out of their aged sockets, and what little colour there had been in his face quickly drained away.

"Yes, I thought that news might shake you! Anyway, under the command of a general called Aulus Plautius, the Romans landed at Richborough and there set about erecting a strong base camp. As doubtless, you can imagine, we had no foreknowledge of the surprise landing and naturally weren't in any position to organise any resistance by which to repel the invader. As news of the landing spread certain of our kings – such as the brothers Caractacus and Togodumnus of the Catuvellani tribe – began to make preparations to throw the enemy back across the Channel. Unfortunately, there are too few kings as patriotic as these brothers, with most of the others having succumbed to the assurances of gold and their retention of power promised by the Emperor's emissaries in return for a total Roman victory." Cerix said pausing to pull the now-roasted hare free from the spearhead. And effortlessly splitting it in two with his dagger, he handed one half over to Vescala who was anxious to know more.

"How far have they advanced?" he asked, grasping hold of the welcome meal.

"They are now firmly established along most of the southeastern coastline. The information I've managed to obtain indicates they're spreading daily, north, and west. Some ten days ago they crossed over the river Thames with a huge army, and in a ferocious battle that took place near to the river Medway, in which they were outnumbered two to one by our own forces, they annihilated our armies, killing King Togodumnus into the bargain. In a courageous attempt to prevent them from advancing further north, the defeated Caractacus has regrouped his forces and is now preparing to wage a do-or-die battle with them at his hometown of Colchester. Naturally, the priesthood is doing everything in its power to unify the kings and tribes into one national fighting force. However, such are the divisions among our kings and nobles, I'm afraid most hold out little hope of success."

"This Emperor Claudius you spoke of, when did he succeed Augustus?" Vescala enquired, tearing into the hare's flesh.

"He didn't," Cerix answered with a surprised look on his face. "Augustus succumbed to Tiberius a long time ago. Tiberius was then assassinated five years ago, only to be succeeded by an even more debauched and demented maniac by the name of Caligula. About a year ago he too in turn was assassinated and replaced by his uncle Claudius who is a supposedly elderly scholar accredited with a brilliant mind. Anyway, this stuttering cripple Claudius decided to add our islands to his already inflated empire and there you have it."

Cerix then stopped talking to begin his meal leaving Vescala to contemplate on the catastrophic effect the invasion would have on the peoples of Britain.

"You say he's supposedly brilliant, Cerix: I hardly think it economically viable to wage an expensive war only to then encumber yourself with the additional cost of having to garrison thousands of occupying troops in a land that's hardly rich in its agricultural output or even precious metals."

"Glory, old man…glory. The Roman emperors are the most powerful men on this planet, believing themselves to be gods. As you know, all gods demand tribute. Our master told us that his action is probably no more than a political exercise to ensure that the old bastard saves his own neck and remains on his blood-drenched throne. After all, there hasn't been a Roman emperor who has yet succeeded in eluding the assassin's hand!"

"Yes, your master may well be right. Still, it's disastrous when one power-mad individual can so easily make such a decision and send so many innocents to a premature death. Now tell me, what tribal region are we in?"

"These are the lands of my own tribe, the Dumnonnii. What tribe do you belong to?"

"The Durotriges. Have the Romans advanced that far west yet?"

"No, both our tribes are hastily preparing defensive measures for when they do come. If you're thinking of returning home, be careful. The entire country is riddled with their spies and collaborators."

Vescala smiled at the youth's concern for his welfare, and throwing the hare's bones away he leaned back on the damp grass.

"Tell me, lad, do you enjoy being a novitiate?" he asked, putting the question forcibly.

"Very much…in fact, I'll be more than happy to return to Anglesey to complete my studies."

"Yes, I wonder if the Romans will take to your masters as much as you obviously do?"

"No, I'm sorry to say that many of our priests have already been massacred. It seems that the Romans intend wiping our religion from the face of the earth. However, they may find that task a little more difficult than they imagined!" Cerix exclaimed, chuckling derisively, and looking into the youth's eyes, Vescala sighed at the blind ignorance that seemed to fill them.

"Yes, that's as may be, now tell me what month is it?" he asked, glancing into the fire.

"This is the first day of the month of the red-backed shrike. But you still haven't told me your name, old man?"

"I am known as Vescala," he declared quietly as the youth's eyes narrowed in a bemused manner.

"That's strange; the only time I ever heard such a name was when our master told us of the proph…"

"You mean the prophecy foretelling the destruction of this, the last bastion on earth of the druid faith and set to occur in the month of the red-backed shrike!" Vescala exclaimed, interrupting him. Cerix now looked afraid with the old man he had befriended having named himself as the very man his master had denounced as the evil one in the prophecy. A name banned by the priesthood for many years. Glancing up from the fire Vescala saw, that the friendliness in the young man's eyes, had been replaced by a haunted quality. Now suddenly discarding the remains of his meal, Cerix leapt to his feet to quickly gather up his belongings.

"It…it's getting late. I must be on my way. I…I still have a long way to go," he stammered nervously as Vescala rose to wish him luck on his journey. But somewhat reluctantly clasping his handshake Cerix then quickly withdrew his hand, before rushing over to the pony to replace his belongings into the saddle-pack and hastily mounting the animal rode off north at a gallop. Unsurprised by the youth's rapid departure, Vescala kicked dirt over the fire until it was completely extinguished. But on leaving the place, his unexpected encounter with Cerix continued to trouble him for the rest of the day until he came upon another wood where he took shelter for the night.

The following day saw his progress hampered owing to increasing pain in his leg, but by the afternoon the pain had eased, and for the next three days he continued his way eastward, living on roots and stream water to stave off his hunger and thirst.

On his journey, he passed by many villages and homesteads, with most of them now lying deserted. Frequently, he spotted long columns of refugees, mainly women, children, and the elderly, who with their pathetic bundles of belongings strapped onto their backs trekked slowly northward in their flight from the oncoming invaders. Seeing the uncertainty of a sterile future imprinted on their faces, he cursed yet again at the seemingly unending legions of tyrants who all too willingly bask in the misguided glory of conquest at the expense of countless numbers of innocents. And steadfastly advancing, he was occasionally stopped by parties of warrior charioteers riding east to face the all-conquering Roman legions, with some of them taking him to be a Roman spy. However, just as he had done in Ireland, he was able to convince them that he was no more than a harmless old man in search of his niece.

With the approach of another evening, he passed beyond the tall carved, weather-beaten totem poles that stood as the boundary markings separating his tribe from the Dumnonni. Soon he came upon the village of his childhood; now no more than a few grass-covered mounds on the barren landscape. There he rested for a short time, reminiscing over his happy early childhood days before hobbling on towards a narrow brook that meandered beside a deserted meadow, where he stopped to wash and drink. With the darkness descending and serenaded by the song of a nightingale and the brook's babbling waters, he lay down on the soft grass from where his weary eyes beheld the mystery of the star-encrusted sky overhead. However, it wasn't long before his heavy eyelids fell to take him into the realms of a calm and dreamless slumber.

On awakening, his alert eyes met the dawn's pink-streaked sky, and on rising from the dew-sodden grass he neither ate nor drank but immediately headed east towards the great forest. He hadn't gone far though when his observant eyes, now sunk deep into their heavily wrinkled sockets, glimpsed ahead of him, a hare limping warily through the long grass; its wounded body trembling in reluctant anticipation of an inescapable death in the mauling jaws of a nearby wolf who, on spotting Vescala, temporarily kept his distance. As the desire to turn back stormed through his mind, his step briefly faltered, but ignoring his momentary indecisiveness his sense of deliverance drove him relentlessly forward. Somehow, he knew that his strange return was taking him into an ultimate confrontation with the truth, and reaching the outskirts of the forest he experienced a light-headed sensation that seemed to breathe new life into his aged body.

"Chaek…chaek!"

Suddenly he stopped in his tracks, although unable to sight the actual bird, its raucous warning cry was easily recognisable to him as belonging to the mysterious red-backed shrike commonly known as the 'butcher bird,' whose dark evil lurks within its renowned physical beauty. A strange, solitary, passerine and aggressive creature, who when food is scarce, has the unique custom of stock-piling its small prey by carefully impaling them by their necks onto thorns, keeping them alive as long as possible to avoid their decomposition. And yet it is also a bird who, when food is plentiful, kills outright before devouring only the innards of its victims, usually smaller birds lured to their destruction by the shrike's cunning ability to impersonate their songs.

His curiosity saw him wander over to a nearby thicket of hawthorn bushes, lying close to the forest edge. Searching feverishly through a stretch of the stinging branches, he soon discovered the bird's thorny larder, which comprised of two living frogs, an unconscious shrew, and a tiny wren twitching agonisingly in its final death throes. The sight of their suffering, as they dangled helplessly on the sharp thorns, saw him shudder, and with a grim premonition of evil now encapsulating him, he quickly replaced the branches. Stepping back, he suddenly spotted, glaring fearlessly down at him, and perched on a twig, only an arms-length away, the male red-backed shrike itself. It was a much smaller creature than he had imagined it to be, with a bluish-grey crown, rust-red back, whitish throat, and a pale pink breast that seemed to intensify its undoubted beauty. Its slightly hooked black bill along with its ferocious-looking talons more than emphasised its predatory qualities. But to Vescala, it was the distinctive black band stretching across both its eyes like some menacing mask that appeared to enhance the bird's sinister reputation.

Drawing his eyes away, he left the thicket to enter into the forest where fierce shards of sunlight slivered down through the majestic trees to spread over the entangled bracken on the forest floor like the strings from innumerable broken harps. By midday, the air hung heavy as he came upon the peaceful lake where, as a child, he had known so much insecurity. However, he lingered there for only a short time, and after leaving its shores it wasn't long before his aching feet once again met the pebbled pathway that would lead him to the sacred glade.

Hearing only the lamenting croon of a solitary wood pigeon, he soon came upon the now deserted crossroads where a terrorised stoat hastily scampered past his feet. Suddenly to either side of him, countless numbers of birds began to screech dramatically in the trees and bushes, as if warning one another of an approaching danger. As he advanced towards his goal, he saw that more creatures were now fleeing towards the forest's outskirts: deer, badgers, bears, otters, squirrels, voles, boars, beavers, wolves, and foxes. All running from some still-invisible danger, as they scattered before him like the spray of violent surf on a distant headland. For a few moments, he stood bewildered at their behaviour. But as he progressed further along the path, he at last discovered the cause, finally detecting the accursed stench of destruction and death. Fire! That most fearsome of words screamed instantly in his mind.

Soon his eyes spotted the wispy trails of smoke curling gently through the branches of the trees ahead, and the further he walked, the thicker the acrid, blue haze became; its malevolence appearing to intensify in the strong sweltering rays of the high sun. By now his leg had become increasingly painful, and he stopped only briefly on spotting the advancing sheet of crackling flames heading towards him and now in the rampant process of devouring the forest's life. However, at the sight of the onrushing holocaust, his determination somehow strengthened, and drawing his cloak over his head, and with the aid of his staff, he forced himself along the path towards the fire, only to then plunge headlong through the blazing embers tumbling down all around him. Once clear of the searing flames, he flung his smouldering cloak back, and gasping for fresh air to ease his burning lungs the sight before him saw him ignoring the discomfort his body was suffering. For as far as his eyes could see lay a charred, desolate landscape now punctuated by the blackened skeletons of trees whose ruination stood exemplified by the scattered diaphanous flames still cruelly leaping up in patches from the smoking tortured earth.

To Vescala it seemed as if all his accumulated nightmares had become one grotesque reality, and panting for breath, he discarded his cloak to briefly look back at the raging inferno behind him, before turning to advance purposefully towards what had once been the sacred grove. Suddenly he spotted a running figure heading towards him, with the person's crimson cloak flailing through the smoke-laden air like the wings of some gigantic bat. Coming to a startled halt, he watched the stumbling figure collapse in a heap by the side of the path. But as the figure crashed down to the smoking earth the dirt-engrained cloak cascaded over its back to effectively cover its head, and limping across to reach the person, Vescala bent down to help.

"Help me…help one who drank from the vessel of power only to become intoxicated in its all-corrupting liquid," the feeble voice implored from beneath the cloak. Now stricken with intense shock, Vescala stood up and stepped back. Even after all these years, he found the voice instantly recognisable, and using his staff, he flung the cloak back over the man's head, but as he did so his heart almost stopped. Just as he had suspected, the face staring back up at him, although deeply embossed with age, belonged to none other than Straval! And as Vescala's bloodshot eyes once more looked upon the black eye patch and the long white scar protruding through Straval's wispy, grey hair, he recalled the living hell that his one-time finest of friends had perpetrated against him.

But as his peering eyes distinguished the unmistakable figure of a man who for so long, he had assumed dead, the cadaverous Straval rose meekly onto his unsteady legs, and from his shoulders, the cloak slipped slowly to the ground. Vescala could only stare in disgust at the grimy, white robes covering Straval's portly frame, but as the two old men stared at one another, it was Straval who broke the cold, lingering silence between them.

"If it be your shade that stands before me, Vescala, then I crave your forgiveness. But if somehow it be your mortal form, then take this golden sickle and with all your strength strike it through my heart!" Straval exclaimed in a terror-stricken drawl. Removing the sickle from his broad leather belt he passed it to Vescala on the palm of his trembling hand. But now having recovered from his initial shock, Vescala calmly took hold of the weapon only to cast it over his shoulder.

"Straval, many long years have passed since we last saw one another and I am neither a phantom nor your murderer. But tell me why you speak in such riddles?"

Straval drew his sweat-beaded eyes away from Vescala's stony glare to look up at the sky.

"Over these past four years, I have held the highest position attainable in the priesthood: arch-druid! It's an indisputable fact that I, and I alone, am directly responsible for the murder and persecution of thousands of our innocent citizens. At this very moment, I am hunted mercilessly by Roman soldiers, with my unenviable position now being that I am the most wanted man in the land." As Straval paused, Vescala detected his one-time friend's words to be spiked with a genuine remorse: Straval having spoken in a low, humble tone that no man could help but pity. "You see, Vescala, I am the protagonist of the old master's dreadful prophecy and not you, as I and so many others had for so long believed. As events have proven, the humanitarian views you were always at pains to uphold were indeed the correct ones. Had it been you who had ascended to my position, as no doubt you would have had you not fallen in love with Delancia, all this devastation might well have been averted. I was given a golden opportunity to change things for the better, particularly for the poverty-stricken masses. However, in my religious fanaticism, I cared nothing for them as I became increasingly obsessed with reasserting our religious beliefs throughout Roman-occupied Europe. You see, it was I who convinced the most powerful of our tribal kings to send guerrilla bands across the channel to Gaul in order to create insurrection; an action that Rome saw as a grave threat to her worldwide domination and inflamed her temper to breaking point. Now they slaughter kings, druids, and peasants alike as if we are no more than animals. As for our sacred forests, they swoop on them like some ecological nemesis, burning and destroying with no consideration of the damage they are inflicting on the future generations of mankind or indeed the many species of life we share our earth alongside. Perhaps the fall of the sacred trees heralds not only the demise of our ancient way of life but much more besides. None but the gods can know the final outcome!"

Leaning heavily on his staff, Vescala stood impressed by Straval's words of repentance, and although for many years he had carried in his heart a vehement hatred towards the man, he now felt a certain compulsion to ease his anguish. After all, was it not a fact that over the course of his own long life, he himself had been responsible for the deaths of so many, he thought feeling an inconsolable remorse.

"That's as may be, Straval," he muttered almost in a whisper, "but it's more than probable that the Roman imperialists would have eventually swallowed up these islands regardless of the priesthood. After all, any empire must continue to expand its boundaries, otherwise it collapses. No, Straval, no man could place all the blame for this present scenario on your shoulders alone."

"Then forgive me, Vescala…forgive me for the dreadful wrong I have done you. I foolishly acted under Durada's orders and when the time came to raise Delancia's remains from the pit, I was told to burn them. I couldn't go through with it though, and so I had her interred beside the knoll on which stood the sacred tree. Please, Vescala, for old times' sake, let me die knowing I have your forgiveness," Straval pleaded, looking at him with a tear welling in his one eye as Vescala's thoughts roamed back over the years to the happy friendship they had once shared on Anglesey. For a few brief self-indulgent moments, he again glimpsed in his mind's eye those early idyllic years of innocence.

"We are now both men of the past, Straval. For what it's worth, you have my forgiveness," he replied softly. But suddenly Straval drew back from him; a wild look now prominent in his one eye.

"How can it be, Vescala, that you stand before me when Durada told me of your death from fever more than thirty years ago?" he asked with his words carried a terrifying uncertainty, but not waiting for an answer, he turned to begin stumbling along the path towards the holocaust.

Taken aback by Straval's strange behaviour, Vescala wanted to stop him only to find his own body inexplicably rooted to the ground, and he could only stand, horror-stricken, as he watched one of the great trees come crashing down to crush the arch-druid beneath its flaming trunk. With Straval dying instantly within the inferno, he found it strangely ironic that as the arch-druid, he should share a fate not dissimilar to many of his victims. This was truly a historic moment, he reckoned. Straval had been the last arch-druid – there would be no more after him – and glancing ominously down to the crumpled cloak, he resumed on his journey through the petrified hell towards the once-holiest of shrines.

Hobbling away from the fire, tears tumbled from his sorrowful eyes as the charred landscape stretching out before him appeared to lie like some perverse monument dedicated to the evil of human folly and war. For the third time in his life, he reached the once hallowed clearing, where a few patches of grass still smouldered; at the same time noticing that some of the carved totem poles leading to the remains of the sacred tree had remained untouched by the fire. However, with the exception of these, the sacred glade was now no more than a vast expanse of noxious wasteland, with the once-supernal oak trees standing like unnatural, blackened dolmens whose shattered trunks watched over a place now truly exorcised of all its evil secrets.

A strange uncanny silence now hung over the smouldering glade; even so he could still imagine the innumerable sacrificial screams that had seen the very trees tremble. Feeling a deep disgust at the senseless slaughter, that for centuries had been perpetrated against his fellow men and women, he expressed his anger by drawing his sword from its scabbard and smashing its blade violently against the nearest totem, he dropped the weapon to the earth.

Slowly, he shuffled towards the knoll where, so long ago, his finest of loves had been taken from him in such savagery. Kneeling at the base, his sorrow-filled eyes rose to meet the stark remains of the once-sacred tree that for so long had witnessed the worst in human depravity, at the same time cursing aloud; infuriated at one Roman emperor's immorality in destroying the very life force of the magnificent forest. But as he did so, he recalled the prose he had been taught as a young novitiate.

The mighty oak trees who harbour three hundred different species of life; the trees whose leaves and branches have, since the beginning of time, shielded the earth from the fierce rays of the naked sun and whose transpiration prevents the creation of worldwide deserts; the trees, whose roots grow to harbour and shelter the forest's animals and whose bark grants so many insects their food and refuge; the trees whose branches, leaves and seeds provide so many birds with the materials and sanctuary by which to continue the process of their essential regeneration; the trees, whose leaf mould gives life to so many plants and whose seeds grow to give men the weapons and farming implements by which to hunt and farm, and the wood necessary to build safe abodes; the trees, whose fundamental and incorruptible existence embraces all the creatures of the land and air regardless of size, breed, beauty, strength or weakness; the trees, whose food and medicinal value bring so many benefits to mankind and whose very beauty alone enhances so many a despairing day.

How ironic it is that the trees, surely the most innocent of all god's multitude of creations, should be forced to suffer as much as the druid's sacrificial victims themselves, he thought sadly as his tear-filled eyes stared up at the long rivulets of molten bronze now solidified into the tree's petrified trunk; remnants of the chains that would hold no more tragic victims. But as he again saw in his mind's eye the golden sickle being raised, and heard again Delancia's dying scream, his mind suffered an excruciating anguish. And yet, had Straval been correct in his assumption that all this destruction might have been averted if he himself had become the arch-druid? He wondered agonisingly. After all, he had once remarked to Brenas that any tyrannical system is best altered through dialogue and debate from within, rather than by the anarchy of intolerance and conflict. But no, he thought, discounting such an idea, now fully recognising that his great love for Delancia had truly been the turning point in his destiny; a mystical true love that each of them had been powerless to deny.

Rising to his feet a spiritual enlightenment now immersed his very being, and as at his trial so long ago, he knew with absolute conviction that the imagined existence of terrestrial and unearthly gods is and always will be a dangerous philosophy for men to pursue. Once again, he felt the absolute certainty that man and man alone governs' all living things upon the earth, but only through the benevolence and guidance of one sole universal creator. For this reason, he knew that it was man — and no other — who was granted the power of free will, imagination, reason, creativity, flair, hope, and above all the faith in his own ability and technological innovation to create for himself and all his planet's inhabitants a true earthly paradise.

"You, priest!" the harsh commanding voice boomed out menacingly around the ruined landscape, interrupting Vescalas contemplation. A startled Vescala quickly turned to see, approaching through the avenue of totems behind him, three soldiers whose bronze helmets and breast armour gleamed and sparkled in the now-dazzling sunlight; the men heavily armed, and all carrying a long, curved rectangular shield as well as a sheathed sword and dagger along with two javelins apiece. Each man now held one of their javelins in a throwing position aimed directly at Vescala, who knew instantly that they were soldiers of Imperial Rome. It was the first time in his life that he had ever seen such uniformed militarism, and he could only stand staring in awe at the resplendence of their red tunics, aprons, breeches, leather boots, and belts that they appeared to wear with such dignity and authority.

"Stand your ground and make no movement," the young Roman in the centre of the group then commanded and as they approached him, Vescala did as he was told, tensely gripping onto the staff by his side. Suddenly the soldier who had issued the order plunged his javelin into the earth close to his feet, and from behind his shield produced the crimson cloak discarded by the fleeing Straval, before throwing it to the ground by Vescala's side.

"None but the highest ordained priest is permitted to don such a garment. We have searched long and hard for you, priest! And by the gods you will pay dearly for your sins." the young man declared angrily. Vescala glanced down at the cloak only for his devastated eyes to rise and meet those of the dark-skinned soldier. And although the man's physical features bore little resemblance, he had no difficulty in recognising eyes identical to those of the centurion whom Trestania had so brutalised some forty-odd years previously. To Vescala, it now appeared as if the eyes, and eyes alone, carried in their essence a vengeance spanning a generation. However, sensing his inevitable death, he courageously laughed aloud when realising that, of all people, they were taking him to be the arch-druid! But now infuriated at Vescala's apparent insolence, the lust to kill masked the Roman's grimacing features, and throwing his shield to the ground he slowly drew his sword.

"Know this, arch-druid: after you die every blood-drenched grove and every bastard priest throughout your lands will be slaughtered and burned until we have rid the earth of your vile practices for all time."

"Hold on, Lancer. We are under strict orders to take the highest of priests alive!" the elder of the other two Romans exclaimed sternly.

"Never, Halvara. Some of my own relatives and many of our good men have died at the hands of scum like this."

"Don't be foolish, Lancer. We can hold this man to ransom and perhaps save thousands of innocent lives, including many of our own men."

Lancer however stood unimpressed by his companion's plea, and as he made to lunge a blow at Vescala, Halvara cast his own shield and weapons aside. Pushing Lancer, he sent him sprawling to the ground, but as he did so, he glanced sideways to the astounded Vescala with his eyes conveying a very genuine and humanitarian compassion. But quickly springing back onto his feet, the much stronger Lancer released his sword to dive headlong at Halvara, and after a short but decisive struggle he rose to stand victorious over his grounded assailant; his gloating eyes absorbing the small silver necklet of a dove in flight now showing prominently through Halvara's torn tunic.

"Well, well, Halvara…the symbol of the Christian faith…the so-called 'new religion.' You could be put to death for belonging to such a sect," Lancer commented through an arrogant sneer, and turning to retrieve his sword, he pushed past the third soldier still guarding their captive. But Vescala could only stand unable to draw his eyes from the simply crafted silver dove dangling on a leather thong from the powerless Halvara's broad neck. What was this 'new religion,' he asked himself standing bewildered as he looked down into the defeated eyes of the fallen Roman. Christian? Never in his life had he heard such a word, and yet at this moment in time he found it to be an inexplicable fact that some common bond existed between the elder Roman and himself. But how could that possibly be, he wondered in awe as Lancer placed the sharp tip of his sword against his now tense diaphragm.

"Arch-druid," he snarled, and bracing himself against the oncoming blow, Vescala drew in a deep breath as he glanced towards the third Roman.

"Christian – what is a Christian?" he asked the man, but no sooner had he spoken the words when Lancer thrust the blade deep into his stomach, and with a ghost of a smile flitting over his pale features, Vescala only flinched when the point of the weapon pierced his spine. On the sword's withdrawal, he released his staff to fall heavily forward; his tense fingers digging frantically into the mother earth. As Lancer easily sidestepped him, Halvara again grabbed him, only this time from around his legs. But kicking free from his companion's grasp, the now-berserk Lancer stepped forward to bury his weapon's blade mercilessly into Vescala's expiring body. Now turning onto his back, and at the revelation of his life's blood flowing out from the savage wounds being repeatedly inflicted upon him from the Roman's flailing sword, Vescala managed to half turn his head, and with his strength rapidly ebbing away, he found enough strength to whisper.

"Delancia…dear god let us be reunited!"

"Your death was long overdue, arch-druid. None of your fellow priests will escape Roman justice," Lancer screamed out, and now perspiring heavily from his exertions, he stepped back.

"God only knows how much innocent blood is destined to cling to your murderous hands, Lancer? You know only too well that we were ordered to take him alive; if indeed he was their highest of priests," the now-upright Halvara muttered in disgust. But turning to him, Lancer intimated his threat through his scowling eyes.

"You, Christian, will keep your mouth shut about this. Get your weapons and I'll burn the cloak; that way all evidence as to his identity will be gone! No one will ever know who he really was."

"Don't you think we should burn his body as well?" the third Roman suggested, only for Lancer to appear uninterested.

"No, we don't have the time. We must get back to the main army. Let the vermin rot where he lies."

Gathering up the cloak Lancer and the other Roman then took it over to where a small patch of ground was still aflame. As Lancer cast the cloak onto the fire, Halvara, stepped over to kneel down and comfort the heavily bleeding Vescala, whose eyes remained open. Halvara saw that the old man was still fully conscious and alert. Suddenly he was overcome with a perception that this man was neither any arch-druid nor indeed any misguided pagan. Having been well schooled in the local dialect he had clearly heard his reference to a 'dear god!' And staring pitifully down into the distinctive glow in Vescala's eyes, it became apparent to him that this was a man who had experienced a great suffering in his life.

"Listen to me, old man, you have little time left before you join your precious Delancia. Many billions of years ago at the silent nativity of time and space, the one and only god of love and light created the universe, heavens, earth, and all living things upon our beautiful and unrivalled planet. However, while the concept of time cannot exist for God, it does to all earthly life through the elemental forces we humans refer to as Mother Nature. Now through this natural process of evolution all life on earth, including man, originated from the oceans over a cycle of time that we mortal beings can neither define or even imagine. Our creator or Lord to whom I now refer is not a mortal being but a spiritual entity. Subsequently, the Lord created man and woman in his own image, not physically

Mother Nature, through our parents, is responsible for that scenario but spiritually! Over a span of millions of years, man, to whom the Lord had granted absolute free will, developed both physically and intellectually, only to become ensnared in the power of the fallen rebellious angel of darkness known as the mentor of all chaos and insanity...Satan! An entity whom the Lord had cast out from paradise at the very beginning of existence. Satan represents evil; this sworn enemy of the Lord and men tempted mankind in his natural environment through the narcotic fascination of the seven deadly sins: known universally as avarice, lust, wrath, sloth, pride, envy, and gluttony. As a result of man's wayward behaviour, the Lord became displeased with his human creation, and in order to bring a true morality into a world, where the madness of evil had reigned for so long, some four thousand years ago he created a perfect man and woman whom he named Adam and Eve. However, although created within the earthly paradise of Eden, even two such unblemished mortals succumbed to the temptations of evil thus falling from the Lord's grace. As a result of their disobedience, they were subsequently forced to live on the earth as ordinary mortals alongside the rest of mankind. Now through Adam's lineage came the patriarchs and fathers of the twelve tribes of the nation we know as Israel. These chosen people were the beginning of the religion known as Judaism, and whose followers are known as Jews. Now only through the law can mankind become conscious of evil, and with the spiritual forces of evil existing at the very highest levels of humanity, the Lord sent to us a powerful Jewish prophet by the name of Moses who he empowered with the commandments, statutes and precepts that would take men and women to the highest levels of morality thus ensuring eternal life to all those who obey his laws! Some forty years ago, our living, spiritual Lord through his grace sent among us his son incarnate – a Jew by the name of Jesus Christ, meaning messiah or saviour. A wonderful counsellor and a man of tender mercies, fathered by the Holy Spirit and conceived and brought forth from the womb of a mortal virgin. This 'King of Kings' obeyed his father's commandments to perfection, and in his short lifetime on earth fulfilled his role as a teacher of love, truth, and justice, performing many miracles among the sick and infirm through the healing power of the Holy Spirit. In the Lord's Prayer taught to us by Jesus Christ, the role of man's destiny is simply defined as creating the will of the Lord on earth as it is in heaven; namely the eradication of poverty, war, famine, pestilence, and plague. However, in order to fulfil the teachings of the Jewish prophets, and through the guile and treachery of his own priesthood, Jesus was then condemned and crucified on a cross by the Romans. Three days later he rose from the dead having overcome death, and some forty days later, ascended to his father in paradise. With this victory over death, mankind, regardless of race, colour, or creed, became the recipient of the Lord's pledge of eternal life to all those who follow the path of his beloved son. We who believe in Christ's immortality are called Christians in his name. Say you believe in him, old man, please say you believe, and through the grace and mercy of our almighty comforter Jesus Christ all your sins will be forgiven!"

"Yes, yes…I believe in such a saviour as Jesus…I feel I always did," the erudite Vescala managed to whimper, instinctively understanding the virtuous Roman's redeeming words. It was to be his final statement, and with his lips smiling for the last time at the glory of the clear blue sky above, his eyes closed into an immeasurable light as his head slumped sideways to rest directly above the very spot where, so long ago, Straval had interred his beloved Delancia.

By the following evening, the great forest's extirpation by fire was complete. However, through the mystical grace of the one universal creator the trees of a virgin forest would once again grow to adorn the earth in their serene, billowing waves. For to the side of Vescala's sprawling body, a solitary surviving acorn lay gently pressed into the charred leaf mould close to the base of the knoll itself; an acorn that he had inadvertently raised to the earth's surface with his dying fingers.

Perched high above on the incinerated pinnacle of the once-sacred tree, the prudent, black eyes of a beautiful bird first stared down at Halvara, before turning its attention towards the other two Romans.

"Chaek…chaek!"

It cried out symbolically in the alien wilderness as if to acknowledge the oncoming world-dominating paganism of the Roman eagle. However, as Halvara rose to his feet, a lonely tear represented his grief for the old stranger as suddenly he felt a tranquil spiritual power flooding over his entire being, bringing to him a peace and serenity that he had never before experienced.

"It's never too late, old man…never too late to embrace the eternal redemption of our faith," he whispered through a contented smile. And with an enlightened Halvara now having a power within him to see beyond the stars, his inspired eyes turned and rose to see the red-backed shrike fly off into the ravaged landscape.

"Halvara! Keep my secret and I'll keep yours. Now collect your weapons and remember, not a word of this to anyone," the now-pacified Lancer shouted over as his avenging eyes turned to watch the last remnants of the cloak burn until it was utterly, destroyed. Feeling no antipathy towards his sadistic companion, Halvara left Vescala's body to retrieve his weapons, and re-joining the others the three men departed the scene.

Before being forced to enlist in the Roman army in his homeland of Greece little more than a year before, Halvara had been baptised into the Christian faith by an elderly stranger whose knowledge, wisdom, and understanding of life had astonished even his village elders. The demise of the red-backed shrike had now convinced him of the long-term invincibility of his beliefs. And as the Lord had appeared in the form of a dove at the time of Christ's baptism, he knew in his heart that the paganism of the Roman eagle must in the future succumb to his faith. Although he and his fellow Christians numbered only a few thousand, in the oncoming centuries their numbers would multiply. Many struggles would have to be undertaken and innumerable martyrs called for the cause, but the inspirational message that they would carry in their hearts would march on forever. The spirit in the light of the dove would pass over the earth in the greatest conversion mankind would ever know!

Thank you for taking the time to read "The Light of the Dove." Over 40 years ago, Ronnie, my late father, began writing this book, meticulously handwriting every page. In a time before the internet made research so accessible, he poured countless hours into gathering information. Born into a working-class family in Edinburgh in the 1940s, Ronald James Rutherford Black was the eldest of four siblings. Although he had a profound story to tell, his struggle with self-doubt and fear of rejection kept him from sharing his work.

Before he passed in 2023, he entrusted me, his eldest daughter, with the promise to honour his writing. Our family is truly grateful for your support in celebrating his legacy.